MOUNTAINS OF GRACE

AMISH OF BIG SKY COUNTRY

Kelly Irvin

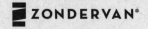

To my husband, Tim. The best copilot ever.

ZONDERVAN

Mountains of Grace
Copyright © 2019 by Kelly Irvin

This title is also available as a Zondervan e-book.

Requests for information should be addressed to:
Zondervan, *3900 Sparks Dr. SE, Grand Rapids, Michigan 49546*

ISBN 978-0-310-35669-1 (softcover)
ISBN 978-0-310-35671-4 (ebook)
ISBN 978-0-310-35672-1 (downloadable audio)
ISBN 978-0-310-36563-1 (mass market)

Library of Congress Cataloging-in-Publication Data
CIP data available upon request.

Printed in the United States of America

21 22 23 24 25 / LSC / 20 19 18 17 16 15 14 13 12 11 10 9 8 7 6 5 4 3 2 1

What do you think? If a man owns a hundred sheep, and one of them wanders away, will he not leave the ninety-nine on the hills and go to look for the one that wandered off?

MATTHEW 18:12

DEUTSCH VOCABULARY*

ach: oh
aenti: aunt
bopli(n): baby
bruder: brother
daed: father
danki: thank you
dochder: daughter
Englischer: English or non-Amish person
faeriwell: farewell
fraa: wife
Gelassenheit: submission to the will of God; attitude of tranquil humility
Gmay: church district
Gott: God
groossdaadi: grandpa
groossmammi: grandma
guder mariye: good morning
gut: good
hund: dog
jah: yes
kapp: prayer cap
kind: child
kinner: children
kitzn: kitten
mann: husband

mudder: mother
nee: no
onkel: uncle
Ordnung: written and unwritten rules in an Amish district
rumspringa: period of running around
schweschder: sister
suh: son
wunderbarr: wonderful

*The German dialect spoken by the Amish is not a written language and varies depending on the location and origin of the settlement. These spellings are approximations. Most Amish children learn English after they start school. They also learn high German, which is used in their Sunday services.

Featured Families

Jonah and Elsie Yoder

Leesa   Mercy   Abraham   Moses   Seth   Hope   Job   Levi

Lyle and Casey Knowles

Juliette   Courtney

Marnie McDonald

Spencer McDonald   Angie (McDonald) Rockford

Kylie   Mikey   Janie

Eleanor Trudeau and Leland Delacroix

Tim   Camille   Victoria   Romy Trudeau

Max and Lou Ellen Brody

Sheriff Emmett Brody (ex-wife: Colleen)   Paul Brody

Jason   Zoe   Bethany   Emmett Jr.

Susannah Hostetler (of Indiana) (widow)

Caleb (of West Kootenai)   Mark   Emma   Rosie   Karen Hostetler

Noah and Joanie Duncan (bishop)

Lucas and Elizabeth Zimmerman (minister)

Tobias and Mary Eicher (deacon)

CHAPTER 1

U.S. FOREST SERVICE BASE
Missoula, Montana

Waddle, waddle, waddle. Grinning behind his face mask's metal mesh, Spencer McDonald hoisted himself into the Shorts C-23 Sherpa aircraft and squeezed into a seat on the bench next to his buddy Dan Martinez. People laboring under the illusion that smoke jumping was a glamorous job should spend some time crammed into these tan Kevlar jumpsuits donned over a uniform made of fire-resistant Nomex, helmets, parachute pack on the back, another reserve parachute strapped to the front, and a personal gear bag with first-aid kit and fire shelter on the hip. They would understand what it felt like to be a guy in an oversized snowsuit in the middle of a sizzling-hot August day. Or an ear of corn wrapped in foil on a gas grill. *Pop, pop, pop.*

"What are you grinning about?" The suit took the bulk of Dan's elbow jabbing his ribs. "It's not funny. So much for taking the kiddos camping for Labor Day weekend," Dan yelled over the plane's noisy engine. "Sheila hates to camp without me."

"She can't be surprised." The wildfire season ran May through September. Which meant smoke jumpers rarely spent the Memorial Day, July Fourth, or Labor Day holidays with their families. It didn't matter to Spencer. In fact, he preferred working the holidays. "You'll make it up to them when you walk them to school in October."

Dan offered a thumbs-up. By now ten smoke jumpers and two spotters in green jumpsuits crowded the bench. The plane taxied and took off, increasing the noise, wind, and heat factors by 500 percent.

The plane headed northwest from the Missoula Fire Base to the Kootenai National Forest near Eureka.

Eureka. Spencer's hometown. He shook off the thought with such force it spun out of the plane and into outer space.

The incident commander rolled out the map. The full-volume chatter ended. The fire, sparked by lightning on August 9, hadn't been spotted by a U.S. Forest Service observation plane until three days later. Efforts by local crews on the ground to contain the fire had been unsuccessful. A U.S. Forest Service Type 2 Incident Command Team would take over containment efforts next.

"The weather conditions are extreme." The commander's deep bass was perfect for briefing in these noisy conditions. "No rain in thirty days, high temperatures, and gusty winds. No rain in the forecast. The fire has shifted to the southeast. Populations in an area called West Kootenai are under pre-evacuation orders."

West Kootenai. Spencer hadn't thought of the folks in that backwater town in years. Amish families mixed in with English families who enjoyed living in one of the few pockets of earth almost untouched by civilization. Hardworking people who also enjoyed the spectacular vistas, hunting, fishing, and boating in the beautiful Purcell, Cabinet, and Salish Mountains.

Now threatened by an adversary that consumed everything in its indiscriminate path.

The spotter talked on his headset. He and his cohort conversed. Radio frequencies, flight restrictions, water sources, safe zones—everything got covered, preparing the way for a safe, effective, efficient jump just outside a raging wildfire that often couldn't be second-guessed.

The plane's engine throttled back to drop speed. The pilot began to circle the drop spot.

"We're getting close." The spotter picked up weighted crepe streamers that would be used to check the wind and the speed of the drop at the proposed jump spot. "Get ready."

They were ready. Intensive PT that included running 1.5 miles in under eleven minutes—Spencer ran it in under eight without breaking a sweat—gave them the physical endurance needed to dig out ground cover down to the mineral level and remove fire fuel in strips a football field wide. Mentally, their heads were in the game the second the horn sounded at the base, giving them ten minutes to suit up, safety check, and sprint to the plane.

Spencer checked out the terrain below through the open door on the side of the plane. Black smoke and fierce red flames billowed along the end of a small meadow. Deer and elk bounded through open spaces. Towering pines in the fire zone ringed the opening. Beyond it a skinny ribbon of hunter's path would serve as egress when they had to pack out all their equipment on their backs.

The streamers fluttered in the wind and sank to the ground.

Forty fire jumps and many more practice jumps under his belt, Spencer still didn't take any of this for granted. Too many variables were beyond his control. Things looked different from the sky than on the ground. Hidden obstacles, rocks, stumps, logs. Gusts of wind. It didn't matter. He lived for this. It had taken three tries to get accepted to the Missoula Smoke Jumper's School after three seasons as a helicopter rappeller in Idaho.

Rappelling into a fire zone produced an exhilarating adrenaline high that lasted for hours. Jumping into that zone was even more fun, but riskier.

Once he hit the ground Spencer had no qualms. He worked with some of the most experienced firefighters in the country. After four years on the job, he was still considered one of the new guys. Only rookie Chase Wilson had less experience. Chase was about to jump for the first time with a chute he'd rigged himself. Twenty-one was the magic number that made him certified to pack the chutes.

Chase's left foot, clad in a heavy-duty steel-toed boot, tapped wildly. His entire leg jiggled. Spencer leaned over Dan and tapped the guy's knee with a gloved hand. "You ready to make those Spam tacos down there?"

Chase's leg quieted. "I've been working on a recipe for Spam sushi I think you're gonna like."

Spam was gourmet food at its finest on the fire line.

"What does your wife think of your cooking?"

"She'd rather I stick to barbecuing hamburgers." Grinning, Chase relaxed against the bench. "She's very picky about smells these days."

The young newlyweds were expecting their first baby—a boy already named Chase Junior. "When this is over, take her home some ice cream." Not that Spencer knew much about pregnant women. Only what he'd heard long distance from his sister. "My sis says it has medicinal effects."

"Got it." Chase twisted the silver band on his ring finger. "She's into Rocky Road."

"Good luck out there, buddy."

Chase shrugged. "Right back at 'cha."

The noise of the engine ratcheted back. The plane began its orbit around the jump spot.

"Get ready." The spotter gave the thumbs-up to Spencer. "No catching a catnap on the way down."

No chance of that.

"Leg straps tight?"

Affirmative.

"Hook up."

Spencer hooked up. He put one hand on the doorframe and the other one on his reserve chute.

The plane turned.

"Static line is clear."

The spotter smacked his back. Spencer grabbed the outside of the frame with both hands, stepped out, and embraced the free fall. His static line would open his parachute automatically. If it didn't he had the backup on his chest. Eighty-five seconds and counting.

The chute opened. The noise ceased. The sky became the most peaceful place on earth.

A time to feast on the majesty of God's earth. A person couldn't miss the Creator's handiwork, not in this business. Spencer did good with nature, not so much with people. Rays of sunlight sparkled around him. Tree canopies looked disarmingly like green pillows.

Thirty seconds. He surveyed the meadow. A nice, soft landing spot in the tall grass would be perfect.

A fierce gust of wind picked him up and hurled him across the narrow opening.

No, no, no. He struggled against a force far greater than any he'd experienced before. He was a toothpick in a tornado.

Nothing to do now but brace for impact.

The Douglas firs that stood guard on the meadow's edge bowed and swayed at his approach.

Twenty, nineteen, eighteen . . . The branches, sharp and unyielding, came at him with the swift, merciless intent of drawn swords.

No stopping now.

Brace for the inevitable.

Love you, Pretty Patty.

Seventeen, sixteen, fifteen . . .

His body rammed a fir with a sickening *thud.*

The collision rattled his teeth. His brain banged against his skull. It scrambled like half a dozen eggs.

Pain unfurled from head to toe.

A bright, white-hot day turned dark and cold.

CHAPTER 2

WEST KOOTENAI, MONTANA

Acrid smoke hung in the air like a visitor who'd overstayed his welcome. Mercy Yoder heaved a breath and immediately regretted it. Her lungs burned. Her parched throat ached. No sunlight shone through the three long windows on the schoolhouse's east wall, making the room seem dreary. It was only Wednesday, halfway through the week. Usually she reveled in the long days. Not today. She glanced at the red fluorescent numbers on the battery-operated clock on her desk. Recess time. Should she send her scholars out to play in smoke that seemed to become more entrenched by the minute? They'd been under pre-evacuation orders since the previous day.

The order to evacuate could come at any moment.

Her father had said to pack a bag as if they were going on vacation. Just enough for two weeks. Her father, the optimist. The sheriff's deputy going door-to-door said to be ready to leave at a moment's notice.

The fire was a giant flame-breathing dragon consuming everything in its path—fourteen thousand acres of Kootenai National Forest north of Lake Koocanusa—in twenty-four hours.

Her childhood home, the homes of her friends and family,

stood in that dragon's path. Everything she'd ever known and loved faced almost certain annihilation.

Yet here she stood teaching ABCs and multiplication and division to a room of antsy, distracted children whose heads were filled with the same worries.

"Leave it to God. He has plans for you, plans to prosper, not harm you." Father had said those words this morning at the breakfast table before he'd sent them to their rooms to pack.

He believed that. So must she. *So, Gott, where does this forest-gobbling, fire-spewing monster fit into those plans?*

God would strike her dead with the same lightning that started the fire for questioning His plans. For worrying. Worrying was a sin.

Mercy heaved another steadying breath. *Focus on the here and now. This minute. This second. Leave everything else to God.*

Hers was not to question, but to teach twenty-seven young scholars English, writing, arithmetic, and a smattering of history and science. Along with hymns, prayer, memory verses, and obedience, humility, and civility.

For as long as she could remember, it had been her job to take care of children. That's what Plain women did.

They did it and they liked it.

She stifled a sigh.

"Teacher, aren't we having recess?" Billy Borntrager wiggled in his seat. The six-year-old was Mercy's youngest scholar. Truth be told, recess was her favorite time of day too. That fact must remain her secret.

Mercy mustered a smile that included all her students, from the oldest, thirteen-year-old Samuel, to her littlest wiggle worm. "Billy's right, I did say that. But I'm concerned about the smoke. It's hard on your lungs. Running around will make it worse. Martha, you have a cold, and Job, with your asthma, it's best you sit this one out."

Her little brother crossed his arms and glowered. "No fair. I have my inhaler."

Teaching her own siblings had its challenges. "It's better to err on the side of—"

Caleb Hostetler pushed through the door and strode into the room.

The words disappeared. Mercy's vocabulary shrank to nothing.

Fortunately Caleb ignored her. He smiled at the children— that lopsided, half-shy grin that never ceased to send goose bumps scurrying up Mercy's arms. "*Guder mariye*, scholars."

"Guder mariye, Caleb." Looking tickled with the interruption, their gazes bounced from Caleb to Mercy and back. They obviously expected her to say something.

She didn't because not a single word came to mind that could be spoken in front of them.

Caleb filled the gap. "I need a word with Teacher."

They had no idea what a surprise those words were to the teacher. Caleb hadn't spoken to her since their last ride along Wilderness Trail almost two months earlier.

Still whispering, her students returned to their work. Which didn't mean some weren't peeking to see what was going on. Nosy little minds.

Mercy instructed her feet to move. Finally, they obeyed. She trotted to the back of the room. "What do you want?"

Besides to be her husband and call her wife?

A pained expression flitted across his face with its high cheekbones and noble nose. "It's time to evacuate. The deputies are going house to house."

His words sank in and squeezed the breath from Mercy's lungs. Light-headed, she managed a nod. The desire to lean into his solid, six-foot-three frame overwhelmed her. She'd lost that right when she said no to his proposal.

He cleared his throat and turned to the students. "I've come to tell you that it's time to evacuate. You need to gather your things and go back to your homes."

A startled murmur ran through the children. It immediately rose until it became a crescendo of high-pitched chatter that filled the classroom.

Amelia jumped from her seat. Her history book and composition notebooks fell to the floor. Samuel grabbed his little brother Carl's arm and started toward the door. Nelly began to sob.

"No need to panic, *kinner*." Mercy took her cue from Caleb and worked to stay calm. "We planned for this."

"Your parents will be expecting you." Even though Mercy was tall for a woman, Caleb towered over her. His loose-fitting clothes were covered with a fine layer of sawdust. His gaze caught hers and offered the same assurance he'd given the children. "No need to panic, but it is necessary to move now."

"Kinner, leave everything. Move quickly to the door, row by row, starting at the front." Mercy nodded and clapped her hands. The children slipped from their desks and flowed past her youngest to oldest. "*Bruders* and *schweschders*, stay together on your bicycles. Go directly home, no loitering, no kickball. Your parents will be looking for you. We've talked about this. You know what to do."

Hannah Plank, a carrot-topped fourth grader, hugged Mercy's skirt. "I love you, Teacher. You go home too."

"I will." A sudden knot lodged in Mercy's throat. This might be the last time they met in this school she'd come to love in three years of keeping the fire going in the wood-burning stove, washing down the chalkboards, and pulling on the rope that made the bell clang, signaling the start of another school day. Mostly, she'd come to love her scholars.

She returned the hug. The little girl smelled like the sweet cinnamon and oatmeal her apron indicated she'd eaten for breakfast. "God be with you, *kind*. See you in Eureka."

Those who had family in Rexford would travel to that small village to RVs or vacation cabins owned by English friends. Mercy's family would head to Eureka, only seven miles farther down the road.

But first they had to traverse the eighteen miles of West Kootenai Road, across the longest, highest span bridge in the state, and north on Highway 37 to Rexford. Suddenly, a drive she'd made hundreds of times in her twenty-two years seemed fraught with peril.

"I could give some of them rides if needed." Caleb jerked off his straw hat and ran his big calloused hands through thick wheat-colored hair soaked with sweat. "It would be faster."

"They have their bikes. They need to take those home with them. They know what to do."

"Right. I'm just trying to help."

Despite everything they'd been through, Caleb had come for her and for the children. She had no right to expect help from him. Yet he'd set aside his pride and walked through that door. He was a better person than she would ever be. She'd always known that. *"Danki."*

"Are you coming?" Her sister Hope, a precocious ten-year-old who was by far the best reader in the school, grabbed her hand. "You'll come with me and Job, won't you?"

"You go ahead." She gently disengaged her hand from Hope's. "I need to close up here. I'll be right behind you. Stay with Job and make sure he doesn't get distracted by a raccoon or a squirrel."

Job loved animals and tended to bring home every garter snake, mouse, and turtle he found.

"Hurry home." Hope put her arm around Job and together the two curly-haired towheads raced out the door. "*Mudder* will come looking for you."

The last words of warning were thrown over her shoulder. They called her Mother Bear. She treated all eight children with equal loving ferocity. Smiling despite everything, Mercy hurried to her desk and stuck her textbooks, the copy of *Little Women* she was reading for the fifth time, and her Bible in her backpack.

"What are you doing?" Caleb strode after her. He thrust his hand out as if to take her arm. His tanned whiskerless face turned ruddier. His hand dropped, but his pale-blue eyes darkened with fierce emotion. "You need to go too."

"I just want to grab a few things. I can't leave my books." She loved her books. They were her prized possessions—not that she should hold possessions in such high esteem. Truth be told, they were her best friends. What would she do without them?

Caleb knew about her secret passion. He was one of the few people in her life who understood her penchant for reading. He had it himself. Those long evenings spent talking about books had been highlights of their eight-month courtship that ended abruptly with an unexpected proposal. "These books are expensive to replace—"

"People are more important than textbooks. Like you told

the kinner, leave everything." He jerked open the door. "I'll give you a ride."

"*Nee*. I mean danki, but I have my bike. I won't leave it." Bicycles cost a lot, and hers, a mountain bike with extra-wide tires, had been a gift from her parents when she started teaching. "Besides, I can cut across the fields. It'll be faster."

"Don't be silly. We'll put it in the buggy." He followed her out the door onto the low porch where he stepped in front of her as if to impede her progress. His hands fisted and unfisted. "It won't hurt you to give in just this once. It's only a ride. It doesn't obligate you to anything."

Didn't obligate her to wed a man who didn't seem to be able to express his feelings in ways a woman could understand. "I know that, but you need to go get your things. It's the opposite direction."

Her throat was tight with unshed tears. Not just because of the fire. The look on his face begged her to change her mind. To let him take care of her. Some days, like today, she wanted that. But it was too late now.

She pulled the door shut as she had hundreds of times at the end of a long day. Instead of feeling replete with a sense of important work done well, she felt anxiety creep up her spine and curl itself around her throat, a serpent whispering words of fear for a future made murky by smoke and flame.

"You are the most stubborn woman I've ever met." Rare emotion ran rampant through Caleb's words. "I have half a mind to throw you in the buggy."

If he'd shown this much fire during their courtship, her answer might've been different. "You wouldn't dare."

His jaw jutted out and a pulse throbbed in his temple. "It wouldn't be seemly, I suppose."

Back to feelings bridled. One step forward, two steps back. "Please go. Hurry. Save what you can. You'll need your tools to rebuild."

She grabbed her bike, propped against the log cabin–style school. Her father and the other men had built it log by log years ago. Mercy and her brothers and sisters all had attended this school.

Please, Gott, please.

She slipped onto the bike's seat. The normal, everyday act steadied her.

"Fine. At least promise me you'll be careful." Caleb hoisted himself into his buggy. "Hurry but be careful."

The picture in her mind of Caleb throwing her into his buggy still loomed in her mind. What would she do if he dared to do such a thing? Unfettered, undeniable feelings rocked her. At least it would show the depth of his feelings. Feelings that hadn't been expressed through a single hug or kiss. "You too. Are you going to Rexford?"

"Eureka. Arthur has friends there who have offered his family a place to stay. He says there's room for Ian and me."

Arthur Duncan was his boss at Montana Furniture. And a good friend. "*Gut.* Our paths will cross there."

Now why had she said that? Heat that had nothing to do with fire burned her cheeks and neck. She forced herself to break away from his stare and took one last look over her shoulder.

A curtain of red-orange flames spewing black smoke fluttered in the wind on the mountain behind her. Six, maybe seven, miles away.

She pressed her sneakers into the bike's pedals, hunkered down, and fled.

From the fire and from the man.

CHAPTER 3

A raging forest fire could help a man get his priorities in order like nothing else. Coughing, Caleb wiped sweat from his face with his sleeve and barged into the rustic, two-bedroom log cabin he shared with Ian Byler.

Ian looked up from the tools he was stuffing into a canvas bag. "Where have you been? You left the shop at the same time I did."

"I stopped at the school to tell Mercy."

"You are a glutton for punishment." Ian snorted and went back to packing. "Or did she swoon at your act of kindness and change her mind?"

"We're supposed to be a forgiving people." With a fire bearing down on this tiny community of four-hundred-plus English and Plain people, this was a good time to try to forgive Mercy and move on. Even if the blow she'd dealt him still kept him awake every night. "At least that's what I learned growing up in Indiana. I'm sure it's the same here."

"It's one thing to forgive her; it's another to expect her to change her mind." Ian thrust the bag over his shoulder, picked up a battered leather suitcase, and headed for the door. "She told you she didn't want to get married to you or anyone else. You're better off to move on."

Mercy had professed to love teaching and her scholars as much as a mother loved her own children. She said she wasn't ready to get married. Not that she would never marry. It had to be something about Caleb that kept her from saying yes.

Her answer had knocked him for a loop. It was made worse by how apologetic and tearful she'd been. She didn't want to hurt his feelings. She felt sorry for him.

No need. He would survive.

He simply had to figure out how to stop caring about this beautiful, long-legged woman with enormous hazel eyes, chestnut hair, and an inquisitive mind that ran rings around most people.

Still waters ran deep was what Arthur had said about her when Caleb first asked what he thought about Mercy. "Very deep" had been the exact quote.

All thoughts Caleb kept to himself now. Ian was courting Mercy's older sister Leesa. He knew all about Mercy and he preferred the more traditional sister. Caleb rushed into his bedroom where he scooped up the bags he'd prepared the night before. Clothes, the biography of Abraham Lincoln, his latest Louis L'Amour Western, his tools, the letters from his family, his wood carvings—mostly animals and toys meant to be Christmas gifts for nieces and nephews back home—and his Bible.

His hand hovered over the tan Stetson cowboy hat. Mercy had given it to him for his birthday in May. He touched the soft felt. An expensive gift that made him laugh. She called him Cowboy Caleb because of his love of L'Amour's books.

Not that he was allowed to wear a cowboy hat. Plain folks didn't dress differently. But the hat hung on a nail next to his bed. It reminded him of Mercy's smile and her giggle when he tried it on. The way she stroked it with thin fingers and stared at his face as if waiting for him to do something.

Like kiss her.

Only he'd let the moment pass in an agony of embarrassment. He was no good at these things. Leyla, his first and only special friend in Indiana, had made that apparent when she chose another.

Dumped by one woman, turned down by another. Plain women were generally eager to marry. Just not him.

He laid the Stetson on top of the bag. He couldn't let it get squished. These were the sum total possessions of a twenty-four-year-old wayfaring stranger from Indiana who'd lived in Kootenai for two years.

He took one last look around. The sparse room held a neatly made bed, a table and mismatched chair, and hooks for his clothes. Once he walked out, there would be no sign Caleb Hostetler had ever lived here. The folks here welcomed him with the same hospitality they did all the visitors who came to hunt, fish, and hike in the mountains. If he left as all the others did, would they notice?

An engine rumbled outside the open window. Shaking his head at his own thoughts, Caleb strode from the cabin that represented his fresh start. His high-on-the-mountain hope. His last resort.

Now fire threatened it all.

Gott, I don't think I have the fortitude to start over yet again. These are gut people. They welcomed a stranger without question. Spare this community, I humbly beg. Put a bubble of protection around them if it is Thy will.

Those last words were added because ultimately God's will

was the only thing that mattered. His plan. They might not understand it, but they would submit to it.

Over and over again. Whether they liked it or not.

He gritted his teeth and forced an attitude of gratitude. Fire was good for the forest. Just not for people who infringed on its beauty with their homes and their livelihoods.

Thy will be done.

He slammed the door behind him. There was no key. People around here didn't lock their doors.

Deputy Tim Trudeau stood next to his Lincoln County Sheriff's Office pickup. "Are you out of here?" He shook a can of spray paint with one big paw. "I saw your roomie hoofing it in his wagon on the road. He had the right idea. It's time to get the heck out of Dodge."

"We got the word over at the shop. I'm headed out as well." Caleb slid his bags into the back of his buggy. His mare, Snowy—so named for her gleaming white coat—pranced and snorted with impatience. "Easy, I'm coming, girl, I'm coming."

"Anybody else in the house?"

"No."

Tim lumbered up the skinny strip of cement that served as a sidewalk leading to the cabin. Sweat darkened the back of his tan uniform shirt stretched tight across enormous shoulders. He spray-painted a thick 0 on the sidewalk.

"What's that about?"

"Number of people still here." Tim stuck the lid back on the can. "We have people who don't want to go. We put the number who stay. We're keeping it simple."

"Staying is an option?"

"Not a smart one. The evacuation is mandatory, but we've got some stubborn folks holding out. They have to sign a piece of paper that says they know we're not coming in to rescue them if the fire sweeps this area." His scoffing tone told Caleb what Tim thought of these folks. He tossed the can onto the seat through his open door and slid in next to it. "They can't move to other folks' property either. And if they've got kids, the kids gotta go or we'll arrest the parents for putting minors in danger."

"Makes sense." Caleb gripped the door before Tim could close it. "Before you go, have you been by the Yoders'?"

"Which ones?"

Mercy's place. "Jonah's?"

"I was just there. The women are loading up the buggies and leaving." Tim tugged the door shut and leaned his bare head through the open window. Sweat beaded on his tanned forehead. It stretched back to a hairline receding before its time. "Jonah and the older boys are staying behind a little longer. They swear they'll leave as soon as they have the livestock and the equipment loaded. I hope they don't wait too long."

"Did you tell them that?"

"Of course I did. Jonah's a smart man. He won't risk those boys' lives."

"Wouldn't it be faster to give Mercy—the women—a ride out in your truck?"

"There's still time, but folks on bicycles are getting a ride, if they'll take it, don't you worry." Tim hesitated. "Have you talked to any of your English neighbors?"

That he adopted the Plain word for non-Amish folks spoke of the fact that Tim had grown up in these parts. Caleb shook his head. "I waved at the Drakes when I passed them on the road. They had their trailer loaded down and the back of their

SUV. Their son was driving an ATV and DeeDee had the truck with a horse trailer."

"You haven't seen the Knowleses then?"

Translation: Had Caleb seen Juliette Knowles? Everyone knew Tim was sweet on Juliette. His personal vehicle, a dark-blue Dodge Ram, sat in the Knowleses' driveway too many evenings this summer for people not to notice. "No. Sorry. But they were notified by phone, weren't they?"

"Yeah, Code Red, Reverse 911." The furl on Tim's forehead said the deputy wasn't comforted by the thought. "Still, people are taking their sweet time getting out of here."

"On that note, I had better get moving." Caleb climbed into his buggy. "Stay safe."

"Same to you. Pray as you go. Don't make any stops. Get off this mountain now."

Good advice.

Tim roared away, the truck bucking on the well-worn ruts of the gravel road. Eating its dust, Caleb followed. At the end of the long driveway, he glanced back. A second later he regretted it. The menacing, fiery glow advanced relentlessly down the mountain toward Kootenai.

"Come on, Snowy, let's make sure everyone gets out safe." He snapped the reins. "Starting with the Yoders."

CHAPTER 4

Kootenai tasted and smelled like a big fire pit. The smell of burnt wood clung to Mercy's nose. The smoke gagged her. Breathless, her lungs aching, her nose burning, she pumped harder. The home she was born in came into sight. A rambling cabin-style home had been made larger over the years with two additions to make room for their growing family. Her dad and the other men in the community built the first piece before she was born. She'd never lived anywhere else.

Her mom had the horse and wagon hitched up. Behind it, Dad stood by the buggy, talking to her older sister Leesa and her younger brother Abraham. Hope sat up front, waiting.

Mercy pulled up next to the wagon and braked hard. Panting, she gasped for air.

"You made it. Thanks be to Gott. The kinner said you stayed behind to close the school." Mother picked up Levi, the youngest of her eight children. He wiggled and clamped his chubby arms around her neck. She shifted his three-year-old body so she could see Mercy. "I suppose it's human nature to tidy a building that may burn to the ground in the next few hours. We were going to come to get you."

In other words, Mother was worried. "I'm fine. I'm here. Do you have everything?"

"Your *daed*, Abraham, Moses, and Seth are staying behind.

They'll load the trailer with what we can't get in the wagon and the buggy." Mother's hazel eyes were wet with unshed tears behind dark-rimmed glasses. "The most important thing is you kinner."

Mercy wasn't a child anymore, but Mother sometimes forgot that. "Is everyone okay? Have you heard from the Beachys or the Masts? What about the Knowleses?"

"Everyone is helping everyone. No need to worry, kind. Gott is faithful."

That was West Kootenai. Friends helping friends, regardless of what church they attended on Sunday morning.

"Where do I put my bike?"

"Daed will bring the bikes out in the trailer."

"I want my rabbits." Job popped from the back of the wagon. "They'll burn up in the fire."

At six, he was old enough to understand what was happening. Mother held Levi up and Job took his little brother into his arms with an exaggerated *hummph*. "I'm sorry, but they were gone this morning. We don't have time to look for them. At least you have Doodles."

Doodles was a skinny stray dog who'd made himself at home in their barn the previous winter. Although he appeared to be the laziest dog God ever placed on the earth, Doodles, a nondescript brown-and-white mutt, stuck to Job's side like a cocklebur when he wasn't at school. The rest of the time he slept on his back, feet in the air, tongue flopping out one side of his mouth. Job plopped Levi down on the seat next to the dog, who licked the new addition as if the child were his own.

"Get that bike in the trailer." His hand on one hip, a look of pain on his sun-reddened face, Father tramped over to the wagon. "Let's go. I want you out of here now."

Mercy did as she was told. Minutes later she climbed into the wagon and sat next to Mother. This time she didn't look back. They joined a steady stream of people on Spring Creek Road. The parade grew when they turned onto West Kootenai Road. The narrow two-lane road wound through the Kootenai National Forest, Purcell, Cabinet, Salish, and Bitterroot Mountains in the distance.

A route too beautiful for words. No matter how many times a person traveled it.

"I wonder how much will be left when we come back." Mercy grabbed the seat railing as the wagon rocked on the cracked asphalt. "All these beautiful spruce, tamarack, aspen, and pine trees. They could all be gone."

"Say your prayers. Gott's will be done." Mudder clucked and snapped the reins. "It's only a precaution anyway. The Forest Service's crews are digging containment lines. They'll stop it from reaching Kootenai."

From her mother's lips to God's ears. *Are You listening, Gott?*

Thankful her mother couldn't read her mind, Mercy waved to the Masts. They'd loaded five kids, two dogs, and a mound of bags into one wagon. Maisie, who was four or five, sprawled across two bags, sound asleep.

Christine waved back. "See you in Rexford. We have to talk." Her excited, high-pitched excitement carried across the chasm. "ASAP."

"We're going to Eureka." Already, they were being spread across the countryside. Mercy groaned and waved harder. "But ASAP."

It was their code for Awful Situation Approaching. It usually involved their parents and men. Christine and Nora, her best friends since they were five and started school, were the only single girls their age left in Kootenai. Still on their *rum-springas* until they found special friends and married.

Again, Gott, are You listening?

"Did you see Nora?" Christine shouted louder. "Or Juliette?"

"Nee. I was at school."

"Stop screaming at each other." A tiny thread of irritation wound its way through Mudder's words. She never showed irritation. Another first in Mercy's life. "It's not seemly."

Seemly? "Sorry, Mudder."

She snapped the reins again. "I'm sorry too. I just want to get there. Is Leesa still behind us?"

Mercy craned her head and looked back. Leesa and Hope waved in unison. "Still there."

"Gut. They need to keep up." Still that brittle tone. "No time for dawdling."

No one dawdled. It simply wasn't possible to move more quickly in a line of buggies, bicycles, and wagons.

It took most of an hour to make it to the span bridge over Lake Koocanusa that connected West Kootenai to Highway 37 North, where they would travel back north to Rexford and then seven miles across to the valley where Eureka lay. The lake's turquoise water sparkled in the early afternoon sun as it lapped against sandstone cliffs. The narrow bridge swayed slightly some three thousand feet above the satin blue-green water.

A hundred memories crowded Mercy. Fishing for rainbow trout and salmon, splashing in the icy water, canoeing, bonfires and s'mores. Happy childhood memories soon to be scorched by fire.

They started across. Sirens screamed in the distance, beyond the bridge, then grew louder, shattering the lovely lake peace.

Mudder's knuckles went white on the reins. Cocoa tossed her head and snorted. "Easy, girl."

The bridge jerked. It was the longest bridge in the state of Montana. The words so often said to the children during her Montana geography lessons repeated themselves in Mercy's head. "What do you think it is?"

"I don't know. More fire trucks?" Mother shielded her eyes against the sun with her free hand. "The volunteer firefighters are already out there."

A second later a white Lincoln County pickup truck barreled toward them. No one ever went fast on the bridge. Partly because it was so narrow and partly because everyone liked to enjoy the view. The bridge rocked. Cocoa's neck bucked. She whinnied and sidestepped. Mercy clung to the seat. "Mudder."

"Easy, Cocoa, easy. You're okay." Mother's grip tightened on the reins.

The truck roared past.

"Sheriff Brody. He's in a hurry." Mother clucked. Cocoa's gait quickened. "I hope your daed and bruders don't dawdle."

"Daed never dawdles."

"Now would not be a gut time to start."

Mercy swiveled and craned her neck. Smoke rolled from the mountains high above her. Dark, black, and foreboding. A wall of orange flames licked at the treetops.

Indeed, it would not.

CHAPTER 5

Deputy Tim Trudeau didn't bother to count to ten.

"What the Sam Hill are you doing still here?" He stormed across the dirt and gravel that served as a driveway in front of the Knowleses' sprawling ranch house to the spot where Juliette Knowles sprayed a greenhouse with a garden hose. "Evacuate means leave. Now."

Juliette turned. The hose came with her. Lukewarm water splattered his face and drenched his uniform. "Oops, I'm so sorry, Tim." Giggling, she lowered the hose and turned off the water at the faucet. "I didn't realize you were standing so close."

"You did too." Tim sputtered and wiped at his face. Truth be told, the water cooled his sweaty face. He would never tell Juliette that. She needed no encouragement. "Get your rear in gear, woman."

Juliette's studied nonchalance as she wrapped the hose around its plastic rack attached to the greenhouse's outer wall threw fuel on Tim's internal flames. He forced apart gritted teeth and breathed. "Juliette—"

"Daddy's still loading the trailer around back with equipment. We're trying to soak everything we can. We've worked really hard to make our buildings fuel poor, but it might not be enough."

Removing trees in a fifty-yard radius around the house, raking leaves and needles, placing firewood piles away from the house, keeping the roof clear of debris—these were all ways the Forest Service recommended making homes more fire defensible for firefighters. But they were no guarantee when homes were built in forests prone to lightning-strike fires.

"That's all fine and dandy. Now skedaddle." He plucked the last remaining feet of hose from her sun-glazed hands and slapped it on the rack. Juliette put those same shapely hands on her beautiful hips and scowled. He glowered in return. "And you did do that on purpose. Let's go. I'll give you a ride. It'll give your mom and dad more room in their SUV."

"I'm not leaving until they do." Juliette stomped in well-worn purple cowboy boots up the steps to the front porch. She whirled, crossed her arms, and stared him down. She might be all of five feet four inches tall, but she packed every inch with determined bravado. "Don't you have other families to notify?"

This skirmish had nothing to do with the fire or the evacuation and they both knew it.

He stared up at the only woman he'd ever loved and took a breath. "I saved the best for last. We went to all the Amish families first since they didn't get the Reverse 911 call. I knew you would be lollygagging behind and I'd have to throw you over my shoulder and hog-tie you to the grill of my truck."

"In your dreams." She rolled her blue-green eyes and laughed. The laugh turned into a half sob. "Honestly, I'm grabbing my suitcase and we're out of here in two shakes."

"Oh, honey, I'm sorry. I know you love this place. God willing, it'll still be here when you get back, but it's out of your hands now. You gotta go."

She bounded down the stairs and hurled herself into his arms. "I can't stand it." The words were whispered into his tan uniform shirt, already wet with water and sweat and smudged with soot. Her long blonde curls smelled of spearmint-eucalyptus shampoo. Clean and fresh. "It's their whole life."

"You and your sister are their whole lives." He tightened his arms around her for a second, then eased her back. "Houses can be replaced. Children can't."

"He's right, baby girl." Lyle Knowles shoved through the screen door and dragged out two enormous, battered suitcases. "Let's get out of here."

Juliette's mother, Casey, brought up the rear with two smaller suitcases. "You can take Juliette off our hands if you want."

The Knowleses had been surprisingly good with their daughter spending time with a law enforcement officer. Even if they found it confusing that most of the time was spent with family rather than typical dating. Watching football games with her dad. Going to the shooting range. Arguing politics and religion. His, not hers, since hers was almost nonexistent.

"Mom, I want to help you—"

"Just get in the man's vehicle and go." Lyle clomped down the steps and headed for the mammoth Suburban parked next to Tim's F-150. "No time to argue."

An F-350 roared up the drive and halted within inches of Tim's. "What the heck?"

Tim's boss, Sheriff Emmett Brody, stuck his head out the window. "You got folks who stayed behind?"

"Yes, sir. Some of the Amish men are still packing equipment and setting up sprinklers, but their womenfolk are all out. I told them they had about a two-hour window."

"That window has closed. The wind has shifted." Emmett gunned the engine. "Backtrack down Wilderness Trail. I'll take Spring Creek Road."

"Got it."

Emmett took off without a backward glance.

Tim whirled and sprinted to his truck. Hand on the door, he looked back. Juliette stumbled toward him. He met her halfway. One quick hug.

"Be careful." She touched his cheek with her warm, slim fingers. "Promise."

A thrill ran through Tim and he swallowed against the lump in his throat. The desire to kiss her and throw her in his truck blazed through him. Nope. Not allowed. Friends didn't act like that. He and Juliette were friends. "Promise. You too."

He raced back to the truck.

"If anything happens to you, I'll kill you." Her words carried on the same windy gusts that brought the fire to their door. "That's a promise."

"Right back at 'cha." He tore down the road, but not without a backward glance. The Knowleses scattered to their vehicles, except for Juliette. She still stood staring after him, her face contorted with conflicting emotions. Ever a study in contradictions. Too complicated for a simple man in search of a simple life to be shared with a woman who wanted the same.

What was he thinking? Giving his heart to her?

"Make plans and watch God laugh." His Nana Trudeau's French-Canadian accent echoed in his head.

Nana was never wrong. He stuck his arm through the window and waved.

Juliette didn't wave back. Stubborn to the end.

CHAPTER 6

The man wanted to kiss her. That was obvious. But he refused to do it. Ignoring the rush of her family around her, Juliette tugged her cell phone from the pocket of her shorts and called him.

"Juliette, I'm driving."

"You have Bluetooth."

"I'm on a mission to save lives."

"I know. I just wanted to tell you something."

"Get out of there. Now."

Her dad's mammoth hand clamped down on her shoulder. "Jules, get off the phone. We have to go. Tim can take care of himself."

Dad knew how her mind worked better than anyone in the world, except Mom. Juliette lowered the phone to her heart. "Coming. Two seconds." His hand released and she put the phone back to her ear. "One of us could die in the next few hours. You never know."

"Nobody's gonna die. And if someone does, I hope it's me."

Her knight in shining armor. A gentleman to the end. Which was why he'd never done more than kiss the top of her head like she was his little sister since she returned from Missoula with a communications degree and no job. "What kind of stupid thing is that to say?"

"I'm saved. I know where I'm going. I'm not afraid to die." Tim's voice cracked. "You, on the other hand, God's still working on."

Same song, fortieth verse. Pain burned through her stomach and throat. Had she remembered to eat this morning? It didn't matter. Nothing assuaged this pain, her constant companion for years. "I love you."

"And I love you." He stuttered the words. "You know I do."

"But I'm a heathen so the only way we can be together is if I get on the religion bandwagon?"

"That's not how I would put it. Nor is loving a man the reason a woman accepts Christ as her Savior." His frustration gave the words a hard edge, unusual for an easygoing teddy bear. "This isn't the time. You need to get your very lovely behind into the Suburban and go."

"I can't commit to something that sounds like a fairy tale. You know what they say: If it sounds like it's too good to be true, it probably is."

"You can't commit, I know. You can't even commit to staying in this area. Or to me." His cough, followed by a gusty sneeze, reverberated in her ear. "Sorry about that. We'll talk later. I promise."

He hung up before Juliette could protest.

Cursing under her breath, she picked up her suitcase and stuck it on top of the others. She could commit. To a pair of purple, soft leather cowboy boots in a size seven and a half. To the gorgeous Appaloosa her dad gave her for her eighteenth birthday. To the University of Montana Grizzlies. To Chicago-style meat lovers' pizza and her mom's huckleberry pie. She committed to many things.

So far, love had not been one of them. Not until Tim Trudeau stopped her on IH-37 one spring day two years ago and gave her a ticket for driving her Ford Ranger seventy miles an hour in a fifty-five zone. And another for passing in a no-passing zone. And another for having a brake light out. And another for an expired inspection sticker. A bouquet of costly infractions.

They knew each other from high school, but Tim had metamorphosed into something quite different from that shy, bumbling football player who never knew what to do with his six-foot-five-inch two-hundred-pound body and who once vomited all over her lunch tray in the school cafeteria.

The brawny hunk who stopped her on the highway was immune to her charms. Professional, kind, borderline sweet. But firm. No, he wouldn't give her a warning. Her actions put others in danger. She deserved the tickets. Which charmed her, even though the last thing an unemployed would-be advertising agency account exec could afford was a moving violation. He even ma'amed her. Which only charmed her more.

"Get in, baby girl." Dad's jaw bulged against his cheek. "Now."

Ignoring the pain in her gut, she tucked the phone in her pocket and climbed into the vehicle.

"He does get under your skin, doesn't he?" Mom pulled her seat belt tight and held on to the dashboard while Dad shot down the driveway and zipped onto the road without a backward glance. All the Knowleses drove too fast. With skill, but fast. "What's the problem with you two? You dance around like two scorpions in a dangerous mating ritual."

"Mom!" Courtney slapped her hands over her ears and sang, "La-la-la-la-la-la-la."

Juliette stared out the window. Mom always did know exactly what was going on in her older daughter's head. It bugged Juliette to no end. "Nothing."

"Nothing you want to tell me about, in other words."

Or Dad. He used to carry her on his shoulders into the Kootenai church when she was little. He gave her jelly beans when she was good and a smack on the behind when she was bad. He praised her for reciting her verses and critiqued her choice of wardrobe. Some of their biggest fights were over what she wore to youth group on Sunday afternoons.

"God's House deserves respect," he roared.

"God gave me this body, didn't He?" she argued.

"How about jeans and a nice T-shirt?" Mom, ever the peacemaker, would intervene.

The show that repeated every Sunday afternoon until Juliette went on a youth group campout on Lake Koocanusa her junior year.

Nope. Her brain did its own version of Courtney's *la-la-la-la* with hands on its ears.

Light receded into a pinpoint beam in a swirling dark world.

She dug through her purse until her fingers wrapped around the remnants of a roll of antacids. Two left. She popped them in her mouth. The chalky taste gagged her.

"Your stomach hurts again?" Courtney's freckled nose wrinkled. "You eat those things like candy."

Juliette glared at her little sister. The last thing she needed was for Mom and Dad to be concerned about her gut in the middle of an evacuation. "It's the garlic bread from supper last night, that's all. Nothing to worry about."

"Fine. Crabby butt." Courtney turned to stare out her window.

No need to bite the girl's head off. Stifling an apology, Juliette did the same.

Garlic, onion, Mexican food, any spicy food she ate resulted in a steady burn.

The story on loop in her head resumed of its own volition.

No more youth group. No more church. No more God.

More fights, more afternoons spent confined to her room, more tears, more dreams of being free.

Until she was. No one ever mentioned how hard adulting could be. A person found out quite suddenly that adulting involved walking a high wire with no net.

Like falling in love with a man who kept a copy of Martin Luther King Jr.'s *The Measure of a Man* in his glove compartment for light reading on his supper break. How did a woman compete with that?

Or coming home to Mom and Dad and speaking those dreaded words. *You were right.* The worst punishment in the world for any child, but especially for Juliette. The last thing she ever wanted was to let them down.

"There's Caleb. Why is he still here?" Dad skidded to a stop and rolled down the window. "Hey, Caleb, you better roll. The fire is moving faster than they expected. It'll be here in the next hour."

"I'm making one last pass to make sure no one needs help." Caleb's horse tossed her head and whinnied, a high, tight sound. Her eyes rolled. She strained against the harness. "Easy, girl, easy. I'm worried about the Yoders."

"Let Emmett and his deputies make that pass. He came by and said to leave immediately. You need to get out."

Caleb shook his head. "You go first. I don't want to hold you up."

"We've got room for you."

"I'm not leaving my horse."

"Understood."

They had moved their horses to a pasture on the other side

of the lake a day earlier. Juliette leaned through her window. "Is Mercy still up here?"

"No, the women and children went first, but Jonah and the boys were still here, last time I checked."

"Tim and Emmett will get them moving."

Caleb gestured toward the road. "Be safe."

"You too."

Juliette pushed the button to roll her window up, but she leaned her head against the glass so she could see in Dad's side mirror. Caleb veered off on Spring Creek Road instead of following them.

Checking on Mercy no doubt. The guy had it bad. Being turned down probably made it even worse. Guys were like that. They wanted what they couldn't have. He was the right height for Mercy, who was tall for a woman. He was wide in the shoulders, narrow in the hips, and had sandy-blond hair, but for some reason Mercy couldn't say yes.

Which took guts for an Amish woman. Mercy liked Caleb, but she said she liked teaching more. Her expression said it was something more than that, but her Amish reticence kept her from spitting out the truth.

Maybe it was because Caleb wasn't much of a talker. Or because he was shy about the physical part. His smoldering expression suggested plenty of heat. Not that Mercy had much to say about that. She turned red as an heirloom tomato every time Juliette asked her about it. She was so cute.

And so was Caleb. So what was the real problem?

If Mercy were here she would say Juliette ought to mind her own p's and q's. She'd rather think about matchmaking for other people.

Mercy would be right. Juliette's complicated man demanded

far too much. Why Tim decided to pick on her was anyone's guess. He didn't like her religion—or lack thereof. He didn't like her clothes—or lack thereof. He didn't like her politics—or lack thereof.

Which begged the question: What did he like about her?

Juliette groaned and snapped her seat belt against her chest.

Better to think about Mercy's love life—or lack thereof. Juliette grinned to herself and took one last look back. Caleb's buggy had disappeared from sight. Headed to Mercy's house to make sure she was safely evacuated.

The battle for Mercy's heart wasn't over. Not by a long shot.

CHAPTER 7

EUREKA, MONTANA

Whoever said life sucked and then you died was a wise man. Spencer jammed the stick shift in park and turned the Tundra's engine off. He leaned back against the warm leather and winced. His left leg—thank God it was his left leg—ached even encased in a boot.

The doctor wanted him to sit around with his leg up in the air, which made sense. The swelling would go down, and with it, the pain of a fractured tibia. Sitting around wasn't in Spencer's DNA. Which made the first eighteen years of life in one classroom after another a hot mess.

His broken ribs, also on the left side, pierced his chest with more pain. Three broken fingers on his left hand were splinted and bandaged. After a night in the hospital, he'd checked himself out against doctor's orders. Bruised and battered, he'd come crawling home to Eureka—at least it used to be home—after an abrupt end to his smoke-jumping season.

His truck sat in the driveway next to his mom's house. It looked the same as it did the last time he was here. Nine, no, ten years ago. The last knock-down-drag-out fight he had with her about her propensity to drink and drive, drink and pass out, drink and miss his high school graduation.

At least she hadn't burned this house down.

The *tick-tick* of the Tundra's engine beat a rhythm in sync with the reel of memories. Slamming doors. The smell of whiskey and cigarettes in the morning. Three-day-old dried egg yolk on plates stacked in the sink next to a skillet filled with congealed bacon grease and two dead cockroaches entombed in it. A stranger in smiley face boxer shorts and an AC/DC T-shirt stumbling past him in the hallway leading to the small A-frame house's only bathroom.

"Hey man, what's up?"

The guy wasn't much older than Spencer. And not bad looking. If a seventeen-year-old kid could be the judge of such a thing. Marnie—he started calling his mother by her name when she stopped being anything he could identify as worthy of the title "Mother"—had always been able to attract decent guys with her hippie-angel looks. She didn't get mean until the third or fourth drink. Like the devil mixed a potion that browbeat the light until it turned dark.

It took Spencer's dad ten years to figure out he couldn't inspire an affection greater than the one Marnie had for cheap whiskey. So he escaped to California where he sold real estate and lived happily in a house by the beach—if his sporadic Christmas and birthday cards could be believed.

The devil made her do it. That was Spencer's sister Angie's explanation. It was easier to believe in such things as evil and the devil than free will gone horribly wrong. Yeah, that red guy with the pitchfork and horns?

Get it over with.

Why did you come here? Are you nuts?

He grabbed the crumpled letter from the passenger seat and smoothed it out on the steering wheel.

Spence,

I hope this letter reaches you. I got your address from Sissy. She keeps me up-to-date on your latest doings since you never call me or write me. Which I totally understand. I hope you'll come see me sometime. Even if you don't, I want you to know, I stopped drinking. I'm doing my steps. As everyone who's ever watched a sappy TV movie knows, one of the steps is asking forgiveness. I hope you'll forgive me for being a rotten, mean drunk instead of the mother you needed. I knew what I was doing, which makes it worse. I couldn't stop myself. Not even for my own kids. You deserved better and I understand if you can't forgive me. I truly am sorry. Take care. God bless.

Mom

P.S.: I love that you are smoke jumping. You're like me. It'll really make you mad to hear that, but it's true. You're a risk taker like me. Maybe sometime we can skydive together or go bungee jumping. I would like that.

So Marnie got religion after all these years. Who would've thunk it?

Spence shifted. Pain stabbed him stem to stern. The docs said he needed to be patient. It would take three months for his fractured shin bone to heal. The ribs and fingers less. The doctor also said he was fortunate to have a head as hard as a brick. That was his medical opinion. No damage to his noggin. All in all, the collision with a tree a hundred times his weight had done no permanent damage.

Patience had never been his strong suit.

He dry-swallowed three ibuprofen and stared at the house. Thanks to the media's coverage of the opioid crisis, nothing

stronger had been offered. It didn't matter. Given his back-
ground, he approached drugs with extreme caution. The
wood-and-stucco house, built in the late eighties, needed a
coat of paint. The brown, patchy grass cried out for watering.
Flowerpots on the porch held droopy, on-their-deathbed dai-
sies and sunflowers. The brass address numbers had slipped
and turned so a nine became a six and the three lay on its back
looking more like a *w*. Sobriety hadn't improved Marnie's station in life.

She must be forty-nine or fifty now. Not old.

Alcohol aged a person beyond her years.

Stop procrastinating, dude.

Okay, okay.

He grabbed his crutches and eased from the truck. The
September sun warmed his face. He jerked his Denver Nuggets
cap down so the visor shielded his eyes. "Here we go."

The words were spoken aloud to whoever might be listening. A contrite God who was sorry for putting a teenager
through hell?

Suffering honed character according to his last girlfriend.
A good, sweet Christian woman who warded off his advances
with a finely tuned sense of humor and pithy proverbs that
made him smile despite his frustration. Pretty Patty wanted
to save him, that was obvious. But a guy had to want to be
saved.

Had to deserve saving.

When it became obvious Spencer believed he was neither,
Patty had kissed his lips, his cheeks, and his forehead with
the sweetest kisses he'd ever received and whispered in his
ear that she would never stop praying for him. A comforting
gift he sometimes held on to in the middle of a dark night

filled with bad dreams. She'd gone back to her life as a bank teller who spent her free time doing respite care for dementia patients and studying to be a physical therapist. Leaving him to fight his own demons.

He didn't deserve her. Yet he still had her number in his phone. She said to call him when he was ready. Whatever that meant.

Ready for what?

You're doing it again. Ring the doorbell, you coward.

I jump out of airplanes for a living. I'm not a coward.

There are cowards, and then there are cowards.

He gritted his teeth and limped up the cracked, weed-infested sidewalk, then hoisted himself up two crooked steps to the tiny wood-slatted porch. A wind chime with a huge but delicate metal dragonfly above it swayed in a tepid breeze, the sound sweet music that matched the rustle of leaves in a weeping willow in the front yard.

Peaceful sounds in a place that had never been peaceful for him. He swallowed and sucked in a deep breath. "Ouch."

He kept forgetting about the ribs.

Knock.

He rapped hard. Too hard. She'd think the cops were at the door telling her to keep the yelling down when she and the latest "uncle" fought over money and the guy who grabbed her behind at the dive bar down the block.

The door opened.

Marnie stood behind the screen. Her long raven hair held streaks of silver and white like ribbons. Time had drawn hard lines around her blue eyes and full lips. The lips pursed, then spread in a smile that revealed those slightly crooked teeth no longer yellowed by tobacco. The aroma of cinnamon rolls wafted through the open door, sweet and yet spicy. Like the perfect woman.

"Spence."

"Hey."

She jerked open the screen door and tumbled out, all thin arms and high-pitched, nervous laughter. "You came. I didn't think you would, but Daphne, she's my sponsor, insisted I try. She said you would come when you were ready and here you are."

She wrapped him in a hug that told him she remained skin and bone under the faded but clean white cotton shirt and denim capris. Her feet were bare, her toenails painted bubblegum pink. She wore no makeup, and for the first time in his life she smelled good. Like Ivory soap and Jergens lotion.

"I just came by to say hello. I'm staying with Angie." He'd come to Eureka to clean up an old mess. His team IC had told him to go home and not come back until his bones and his attitude were healed. "Where is she? She said she'd meet me here."

Marnie grabbed his hand and tugged him inside the house. "She got called down to the church. They're opening as a shelter for the families evacuating from the fire in West Kootenai. She's sorting donations of clothes and food and such. You know her, she never misses an opportunity to help. The kids are with her."

Spencer stumbled over a Tonka truck left in the foyer that opened up into a living room. Barbie dolls, Matchbox cars, and coloring books were strewn across the carpet. Pain pulsed through his leg. He cursed.

"No need to be a potty mouth." The gentle remonstration was laughable. Where did she think he learned to swear like a barfly? "Sorry, the kids spend a lot of time here now that I'm taking care of them while Angie works."

His sister had stopped short of moving home when her husband left her and their three kids for a waitress at the truck stop on Highway 2. Instead, she took a job as a secretary at a church during the week and a cashier at a convenience store on weekends. She hadn't mentioned Marnie was taking care of the kids. Spencer's stomach launched itself into his throat at the thought.

"I know what you're thinking." Marnie motioned to a brown faux-leather recliner with a back covered with white embroidered doilies. "Take a load off. She trusts me. She knows I'm done drinking."

She frowned and pushed skinny reading glasses up her nose. "What happened to you, Son? You look like you got throwed by a bull at the rodeo."

"Jump went bad." He leaned on his crutches and surveyed the house. It seemed smaller than it had when he was a kid. It definitely smelled better. "I'm out on medical leave until I heal."

Which meant the season was over for him. Being at loose ends during a fire season, or any season for that matter, did not suit him.

"You look like you need one of my super-duper cinnamon rolls and a nice cup of coffee. Angie got me one of those fancy Keurig machines for Christmas last year." Marnie motioned to the recliner again. "Let me take care of you."

For the first time, her happy-go-lucky, long-overdue-reunion-with-son facade cracked. "I can't make up for what I didn't do before. But I can try to do better now. I hope you'll let me."

"Are you dying or something?"

Her forehead wrinkled. "What?"

"Is that why you got religion and stopped drinking? Do you have cancer or something?"

"No. No, it's not that at all." She edged back into the room. Her hands twisted in front of her. She cleared her throat. "Although, after my last blackout, the doctor did tell me I would die if I didn't stop drinking." She rolled her head from side to side as if her neck hurt. "But I already knew that. For a long time I didn't care. I liked the way alcohol made me feel. People who aren't alcoholics can't understand that. I liked drinking. If one drink made me feel good, how much better two or three or four? It's a disease. People like to think it's lack of willpower or discipline or sheer weakness. It's not. I've learned that with the help of my group."

She let her hands drop to her side. Her face cleared and her posture straightened. "It was Angie's kids who made me want to stay around a little longer. She wouldn't let me see them anymore. She couldn't let them see me like that. They already didn't have a daddy or a granddaddy. And you were gone. I'm the only family they have here in Eureka. Angie was hurting. She needed help. They needed me. For the first time in my miserable, godforsaken life, I thought of someone else and got the help I needed."

She whirled and strode away.

Miracles did happen. Pretty Patty always said they did.

Just not in time for him. He didn't have a daddy or a granddaddy either. Or a mother like Angie.

Stop feeling sorry for yourself.

Spencer eased into the chair and cranked the lever to lift his aching leg.

The miracle came in time for Angie's kids. That would have to be good enough for him.

CHAPTER 8

EUREKA, MONTANA

What did the *Ordnung* say about using electricity when a fire was about to consume your home? Mercy's hand hovered over the light switch in the Knowleses' rental house kitchen. Dusk made it hard to see Grandma Knowles's place, which now served as a rental property on Second Avenue near Eureka's small downtown business district.

"I'll light the lantern. You can start unpacking."

Mudder squeezed past Mercy. She dumped a box of canned goods and kitchen essentials on the table and pulled out a kerosene lantern. Despite the remaining light outside, the room seemed dark and unlived in. A few seconds later, the flickering flame revealed a large country-style kitchen. A rustic table with four straight-back wooden chairs filled one corner. Myriad cabinets lined two walls around a double kitchen sink, a mammoth stainless-steel refrigerator, a stainless-steel dishwasher, and a gas stove.

The sparkly white-and-silver granite-top counters were slick and barren, as if waiting for the appliances, pots, and pans of a future renter. The Knowleses had upgraded this room. It seemed unlikely Grandma Knowles had need for such a fancy kitchen.

It didn't look like home. No one expected it to, but a fierce ache in the vicinity of Mercy's heart made her rub her breastbone. Suddenly, misery sucked the air from the room. She couldn't breathe. "Juliette said they're setting up an information center and shelter at the First Church of God. That's only a few blocks from here." Mercy began to pull jars of peaches, cherries, tomatoes, and green beans from the box. She set them on the table with care. *Do normal things like it's a normal day.* "I could walk over there and see if there's any news."

Any news of Father and the boys.

Mother trudged to the sink. She turned the water on and let it run. Her shoulders slumped. Mercy slipped to her side. "I'm sure they're fine."

"Gott's will be done." Mother grabbed a bottle of dish soap and squeezed some into her hands and began to wash them. "I feel so dirty from all the soot and ash in the air. The kinner will need baths tonight."

Pushing back a strand of silver-blonde hair that had escaped her *kapp*, Mother glanced around as if seeing the room for the first time. Mercy handed her a flowered towel from the rack next to the sink. She dried with more vigor than needed. "It will be strange to cook in someone else's kitchen."

"At least Grandma Knowles used a gas stove." Mercy took the towel from her mother and returned it to the rack. Acutely aware that neither the towel nor anything else in this sprawling two-story brick-and-wood frame house belonged to her or her family, she smoothed it into place neatly. "We can fix hamburgers for supper. The kinner will like that. I'll cut up some potatoes and make fries."

"Go to the church. But take Leesa with you." Mother's voice

trembled. "And come right back. I don't want you traipsing around the city in the dark alone."

Mercy hid her smile. Eureka, population 1,086, could hardly be called a city. They'd been coming here their entire lives to Montana Market to buy goods they couldn't get at the Borntragers' store in West Kootenai or the Kootenai Store in Rexford. Suddenly even the familiar seemed fraught with danger. "We'll be fine."

"So will your daed. He knows what he's doing." Mother tucked a package of ground beef in the refrigerator. So big for an elderly woman who'd lived alone the last few years of her life. "They'll be here before you get back."

"You're right." This time Mercy smiled and hugged her mother's neck. "You're always right."

Her hazel eyes wide with surprise, Mother hugged back. "What's gotten into you? Do you have a fever? You must be sick if you're admitting I'm right about something."

"I admit you're right all the time."

"Are you ready to admit I was right about marrying Caleb?"

Mercy let go of her mother and edged away. "I'm happy teaching. I love my scholars." Now was not the time to rehash why she simply could not bring herself to say yes to Caleb's proposal. A girl didn't discuss such things with her mother. She grabbed a flashlight from the box and headed for the door. "We'll be back soon."

Leesa was happy to get out of unloading and unpacking boxes. As the oldest, Mercy's sister liked to pick and choose her chores. Which meant Mercy often got stuck with the less desirable ones, like cleaning the chicken coop or mowing the yard.

"Mudder is worried about Daed and the boys." Mercy shortened her stride to match Leesa's petite prancing. Everything about her older sister was smaller and more girlish. "She won't admit it, but her eyes were all teary."

"She won't admit it because worrying is a sin." Leesa skipped to keep up. "Slow down, will you? I don't know why we're going to the church. Daed had the directions to Grandma Knowles's. He'll be here when he gets here."

"Aren't you worried the house will be gone when they let us go back?"

"It's only logs, Sheetrock, and planks." Leesa lifted her apron and patted her face. Despite the long day and the trip into Eureka, her clothes were clean and neat, as usual. "We'll rebuild, and knowing Daed, the new house will be better than the old one. He has so much experience with building. He knows what he's doing. Just think of it, brand new. Maybe the bedrooms will be bigger and the kitchen too."

Leesa had the ability to see the positive in everything. It was as if God had given her an extra-large helping of rose-colored happy, while He skimped on Mercy's portion.

"I liked the old house."

"Me too." Leesa's stride slowed. "I liked the chair where Daed sat to tell us stories at night by the fireplace in the winter."

"And make s'mores or popcorn over the fire."

"*Jah.* Gut memories. We'll always have those. The fire can't burn those up." The older she grew, the more Leesa sounded like Mother. She looked like her too. God knew what He was doing. Somehow Mercy had received the short end of the stick. Tall. Skinny. Overly opinionated.

"How come Mudder doesn't give you a hard time about not being married?" Mercy kicked at a grizzled tennis ball someone had left on the sidewalk. It rolled into the weeds and disappeared. "You're a year older than me."

"She used to." Leesa wrinkled her perfect upturned button nose. No one ever believed they were sisters. Leesa had blonde hair and dimples. While good looks were unimportant in the Plain way of thinking, a person couldn't help but notice. Mercy was a giant next to Leesa, who always knew what to say and do in every situation. "But now she knows—or suspects—that I'm about to change my status."

"Ian proposed?" Mercy squeezed her sister's arm. "Did you talk to Tobias about it?"

The deacon loved playing the role of informing parents of impending nuptials.

"Ian didn't actually say the words yet." Leesa's satisfied smile said she wasn't worried about that wrinkle in her plan. "But he will. Any day now."

"How do you know?" Mercy had been blindsided when Caleb popped the question. They'd been courting for only eight months. They took buggy rides, hiked, fished, ate together, and talked endlessly, mostly about books they'd read. Caleb was a fountain of information about everything except his own family and his feelings.

He never opened up to her the way she thought a beau—a future husband—would. Nor had he seemed in a hurry to explore the physical side of their relationship. No one ever explained how the pieces fit together—shared views of faith and family, the desire to spend the rest of her life with someone, and the physical romance.

That last part was a complete mystery to Mercy. She had all these feelings—every time Caleb's hand brushed against hers, they exploded in chills up her spine. His full lips mesmerized her. She lay in bed at night and imagined what it would feel like to be kissed by him.

Her cheeks burned at the thought. "How can you be sure Ian is the right one?"

"We fit together like macaroni and cheese." Leesa giggled. "Or oatmeal and raisins. Or peanut butter and jelly, or—"

"Okay, okay." Mercy laughed with her. "I just have one more question. Are you the elbow macaroni or the cheese?"

Entertaining themselves with silly food similes, they passed the First Interstate Bank and the church came into view at the end of the block. Despite the hour, cars, trucks, RVs, and buggies crowded the parking lot. A U.S. Forest Service van sat perpendicular to the curb, taking up five or six slots. A Lincoln County sheriff's truck hugged the line next to it. Leesa and Mercy picked up their pace.

The church was a narrow, L-shaped white building with a brown cross at the foot end of the L. A nearby sign spelled out the Ten Commandments in a font large enough for passersby to read if they weren't driving too fast.

Inside, a handmade sign pointed to a set of white double doors on the right, which led to a big room that didn't fit with Mercy's idea of English churches. No stained-glass windows, no statues of Jesus or Mary. It looked more like a meeting room with a laminate wood floor and a stage at one end. Some of the people were familiar, her neighbors from West Kootenai, some she'd seen in Libby. They congregated around maps on one wall, where a U.S. Forest Service ranger was pointing and talking.

A pretty, plump lady wearing a purple shirt that read TEAM JESUS and a long white skirt stood behind a table next to a folding chair stationed by the doors. Purple-rimmed glasses stuck in curly hair dyed a startling magenta, she hummed a song as she shuffled a stack of papers and stuck crayons in a box. The song turned out to be "Jesus Loves the Little Children."

A blond-haired boy about two made siren sounds as he crawled around under the table pushing a large toy fire truck. Despite the noise, a baby clad in a pink onesie slept in a car seat.

The woman glanced up when Mercy and Leesa reached the table. "Hello, hello, welcome to First Church of God. Mikey, hush, hush those sirens for now." She stuck her head under the table and shook her finger at the little boy and then straightened. She held out her hand. Leesa and Mercy took turns shaking it. Her skin was soft but her shake firm.

"Sorry about that. Mikey wants to be a firefighter when he grows up. He practices. A lot. I'm Angie Rockford, the church secretary, here to make you feel at home. Let's get you signed in. The Red Cross folks are right there at the next table. They have motel vouchers and vouchers for food. Just fill out this form to get started. We also have food donations from our church members and a ton of donated clothes. Grab a grocery bag and pick out whatever you need. Of course, you probably won't find much that suits your style. But we do have packages of new socks and underwear. We might have your size. We also have blankets and sheets and towels, if you need those." Her cheeks pink, she paused for breath. The woman must have enormous lungs.

Leesa jumped in. "We're good for now. We were mostly interested in information. What have you heard about West Kootenai? Did the fire reach it? Has anyone come by here—?"

"The Forest Service is coordinating containment of the fire," a familiar deep, unusually raspy, voice boomed from behind them, "but the sheriff's office made sure everyone was evacuated who wanted to evacuate."

Mercy turned to find Deputy Tim Trudeau approaching. His shirt was wet with sweat and dark circles under his eyes spoke of exhaustion. "Did you talk to my father?" Again Leesa spoke first. "Did you see them? Did they leave?"

"They were still loading the trailer when I drove by." Tim lifted his tan cowboy hat, stained with sweat and soot, and ran his hand through thinning brown hair with auburn highlights. "Your dad said he was almost done."

"You didn't demand that he get moving?" Mercy hated the way she squeaked when she felt upset. She drew a breath. *Calm.* "What if they didn't get out before the fire came?"

"They did." Caleb strode across the room in that long-legged gait that always made Mercy stop and look—even when she shouldn't. He halted next to Tim. His gaze enveloped Mercy. As if she were the only one in the room. His smile was lopsided, but a smile. How hard it must be for him to pretend nothing had happened between them. "I also stopped, as did Sheriff Brody. Your daed and bruders were setting up sprinklers. We headed out at the same time. It takes longer when you're pulling a trailer."

He'd come for her at the school. Then he'd gone to check on her family instead of rushing away from Kootenai and the fire. Despite everything that had happened, he still cared. He was a good man. A kind man, and she'd hurt him. The thought broke her heart. All the words she hadn't said before threatened to spill out. *Not now. Not now.*

She grasped for something that made sense right at this moment in front of Leesa and Tim. "Was the fire close?"

"Close and getting closer. After Emmett stopped and told us to get out, we all saw it coming." Caleb's fingers gripped his suspenders. His knuckles turned white. "We all froze for a second."

"What did you see?" Mercy had viewed the fire at a distance. That was enough. She didn't need to know more, but she couldn't help herself. A person had to face the worst to get past it. "How bad was it?"

"The fire was only a mile or two away and eating everything in its path." Caleb crossed his arms over his broad chest. "Jonah ran past me to your bruders. He told them to go, go, go. They went. So did I."

"So you think our house is gone?" Mercy's voice sounded strange in her ears. Like a little girl's. Small. "The barn, the sheds?"

Caleb shuffled his scuffed, dusty work boots. "I don't know, but I do have something that will make Job happy." He smiled, but it didn't hide the misery on his face.

Mercy summoned her own smile. "You found Nickle and Dime?"

"Nee. I'm sure they raced away on their own, but I do have Lola. She's out in the buggy, making a mess of my clothes."

"Job will be happy. Of course, she's really Mudder's cat, even though Mudder won't admit she's attached to her. Danki for bringing her." Mercy tried not to stare at Caleb's big calloused hands. He had broad shoulders and big biceps. The kind that would make a hug truly felt. The only time he ever touched her was to help her into the buggy. Never a hug. Never a kiss. How could he expect her to say yes?

What were they talking about? Cats. Lola. "She's a gut mouser. Daed and the boys will be at the house by the time we get there. We should go."

"When can we go home?" Leesa wiped at her face with the back of her sleeve. Mercy patted her back. Leesa sniffed.

Her sister didn't form the rest of the question, but it banged around in Mercy's head. When could they go back to see if the house still stood? And the school? And the Borntragers' store? And the Knowleses' house? Caleb's cabin? All their friends and family. Their community. Their entire lives.

"When the danger is past." Tim's tone softened. "When it's safe."

Not an answer.

"If the wind shifts, the fire may circle around and make another pass." This time the observation came from behind Tim and Caleb. "They'll have to wait to see what the weather does."

Mercy tore her gaze from Caleb. The newcomer was a tanned, muscle-bound man who was tall, even hunched over metal crutches. He balanced on his right leg. His lower left leg and foot were encased in a medical boot that stretched from below his knee to just above his toes. His handsome face—even a Plain woman couldn't miss his dimpled cheeks, nice teeth, dark curly hair, and blue eyes—was bruised. A bandage covered part of his forehead above his left eye. Splints covered three fingers on his left hand. Lines around his mouth suggested pain he was determined not to acknowledge.

"Spencer McDonald, what are you doing here?" Tim didn't sound particularly happy to see the man. The deputy was usually as friendly as a rambunctious toddler.

"Passing the time." Spencer swung toward them more gracefully than anybody on crutches should. "Checking on my sister, if that's okay."

His gaze landed on Mercy. His eyes were the darkest sapphire blue she'd ever seen. He looked like he was in his mid to late twenties, but he had the solemn eyes of a much older man. A person could disappear into their cavernous depths, following trails that led to a place where he finally let go and allowed entry. He didn't smile, but his full lips parted. His lower teeth were slightly crooked. "Hi."

Her hands fluttered to her own lips. She corralled them back to her sides. "Hi." Nothing else occurred to Mercy. She closed her mouth.

"What happened to you?" Tim looked wary. "Wreck your motorcycle?"

"I got rid of that thing a long time ago." Spencer smiled. "I'm a smoke jumper now. I got hurt jumping with the team sent in to fight the Caribou Fire."

"That's a good job for you." Tim's mouth clamped shut for a few seconds. "I mean, you always were crazy."

"That's not very nice." The words were out before Mercy could swallow them. "Some people might think being a policeman and going after bad guys with guns is crazy in this day and age."

The newcomer smiled. His whole face changed. Time, years, disappointment, and uncertainty fell away. In a singular moment Mercy stood on the shores of Lake Koocanusa and watched the sun rise over the water. She swallowed and slipped her hand into the crook of Leesa's arm, lest she fall flat on her face—Mercy, not Leesa.

"It's okay, Amish girl." Spencer shrugged. "People who don't know what they're talking about might call smoke jumping crazy, but smoke jumpers are actually highly trained individuals. It requires tremendous physical fitness, presence of mind, and the ability to think independently and creatively."

The words he strung together echoed somewhere in her brain while she focused on *Amish girl*. He made them sound like a designation for someone special. Plain girls weren't supposed to desire to be special. To stand out. Mercy tried to hide the smile his words prompted. *Demut* not *hochmut.* Humility not pride.

"Why don't I give you a ride home?" Caleb broke the sudden silence. "It's getting late. Your daed is probably there by now."

A buggy ride with Caleb. *No. No way.* "You don't have to do—"

"That would be *wunderbarr.*" Leesa tugged at Mercy's arm. "I'm starving. We missed supper."

"Wait." Spencer swung forward a step on his crutches. "Tim apparently forgot the manners his mama taught him. He didn't introduce you—"

"Spence!" Angie Rockford sped across the room and launched her roly-poly body at him. "You came. You came. You came."

"Whoa, easy, Sissy, easy." Spencer's face turned red under the deep tan. His arms opened. One crutch toppled to the floor with a bang. He tumbled back a step but managed to stay upright in his sister's embrace. "I told you I would."

"Mikey, Kylie, look, it's Uncle Spencer. Wake up, baby Janie, your uncle is here."

"They don't know who I am." Despite his protest, Spencer grinned that same all-out grin that lit up his face and the room. He allowed Angie to tug him away from their group. "How many kids do you have now? Forty?"

Angie howled with laughter. She had one of those laughs that made everyone within hearing distance want to laugh too. It started as a soft tinkle, then grew and grew until it became a snort-slash-deep-belly-chuckle.

Mercy chuckled. Leesa joined in. Neither Caleb nor Tim seemed amused.

"I wonder what he's doing here." His gaze on Spencer's

retreating figure, Tim grimaced. "Whatever it is, it can't be good."

"What did he do that has you so riled up?" Mercy had no business asking about an English man. A long day, an uncertain world, and a ridiculous smile combined to make her reckless. "You don't seem to like him very much."

"Spencer used to live around here. He was one of those bad boys all the girls drooled over. I guess I still resent the fact that they couldn't see how much better off they'd be with the good guys." Tim looked at his watch. "I have to get back to Libby. Have you seen the Knowleses since you got to Eureka?"

"That seems harsh."

"Trouble follows him around and slops over on other people."

Leesa glared at Mercy. Caleb looked none too happy either. "The Knowleses left ahead of us. They would've arrived in Eureka long before we did."

Mercy peeked over her sister's shoulder. Angie hugged her brother's neck. The woman had tears running down her face. Not everyone thought Spencer's return was a bad thing.

Besides, boys grew into men. They changed. Didn't they?

"Come get Lola and I'll give you two and her a ride to your house." Caleb stepped into the space beyond Leesa, blocking Mercy's view of the happy reunion. "It's dark out there."

"Lola is never glad to see anyone." Nevertheless Mercy allowed Caleb to lead them from the room. She grasped at her scattered thoughts. They were like leaves somersaulting on the autumn wind. A safe topic presented itself. "How are things where you're staying? It must be crowded with Arthur's family and everyone."

"Arthur's brother has an RV parked behind his house."

Caleb held the door for them and they strode from the church. If he wondered why she cared about where he stayed or what he did, he was kind enough not to throw it in her face. "We're borrowing it."

"That's gut. You should be comfortable there."

If they'd married, the two of them would be staying in that RV now. Instead he had no family here and had to ride out the fire with Ian.

His expression told her nothing. He didn't share his feelings when they were courting. Why would he do it now?

Caleb's buggy was parked on the other side of Tim's truck. Snowy looked happier than she had earlier in the day. Morning and arithmetic lessons seemed years ago. Mercy petted the horse's graceful neck. She rested her forehead on the silky mane and breathed in a scent as familiar as her mother's or coffee or spring breezes.

"She's back here."

Mercy inhaled one last healing scent and trailed after Leesa to the back of the buggy. Caleb pulled a box toward the edge and unfolded the flaps. Lola screeched and leaped into Mercy's arms. Her pitiful meows said, "Where have you been?" and "How could you leave me?"

Mercy staggered back, but she hung on to the writhing cat's bony body. "You're fine, *kitzn*. You're fine."

Lola climbed up Mercy's chest and buried her wet nose in her neck. Her heart pumped in a rapid beat against Mercy's collarbone. "You sweet thing, Job will be glad to see you too."

"She really likes you." Caleb's words had sharp edges. His features were etched in stone.

"She recognizes me, that's all." Mercy stroked Lola's silky fur, more to calm her own emotions than the animal's. Why didn't men say what they meant? How was she supposed to know what Caleb's feelings were before that momentous question that caught her totally off guard? "Cats choose their owners, not the other way around."

"She's not the only one who likes you." Leesa giggled. "Unless I'm mistaken, but I'm not."

Her cheeks as hot as any fire that burned in the Kootenai National Forest, Mercy glowered at her sister. "What's so funny?"

"Nothing." Leesa giggled again. "We better go. I'll bring the box."

In an awkward silence they climbed into the buggy. Leesa insisted on sitting in the back with Lola safely ensconced in her box on her lap.

Mercy kept her gaze on her hands and her thoughts off the man sitting next to her. He was simply giving them a ride. More importantly, he was the last one to see the home she and Leesa grew up in. "How bad was it?"

Caleb snapped the reins and the buggy jolted forward. "It's best to leave it to Gott. His will be done."

Platitudes she'd heard her entire life. "But do you think our house burned?"

"I don't know." His glance brushed against her, full of sadness. "I wish I could tell you more, but we were blessed to get out alive."

"That's what's important."

"You don't sound convinced."

Was he suggesting she valued the house more than his life? The man had pea gravel where his brain should be. "It's hard. I grew up in the house. You're new here. You don't have the same connection to the place."

He didn't respond. She gave him a sidesweep glance. The sadness had grown and taken root in the lines around his mouth and eyes. He seemed years older.

"I don't mean you have fewer feelings. It's just—"

"I know I've only been here two years, but it's home for me too."

"I know. I'm sorry."

"We have to believe Gott has a plan." The stone fell away, replaced by an uncertain smile. "For all of us."

Something about the way he said "all of us" with a hint of inquiry sent a wave of warmth flooding through Mercy. Maybe he could forgive. Maybe there was hope for a new start somewhere in their future. She hadn't meant to end their relationship. Only slow it down until she could be certain Caleb was the one. He simply hadn't given her the opportunity to say that.

Turning down a man's proposal surely hurt his pride as well as his heart. How could he forgive that? She studied her hands in her lap. Even if she could go back to that evening down by the lake, she wouldn't change her answer. She couldn't. Caleb, whether he could see it or not, hadn't given her enough of himself to warrant another answer.

A yowl ripped the air.

"Lola!" Leesa screeched. "And she's gone again."

Mercy swiveled. Her sister bent over, peering into the street. "What happened?"

Leesa held up her hand. "She scratched me. Then she dove out of the buggy."

Caleb pulled over to the curb and halted. "Shall I look for her?"

"In the dark?" Mercy shook her head. Maybe Lola wasn't

happy with God's plan either. "Poor thing is probably trying to get back home."

Caleb clucked and shook the reins. The buggy jolted into the lane again, headed for Grandma Knowles's house.

No one spoke. Maybe Lola had the right idea.

CHAPTER 9

EUREKA, MONTANA

Two hugs from family in one day exceeded Spencer's daily quota. He kept his distance from Angie in case she decided to make another run at him. His sore ribs couldn't handle it. Or his rusty emotions. He shouldn't have come to the church. The look on Tim Trudeau's face said as much. Ten years and Tim assumed Spencer was still the troublemaker who broke into Libby's high school and herded a cow into the principal's office after they beat Eureka High School in their annual cross-county rival football game. He hadn't acted alone, but he was the one who got caught and suspended.

A stupid high school prank. Then there was the smoking under the bleachers after a football game. And drag racing on Saturday nights. Not much else to do in Podunk towns like Eureka and Libby. The tourists had the money to boat and ski and kayak and camp. Local boys like him didn't. Especially ones who didn't have dads to take them hunting and fishing.

On the other hand, if he hadn't come, he wouldn't have run into an Amish girl with eyes that could slay a man in under fifteen seconds.

She reminded him of Pretty Patty.

"So who's this big boy?" With one last glance at the two

sweet-faced women who scurried toward the doors, he plopped into the folding chair next to the boy who hid half-in, half-out under the table. He had Angie's round face and his dad's blond curls. "He looks about thirty or forty years old."

"I'm Mikey. I'm three." Mikey burped and giggled. "I want juice."

"I like your fire truck."

"Me too. I want juice."

"No juice. It's bad for your teeth and it makes you poop too much. Here's your water." Angie handed the boy a Paw Patrol water bottle and patted his head.

He frowned. "Want juice."

"No juice."

He sucked from the water bottle, but fat tears rolled down his round cheeks.

Ignoring them, Angie turned to a little girl who wrapped her body in Angie's voluminous white skirt. She was four or five. With her gorgeous black hair past her skinny shoulders and blue eyes, she looked nothing like Angie or her daddy. A throwback to Marnie. "This is Kylie. She's a budding artist and she loves to dance. Her favorite singer is Taylor Swift and her favorite show is *Fancy Nancy*. She wants to be a veterinarian when she grows up."

Taste in music aside, the little girl was a sweetie. She chewed on her lip and gave Spencer a serious once-over. "Are you Mommy's daddy?"

"No, I'm her brother. Like Mikey is your brother."

"Do you have a dog?"

"Nope." No dog, cat, gerbil, or goldfish. A guy who was gone for chunks of time during fire season couldn't have pets. They might starve.

"What's wrong with your leg?"

"I hurt it jumping out of a plane."

"People don't jump out of planes. They fly in them."

"I promise you, I jump out of planes. To fight fires."

"Firefighters use trucks, not planes."

Sane people did. Or so he'd been told. He gave Kylie the thumbs-up and pointed to the baby in the car seat. "And who is sleeping beauty?"

"My little sister. Janie. She can't talk. All she does is sleep." Kylie wrinkled her small nose in disgust. "She can't even feed herself. Even Mikey feeds himself. Her diapers stink."

"Give her time. She'll catch up." Like Spencer knew anything about babies. He'd never been close to one. He smiled up at Angie who was busy wiping her face. She blew her nose with a squawking honk. "You did good, Sis."

"Thanks." She smiled, but the waterworks started all over again. "I guess Rocky didn't think so."

"Rocky is a—"

"Not in front of the kids."

"Right. Sorry." He took the crutch she offered him and pulled himself to his feet. "By the way, who's the girl?"

Angie swiveled and glanced over her shoulder. "Which one? Why?"

"The one in the blue dress." He had plenty of experience with Amish folks. Everyone in Eureka and Rexford did. He'd never given them much thought before. Too quiet. Too shy. Too religious. But this girl had a straight-on gaze that didn't look away even as her cheeks went red. The blonde was pretty, but the tall woman had something her friend didn't. A steady but inquisitive gaze that told him she saw more than most. And maybe even liked what she saw. "With the eyes."

Angie scrunched up her face the way she always did when he said something she couldn't understand. Angie was a people person, but she didn't pay attention to the outside. She was only interested in their inner workings. She rattled through a bunch of papers on the table until she picked up one. "That's Mercy Yoder. Her sister is Leesa."

"Mercy me." He hummed under his breath. "Mercy, Mercy."

Angie smacked him on the arm. "Don't even think about it. They're Amish. They don't mix and there's a reason for that. You don't even believe in God."

The beautiful, eerie silence after his chute opened filled Spencer's head. The tops of towering trees. Open meadows. Streams. Fleeing deer loping across the landscape. "We haven't really talked in ten years. You don't know what I believe. You don't even know me."

"Whose fault is that?" Angie grabbed a wipe from a bulging pink Barbie backpack sitting on the table. She proceeded to wipe up the stinky spit-up coursing down Janie's chin onto her onesie. "I've written you and called you and sent you birthday and Christmas presents. What do I get from you? An occasional postcard and an obligatory call on my birthday."

"Obligatory. That's a big word."

"Don't try to make me feel stupid."

"I'm not. You've changed, that's all. How much are they paying you to work in this church?"

"Better than the day care. I've been taking some online courses. I want to get my bachelor's degree in social work." Janie started to wail. Angie unbuckled her and picked her up. "I need to change her. Can you keep an eye on the other two for a few minutes? If folks come in, give them the registration form to fill out and send them over to Lori, the Red Cross representative."

"You really think it's a good idea to leave your kids with *me*? Which reminds me, how could you possibly leave them with Marnie?"

"*Mom* has changed." Angie tucked the backpack over one shoulder and walked away. "You just said you have too. So put your money where your mouth is, put up or shut up, and prove it."

Wow. If anybody had changed, it was his sister. She had gained ten pounds with each child, but she carried it well. With the magenta hair and bright-purple glasses, she was a walking billboard for free spirit, something his sister had never been. Gone was the scared kid who hid in her closet at night, fearful of the strangers who traipsed from the bedroom to the bathroom or danced to old-timey rock 'n' roll in the living room at three in the morning.

He winked at Kylie, who returned the favor by wrinkling her entire pixie face in an effort to squeeze shut one eye. "Do you know how to do the hokey pokey?"

"Yep." Kylie sounded scornful. "Since I was little."

Crutches would add spice to the song.

"Give me a minute and we'll play." He riffled through the registration forms. Mercy Yoder of West Kootenai. Daughter of Jonah and Elsie Yoder. Sister of Leesa. They were staying at a house a few blocks down on First Avenue that used to be Sally Knowles's place. She'd been ancient when he was in high school.

Grandmother to Juliette Knowles, trouble on two legs, who'd spent her every waking moment making the lives of boys at Eureka High School miserable. Thankfully, she'd been too young for him.

And probably long gone from Eureka. It wasn't large enough for a personality like Juliette's. She needed a bigger pond.

Unlike one Mercy Yoder. Still waters ran deep and were far more interesting.

CHAPTER 10

EUREKA, MONTANA

A car honked. Mercy jumped. Caleb pulled up on the reins and moved to the right, letting the car pass. After Lola's decision to bail out, the ride had been mostly silent. The longest day of her life had turned into the longest evening. They turned onto the block where Grandma Knowles's house sat. Mercy couldn't think of a thing to say to Caleb—nothing she could say in front of Leesa, that was sure.

"It's been a while since you've been in a buggy in the city, hasn't it?" Caleb's glance sideswiped Mercy. "I promise you I'll get you home safely."

No sarcasm wound itself through the words. In fact, they almost sounded tender.

He knew how awful she felt because he surely felt the same way.

"I wish it were home." Mercy regretted the words as soon as they escaped. "I mean, Grandma Knowles's house is nice and it's nice of the Knowleses to let us camp out there, but I hope we don't stay long."

"I'm trying to think of it as an adventure. It was an adventure to move to Montana from Indiana. This is part of that adventure."

Mercy studied his expression. Bravado replaced tenderness. He always put on a good show. His real feelings remained a mystery to her.

An adventure was hiking in the mountains and spotting a grizzly bear or a huge elk or a mountain lion. An adventure was camping by the lake and hearing the howl of the wolves. An adventure was catching a big rainbow trout and frying it over an open campfire.

"I could do without this kind of adventure."

"I know you're not one for it in general."

The sarcasm had returned. A woman didn't enter into marriage as an adventure. It was a sacred union that had to last a lifetime. "What is that supposed to mean?"

"Nothing."

A smothered snort of laughter from the back. Leesa seemed to be enjoying this.

More awkward silence.

The chorus of raspy crickets accompanied the *clip-clop* of the horse's hooves on the asphalt and the squeak of the wheels. Maybe they had colds. For reasons she couldn't fathom, Mercy found this funny. She chuckled. The chuckle of an exhausted schoolteacher who'd left her job and her home to stay in a stranger's house.

"What are you laughing at?" Caleb sounded offended. "I'm glad you find this conversation funny."

"It's not—"

Squealing tires and the sound of a revving engine saved Mercy from having to share her silly thought.

Juliette's little white pickup swerved in front of them and pulled into Grandma Knowles's driveway. The windows were rolled down and country music blared. Juliette stuck her head through the window and waved. "Just the people I wanted to see."

"Whoa, whoa." Caleb fought to control Snowy. He eased the buggy to the right and parked at the curb in front of the house. "Easy, girl, it's just a lady who should know better."

"Sorry about that." Juliette's blithe expression belied the words. "Mercy, your dad called my uncle Rod's house."

Feeling like an old woman, Mercy climbed down from the buggy. Her legs threatened to buckle. She clutched her skirts and willed her body to cooperate. "What did he say? Where is he?"

"In Rexford." Grinning, Juliette popped from the truck. "He asked us to tell you they're staying with the Wamplers until tomorrow. It got so late, he didn't think it was a good idea to drive the wagons and trailers on the highway after dark."

"Praise Gott. I'll tell Mudder." Whooping like a ten-year-old, Leesa scrambled down from the buggy, scampered up the steps, and disappeared through the door without a backward glance.

Juliette turned to Caleb. "Are you staying here?" Her shapely eyebrows lifted under blonde bangs. "That would be cozy."

"Nee, no, no." Caleb ducked his head and wrapped the reins around his hands. "I'm headed to some friends of Arthur's. Ian and I are staying in their RV."

"Ahh." With an exaggerated sigh, Juliette leaned against the bumper, one cowboy boot propped behind her. "Too bad. No man of the house here tonight."

"We can take care of ourselves." Mercy glared at her friend. Juliette grinned in return. Mercy turned the heat up on the glare. "Do you want to come in and say hello?"

"I'm pooped. I need to get to Uncle Rod's before they lock me out. They're big on early to bed, early to rise." Juliette glanced at the phone in her hand. Disappointment flittered across her face. She stuck it in the back pocket of her jean shorts. "Did you see Nora or Christine?"

"I saw Christine on the road. She yelled something about needing to talk ASAP. I haven't seen Nora."

Mercy would miss their regular powwows to discuss the mysteries of love. What did Christine mean about the ASAP? Had something happened?

"Did you have a chance to stop by the church?"

Knowing Juliette, she only wanted news of one person. "Tim was headed back to Libby."

Disappointment returned to her dimpled face, but she shrugged. "No biggie. I just wondered if he knew the latest evacuation status."

"He's fine, Jules."

His face red, Caleb cleared his throat. "I should get moving." He clucked and shook the reins. The buggy started forward. For a second it looked as if he would say something else. Instead, he pulled from the curb and drove away.

"Take care. Don't be a stranger." Juliette waved after the departing buggy. Caleb didn't look back. "Mercy might need your help moving boxes tomorrow."

"Juliette!"

"Caleb still loves you."

"He's doing what Plain people do. We help each other." Mercy popped the tailgate and hoisted herself onto the truck's bed. "And we forgive—even *Englisch* women who drive like crazy people."

Even the seemingly unforgivable.

"Hey!" Juliette nudged Mercy with her elbow. "He's waiting for you to change your mind. You could, you know?"

"No. That door closed." Mercy fanned her face with her fingers. "I wasn't ready when it opened, and just like that, it closed again."

"You haven't done a very good job of explaining why you let it close." Juliette hopped onto the truck bed next to Mercy. She swung her shorter, bare legs. "You claim it's because you don't want to give up teaching, but I'm not buying that. Plain women have one goal in life and that's to get married and start popping out babies."

"Juliette!" Her friend had a way with words that could still make Mercy cringe, even after all these years. They'd become friends over cookies at a volunteer fire department fund-raiser at age five. Other English girls lived close by, but Juliette was the one who stuck. If anyone would understand, Juliette would. "It was so unexpected. He went from talking about books and taking me fishing and hiking to asking me to marry him. There was no . . . in between."

Juliette wrinkled her perfectly shaped nose. "No in between? You mean like no necking."

"Juliette!"

"You are turning the prettiest shade of red, girl." Juliette laughed. She had a big laugh for a small woman. "There's no shame in wanting to kiss a man before you marry him. What if he slobbers all over you? A woman needs to know. It's called compatibility."

"I can't talk about this." Mercy really couldn't. Thinking about it embarrassed her. Say the words aloud and she would melt into a puddle on the ground. "He probably thought he was being considerate."

"Maybe he doesn't have any experience and he doesn't know how to get started. You could start and let him follow."

"We don't do that." At least she didn't think so. Her mother never talked about it. They learned that physical love was between a husband and a wife. To do otherwise was to sin. How couples got from point A to point B before marriage wasn't clear.

"It could be that Caleb is something special. Really special." Juliette's voice quivered. Mercy peered through the dusk, trying to see her friend's face. Juliette looked away. "The physical stuff is overrated. A man who's willing to wait is special. Maybe Caleb has a hard time expressing his feelings. Some people do."

Juliette rarely strung ten serious words together. Something about Caleb had touched a painful chord in her heart. Mercy sought a way to take that road with her. "Is something wrong? You seem . . . sad."

"Life is too short for sad. Caleb's world is turning to ash and he'd like to go down in flames with his honey." Juliette tugged her phone from her pocket and studied it again. "He's regretting not getting a kiss or two, that's all."

Juliette was back. No point in trying to drag anything out of the queen of stubborn. If Caleb's feelings were locked up like prisoners in a county jail, Juliette's were in a vault in her own personal bank. "Call Tim."

"Nope."

"Why not?"

"He's working. Besides, I don't really care if he calls or not." Her attempt at nonchalance was pitiful.

They sat quietly then, staring up through the willow and birch trees at a sliver of moon that cast fleeting shadows between wind-driven clouds. "I can still smell the smoke," Juliette whispered. "Am I crazy?"

Mercy studied the branches that bent and bowed in the

wind. "Not crazy. I don't think we'll ever get the smell out of our clothes."

"Or our noses."

They laughed together.

Her eyes burned—from exhaustion and smoke, not tears. Mercy ran her thumb over a black smudge on her apron. "I'm so happy Daed, Abraham, Moses, and Seth are okay."

"Everyone got out okay, except Dillon Rodgers and his boys. And Andy Martin and Chris Sandalwood. They all refused to leave."

"A few of the Plain men stayed behind too." Mercy bit her lip. *Don't ask, don't ask, don't ask.* "Do you know a man named Spencer McDonald?"

"Oh, wow, I haven't heard that name in forever." Her face gleeful, Juliette clapped like she had a new pair of cowboy boots. "Spence. He was a senior when I was a freshman in high school right here in Eureka. He was a hottie. That seems like a hundred million years ago. Why do you ask?"

"No reason." A hottie. *Sorry, Gott, but she's right.* Mercy leaned back and stared at the sky. "He was at the church. Tim didn't seem to like him much. He said he was trouble. How does he know Spencer? I thought he grew up in Libby."

"Tim's parents are divorced. His mom lives in Libby and his dad used to live in Eureka when Tim was a kid. He's somewhere in Missoula or Helena now, I forget which. Anyway, he and his sisters split their time between the two for a while. He went to school here some."

Divorce was an alien concept. To have parents who didn't live together or even see each other must be hurtful for a child. Vows were for life. Another reason to enter into them with great forethought. "Did you know Tim then?"

"He was a junior when I was a sophomore." Juliette's giggle turned into a full-on laugh.

"What's so funny?"

"It's not funny really. I shouldn't laugh. At the time everyone did, though." She turned her phone over so the sparkly purple case shone in the porch light. "He asked me to go to a dance with him once."

"Why is that funny?"

"Before I could answer, he barfed all over my bowl of chili and the cinnamon roll on my tray in the cafeteria."

Mercy's mom always said to walk a mile in the other person's shoes. If she'd been born a boy, would she have the guts to ask a girl out? Never. Mercy's heart thumped in a painful one-two-three beat. Romance didn't openly blossom in her classroom, but that didn't mean feelings didn't sometimes spill out among the older students during recess or lunch. Plain teenagers were taught to be respectful of others' feelings, but they were teenagers. "Poor thing. I could never go back to school if that happened to me."

"It was awful, but you know how kids are. Everyone in the cafeteria thought it was the funniest thing since farts." Juliette rubbed her already-red eyes. "They didn't have barf all over the front of their shirt. It stank. I almost hurled myself. I had gym fourth period so my teacher let me shower."

Kids could be meaner than rabid raccoons. "What did he do?"

"He ran out of the cafeteria. He never talked to me again."

It seemed easier to speak of these things in the dark in a strange place on a strange day. Juliette wasn't like Nora and Christine. She'd been to college in Missoula. She'd dated lots of men there. "Are you going to marry him?"

"Probably not. He won't ask."

"Why not?"

"Because he's an old-fashioned guy. He says we're unevenly yoked. Who even talks like that anymore?" Juliette plucked at a thread on her denim shorts. "No offense. Besides you guys, I mean."

Tim was a smart man, even if it hurt Juliette's feelings. "You grew up going to church. Don't you believe in God?" Mercy hesitated. Her community didn't talk much about these things. Their faith focused more on how they lived than what they believed. Despite having been baptized, she wasn't always convinced of God's presence. *Sorry, Gott.* "Don't you believe God has a plan for you?"

"Streets of gold and pearly gates and a sixteen-year-old virgin who gives birth to the Son of God? Why would I find that hard to believe?" Despite her sarcasm, Juliette sounded wistful. "I went to Sunday school and vacation Bible school and youth group and on mission trips and all that stuff. Then I stopped going. When I went to college, no one could nag me about not going. It was a relief."

One of the reasons Plain families didn't want their children straying far from home. It was too easy to be sucked in by worldly temptations. What would it be like to not go to church on Sunday morning? Not to pray before and after meals and at bedtime? A person would have a lot of free time. "Don't you miss it?"

Him. Didn't she miss Him. Gott.

Juliette grabbed a handful of her long, shiny hair and braided it with deft fingers. "I miss certain people. And I hate the way my dad looks at me on Sunday morning when he comes back from church and sees me sitting in my pj's at the kitchen table drinking coffee and reading the funnies." Her fingers faltered. "It would be nice to think there's a God who cares about what happens to me, but I just spent four years getting a degree in communications and marketing. I've sent my résumé everywhere. You know how many job offers I've received?"

"None?"

"Bingo. You know how many interviews I've done?"

"None?"

"Two, and neither place has called me back."

"And that's Gott's fault?"

Juliette's laugh had a bitter sound. "According to my dad, it's my fault. He says I should've looked at the job market when I chose my major. He says teachers get jobs—that don't pay squat—and the medical professions like doctors and nurses are needed. My mom wanted me to be a nurse. Can you imagine me as a nurse? I hate needles and blood and vomit and bodily functions. Plus, my bedside manner sucks."

Juliette was as brutally honest about her own faults as she was about those of other people. One of the traits Mercy liked about her. She spoke her mind when Mercy couldn't get up the nerve. "I like teaching. At the end of the day, I feel like I've accomplished something." Even though she longed for adult conversation some days. "At the end of the school year, that something really adds up when you have twenty-seven students."

"Honey, you were made to be a teacher. Me, my best talent is talking."

"Teachers talk."

"To little kids."

The screen door banged behind them. Mercy swiveled. Mother stood on the porch, her arms wrapped around her middle. "Aren't you two coming in? I saved some hamburgers and cottage fries for you."

"Thanks, Elsie, but my stomach is cranky today." Juliette blew Mother a kiss. "You're sweet to ask."

"I'm not hungry, but danki." Mercy slid from the truck bed and dusted off her hands. Mother lingered at the door for a second, then disappeared again. She probably felt as discombobulated as Mercy did. "Do you want to come in for a glass of tea at least? We have ice."

It felt strange to invite Juliette into her own grandmother's house. "I mean—"

"Don't worry about it." Juliette hopped down. "It's getting late and I know you guys get up at the crack of dawn. I should head back to Aunt Tina's before Dad comes looking for me. You'd think I was still a high school kid."

Without thinking, Mercy wrapped her friend in a quick, hard hug.

"Hey, what's that all about?" Juliette grabbed Mercy's arms and gave her a once-over look. "Are you sick?"

Embarrassment burned through Mercy. Maybe she was sick. "I'm glad you're okay, that's all. Everything is so—"

"Up in the air?" Wincing, Juliette rubbed her stomach. "My dad says change is good. But what does he know?"

She laughed. Mercy forced a smile.

They were about to find out.

CHAPTER 11

One more extra-large Styrofoam cup of Pepsi and Tim could catapult from a cliff and fly. He clomped into his home base at the Lincoln County Sheriff's Office with the sweating cup in one hand and his cowboy hat in the other. Could it still be the same day? Rising before dawn. Miles driven to and from towns in the county. Evacs. Juliette with her full lips and piercing stare. His shirt stuck to his back. His boots weighed thirty pounds each. His eyes felt like dirty, dried-up cotton balls.

The drab tan room, crowded with desks, was a beehive of activity despite the late hour. Deputy Sal Quinones stood at maps taped to one long wall pointing at Kootenai National Forest. Deputy Kimberly LaFortune nodded as she rewound her jet-black hair into its usual bun. She removed a bobby pin from her mouth and jabbed it into the bun.

"You made it." Emmett held a sheaf of papers in one hand and a Grizzlies mug in the other. Coffee spilled on the laminate flooring as he lumbered toward Tim. "Want some mud? I just made a fresh batch."

Tim held up his twenty-ounce cup. "I'm good."

"Gotta pick your poison, I reckon." Emmett shrugged. "Let's huddle up, guys."

No matter how many women served as deputies, they were all guys to Emmett, who treated everyone the same, like the high school football team captain he'd been twenty-five-plus years ago. He shoved aside a stack of folders on Sal's desk and perched his backside on the corner. "Let's make this quick. By daylight, it's likely we'll be doing evacs for the West Fork and Gibralter fires. I've got the dispatchers standing by for the Code Red notification.

"The mayor is working on getting the high school ready to open first thing in the morning to serve as a shelter. The Emergency Operations Center will be open in a couple of hours in the Ponderosa Room at the city building. Police, fire, USFS, the county commissioners, PIO, Fish and Game, etc., will have reps there."

"Emmett, we've all got family—"

"I want each of you to take fifteen minutes as soon as we're done here to call your family, friends, significant others—whoever you need to talk to." Emmett cut Sal off with a firm but sympathetic look. "I got family too, guys, I know this is tough. Do what you've gotta do, but remember, your job is to keep everyone safe, not just the people you care about."

"What about the Caribou Fire?" Kimberly threw out the question amid the murmur that spread through her colleagues. "We don't have the resources to evacuate around three fires at the same time."

"Up north, we've got ICE, Border Patrol, reserve deputies, police, and volunteer fire as well as USFS." Emmett reeled off the agencies with the practice of a man who had to please constituents and politicians on a regular basis. "It's all hands on deck for every agency, not just us."

"What about community meetings?" Tim worked to keep his tone neutral. Emmett had underplayed his own concerns, and everyone in the room knew it. The sheriff's mother was just out of the hospital after a bout with pneumonia. His brother suffered from bipolar disorder and couldn't be trusted to stay on his meds. "Do you need some help covering those?"

Emmett took a long sip of his coffee. It dribbled down the front of his shirt, joining dry sweat stains. "Yeah, I do. Thanks. We've got one at the high school here in town coming up. There's another at the high school in Eureka. I expect I'll need to go to that one."

"Why that one?"

"Got word a few hours ago from the USFS IC that at least thirty structures in Kootenai burned this afternoon. Right after we got people out."

Tim's gut knotted. He closed his eyes for a second. *God, You reign. Your ways are not our ways.* He opened his eyes. "Homes?"

Juliette's home, lovingly constructed by Lyle and his family and friends.

"At least ten. We don't know which ones right now, but you can be sure the word will spread quickly. One way or another, folks will want back in there as soon as possible."

"When will that be?"

"We'll know more tomorrow." He settled the coffee mug on Sal's desk and glanced at the papers in his hand. "Day shift guys, you need to go home and grab a few hours' shut-eye. Kim and Sal, you head to Rexford and then on to Eureka. Make sure everyone understands there's no going home until we give the word."

He went down the list assigning officers to the shelters and to the roads that led in and out of evacuated areas. In the case of Kootenai, access was limited to one road.

Tim waited until the group dispersed to follow Emmett into his office. A large framed photo of his ex-wife, Colleen, and the kids hung on the wall over his head. The divorce had taken them all by surprise, but none more than Emmett, who assumed his wife had accepted his long hours and inability to sleep as part of the territory. Emmett plopped in his chair and rubbed his eyes. "I thought I told you to get some sleep."

"You should listen to your own orders." Tim glanced over his shoulder. The hum of the beehive had resumed. "You sure you don't want to take your parents to Polson now rather than waiting until the evac comes down?"

"Paul can keep an eye on them for now. He's on his meds." Emmett scratched at his orangey-red five o'clock shadow. "What about you? Have you talked to your mom?"

"No."

"You'll hate yourself if you don't."

"And I'll hate myself if I do."

They commiserated in silence for a few minutes. "It took us way longer to get those folks out of Kootenai than it should have."

What was really bothering the man? "It's to be expected when you're dealing with people who have no phones."

"I pulled into Jonah Yoder's yard and they were still trying to set up sprinklers."

"They work hard for what they have."

"The fire was on top of them."

"We evacuated almost four hundred people in twenty-four hours. That's pretty darn good. Even the Forest Service couldn't have predicted the fire would cover two miles yesterday and another four today." Everything IC Mark Stover told Tim at the command center in Libby bubbled up. Emmett already knew it, but sometimes it helped to have someone reiterate the facts. "The control lines did nothing. Neither did the patches of forest that had been cleared. Between the dry conditions and the winds, everyone did what they could."

"Tell that to the people who lost their homes."

"I reckon we will at those community meetings."

"About that. I'll take these first two, but you're welcome to provide backup."

"Whatever you need. They will want to know when they can get back in there."

"We should be able to escort one person per household in tomorrow to get what they can." Emmett grabbed his coffee mug and sipped. He grimaced. Nothing like cold coffee dregs. "Nobody stays until they get this fire under control. Nothing says it won't circle back around."

"Got it."

"Now go to bed."

"I have a phone call to make." Tim glanced at his watch. "Or maybe it will wait until morning."

"Timothy."

Only his nana, who now resided with her Savior, had called him that. "Fine."

In the bull pen, he waved off Sal's attempts to stop him for one of those middle-of-the-night talks that only served to put off the inevitable and pushed through the double doors. He didn't let up until he settled onto the leather seat of his pickup.

A glance at his phone revealed Juliette hadn't called or texted. When he wanted her to call, she didn't.

It was late. Mom first.

He tapped his mother's name listed in his favorites although she was far from it.

"It's late. What happened? Are you hurt?" Eleanor Trudeau's reedy voice rose to a whispered shout. "Did someone shoot you? Did you shoot someone? Am I going to see body cam videos on the six o'clock news—?"

"Mom, Mom, Mom!" Her breathing filled the line. She had COPD and spent her days hooked up to a portable oxygen tank after thirty years of a two-pack-a-day habit. "Mom, I'm fine. No one shot anyone. Is Leland there with you?"

"Of course not. It's late."

"As if that makes a difference to you two."

Mom labored under the illusion that Tim didn't know her longtime significant other, Leland Delacroix, lived with her in the worn three-bedroom house she'd occupied since her divorce from Tim's father. Unlike his dad, who took his children to church when it was his weekend, Tim's mom had little interest in organized religion. "Don't get snippy with me, young man. I can still turn you over my knee and use a switch on your behind."

Not since a growth spurt the summer before his freshman year of high school turned him into a giant who towered over her. "Sorry, ma'am. Did you pack?"

"Pack what?"

"Mom. You received a pre-evac notice, didn't you?"

"Maybe. I'm not sure."

"Pack enough clothes for a couple of weeks. I'll drive you and Leland, if he wants, up to Eureka in the morning. You can stay with Aunt Maddy until they get this thing under control."

"Maddy's allergic to dogs."

Aunt Madeleine wasn't allergic to dogs. She simply didn't like her sister's taste in a yappy dog with wet, slobbery fur on her chin. "I'll take Snickers."

"You'll neglect her."

"Pack, Mom. I'll be by first thing in the morning to pick you up. Tell Leland I'm happy to give him a ride as well."

He prayed daily for a change of heart in his mother, but it wasn't his place to judge. Or let his beliefs stand in the way of offering help to a veteran who'd served his country in the U.S. Army for thirty years, including two tours in Iraq during Operation Desert Storm.

"You sure are bossy."

"Got it from you."

"I could call one of your sisters."

"Camille is working the night shift now at the ER in Butte. Vic and Romy just went back to school. They'll miss class if they come back up here." And all three would call him to complain that Tim hadn't dealt with the situation. Why inconvenience them when he was still in Libby? Would always be in Libby. "I don't mind and I'm right down the road."

"Fine."

It took a second to realize she'd hung up. He laid the phone on the dashboard and considered the September sky. Smoke drifting from the west made it look like a foggy night. No stars twinkled. No moon shone. If a person didn't know better, he'd think rain might be on the way. Sweet, wet, cooling rain.

Memories inundated Tim. The smell of wet earth. Shivering as the wind whipped the rain across his face and soaked his

T-shirt. The high-pitched giggles of his little sisters. They wore dinky swimming suits and jumped barefoot in rain puddles in the front yard.

Then Mom came home from work and spanked him for letting them play outside in the rain. He was the oldest. He was the one in charge.

The man of the house from the time he was ten.

He, Camille, Victoria, and Romy shared one thing in common besides parentage. They all wanted out of that house. They'd worked hard for it—outstanding grades, summer jobs, perfect test scores. Scholarships. Camille was a first-year ER nurse. Victoria and Romy were freshman at Montana State. Vic was premed and Romy prelaw.

Good professions. They would earn a decent living. Libby had nothing to offer them. They would not be back.

Tim had made his choice, and God had blessed him with a good job in his hometown. The girls claimed that because Mom favored him, he didn't know what it was like to live with her as her health deteriorated. Then she had to quit work and go on disability. At which time she became more querulous, according to the fearsome threesome.

They were wrong. He did know. Behind the cranky, old-broad facade was a scared woman who loved her children and would go to great lengths to get their attention. She claimed her short-lived fling with a married acquaintance that ended her marriage with Tim's dad had occurred because Dad didn't pay enough attention to her. Somehow she'd never outgrown the childish idea that negative attention was better than no attention at all.

A cricket chirped. He grabbed his phone from the dashboard.

B that way.

Juliette. Finally. He heaved a breath and thumbed a response.

What way?

U don't call. U don't write.

Working.

Pouting.

About what?

I don't want to fight.

Tim jabbed her name just below his mother's on his favorites list. She picked up immediately. "Where are you?"

"Sitting in my truck outside the office."

"Why? You sound down."

"Tired."

"I wish you were in Eureka right now. I'd come give you a back rub."

Tim stifled a groan. "That would not be a good idea."

"Why? Because you might like it too much?"

Lord, give me strength. "Get some sleep."

"I'm in bed. Do you want to know what I'm wearing?"

"I'm hanging up now."

"Don't hang up. I'm sorry." The teasing quality disappeared. "I don't mean to make things harder. I just don't understand why you don't want me like that."

He closed his eyes. Juliette's need to seek affirmation through the ways of the world was sad. Two years of friendship and he still hadn't found a way to convince her that not taking her up on her offer reflected how much he *did* like her. His feelings for her made it harder every day to stick to his convictions—

harder than it had ever been with any other woman. "You know that's not true. Stop fishing for compliments. The ways I like you are too numerous to mention, but the most important way has nothing to do with the way you look or what you wear."

"I want to be with you." She sounded like a little girl denied a candy bar. "Forever."

"I'm bringing Mom and Leland to Eureka in the morning. Maybe we can meet at the Front Porch Grill House for a quick bite—if I don't have to go to Kootenai."

"Are they letting us back in?"

"One person per household will be allowed to pick up some things, but no one will be allowed to stay. Now go to sleep."

"Call me when you're on the way."

"Sweet dreams."

"I'll dream of you."

He disconnected and held the phone against his chest for a ten-count. His heart thumped. He tried not to picture Juliette with her hair down, laughing, her bare legs and feet splashing him with water the last time they took a picnic lunch to the lake.

She was the most beautiful woman in the world.

He leaned over and tugged open his glove compartment. His hand rested on his well-worn copy of *The Measure of a Man*. Not tonight. He selected the Reverend Dr. King's *Thou, Dear God*, a collection of Dr. King's prayers, instead. Tim's own words seemed inadequate tonight. He thumbed through his favorites, read several, and closed the book.

I know, Lord, it's my fault. I did this all wrong. But I've never asked You for much. I'm asking You now, please heal her heart. Whatever it is that keeps her far from You, remove that obstacle.

I can't walk away from this one. I'll wait as long as I have to, but she's it for me.

Dr. King and Pastor Matt would have all kinds of things to say about that prayer. Starting with "His will be done, not yours," followed by "Don't be unevenly yoked," followed by "Be more concerned for her spiritual well-being than what you want."

All true.

No way he would sleep now.

He slid from the truck and trudged back inside.

. . .

Tears slipping down her temples into her tangled hair, Juliette clutched her phone to her chest. She stared into the darkness. Her throat ached. Her jaw hurt from gritting her teeth. Permanent heartburn had taken up residence in her stomach and throat. Plenty of men—college boys, really—had said the magic words to her. But they would've said anything to get what they wanted.

When did it start? She couldn't put her finger on the exact moment. Freshman cheerleader. Homecoming court. Head varsity cheerleader by her junior year. Homecoming queen her senior year. Hers had been the stereotypical rise in popularity in a small town. Big fish in a small pond. An average student at best, her grades suffered from the hours spent practicing and performing at games followed by victory celebrations.

She liked being liked. She liked being pretty.

Until being pretty led her down a dark path away from a bonfire at the lake one night to a place that still haunted her dreams.

"You're the shallowest woman on the face of the earth." She tugged a pillow over her face. It smelled of Aunt Tina's cedar chest and lavender potpourri sachets. Her stomach roiled and burned. She tugged the pillow down so she could wrap her arms around it. Soft pillow, not Tim's thick chest and biceps inflated by years of pumping iron and doing push-ups in his spare bedroom. So he said. She'd never been invited to his house. He liked his boundaries. "You just want what you can't have."

She rolled until her body plopped over the side of the queen-size bed with its Amish Nine Patch quilt and landed on her knees. She faced the bed and clasped her hands the way she had as a little girl when Dad came in to hear her prayers at bedtime. "Okay, God, here's the deal. What do I have to do?" This was stupid. She cradled her head in her hands. "Tim says we can't be together until I figure out things with You. So here I am. What do You want from me?"

Silence.

The door popped open and slammed against the wall. "Hey, you're awake." Courtney barged into the room. "I thought you might be asleep already."

"I figured from the way you tiptoed in all quiet."

"Sorry." Courtney sprawled across the bed. "What'cha doing down there?"

"I lost an earring. I was looking for it."

Courtney rolled over onto her back and tugged her oversized, blue GOD'S NOT DEAD T-shirt down around her skinny thighs. "For a minute, I thought you were praying. Feel free to pray for me that I get these stupid braces off next month. They hurt."

"Me? You know better. Get Mom to pray for you."

"She already does. It would be nice if you would do it too."
Courtney rolled over on her side and propped her head on her
hand. "We could go to church together again."

"That's not happening."

"Everyone knows you stopped going to church to tick off
Mom and Dad because they grounded you and wouldn't let
you go to the tailgate parties anymore after you got that ticket
for underage drinking." Courtney grinned. "It worked. But I
figure by now you're over it."

It had nothing to do with ticking off Mom and Dad. If only
it were that simple. The memories pounded against the barri-
ers erected to keep them from drowning her in the sick shame
of knowing she had only herself to blame. What had happened
to her that summer night was all her fault. She grabbed a jumbo
container of Tums from the table next to the bed and popped
three in her mouth.

"You've been eating those like candy for days now. What's
the matter?" Courtney frowned. "You look green around the
gills. Are you sick?"

"Nope. Too much chips and salsa at supper. I can't believe
you remember all that stuff with me and Mom and Dad. It
was a long time ago. You were in grade school. Now you have
your own battles to fight."

She might be in high school now, but Courtney still had that
fresh, naive innocence that people loved. Her platinum-blonde
hair was cut in a layered bob. A smattering of sun-induced
freckles decorated her upturned nose. She was all arms and legs
and most of the time seemed to have no cares beyond when her
next softball game would be. She wore no makeup and hadn't
donned anything besides jeans, shorts, T-shirts, and sports
uniforms in years. Juliette had never looked that innocent.

"All that yelling and crying, who could forget?" Courtney scooted across the bed and squeezed onto the floor next to Juliette. "I want to pray that our house is still there. And the tree with the tire swing. And the trampoline. Oh, and the basketball hoop and the barbecue pit. Do you think the old green pickup is still there?"

Dad had taught Juliette to drive in that 2003 Ford F-150. In a year it would be Courtney's turn. "I don't know. Let's hope for the best."

"Let's pray for it." Courtney laid her head on Juliette's shoulder. "I know stuff isn't important, but I really want our house to still be there. I've never lived anywhere else."

Juliette swallowed the knot in her throat. She was not only shallow but selfish. "You start, sweetie. I'll chime in."

If her little sister needed her to pray, then Juliette could at least pretend she believed it would help.

It couldn't hurt, could it?

CHAPTER 12

WEST KOOTENAI, MONTANA

The forest of blackened toothpicks stretched as far as the eye could see on both sides of the highway. Caleb's breakfast of oatmeal and two cups of coffee, black and strong enough to burn the enamel from his teeth, roiled in his stomach. In a mere twenty-four hours, their beautiful, pristine world had disappeared.

He focused on the road ahead of Sheriff Brody's SUV. Maybe if he didn't look left or right he could block out the ravaged wasteland. Neither Brody nor Jonah had spoken in the last twenty minutes. The closer they came to Kootenai, the quieter it became. Caleb sought words, but none appeared. They'd turned to ash.

The sheriff had warned them this quick trip to salvage anything worth salvaging would be hard. Hard didn't do this new world justice. The majestic Douglas fir and ponderosa pine, the birch, the tamarack, the spruce—they were all gone. Despite rolled-up windows, the stench of smoke and burnt earth crowded the car's interior and squeezed into the spaces, blanketing the air around the three men.

The stench of death and destruction permeated everything and everyone.

Caleb glanced in the passenger side mirror. Nearly three dozen trucks, trailers, and SUVs followed. Kootenai's men hoped for the best, expected the worst, and were ready to pick up the pieces. Ian was in Tim Trudeau's truck behind them. They'd prayed together before heading to Kootenai. Tim prayed for the strength to accept whatever lay ahead of them.

"We'll go to your place first, Jonah." Sheriff Brody eased his vehicle onto Wilderness Trail. "Then yours, Caleb. After that we can circle around and see if anyone else needs help."

"I'd like to go by the school." Caleb strove to match the sheriff's matter-of-fact tone. Mercy would be devastated at the building's loss. She claimed to want to dedicate her life to teaching. Even if that had been an excuse to turn him down, she really cared for her job and her scholars. They would have to make plans for rebuilding if it didn't survive. The school board would need to meet about replacing desks, books, and materials. Another auction fund-raiser would be necessary. "It would be good for the children to have lessons in town so they don't miss too much."

"Gut idea. If it's still there, we can bring back the desks and books." Jonah spoke for the first time. "Mercy will appreciate keeping busy too. We can set up in Mrs. Knowles's garage."

Many of the children had gone with their parents to other Plain families in Libby and St. Ignatius. Still, a few would need lessons. Mercy wouldn't want them to get behind. She was that kind of teacher. That kind of person.

Caleb rubbed his aching temple. Time to move on. Just like he had in Indiana. By now he should be an expert at failed attempts at courting. With Leyla he'd thrown himself into courting with all the fervor of an eighteen-year-old. A year later Leyla had broken up with him. All those rides, those stolen moments for kisses and hugs behind the barn. The secrets whispered under the stars. It had been perfect. At least he'd thought so.

Six months later, Leyla married a man from a neighboring district and moved away.

She'd never explained what he did wrong.

Neither had Mercy.

Emmett pulled onto the gravel road that led into the twenty-acre parcel that had been in the Yoder family for twenty-five years. He stopped at the end of the drive. No one spoke for several seconds.

"Let me out." Jonah's bass deepened. "Please."

Caleb pushed the door open and hopped out. He held it for Jonah, who didn't look his way. His expression had gone doggedly blank. It seemed likely he didn't know tears rolled down his lined cheeks.

Hands on the gun belt tucked under his big belly, Emmett trudged around to the other side of his SUV. "Let's give him a minute."

Caleb followed. The thick layer of gray-white ash under his feet felt like snow. His brain refused to comprehend the frantic messages sent by his eyes.

His shoulders slumped, Jonah slogged through the ash past charred trees to a pile of mangled metal and debris where his family's home had once stood. Their everything was gone. Only a heap of metal remained.

The woodworking shop no longer existed either.

Simply gone. Like a tornado struck—only this one used fire to reduce rubble to ash.

How could the sun shine on a scene of such destruction?

An eerie silence haunted the remains. No breeze brushed

leaves on trees. No birds sang. No flies buzzed. No crickets or cicadas or chorus of bullfrogs. Not even a dog barked.

Only the sound of Jonah's harsh breathing filled his ears. His heart ached for this man who would have to return to Eureka to tell his wife and children that their home had not survived. What would it be like to have that burden on his shoulders?

A house was not a home. A family made a home. Years of living in a house with people who remained distant no matter how hard he tried to get closer had taught Caleb that. Jonah still had his family. He would make a home for them, even if it was a trailer or a two-room duplex. He was that kind of a man.

The kind of man Caleb longed to be.

"Look." Emmett pointed to a spot to the left of where the four-bedroom house once stood. A simple lean-to where Jonah had parked his buggy had survived.

"How is that possible?"

"A shift in the wind? Fire is capricious and irrational." Emmett leaned against his truck and rubbed stubble the color of copper pennies on his cheeks. "In all the years I've been doing this, I've never seen a fire run like the one yesterday."

The lean-to stood out like a lantern on a dark night. It served as a sure sign that life would go on.

"When can we start rebuilding?"

"The threat isn't over. The fire is only partially contained."

"Is it safe for us to be here?"

"For the moment." Emmett held up his phone. "The IC will call me if it makes a turn in this direction, but we shouldn't linger too long."

Caleb turned to look for Jonah. The older man had removed his straw hat. He squatted next to the pile of debris that had been his home. His fingers touched the ashes. Caleb straightened. "Should I tell Jonah?"

"Jonah and I've known each other a while." Emmet straightened his hat. "Let me."

The sheriff was a kind man. Caleb squatted and touched the ashes at his feet. Cold. *Gott, Thy will be done. Your will, not mine. Give us strength and stamina for the road ahead. Give us the peace that passes understanding.*

He rose as Jonah and the sheriff approached. "I'm sorry for your loss, Jonah."

"No need." Jonah returned the hat to his iron-gray hair and dusted his hands on his pants. "Did you see the lean-to is still there?"

"I did. Amazing."

"A miracle." Jonah pulled the SUV's door open. "Let's go see what we can salvage at your place."

Not much, as it turned out. When they drove up, Ian stood, legs spread, arms crossed, staring at a pile of debris much like the one at Jonah's, only smaller.

His throat tight, eyes burning, Caleb took his time approaching the man who'd been his cabin mate for almost two years. At his footsteps Ian turned. Caleb waved his hand at the remains. "Not much to salvage."

"Nothing." The two syllables held no hint of emotion. Ian removed his straw hat and flapped it in front of his face. "The other cabins are gone too."

"Much work to be done then."

"It's so hot." Ian settled the hat back on his sweaty hair. "I'm tired of summer. It's time for autumn."

Caleb searched for words of comfort for a man who reserved words as if they were as scarce as water in the desert.

"Autumn will be here any day. Morris will want to rebuild, I reckon." Morris Tanner owned the cabins and rented them out for income. "Cool weather will be gut for rebuilding. We'll want to get at least the walls and roof up before winter comes."

"I'm thinking of going home." Ian's gray eyes filled with unshed tears. He wiped his face with his shirtsleeve. "I can stay long enough to help rebuild, if you need me to."

"You'll go back to Kansas then?"

"I missed Haven even before this." His hand swept out toward the cooling metal twisted into strange shapes like a fancy sculptor might make. "This seems like Gott's way of pushing me that direction."

"What about Leesa?" Ian hadn't said much, but Caleb had gathered from the giggling conversations between Mercy and her sister that Ian and Leesa were courting. "Will you ask her to go with you?"

"Jah, if she'll have me."

"Gut for you." He searched for the right words. "Don't worry about helping us. Go on."

"You'll settle down and take a *fraa*. You won't be living in a cabin much longer anyway."

From Ian's lips to God's ears. Caleb's longing encapsulated in one sentence, thrown out for the world to hear by a man determined to drift away. Caleb's throat tightened. He took a breath. "Are you sure you want to go home?"

"My daed will be happy to have me back on the farm." Ian took two steps back from the cabin remains. "These mountains are beautiful, but they can be brutal. Farming is simple and straightforward. Kansas is flat and easy."

He removed his hat and flourished it in a strangely formal

bow. "I'll leave all this to you." He slapped the hat back on his head. "The Planks, the Schwartzes, and the Borntragers still have their houses."

"Praise Gott." The conversation was over. Ian had made his decision. While he withdrew, Caleb would move forward. "We're headed to the school next."

"I'll help."

They joined Emmett, Tim, Jonah, and the others in a small, sedate parade—it brought funeral processions to mind—past other Plain properties where sheds and outbuildings had burned, but no other houses. The English families hadn't fared as well. Jonah leaned forward and pointed past Caleb. "The Drakes lost their place."

"I feel for Mike and DeeDee. They were fixing to be empty nesters in a few years. Their three kids grew up in that house." His gaze straight ahead, Emmett drummed his thumbs on the wheel. "I know your young'uns will be torn up too, Jonah."

"Job will take it hard. We never did find those rabbits of his." Jonah managed a terse smile. "He'll have the chance to see the forest return. The wildlife will come back. By Gott's grace, no one was hurt. Life will go on, better than before."

A true statement by a strong believer. Caleb studied the road ahead. He longed to be the stoic, stalwart believer that Jonah was. His own father and his uncle had died in a freak accident when Caleb was still in school. The community rallied around them. He and his siblings never wanted for anything.

His mother never remarried. She worked hard and had no time for affection. A house did not a home make. A hole always remained where his father's love had once been.

The loss of the cabin must have stirred up those memories. It had been a long time since the images assailed him. The procession to the graveyard. The two gaping holes in the ground. His mother's stoic face.

The empty chair at the table.

No more silly jokes. No more claps on the back. No more instructions on how to do the things a man must know how to do.

Gott, help me.

As a child he'd prayed those three words hundreds of times. Lying in his narrow bunk in a room shared with his brother. Ashamed of the silent tears shed into the pillow.

Eventually, he became accustomed to the cool quiet that seeped into the cracks and crevices of their once warm, joyful home. To the way his mother never quite looked at him when she talked. She was busy, dishwater up to her elbows or hanging clothes on the line or digging up potatoes in the garden or rushing to take pies to the church dinner.

A boy couldn't complain because his mother worked hard.

Not a Plain boy, certainly.

Emmett pulled into the open field where the log cabin school stood amid the ashes. The outhouses were gone, but not a stick of the brown rectangular building had been marred.

"Praise Gott." Jonah pushed the door open. "He is gut."

Caleb followed. How would Mercy feel when she found out their family home was gone but the school remained? Should a person read a message or a sign into this? That she should continue her work with the scholars?

His pea-sized brain hurt. He'd never been good at schoolwork. He loved to lose himself in books, reading for hours on end, but the monotony of schoolwork had sent him into a world of daydreaming that irritated his teacher to no end. To spend time in a classroom after the allotted number of years would be downright torturous.

Mercy would beg to differ.

He hustled into the building. Smoke damage, but flames had touched nothing. Add some paint and it would be good as new. He went to Mercy's scarred oak desk first. Her lunch box still sat on one corner. The image of her startled white face the day before filled his mind. How quickly she'd recovered. Such presence of mind. Such concern for her charges. No matter how scared she was on the inside, on the outside she remained cool and collected. He respected her. How did a Plain man say that to a Plain woman?

"I'll help." Ian approached and grabbed the other end. "You want to go backward or forward?"

Puffing, they hoisted the desk into the back of Emmett's truck. Ian wiped his red face with a bandana and stuck it in the pocket made by the button flaps of his flat broad pants.

"Mercy will be happy to have her desks and her books." He brushed past Caleb. "Maybe she'll appreciate your bringing them to Eureka enough to offer you a piece of her huckleberry pie."

"She's not a great cook, truth be told."

"Leesa's piecrust is tender, and so is her pot roast."

Not so with Mercy's, but a lifetime with the woman he loved would be worth all the tough piecrust in the world. Caleb stared at the mangled metal that had been a swing set. Life was short. Nothing mattered more than spending it with the people a man loved.

Time to rebuild. Houses with lots of room for little ones to sleep. Swing sets for when they played outdoors.

And the room where husband and wife snuggled in the dark and spoke words of love. Caleb would not give up on that dream.

Or on Mercy.

. . .

The half-muffled sobs of a grown man would pierce hearts made of the heaviest stone. Tim swallowed against tears that threatened to escape. He gritted his teeth and waited. Head bowed, Lyle Knowles stood at the edge of his family home's ruins. Lyle lifted his purple Colorado Rockies baseball cap and settled it on wild silver-streaked blond curls. He turned and trudged through thick ashes into the greenhouse only a few yards from the pile of debris. It stood as sun filled and bright as ever.

"Tim, come here." Lyle's voice, hoarse with emotion, floated from the interior of the aluminum frame and polycarbonate shelter that held everything from fragrant herbs to pansies and Boston ferns to cucumbers and green peppers. "You have to see this."

Dodging the remnants of trees, an old truck, and a riding mower, Tim sloughed into the nursery. Lyle held out a perfectly round, perfectly red tomato. "Isn't it beautiful?"

Tim accepted his offering. The tomato's silky skin felt warm.

"Do you like tomatoes?" Lyle tugged another from the plant that sprawled over a wire cage intended to keep it up off the soil in the plant bed around it. "I love fresh tomatoes. I wish I had some salt and pepper. Go on, eat it."

"Thanks. There's nothing better than a fresh tomato." Tim took a big bite like he was eating an apple. Juice and seeds ran down his chin. He laughed and slurped them up. "Hmmm, so good."

Busy with his own tomato, Lyle didn't answer. He walked farther down the aisle and stopped by smaller pots of basil, oregano, and thyme. He leaned down and inhaled. "Amazing, isn't it?"

"That it survived. Yeah." Tim inhaled the warm scents of earth, peat moss, decaying leaves, and herbs. "It's amazing, too, that come spring we'll see all kinds of green sprouting where there's only black, burnt remains now."

Lyle wiped his hands on his pants. He sighed. "I loved that house."

"I know."

"We'll rebuild."

"I'll help."

"I'll borrow my brother's RV in the meantime. Casey and the girls can stay in town, but I need to be out here."

"As soon as they give the all-clear."

Lyle clapped Tim on the back. "Thanks."

"I haven't done anything yet."

"You put up with my oldest daughter." Lyle snorted and headed for the door. "Only the Lord knows why."

Tim followed him out to the truck. "About that."

Lyle tugged his door open and then paused, his gaze on the pile of debris that had once been his home. "Son, I'm not trying to get in your business. I know she's a handful. Always has been."

Now. He wanted to discuss this now. Maybe it made sense. The home where Juliette grew up lay in ruin. They couldn't go back. The only way left was forward.

Tim waited until the other man climbed into the cab and did the same on his side. "Truth is, sir, I'm stuck."

"Don't sir me. I told you, call me Lyle."

"I'm stuck. I thought maybe you could give me some insight into why she's the way she is."

"And how is that?"

His grimace said it all. *Tread softly.* Juliette was the man's daughter. Lyle could say whatever he wanted about her. Let someone else bad-mouth her and that was a bear of a different breed. "Why do you think she stopped going to church?"

"Good question." Lyle sank against the leather seat. "She was never an easy one to figure. Juliette always chafed at being told what to do. But it got worse in high school. From one day to the next. Seriously, she came home from a trip to the lake with her youth group. She basically dug in her heels and refused to go back. No matter what we said or did, she flat-out refused. She said we could ground her for life and it wouldn't matter. I always wondered if something happened or if it was just female hormones in a dither."

No way discussing female hormones with Juliette's dad sounded like a good idea. Tim punched the starter and the truck roared to life. He circled around until the decimated property appeared in his rearview mirror. "She doesn't talk about her issues with church or religion unless I push hard. Then she gets really defensive."

"I've tried. Her mom has tried." Lyle sounded weary and sad. "Casey has a book on praying for your adult children. We did a lot of that when she was in high school and then when she left for college. We'll keep praying. Our pastor says to take it to the Lord and let Him do the work."

"I try to do that. Every time I think I took it to the altar and left it at His feet, I discover I've picked it up and started carrying it around again."

"You're a good man."

"I try."

Lyle pulled his hat down over his eyes and leaned his head back on the headrest. "Do me a favor."

"I'll do my best."

"She's worth the effort. Don't give up on her."

"I won't."

A few seconds later Lyle's snores rattled the windows and kept Tim wide awake for the rest of the drive.

That and the thoughts that fenced in his head. *Don't give up. Pray. You're gonna get your heart broken. She's worth it. She'll never change. God's will. Broken heart. Worth it.*

What he wouldn't give for a decent radio station in this neck of the woods.

CHAPTER 13

Uh-oh. This didn't look good. Juliette widened her smile. No dice. His expression somber, Tim threaded his way through the square wooden tables at the Front Porch Grill House. His boots clomped on the varnished wood floor. Usually the scent of hamburgers on the grill and french fries made him grin. Not today. He had all the trappings of a man on a mission. He also filled out his tan uniform quite nicely.

Stop that.

She picked up her menu, then laid it down. She always had the peanut curry salad. The Grill had the best burgers in town. Maybe she should get a vegan burger on a gluten-free bun. Her stomach might appreciate it, but her taste buds would scream bloody murder. If she were a betting woman, she'd bet on Tim having the cowboy burger. Why a man would put barbecue sauce on a perfectly good burger was beyond her. Thinking about food didn't help. In fact, it only made the pain that lived in her gut worse.

It was now or never. She'd always been able to move mountains with a toss of her long blonde hair. Not this mountain. He would never go for it. Changing jobs. Following her to Billings. The call offering her a job came at nine o'clock, also known as the crack of dawn in Juliette's book.

After fleeing her childhood home with her entire family and a few possessions the day before, the call had been anticlimactic. She'd had to think about who the headhunter was. When the painfully cheerful words penetrated the fog, she hopped from bed and did a Snoopy dance. She needed gainful employment badly. Tim had a job, but he was in law enforcement. Surely he could work in law enforcement or security in Montana's largest city.

But would he want to?

The billion-dollar question.

Tim towered over her. His swoop-down kiss on her forehead came and went so fast she had no chance to turn her face and try to catch his lips on hers.

"Why so grim?" She caught his hand and tugged. "A decent kiss isn't too much to ask."

"You know better." His tanned face now red, Tim settled his cowboy hat on an empty chair, grabbed a menu, and eased into the chair next to her. At least he hadn't sat across from her like he usually did, keeping safe real estate between them. "Have you talked to your dad?"

"No small talk. No how are you." She reached up and smoothed his mussed hat hair. Someday there would be no hair to muss, but that didn't keep him from being a handsome man. "No I've missed you."

"Juliette, I'm serious." He wore his sheriff's deputy air, but his deep-blue eyes were filled with warm empathy and something that seemed like dread. "Have you talked to him?"

"He called a couple of times, but I didn't pick up."

Tim met her gaze head-on. "You should probably go to your aunt's."

"So he can pick at me about what I'm doing and where I'm going and my life in general? Not until I have a burger with my guy. Or a salad, as the case may be. I ran five miles this morning and worked out with my cousin's equipment. I feel good. I don't want to blow it—"

"We went out to Kootenai this morning. That's why I had to push back lunch to an early supper."

Juliette's throat began to ache. Her heart hammered in her chest. Salad no longer sounded appetizing. "And?"

"It's gone. I'm sorry."

"Everything?" The words seeped out in a high-pitched squeak she didn't recognize as her own. "All of it?"

"Except for the greenhouse."

The greenhouse she'd spent so much time watering with a hose. "Maybe I should've watered the house more and the greenhouse less." Saving stupid plants, when everything her parents owned went up in smoke. The table and chairs where they played Monopoly and dominoes and cards on cold winter days. The pool table where she learned to beat her father at his own game. Mom's library of what she called "clean" romances. Grandpa Knowles's grandfather clock that reminded them it was time to catch the school bus.

Their clothes, their shoes, their coats, their blankets, their beds.

Their everything.

The family photos taken every year at Christmas. Baby photos. Her paintings that Mom had proclaimed so good they had to be framed. Mom and Dad's wedding photos. Grandma's baby photos.

Mementos that couldn't be replaced.

"Nothing you did or didn't do caused this to happen." Tim's big hand enveloped hers. She held on and breathed through tears not allowed to fall. "I promise you that."

"I should go home. Mom will need me."

"Right." He squeezed her hand, let go, and rose. "I'll walk you to your truck."

"Wait." She couldn't put this off. Not and sleep tonight. "We need to talk."

Hat in hand, he wavered. "Can we talk and walk?"

"Not for this. I want to see your face."

"That is serious." He sat. "I imagine I'll want to see yours as well."

Juliette waved the waitress over. "Could we get two diet Pepsis in to-go cups?"

"No burgers today?"

"No time."

"I'll get those drinks right away."

"Stop procrastinating." Tim squeezed her hand. "There's nothing you can say that will make me care for you less."

Care, not love.

"I got a job offer."

"That's great." Despite the words, his expression turned wary. As if he knew what was coming. And he did. How many jobs were there in Podunk Eureka or Libby, for that matter? "Doing what? Where? Here in Eureka?"

"Not in Eureka."

"Kalispell? That's still close enough. Even Polson would work."

Juliette shuffled the ketchup and mustard bottles so they flanked the salt and pepper shakers. She cleared her throat and met his gaze. "In Billings. It's a great offer for someone with no experience. It's an assistant account executive at a marketing firm. The pay is good, enough to live on at least. It's a foot in the door."

"In Billings." His lips barely moved. His face had turned to concrete. His blue eyes were as cold as the water of Lake Koocanusa in winter. "Congratulations. When do you go?"

"Don't be like that." She grabbed his hand. He jerked it into his lap under the table. "Come on, Tim, you knew this was a possibility."

"It's for the best."

"What do you mean?"

"I've prayed and prayed." His Adam's apple bobbed. He scanned the surrounding tables as if seeking a way to escape. Seconds passed. "I think I just got my answer." He pushed back the chair ever so gently and stood. "Have a good life, Juliette."

"Come on, Tim. It's only eight hours away." She shoved between tables. His long stride forced her to scurry past other customers who stared unabashedly. She was making a scene. It would get back to her mom and dad. So be it. "Tim, Tim, stop." She grabbed his arm as he pushed through the door and onto the sidewalk.

"There's nothing more to say. I knew this was a crap-shoot." He tugged his arm free and glowered at her. He never got mad. Never. Frustrated. Sarcastic. Borderline broody. But never angry. Until now. "I won't stop praying for you. But I understand now. This wasn't meant to be more than friend evangelism. I allowed myself to cross that line so I'm learning a hard lesson."

"Come with me. There's so much to do in Billings. It's a big city." By Montana's standards, Billings was a sprawling metropolis with 170,000 residents. "We can explore it together."

"Come as what? Your buddy?" His jaw worked. The pulse in his temple jumped. "You don't get it. Playing with people's feelings is dangerous. And wrong. Just wrong."

"I'm willing to make it more. You're the one . . ." She paused to let the Wilkenses, who lived down the street from Aunt Tina, pass. They smiled and nodded. Tim smiled and nodded. Then went back to scowling at her. "You're the one who can't get past our differences. Every couple has differences. I have friends who are married, and one is Catholic and the other is Lutheran. They make it work."

He pivoted and started toward his truck.

"Tim, come on. Can't we at least talk like civilized human beings?"

"This isn't about differing denominations and you know it." He jerked open the truck door and turned back. His stare would melt rubber. "It's about believing or not believing. I can't force you. You have to come to Jesus of your own accord. And until you do, we're never going to be together."

He paused. His gaze softened. He ducked his head and stared at the sidewalk. "It breaks my heart." He whirled, slid into the truck, and slammed his door. A second later the window whirred down. He stuck his head out. "You break my heart."

Then he drove away and left her standing there.

"Love you too."

The truck disappeared and she still couldn't move. Her throat hurt. Her head hurt. Acid burned her stomach.

"Man troubles?"

She jumped and turned. The waitress stood halfway in,

halfway out the Grill's door. She held out Juliette's phone. "You forgot this. It's been blowing up. I figured you decided against the Pepsis."

Juliette thanked her. Three texts from her mother.

Come home.

Come home now.

Please come home now.

Two more from Courtney.

Whr r u? I need u.

Mom's crying. Come home.

Didn't they get it? Juliette couldn't come home. Home was gone. Aunt Tina's house was not home. She wished she could go home.

Or anywhere but here.

On my way sweetie.

CHAPTER 14

Language escaped Mercy. Did her father speak in German or English? His mouth moved, but the words were gibberish. She bit her lip and concentrated on the tiny burst of pain. Better than acknowledging the enormous, looming, agonizing ache that permeated every bone and muscle in her body. The stoniness on her father's face when he returned from the trip to Kootenai had told the story.

Gone. Obliterated. Leveled.

Leesa's hand crept into hers. Mercy squeezed. Her sister squeezed back.

Don't cry. It's only stuff. Don't cry.

Father sat at Grandma Knowles's walnut dining room table, Moses on one side, Abraham on the other. Her hands spread, palms down on the embroidered tablecloth, Mother sat across from him. Despite her pale face, her expression never wavered when Dad delivered the news.

The fire took everything except the lean-to where he stored the buggy.

Did God call that a sense of humor?

"What about Nickle and Dime?" Job climbed into Dad's lap and snuggled against his chest. "Did you find them?"

Dad's rough-skinned hand rubbed Job's back. His gaze dropped to the table. "We didn't see them. All the animals, even the rabbits, are smart enough to know they have to leave when fire comes."

"What about the others?" Abraham asked. "Who else lost homes?"

"At last count, Emmett said thirty-one buildings were lost, but many of them were outbuildings. We're the only Plain family to lose a home." Dad's tone didn't change. He might have been discussing the weather forecast. "Ian and Caleb's cabin is gone. So is Luke and Samuel's cabin and the one Andy shares with Henry. The rest are all Englisch homes."

"So the Beachys and the Masts have homes to return to?" *Thank You, Gott.* A tiny, insistent voice refused to be silenced. *But why not us? Why not the Yoders?*

"Daniel's shop is gone and their sheds. Robert's outbuildings are gone, but the house still stands."

The grandfather clock next to the hutch dinged the hour in the silence. Five o'clock.

It's not fair. Life's not fair.

Mercy sneaked a gander at her siblings. Their faces ran the gamut. Shocked, stoic, worried, sad. But no one seemed angry.

Am I the only one, Gott? The only one who wants to stomp my feet and throw myself on the floor in an epic tantrum?

No answer.

She should be thinking of others, not herself. "The Knowleses?"

"The house is gone. The stable. The sheds. Only their plant nursery survived."

"Where will we live now?" Hope leaned against Mom. "Will we stay here? What about our clothes and our books and our beds?"

"And Grandma Zook's cedar chest." Leesa would be thinking of marriage. Her time was at hand. "It had the quilts in it that I was to have when I marry."

"And the table and chairs that were Grandma and Grandpa Yoder's." Mercy gripped her hands in her lap. "It's hard to image our house without them."

"All things we can do without." Dad's stern gaze skipped from child to child. "It doesn't matter if we understand these things. Gott's will be done. We are blessed. We have each other. We have all we need."

"Your daed is right." Mother wrapped her arm around Hope. She smiled. Her voice held steady. "I'll use Grandma Knowles's old Singer and get started on more pants for the boys. Leesa, tomorrow we'll go into town for material. I'll put together a list."

"Pots, pans, dishes, silverware." Hope got into the spirit of things first. "Sheets and blankets and pillows."

"We don't have beds . . ."

Mother's scowl stopped Seth from finishing his sentence.

Starting over from scratch. Where would the money come from? How could this be God's will? What made it a blessing?

The questions tumbled over each other, trying to escape. Mercy gritted her teeth. Father's expression said he expected them to fall in line. Especially his older children. The younger ones would follow suit.

She counted to ten twice, then backward. "What about me, Mudder? What shall I do?"

"You, I have a surprise for." Dad stood, Job clasped against his side like a sack of potatoes, and strode from the room. "Don't just stand there, come on."

Mercy did as she was told. Of course, everyone followed behind, their procession set to the music of Job's delighted giggles. Through the kitchen, out the back door, and across the driveway to the freestanding garage. Emmett's truck was backed into the driveway. The tailgate stood open in front of the garage door.

Caleb leaned over a stack of desks in the truck's bed. Her scholars' desks.

"They survived." This time the tears threatened to escape. Mercy raised her hand to her mouth and swallowed hard. *Breathe.* "The school survived."

"It did." Dad's awkward pat on her shoulder served to make the tears that much harder to stymie. "Caleb and Ian and the other men helped load everything up to bring it here. Emmett let us use his truck. We figure you can have school in the garage until we're allowed to go back."

At the sound of their voices, Caleb turned. He shoved his straw hat back. Sweat soaked the brim. His shirt was wet as well. "We could use some help here. Mercy, show us how you want them arranged."

"Jah. Of course. Danki for this."

Mercy whirled and scampered into the garage before he could see her face. He'd come to the school to warn her. He saved Lola—at least tried to save her. He gave them a ride home from the church. He gave no hint of the terrible hurt she must've caused him. He was such a good man. Her heart pounded in her chest. He showed her how he cared in so many ways. Why could he not take that one step further? To be vulnerable to her in a way no other person would ever be? Wasn't that what husband and wife did?

Nor did he raise the topic again. Confusion at his behavior ran circles around her. If only she could ask him. Did he not find her appealing enough to kiss? To touch? And why was that so important to her? Should it be?

She had no one to ask.

The dark garage smelled of car oil and grease even though it had been years since either of the Knowleses drove a car. Intricate, lacy cobwebs festooned boxes that lined one wall. Shelves on the other side displayed gardening tools, a Weed Eater, a blower, and all manner of household cleaners, paint, and varnish. This had served as Grandpa Knowles's domain before his death three years earlier at the ripe old age of eighty-five.

"I'll wipe off the window above those boxes and see if I can get it open." Caleb paused next to her. "Don't worry. You'll have it whipped into shape in no time."

The soft concern in the words loosened sadness's grip on Mercy. Breathing came more easily. "I'm sorry about your cabin."

"I reckon it's not the same as losing the house you grew up in." His face somber, he set the desk to one side and scavenged in a box on top of a workbench until he came up with an old rag. "I only lived in that cabin two years. For you, it's your whole life. That must be a bitter pill to swallow."

"Did you have mementos from your life back home there?"

His face lined with sadness, he shook his head. "Some clothes, some household goods, that was it. I brought my tools and my books with me."

His books. He saved his books after telling her to leave hers at the school. "What are you reading right now?"

A question she asked him every time she saw him when they were courting. Talking about books had been the highlight of many of their jaunts around the lake or hikes in the Cabinet Mountains. She missed that more than she thought possible. "I'm sorry. That's none of my—"

"A biography of Abraham Lincoln. It's really good." His face turned red as if caught in a naughty prank. "I finished another Louis L'Amour Western last week."

She had teased him about wanting to be a cowboy. She even bought him a cowboy hat for his birthday. They'd laughed so hard her sides hurt. His blue eyes turned dark with emotion. At that moment she'd been sure he would kiss her.

So sure, she couldn't stop staring at his lips.

But he hadn't. Instead, his face a deep red under his tan, he laid the hat on the table and offered her a piece of cake. "Did you save the hat?"

His smile died. "I did."

She tore her gaze from his face and stared at the dirty cement floor. "It won't be much use when it comes time to rebuild."

"It reminds me of better times."

The words were replete with bewilderment.

She didn't dare sneak a peek. A tiny flutter of air brushed her cheek.

As if he might touch her.

She squinted his direction. He turned away.

"Gott's will be done." Glancing toward the door where her father stood talking to Aaron Plank, Mercy pushed a mower into a corner and out of the way. "That's what Daed says."

"But that's not what you say, is it?" Caleb popped open a wooden ladder and scooted it closer to the window. A few seconds later he had the narrow single pane open. Fresh air wafted through the stuffy garage. "It's all right. I promise I won't rat you out."

He knew how her mind worked. Even when she didn't say anything. Perplexed, she studied Caleb's face as he slid the ladder aside and began stacking boxes to make more room for desks. He was sincere when he said he wouldn't tell on her. "It's hard for me to understand how Daed can be so certain that this is Gott's will. And why would Gott want us to be homeless? Why would He want us to lose everything we've ever had in a few short hours? What purpose does this suffering serve?"

"I can promise you one thing. Your daed feels the loss strongly." Caleb dusted his hands on equally dusty pants. "I don't know what Gott's plan is. None of us do. But Scripture says He 'is able to do immeasurably more than all we ask or imagine, according to his power that is at work within us.' I try to hold on to that."

She'd caused him so much pain and yet here he stood, trying to make her feel better. "I'm sorry—"

"It's okay. I reckon your daed would like something cold to drink."

The door slammed shut on that conversation. "I'll bring out some cold tea. For you too."

He slipped from the garage and began helping Abraham and Seth pull her big oak desk from the truck.

Mercy surveyed the garage quickly filling with a hodge-podge of desks and boxes of books. Her new classroom. The swirling emotions didn't abate. The fire, the destruction of her childhood home, Caleb, a stranger named Spencer McDonald whose face appeared in her mind's eye at odd moments. Everything seemed to conspire to send her life spiraling out of control.

The only thing she could do was bring cool drinks to a group of men who were hurting and trying not to show it. Think of others instead of herself. Caleb had shown her that by his example.

It always came back to Caleb.

CHAPTER 15

Grandma Knowles's guest bedroom made escaping into a book easy. Mercy should've been asleep. Instead, dressed in a nightgown, she sat with her knees up and the gown pulled around her feet on the wide cushioned ledge next to the bay window. Floor-to-ceiling shelves filled with hardbacks, paperbacks, and children's books surrounded her like a lovely group of friends. Deciding which book to read had been her biggest challenge. If she lived here, she would never leave. Never set foot in the garage that—as of a few hours earlier—served as her schoolroom.

Hope snuggled against a pillow, her back to the light cast by the kerosene lamp Mercy stuck on the end table next to her perch. The little girl had been asleep the second she crawled under the rose-flowered comforter, a small lump in a king-size cherrywood bed.

The book by an author named Janette Oke—Grandma Knowles had an entire shelf dedicated to the novelist's works—was entitled *When Calls the Heart*. The novel told the story of a woman who left her home in Canada to teach in a coal-mining frontier town where the children were poorly educated and spoke little English. She did it because she had a calling.

In this new town Elizabeth—that was the heroine's name—had caught the interest of two men. Both were Mounties. Canada was only eight miles from where Mercy sat, so she understood what Mounties were and what they did. What she didn't understand was how Elizabeth was supposed to know which one to choose.

Mercy liked Caleb. A lot. He was sweet and kind and, to her inexperienced eyes, handsome. But an invisible wall separated them. No matter how much she whittled, pried, and hammered, the wall wouldn't come down. Caleb never talked about his family or Indiana. He never talked about his feelings for her. Even when he asked her to marry him, he hadn't said he loved her. What kind of proposal was that?

She would stick to pioneer stories and leave the fictional romances to the English ladies.

Curling her bare toes in sudden frustration, Mercy raised her head and brushed aside the gauzy shell-pink curtains to stare at the trees outside the window. A cool breeze brushed her face. September brought autumn weather. If only it would bring rain and douse the fire. Then they could go back to their lives. She leaned against the solid wall of the old house and searched for stars blinking between tree branches that danced the night away.

"You should be asleep." Her hands already removing pins and releasing the bun that had spent the day hidden under her kapp, Leesa padded into the room. "You disappeared as soon as the kitchen was clean and prayers were said."

"I thought I would get to sleep early. It's been such a hard day."

"But you couldn't sleep. Not surprising. Everything is topsy-turvy." Leesa pulled her dress over her head and hung it on a hanger in the closet at the other end of the room. Their first closet. "I'm pretending it's a vacation in a faraway town. We have a hotel room with all the Englisch stuff we don't have at home. Even your silly books."

"They're not silly." Mercy closed her mouth. Leesa always made fun of her reading. Mercy had learned not to rise to the bait. "Where have you been? It's late."

"Ian came by. We talked." Yawning so wide her jaw cracked, Leesa wiggled into her nightgown and slid onto the bed next to Hope, who didn't move a muscle. "When things settle down, he wants to get married. He wants me to move to Kansas with him."

"That's . . . wunderbarr. I'm so happy for you." Mercy hugged her book to her chest. She would miss her sister terribly, but her happiness was far more important. "Have you said anything to Mudder?"

"Nee, it's a secret until we talk to the deacon. You can't say anything."

"I won't." Sisters kept secrets. Especially this one. "Can I ask you a question?"

Leesa tugged the sheet up around her neck. "I'll try. I'm so wound up, I won't be able to sleep anyway."

"Does Ian . . . I mean, do you . . . are you and him . . . ?"

Leesa sat up. "Goodness. Spit it out, Schweschder. What's got you all tongue-tied?"

"Did Ian kiss you? Before he asked you to marry him? Did he . . . touch you?"

"Of course he did." Leesa giggled. The giggles stopped. "Didn't Caleb?"

"Nee. Not once."

"Now I get it. I'm sorry, Schweschder." Leesa sighed. She rolled over and closed her eyes. "Can you lower the light? I'm . . ."

Two seconds later she was snoring. Mercy didn't bother to turn down the kerosene lantern. She flipped the page in her book and settled against the wall. At least she wasn't crazy. She was simply confused.

Sobs filtered through the open door. She laid the book down and cocked her head. The sound, muffled this time, seeped into the room from the hallway. She grabbed her hair, twisted it in a knot, and stuck it under the collar of her nightgown. On tiptoes she slipped from the room.

Two doors down, the sobs had turned to sniffles. She peeked into the room shared by Seth, Job, and Levi. The boys had squeezed a bunk bed in next to the double bed. The only other furniture was a dresser. Light from the street shone through a single window.

Levi curled in a ball in the bunk bed, sound asleep, but Job sat straight up, his arms wrapped around a pillow as big as his six-year-old body. He laid his head on the pillow and hiccupped a sob.

"What's the matter, Bruder?" Mercy whispered as she eased onto the bed. Levi had a penchant for waking in the middle of the night to play with his wooden blocks for an hour or two before he returned to bed. "Why are you crying?"

"I don't think Nickle and Dime ran away. I think the fire killed them." Tears ran down his chubby cheeks. "All the deer and the elk and the antelope and the mountain lion don't have homes anymore. They're just like us, homeless."

"They're fine, Bruder. Animals are smarter than humans. They know exactly what to do when fire comes." Mercy spoke truth. Animals had been dealing with forest fires since the beginning of time. True, some fires were started by humans, but others began from natural causes that cleaned up the forest floors and created room for new life to flourish. "It's hard to understand when you're six. Or twenty-two, for that matter, but Daed's right. Your bunnies are fine."

"I want Lola."

"Lola can take care of herself." Cats were natural scavengers, and Lola had been a feral cat before she showed up at their back door in Kootenai, searching for scraps. "Lola would want you to get some sleep so you'll be ready for school tomorrow."

"I want my bed. The roof makes squeaky noises here, and the sheets smell different."

"We can't always have what we want." Almost never. Job was learning this hard lesson much earlier than Mercy. She was spoiled. And ungrateful. "Lie down and I'll sit with you until you fall asleep."

"Can you sing me a song?"

"If you want."

"What are you doing in here?" Seth tromped into the room. She couldn't see his expression in the darkness, but he sounded as cranky as his six-year-old brother. "Are you like Goldilocks, trying out all the beds?"

"Just checking on the little ones. Job is having trouble sleeping."

"He's too old for that." Seth slapped his hat on the dresser. His curly brown hair stood on end. "I can't believe I have to go to school tomorrow."

"This is your last year." Mercy hugged Job and kissed his silky hair. "You should take advantage to learn as much as possible."

"I'd rather be with Daed and my bruders. They're going hunting. Even Leesa is going. Daed figures we shouldn't waste this time. Mudder can put up meat for the winter in this kitchen just as gut as at home."

No wonder Seth was out of sorts. He loved to hunt. They all did. "Did you ask?"

"He said the Ordnung is the Ordnung. Wherever we live."

"Maybe this weekend you and I can have a turn."

"That's what he said."

"See there."

"Jah, Teacher." Seth's tone softened. He chuckled. "It's very strange to have a schweschder for a teacher sometimes. Here you are talking to me in your nightgown and tomorrow you'll tell me I have to write an essay or spell some stupid word like *parsnip.*"

"*Parsnip* is an easy word to spell—"

"You know what I mean."

It was weird. But they'd adjusted to it. "Good night."

"Feel free to oversleep in the morning," Seth called after her. "We can always start school late."

No, they couldn't. Somehow they had to find some semblance of normalcy in this place. Even if the comforters smelled like dryer sheets and the beds were so soft a person sank to the bottom or an entire wall of books called her name.

Not even if nothing—not even Mother's sourdough bread—tasted the same.

This life was temporary.

A new life lurked around the corner and down the road. If only it would quit messing around and get here so she could breathe again.

CHAPTER 16

Fourteen children from age six to thirteen stared at Mercy, their faces expectant. Far from the twenty-seven who normally joined her at the beginning of a school day. So much had changed since Wednesday. Their entire world had tilted and spun on its side. Many of the desks were empty, silent testimony to the scattering of families across northwest Montana due to the fire. Some were staying with friends and family in Rexford, Libby, St. Ignatius, or wherever they could. Despite the September sun outside, the garage seemed dank and shadowy. Should she turn the light on? What did the Ordnung say about that?

Summoning a smile, she lit the kerosene lantern sitting on her solid oak desk. She ran her fingers over the scarred wood, took a breath, and let her gaze flow over her scholars. "Guder mariye, scholars."

"Guder mariye, Teacher."

The response was as halfhearted as her own effort. Job sank farther into his seat. Seth leaned over and whispered something to his friend Zeke, the only other boy his age. Zeke smirked. Only Hope smiled. Her cheerful face sent shame coursing through Mercy. The teacher should set the example. "Come now. It's Friday, the last day of the week. You'll have all weekend to rest up. Today, we study. Whose turn is it to pick the songs?"

"Teacher, it smells like car in here." Emma wrinkled her nose. "And something moldy."

"I have the window and the door open. The breeze will air it out. Besides, you'll get used to the smells."

"I like the schoolhouse better." Job leaned back in his chair and crossed his arms. He'd been crabby and tearful at the breakfast table. He didn't touch his oatmeal, which irritated Father, who didn't eat much either. "This is a garage. You park cars in a garage."

"Plain people don't park cars anywhere." Her eyes bright with anticipation, Hope picked up her pencil and tapped it on her composition notebook. "We can have school anywhere, can't we, Mercy, I mean, Teacher?"

That was Hope. The eternal optimist. Like their father.

"We can and we shall. Come, we'll practice our English by singing 'How Great Thou Art' and then 'Jesus Loves the Little Children.' Then we'll get started with our reading for first through third, math for fifth through eighth."

Their groans weren't audible, but some couldn't keep their distress from their faces. Academic subjects didn't seem to have much meaning when fires threatened their homes.

"After that it will be time to work on essays. The topic of the essays will be My Favorite Frolic This Summer. This will be your first essay since we returned to school. Give me your best handwriting, your best grammar, and make it clean and neat. I want to see how much you forgot over the summer."

The essay would also give them the chance to think about something besides their current circumstances. Maybe they would realize those frolics would happen again. Whether it was canning vegetables from the garden, quilting, building a new shop, or clearing a piece of property for a bigger garden, the frolics would happen because their friends and family were still there, alive and well.

She should take a page from this lesson.

The children sang with gusto and the words of "How Great Thou Art" filled the room. The lyrics were difficult for the little ones, but what they lacked in pronunciation they made up for with enthusiasm. English hymns were fun because they moved so much more quickly than the Plain hymns. Mercy joined them.

Doodles wandered through the open garage door. Still singing, Mercy trotted down the single aisle between the girls' and boys' desks. Endeavoring to not miss a note, she shooed at him.

Doodles lifted his snout and sniffed. His silly mutt face widened into a smile. Dogs smiled, didn't they? "Shoo, go on, go on, *hund*."

The singing broke down. The children giggled and pointed. "Doodles wants to learn Englisch too." Hope leaned over and snapped her fingers. "Sit next to me, Doodles. You can help me write my essay."

The other children tittered.

If it lifted their spirits, maybe a dog in the classroom was a good idea.

Doodles licked Hope's fingers, then her face. She squealed. "Stop it, you silly goose."

"He's not a goose, he's a hund." That from Job, who slipped from his seat and scampered to his sister's side. For the first time in days, his chubby face lit up in a grin. "I want him to sit with me."

Control was slipping away. "Go back to your seat, Job. Doodles will sit with me while you work on your papers. You can play with him during lunch."

She grabbed the dog's collar and tugged. Doodles planted his behind on the floor and refused to move. She tugged harder. He responded with a low whine.

"What is wrong with you, hund? Let's go."

He stood, raised his snout, sniffed, and barked.

This would not do. No barking in the classroom. "Hush."

His claws *clickety-clacking* on the cement floor, he bolted toward the driveway.

Maybe that was for the best. "Let's get to work, shall we?"

His barking turned to soft woofs. The kind that signaled a welcome usually reserved for a friend.

Curiosity and a certain longing on their faces, the children, from littlest to biggest, swiveled to peer outside. Mercy sighed and trotted to the back of the garage for a second time.

Bedraggled and somewhat worse for wear, Lola the cat pranced toward her. Tail high, she stalked past Doodles and straight to Mercy, where she wound herself around Mercy's feet with a pitiful meow.

"Where have you been, kitzn?" Mercy scooped the ragged tabby into her arms. Lola's orange fur was caked with mud and other stinky remnants of who knew what. A scratch across her eye and another on the white patch over her nose made her look like a wounded soldier. Or Spencer McDonald. Where had that thought come from? "Did you bump into a tree or get into a fight?"

Lola yawned and then yowled, the complaint obvious in her screechy dialect.

"It's Lola. She's back, she's back."

Job rushed from the garage, followed by the other students, who crowded around Mercy. Everyone wanted to pet the wayward cat. "Easy, easy, you'll scare her into running again." Mercy handed the skinny bag of bones, fur, and teeth to Job. "She has some wounds but nothing that appears life threatening."

Mercy stood back. With amazing care and soft touches, the children took turns welcoming Lola to her new, temporary home.

"How do you think she found us?" Hope put her hand to her forehead as she squinted up at Mercy. "She's never been here before."

"I don't know. Instinct. Scent. Process of elimination."

Would Father say it was God's provision? Job needed his animals around him. He'd lost Nickle and Dime. Which might seem a small loss compared to the house, but to a little boy suddenly without a home, those little losses loomed big. His sense of security had been ripped away.

The essay could wait.

Arithmetic and spelling could wait.

Making little boys and girls feel secure in their new world was far more important.

CHAPTER 17

The unusual September heat outside the Eureka High School had nothing on the heat in the auditorium caused by the churning emotions of West Kootenai folks affected by the Caribou Fire. Mercy stuck close to her father, mother, and brothers as they squeezed into the last row of seats next to the Beachys and the Masts. Leesa had stayed back with the little ones. Nora and Christine immediately forced their brothers and sisters to rearrange so they could sit next to Mercy. Three days had passed since the evacuation, and it was obvious from the steady murmur that people wanted questions answered.

"We've been dying to talk to you." Excitement made Nora's pretty cheeks pink. She wiggled in her seat. Her dark-blue eyes were wide. "We heard about your house. We're so sorry."

Nora often spoke for Christine, who mostly didn't get a word in edgewise, but this time Christine added a one-armed hug around Mercy's shoulders. "I've been praying."

"I know you also lost several buildings."

"But not our homes." Nora squeezed Mercy's hand. "Which is why I don't understand why we have to go to Libby for a while."

"You're headed to Libby?" Tired from a sleepless night and a day spent in the garage-turned-classroom with her students, Mercy sank lower into her seat. Christine and Nora had been her best friends since they were old enough to trot around barefoot in saggy diapers chasing kittens who knew better than to be caught in their sticky, plump hands. So said their mothers. "I don't want you to go."

Stupid thing to say. It wasn't up to any of them. They were unmarried and living in their parents' homes. That summed it up. Her expression resigned, Nora shrugged. "Mudder says it'll be good for *groossmammi* and *groossdaadi* to have us around to help out. I'm pretty sure what she really thinks is I might learn something about the old ways from them."

"Doesn't your groossdaadi drive?"

"Jah, but Groossmammi still embraces the old ways."

"Isn't she worried you might end up evangelical?" No meanness permeated Christine's words. The Libby Amish were different. They'd left Kootenai to worship the way they saw fit. Mercy didn't know much about it—her parents saw to that—but many of Nora's extended family members embraced the new way of thinking while still calling themselves Amish. "My parents won't let me visit my cousins."

"Maybe they think we'll rub off on them."

Plain folks never lost hope for those family members who had strayed.

"I was hoping you both could come over for a visit." Mercy missed being down the street from her two best friends. "I'm teaching school in Grandma Knowles's garage now. I thought it would be fun for you to stop by tomorrow and help out."

"We're leaving for St. Ignatius tomorrow." Christine's shoulders slumped. "My family is moving back to Kansas. They're dropping me off at my *aenti's* to help in the store. After a visit, they'll go on to Haven."

"Nee!" Mercy squealed in unison with Nora. "They can't. You can't."

"St. Ignatius isn't far. At least I don't have to go to Kansas."

"What does Andy say?"

Everyone knew Andy and Christine were courting. Even if it was supposed to be a big secret. "He's going to Lewistown to stay with his family. We're still trying to figure things out. I'm hoping to see him here today."

More victims of the fire. Friendships. Courtship. Everything upended. Mercy clamped her mouth shut. Nora's and Christine's homes had survived. Still, their lives were changed.

A loud hissing sound followed by a whistle forced Mercy to tear her gaze from Nora and Christine and focus on the row in front of them.

Waving, Juliette made an exaggerated face and whispered loudly enough for a dozen people to hear, "Look who's here."

She swiveled and pointed to a group of people clustered in the open area behind the auditorium seating. Mercy twisted her body and peeked. Spencer McDonald leaned on his crutches and tickled the little boy in Angie Rockford's arms. The little boy pulled on his ear. They both laughed. He seemed more re- laxed than he had last week. Mercy tore her gaze from the scene and shrugged. "So?" Aware of her mother's penetrating gaze, she mouthed the single syllable and faced the stage where Sheriff Brody and other officials congregated near a U.S. flag on a stand by thick dark-blue curtains.

"What's that all about?" Nora asked as both she and Christine craned their necks to stare. "Who was she pointing at?"

"Nobody." Nobody her friends needed to know about. They

would agree that Spencer was a cute English man. Their rum-springa technically didn't end until they married, baptism or not. They would also be horrified to think she might gaze his way more than once. Which she wouldn't. Of course not. Would she? "Hush up, you two."

Something about his dark eyes ran circles in the back of her mind, chanting, *Look at me, look at me, you know you want to look at me.* Mercy sighed. *You hush up too.*

"Sorry, excuse me, sorry." Juliette squeezed past Abraham, Moses, and Seth in her red strapless sundress and leather sandals that allowed her to display matching red toenails. "I need to talk to the girls."

She paused long enough for Nora to sigh and move down one seat so Juliette could sit next to Mercy. She slid down into the seat and leaned close enough for her breath to tickle Mercy's ear. "Spencer was staring at you."

"Hush. They're starting."

"Be careful with him, my child. He has a bad boy history."

Juliette liked to act as if she were so much older and wiser because she'd been outside of their little hamlets in northwest Montana. All the way to Missoula.

"He's Englisch." Mercy pointed out the most salient detail about the man. She'd only met him once, yet every detail of that brief conversation stood out in her mind. *Be good. Be good.* The voice in her ear that always spoke when she knew she was tiptoeing over an invisible line blared. She shivered. "I'm sorry about your house."

Juliette's smile turned brittle. "It's just a bunch of stuff."

"That's what I keep telling myself."

The table and chairs made by Grandpa Yoder. The Prairie Star Patchwork quilt in navy, burgundy, and purple quilted by

Grandma Yoder. It had adorned Mother and Father's bed as long as Mercy could remember. Mercy's books bought with her hard-earned teacher's salary. Job's rabbits. The cedar chests that contained Leesa and Mercy's quilts and hand-me-down treasures to be used one day in their own homes. The snippet of hair and single nightgown kept when baby Esther died a few days after birth.

Material things weren't important. Yet Mercy's heart ached for the familiar that represented so many good memories.

Why did God let small, tight-knit communities burn? It couldn't be punishment. They'd done nothing but work hard, mind their own business, and follow the pillars of faith. Obedience, humility, *Gelassenheit*.

Juliette squeezed Mercy's hand. "So I think Caleb was looking for you the other day when—"

"Hush, they're starting."

Every bone in her body wanted to turn around and stare at Spencer. She chewed on her fingernail. Nora swatted at her fingers. Mercy rolled her eyes and gathered her hands in her lap. No peeking. The important information would come from the stage. The hair on her arms stood up. Goose bumps rippled across them as if someone had run his fingers across her skin.

Stop it. Pay attention. Gott, forgive me.

The briefing served as folks' first opportunity to get their questions answered and vent their frustrations. The important question—in Mercy's mind—was when could they go home? The men from Kootenai seemed more concerned with quibbling over how the fire was being contained.

Miles Rutgers got the ball rolling. "Are we a test bed for not suppressing fires in their infancy?"

A man who was introduced by Sheriff Brody as Incident

Commander Mark Stover rebuffed the idea with the shortest answer on record. "No."

"Tell the truth, we're the sacrificial lamb. This fire was at forty acres at one time. It seemed to me like it was 75 percent observed and only 25 percent put out. That was negligent." Rutgers, who lived down the road from Mercy's family, picked up steam. He leaned too close to the microphone on a stand near the center of the auditorium. It squealed. Mercy slapped her hands to her ears. Rutgers backed off. "That's negligent. It should have been put out at forty acres. Every kid knows you put the campfire out. That's the kind of leadership we're getting?"

"With all due respect, Mr. Rutgers, this isn't a campfire." District Ranger Eugene Rader, from the Forest Service, took the question. "There was a delay in detecting this fire because conditions were so smoky. One of our observation planes just happened to fly by and spot it."

The fire operations guy picked it up from there, giving the crowd a rundown on the crew fighting the fire. Bottom line, they were short staffed because of twelve outstanding orders for twenty-man crews. Only three crews were on the Caribou Fire.

"Crews are struggling to hold the dozer line that extends around West Kootenai and eastward to Lake Koocanusa," Stover added. "We're holding a ton of line right now with seventy people. They're holding on by their fingernails. They're bumping from one spot to another spot. We're trying to patrol the lines. It's not what you want to hear, but that's what we're dealing with."

Mercy stifled the urge to catapult from her seat and race to the microphone. Her parents would be shamed. Her *Gmay* shamed. Still, the desire to shout it out raged. That place these men were talking about held the homes of her family and friends. Once it had. They had been trusted to hold the line. It was their job. Now, she and her family had nothing to return to.

"Daed—"

Her eyes daggers, Mother shook her head and put her index finger to her lips.

Mercy subsided in her seat. Her face a reflection of Mercy's seething emotions, Juliette wiggled. "Easy for them to say, right?"

"I'm sure it's not, but—"

More daggers from Mother.

Mercy chewed her bottom lip and stared straight ahead.

Juliette's dad stood and stomped down the aisle to the microphone. "Oh boy." Juliette sank into her seat and covered her eyes. "This should be good."

"Lyle Knowles here." Lyle sounded like the disc jockey on the country music station Juliette liked to play in her truck. Warm, deep, and smooth. "I think what these folks mean to say is thank you. Me and my wife and daughters got out safe. I'm thankful for that. We're blessed. My thanks to Emmett for his efforts and the efforts of his deputies to get everyone out safe. That's what is important. I'm speaking as a husband and father who lost his house but still has what's most precious to him. Family." He swiveled, taking his time, and peered around the darkened auditorium. "I suggest everyone go home and say their prayers and be thankful. Be a good neighbor. We've still got each other. That's what's important."

He stalked back up the aisle. At the top he cocked his head. Juliette's mom popped up from her seat. "Let's go, girls."

"That's my cue." Scowling, Juliette squeezed past Mercy and Christine. She scanned the crowd. "I was hoping . . ."

"Tim's probably in Libby since the sheriff's here."

"He's mad at me."

"Why?"

Juliette leaned against the seats behind her and studied her manicured fingernails painted a shimmering red that matched her toenails. "I have a job offer in Billings. As a lowly assistant account exec with a marketing firm, but it's an offer." Her grin seemed forced. "A paying job in a big city with nightlife and culture and stuff for a single person to do. It's all good. 'Course Tim doesn't think so. He congratulated me and walked away."

Good and bad. A double-edged sword of the worst kind. No doubt Tim wanted Juliette to stay, but he couldn't ask her to marry him. Not with her views on religion. And if she left, he couldn't continue to try to change those views. "So you're accepting the offer?"

"That's the thing. They gave me a week to decide. The horse's behind didn't give me a chance to say I haven't decided yet."

Juliette was always careful not to curse in front of them, but her substitutions always made the girls grin at each other. Nora's smile faded. "But you want to."

"Yeah, I do. But I thought maybe Tim could come with me."

Big assumption. Tim seemed to love his job as a sheriff's deputy. How easy was it to get these law enforcement jobs in other places? The English world of jobs was hazy at best, but especially when it came to a workplace that the Plain community took great pains to avoid in its official capacity.

Tim and Emmett and the others were good friends, but no one wanted to talk to them about crimes.

"All things considered, I don't think he can." Mercy dug for the words she should say. They seemed hypocritical at best.

"You should pray about it. You know he will, when he's over being mad. He's only mad because he cares."

"Do it for me. Ple-eeezz." Juliette's gaze took in all three women. She drew the word out like a little girl begging for a cookie. "You're the supreme prayer warriors."

Whatever that meant. They prayed as Jesus taught all Christians to pray. The Lord's Prayer was at the top of their list. "I'll do my best." Even if she had her own bones to pick with the Great I Am. "But you have to promise you'll try too. For Tim's sake."

"I second that." Nora nodded in vigorous agreement. "Gott's will is Gott's will. If His plan involves Tim going with you, then He'll make it known."

The scowl flew away. Juliette passed out hugs like jelly beans, small and sweet. "You're the best. If God hears anyone's prayers, it's yours."

Ignoring the admonition to pray herself, as usual.

Still, a point for Tim. Juliette had acknowledged God's existence and that He answered prayers. On the other hand, Tim couldn't ask her to stay if he didn't intend to propose. He couldn't propose unless she was a believer. The Amish understood that, even though they saw it in a different light. Mercy couldn't marry someone who hadn't been baptized and joined her faith.

They also didn't evangelize. At least her Old Order Gmay didn't. That didn't mean Mercy didn't worry for her friend's happiness. "Do one other thing for me?"

"I wish you had a phone. You could text me." Juliette edged closer to the aisle. "Tell me quick. I gotta go."

"Come over Monday. Spend some time with me in the classroom."

"Why?"

Because Juliette had talents she'd yet to explore. Because teachers were always in need. And a person didn't have to travel to the largest city in Montana to fill the need. "Just come help me out for a while."

"Whatever you need, sweetie."

"Go—your dad will be cranky if you keep him waiting."

Juliette slipped into the crowd, which parted for the pretty former cheerleader known and loved by everyone.

Mercy turned to her other friends. "You didn't tell her you're leaving."

"She would've thrown a fit." Nora giggled. "You know Juliette. She's used to getting her way. We'll let you tell her."

"We're going," Abraham called from the end of the aisle. Mother and Father were already on their way to the door. "Hurry up."

Mercy stood and moved toward the aisle. Her friends did the same. "I can't believe you're leaving me."

"Only for a while. I'll be back." Nora hugged her first and then Christine. "There's a certain person who'll be waiting for me."

"Me too." Christine put her arms around both Nora and Mercy. "I'll stay as long as Aunt Lucy needs me at the store, but I have unfinished business here too."

What if God had other plans? If God's will was for them to be separated? What they wanted seemed to have nothing to do with anything. Mercy swallowed the negative thoughts that bombarded her like stinging hornets riled up in a strong wind. "See you soon, then."

"See you soon."

God's will be done.

Even if she didn't like it.

CHAPTER 18

EUREKA, MONTANA

S he looked really good.

Spencer kissed Mikey's sweet cheek, adjusted his crutches, and began the slow trek through the auditorium crowd toward Mercy Yoder. The tight knots of English and Amish folks from West Kootenai, Libby, and Eureka parted for the gimp on crutches. What did an English guy say to an Amish girl?

A woman in a red sundress fitted to show off her body sauntered directly into his path. She didn't seem to realize it until she bumped his crutch and he stumbled back a step.

"Oops, sorry, sorry." She slung long, wavy blonde hair over her shoulder and fixed a dazzling smile on him. "So sorry. Oh hey, it's you. Spencer McDonald."

Juliette Knowles. A lovely vision from the past.

A past he tried to forget. "Hey, it's you. Juliette."

Her gaze swept Spencer head to toe and then did a slower sweep in reverse. She didn't even try to hide her assessment. "You've aged well."

"I could say the same for you."

Even as a ninth grader, far too young for a senior who was much too old for his eighteen years, Juliette had exuded feminine wiles. Her sideways glances while practicing her cheerleader moves on the football field at Eureka High School left no doubt she knew exactly what she was doing in her tight white T-shirt and miniscule gym shorts. Flips, cartwheels, handstands, and dance moves normally reserved for nightclubs, all designed to show off her tanned, nubile body.

That was a long time ago. Not that a hot body didn't still push his buttons. He managed to close his mouth after a full five seconds.

"Thank you." She grinned the famous Juliette grin—half angel, half demon. "What are you doing back in town, and how long are you staying?"

"Do you work for the hometown newspaper, or are you just nosy?"

She smelled like coconut oil. A sudden flash of sandy beach, a lazy breeze, and seagulls cackling assailed him. Chuckling, she leaned closer and touched his bare arm. "Are you still the same brooding bad boy you were ten years ago? Why are you back?"

"Again with the questions." The hair on his arm stood up. Goose bumps marched down his biceps and hid in the hair. "Visiting family."

Mercy slipped from the last row of seats with a cluster of folks dressed in Amish garb. Must be her family. And they were leaving.

Juliette swiveled and glanced over her shoulder. "Interesting." She stepped aside. "Just remember, Mercy is a sweet, innocent Amish woman. And she's a friend of mine."

"I don't know what you're talking about." He swung past her. "See you around."

"See you around, Spence."

Her words held a faint inquiry. And a dash of laughter. A recipe for disaster.

His interest in women like Juliette had abated long ago. The first time he walked into the Missoula First Bank of Montana and gazed into the soft, earthy-brown eyes of a teller dressed in a prim, white, long-sleeved blouse, wearing pearl earrings and a touch of pink lipstick. Her name tag read Patricia. There'd been a mix-up with his check deposit. It took long enough to figure it out for him to ask for and receive her number.

The rest, as they say, was history. Unfortunately.

The older couple, probably Mercy's parents, stopped to talk to some other Amish folks. Three boys who had her same nose and chin went on ahead while Mercy lingered as if caught between being an adult and a teenager.

He sidled closer. No way to be graceful with clunky crutches under both arms. "I'm Spencer, from the other night at the church."

"I remember you." Her hazel eyes flashed and her peaches-and-cream complexion turned pink. "Angie's brother."

"They really had a big turnout for this meeting." What a stupid thing to say. Of course they did. No turning back now. He made a show of surveying the crowd surging up the aisles. "It appears as if the entire towns of West Kootenai and Rexford showed up."

Not that the combined population of those specks on the map could fill this auditorium. Plenty of the good citizens of Eureka had attended as well.

"Everyone's concerned." She ducked her head. Strands of her chestnut hair had escaped her prayer kapp and lay on her neck, shiny in the fluorescent lights. "Some have lost so much."

Her hazel eyes were fierce. Something hummed inside Spencer, like the thrumming of guitar strings. "Are you one of the ones who lost your home?"

"The only Amish family. Some single men lost their cabins." She glanced away. "And several of the Englisch—non-Amish—families lost their homes. We're all family in Kootenai."

"I'm sorry. I know it's rough."

Even after seven years as a firefighter, four of those as a smoke jumper, he never lost sight of the people who stood to lose everything if his team's efforts to contain a fire failed. But the more people built their homes near the forests, on the mountains, instead of the open valleys, the less the Forest Service could do to protect them. Education campaigns helped some, but mostly people continued to build where nature had its own ways of pruning and weeding out the weak and the overgrown. Lightning had been used as nature's fire starter since the beginning of time.

People didn't want to hear that.

"It's okay. My father says it's Gott's plan."

Another way of putting it. Her halfhearted answer said she wanted to believe but couldn't quite wrap her head around a God who chose this plan. That he could understand.

"More like nature's way of cleaning up her front yard and sending a message."

Her pretty forehead wrinkled, she glanced up at him. "What message?"

"Back off. You're getting too close."

"We live in harmony with nature." She edged behind two women chatting over matching strollers. "We don't even have electricity. We don't even litter."

Chuckling, he shook his head. "I'm not talking about you specifically. But you are living on the edge of a national forest."

She began to move toward the door. "I never thought of that as a bad thing."

"It's not bad. You just have to recognize and accept the forces of nature at work here."

He leaned into the crutches and matched her stride as she dodged men talking, hands on their hips or rubbing their beards, and then women chattering like a bunch of happy hens in the hallway that led to the double doors and into the parking lot. Outside, the noise died a quick death, replaced by car engines rumbling and cicadas singing. The evening air held a hint of autumn.

All the while, she seemed to be working over his words, digesting them, giving them more thought than anyone ever did. Finally, she raised her hand to her forehead and shielded her eyes from the setting sun. "You sound like a philosopher. Are you a teacher?"

"Nope. A smoke jumper."

Her eyebrows rose and her eyes widened. "Is that how you hurt yourself?" Her fingers fluttered near the metal stents on his fingers, but she didn't touch them.

"Yep. I had a midair collision with a ponderosa pine."

"Ouch."

"That about sums it up."

"How come your smoke jumper team didn't put the fire out?"

"You don't put forest fires out. You contain them so they burn out on their own."

"I don't understand what that means."

"We remove fire fuel from the fire's path. We dig down until we hit minerals and create a barrier so the fire doesn't have anything to eat."

"It doesn't seem to be working."

"I'm sorry for your loss." He craned his head from side to side. Her grief was fresh and new. She still labored under the shock of it. He rarely dealt directly with the people affected by the fires he fought. Her horror and righteous anger were good reminders of why he and his buddies put themselves in harm's way. So people like Mercy didn't have to feel like this. "I promise you every hotshot crew, all the volunteer firefighters, every line crew, all the smoke jumpers working this fire are doing everything they can to make it stop. Because that's what we get paid to do, but also because we care."

Her troubled gaze penetrated to the bone. After a few long seconds she nodded. "Thank you."

Mercy moved toward a long string of buggies and wagons near the perimeter of the parking lot. He kept pace. She glanced his way. "You look like you're in pain. You don't have to walk with me."

"Am I bothering you?" He stopped. "I didn't mean to make you feel uncomfortable."

Her expression unfathomable, she halted. "I'm not used to talking to Englisch men . . . alone." She studied the asphalt for a second. "But I want to understand about the fire and what you do. If I could go out there and fight it myself, I would. I would put it out. I wouldn't wait."

"I understand the desire." Her urgency touched him. Smoke jumpers picked up and moved on to the next fire. People like Mercy lived with the results of their efforts. He selected his words with care. "If you were a firefighter and you were out there on the line, you'd see what I see. Fires are like living, breathing creatures. They seem to ponder how to stay two or three or four steps ahead of you. They zig and zag. They die down and then—boom—they're back."

She resumed her steady pace toward the buggies where her brothers stood and leaned. The one squatting stood as they approached. All three stared.

"These are my brothers." She introduced them. They nodded but didn't speak. "Spencer is a smoke jumper."

With regular folks, this always jump-started the conversation. With these three, more nodding. "He was going to work the Caribou Fire when he got hurt."

"Doesn't seem to have mattered." Abraham, who appeared to be the oldest, finally spoke. "It's still going."

"This fire is a beast." Being defensive didn't help. Spencer paused and slowed his words. "I was just telling Mercy it's a point of honor with every firefighter to do everything possible to contain a fire. They won't stop until they do."

"Good to know." Abraham cocked his head toward the buggy hooked to a strawberry roan. "We'll get you home, Mercy. You probably have school stuff to do. Mudder and Daed will bring the wagon."

What Spencer knew about the Amish would fit on a stick-um. "I thought you quit school after eighth grade."

Mercy climbed into the buggy with the grace of someone who grew up doing it. She swiveled. "I teach."

"At a school in Eureka?"

"We're holding our Kootenai school here in Grandma Knowles's garage."

Grunting, Abraham hoisted himself into the driver's side of the buggy. "Nice to meet you. We have to go."

The other boys hopped into the back with oblique nods. They were nothing if not protective of their sister.

Spencer stood and watched them drive away. *Come on, come on.*

They reached the end of the parking lot and halted at a stop sign before they turned onto the street. Mercy leaned out and waved.

He returned the favor. *Thank you.*

Grandma Knowles's garage. Everyone knew where the senior Knowleses had lived for fifty or sixty years.

It was a start.

Of what? A conversation? An interesting friendship? A question to be pondered.

. . .

Twice in three days. Caleb rubbed his throbbing forehead and inhaled the smoky air only slightly better than the refrigerated air in the auditorium. He leaned against the building's blond brick and stared at the man waving good-bye to the Yoder boys. And Mercy. Why did this guy named Spencer McDonald seem so taken with Mercy? He'd stared at her in the church fellowship hall and now he sought her out at a community meeting. He didn't just seek her out; he walked her to her buggy and spoke to her and her brothers.

He's simply being neighborly. The voice in his ear chided Caleb for being so suspicious.

People around here were like that. Friendly. And they didn't make a spectacle of their Amish neighbors. They went about their business.

Which was what he should do.

He weighed the letter in his hand. At loose ends with no work to do, he'd driven over to the Rexford post office to pick up his mail on Friday. Now he wished he hadn't.

A letter from his mother, which he had now procrastinated more than a day in opening.

"Are you holding up the wall or is it holding you up?"

Caleb glanced up to see Juliette traipsing his direction. He let his gaze drop to her sandaled feet. "I reckon it's holding me up at this point."

"I'm sorry about your cabin."

"Thank you. Same with your house."

"We'll all be tired of saying that after a while." She leaned against the wall next to him and stuck her sandal against the brick exterior. She smelled like suntan lotion. Thinking about how a woman smelled seemed wrong, but a nose did what a nose did. Juliette fanned her face with her fingers. "We should just have a signal or a sign we can whip out. So Sorry. And move on."

"That would be okay with me." Except people needed to say something. It made them feel better. And the recipient somehow felt better, too, that someone cared. "Did you learn anything in the meeting?"

"It's what I'm learning out here that interests me." She gave him a sly sideways glance. "Was that Mercy I saw walking with Spencer McDonald to her buggy?"

"I don't know what you saw. Only what I saw."

He'd seen the girl who had his heart in her hands walking across the parking lot in broad daylight with an English man. It wasn't like they were holding hands, but something about the way this Spencer McDonald bent down to hear her words seemed like he knew her better than Caleb did. Like he was hanging on to her words. They walked closer together than casual acquaintances should. In Caleb's opinion, not that anyone had asked him for it.

"I saw an Englischer putting out feelers to see if Mercy is interested in courting him." Juliette pushed off from the wall. She turned to face him. For the first time since he'd met her, the woman's face was serious. "If that doesn't give you a kick in the behind, I don't know what will. Nothing, I guess."

"I don't know what you're talking about." That Juliette employed the Amish vernacular didn't surprise Caleb. She'd grown up playing with Mercy, Nora, Christine, and the other girls in the tiny community where they were all born. No one thought much about it. They were all just kids, regardless of church affiliation. As a newcomer he didn't have that advantage. Even after two years he was still trying to figure out the nuances of the relationships in this tight-knit Gmay. Plain folks didn't talk much about that sort of thing. "Amish women don't court Englischers."

"Maybe Spence doesn't know that. Or maybe he doesn't care."

"It's not your business. Or mine."

"It's my business because Mercy is my friend and I know what a player Spence is. It's your business because you are in love with Mercy. You took no for an answer instead of fighting for her. Wake up and smell the coffee, buddy."

"Courting is private."

"You have to actually court before it can be private. Food for thought, my friend." She waved her red-tipped fingers, whirled, and sashayed toward the white Ford Ranger parked next to her parents' Suburban. "Toodles."

"Wait."

She turned. The sly smile was back. "Your wish is my command."

"What does it mean to say Spencer is a player?"

Juliette traipsed closer. Closer than she should. Caleb straightened and edged away.

"It's been a lot of years, I'll give you that, but a tiger doesn't change its stripes, does it? I was a freshman when he was a senior. He played sports, but he wasn't one of those clean-cut athlete types. He had girls hanging all over him—all the football players did—but he did the whole brooding, bad-boy thing. He ignored them and went for the bad girls. They hung around under the bleachers after practice smoking and making out—"

"I get the picture." Caleb rushed to stop her. Drawing a picture was unnecessary. Gossip was wrong under all circumstances. "I'm sorry I asked. Like you said, that was a long time ago."

"I'm just saying Mercy may be my age, but she's led a sheltered life. She won't know what hit her."

"You should talk to her."

"I know, but she's been so sad since you broke up with her."

"She turned *me* down. She broke up with *me*." There he went again. "Never mind."

"Mercy said she wasn't ready to get married. She said she didn't want to give up teaching." Juliette went on as if Caleb hadn't spoken. "You didn't bother to dig deeper. You didn't bother to find out what was really freaking her out."

"Freaking her out?" They'd been courting for eight months. Surely Mercy had given some thought to the possibility of marriage. He'd been so careful to be respectful and get to know her. To listen to her. To truly know her. He hadn't allowed himself to be carried away by feelings the way he had with Leyla. "Every Amish woman wants to marry. Why would a proposal 'freak' her out?"

His feelings for Mercy were deeper and stronger because they were based on really knowing her, but she obviously didn't feel the same way.

"My question exactly." Juliette stood on her tiptoes and patted his cheek. "It may not be what you did but what you didn't do. I get the impression she was totally surprised that you were moving right to marriage. Did you forget something in the middle? I mean, seriously, did you even kiss her?"

Caleb touched his cheek. The man who fell for Juliette would have to be more than a little bit crazy. The woman had no boundaries. "That is not your business."

"I can tell by the expression on your face you didn't."

Kissing might scare her off. Kissing might muddle her feelings. Trying this hard was exhausting. His head hurt. His fingers tightened around his mother's letter until the envelope folded in his hands.

"What's that?"

"What's what?"

"That letter you keep fondling."

"It's from my mother."

"What does it say?"

Yet another piece of information that wasn't Juliette's business. "I haven't opened it."

"Why not?"

"Because I know what it says."

Juliette snatched the letter from his hand and held it to her forehead. Eyes closed, she hummed for a few seconds. "My dear son, your dad and I miss you terribly. Even the dog misses you. Take the next train to Georgia. Hey, I'm writing a country music song. Am I right?"

"Close." Except his father passed away years earlier, his mother and siblings lived with his aunt Teresa, and the dog had gone blind. "I thought maybe my family might want to come out for a visit. I invited them."

They might like it here. They might even settle here. It was a stupid idea, but a man needed family around.

"You who have no house." Juliette returned the letter. "I'm sorry."

"We're not saying that anymore, remember?"

"I'm sorry I'm obnoxious. It's a habit my boy—my friend—says I need to break."

"Tim's right."

"What makes you think it's Tim?"

"It's none of my business."

"You got that right." Her smile gone, she backed away. "You should swing by Mercy's tonight. Take her for a ride. I'll be rooting for you. Team Caleb. You're like Team Edward. Spence is Team Jacob, all dark and broody. You know what I mean?"

"I have no idea."

"It doesn't matter. He who snoozes, loses. Don't make me say I told you so."

"I won't." She didn't need to say anything. Ever. "Good-bye." She strolled to her car.

He studied the letter. Might as well open it. Tear the bandage from the wound.

Dear Caleb,

We hope you are well. We read about the fires. We are praying for your safety and the safety of the other families in West

Kootenai and Libby. I also pray that you aren't taken in by the exhortations of the Libby community. But I leave the future to God who is faithful.

I read your letter inviting us to visit and imagine the mountains and the lakes and the wildlife. But Montana is a long way from Indiana. Your brother's wife is in a family way. The baby will come this spring. I'll have a garden to plant. And canning to do. I can't imagine us making such a long trip. Maybe you can come home in the spring instead.

Take care of yourself. God's blessing on you.

Mudder

Caleb folded the letter and stuck it back in the envelope.

Some things never changed. His mother was one of them.

He came to Montana for a fresh start. He came in search of affection he missed at home. He would never go home and his family would never come here.

He would build a new house here and fill it with the love and affection a child needed to grow up happy and healthy.

To do that, he needed to take Juliette's advice. Starting now.

CHAPTER 19

People were idiots. Not a very Christian thought. But true. Making a circling motion with one hand, Tim slapped the side of the fire engine–red Ford F-350 with its oversized tires and diesel fumes with his other hand. No entry meant no entry. What part of the sawhorses and orange cones across Piper Road didn't the guy understand? Closing the road to prevent residents from returning home to this area only seven miles north of Libby because of the West Fork Fire was for their own safety. As difficult and as scary as that was. A guy also had to do his job, whether people liked it or not.

"Hey, man, we just want to pick up a couple of things." The guy in a Dodgers ball cap stuck his head through the open window on the passenger side. "No need to be such a jerk about it."

"Everyone thinks they should be the exception," Tim yelled back. "The evac is for your own good."

The man said a few things he ought not to spout about law enforcement, but Emmett wouldn't approve of Tim slapping cuffs on a guy for utilizing his First Amendment rights.

What would his hero Dr. King say about it? So much for his "beloved community." The truck rumbled away, leaving Tim and his county pickup in billowing dust. Coughing, he hid his face in the crook of his elbow and waited for it to subside.

"Who peed in your Cheerios?" Kimberly wiped her face with a red bandana soaked with melted ice from the small cooler Tim kept in the truck. "I've never seen you act like this. You're never cranky. That's Sal's schtick."

"I'm not cranky. Just dirty and tired." Tired from working a full week and now manning a barricade on his Saturday morning instead of sleeping in.

"And cranky."

"Okay, a little cranky." No way Tim would talk to the first-year deputy about his woman problems. They weren't even problems anymore. It was over between Juliette and him. Kaput. No excuses. Time to get over it. He glanced at his watch. "I need to head over to the community meeting in Libby. You got this?"

"Come on, talk to Auntie Kim. I'm a good listener, and I have experience with relationship issues." Kimberly stepped into his path and stuck both hands on her hips. "Besides, you can't be allowed to attend a community meeting with your attitude. You're like a keg of dynamite about to blow."

He could handle himself. "There are no relationship issues."

"Fine, good to know. Have a drink with me after all this is over."

Hand on the door, Tim stopped. So engrossed in walking the tightrope of emotion required not to have a relationship with Juliette, he'd totally missed the signs. Kimberly was a sight to behold. When she removed the pins from her bun, her jet-black hair fell in waves to her waist. She had soft milk chocolate–brown eyes and a deep tan. Not to mention she filled out her uniform nicely.

Even good Christian men noticed that sort of thing. Whether they admitted it or not.

"I don't drink."

"I'll buy you a Pepsi or a cup of coffee, pick your poison."

"We're fighting fires on three fronts right now—"

"If you're searching for excuses, you can just say no. It won't hurt my feelings."

"I'm just surprised."

"You're one of those guys who doesn't realize he's a catch. You're still stuck in that high school mentality where you were the class goof or your brain hadn't caught up with your size and kids made fun of you or you had braces and pimples." Kimberly pantomimed casting a fishing rod and reeling in a big fish. "What you don't see is that the ugly duckling has become a swan."

"A swan?" He laughed, something he hadn't done in a long time. "I've been called a lot of things, but swan is not one of them."

"Women like a man in uniform with a gun on his hip." She had a toothy grin. "Part dangerous, part protector."

"I've seen you at the gun range. You don't need protecting."

"Nope. I like my men manly."

"I gotta go."

"You're welcome."

"For what?"

"For taking your mind off your troubles for a minute. Now you owe me a drink. As friends."

A guy could never have too many friends. With a mock salute Tim slid into the truck and took off for Libby. Taking his frustration out on some dude who just wanted to get into his house wasn't cool. Unprofessional. The first notes of Luke Bryan's "Play It Again" sounded on his phone.

Juliette.

That song had been playing on her Ranger's radio the night he stopped her two years ago and gave her a bunch of tickets.

He picked up the phone and pushed a button, and the notes died away. That made fifteen times. Fifteen times she'd called in one day. Fifteen calls he hadn't answered.

Plus six increasingly irritated texts.

But who was counting?

Maybe he could have her arrested for stalking.

Twenty minutes later, he tromped into the Libby High School gym. About two hundred citizens packed the bleachers on one side. Nathan Kuntz, the Kootenai National Forest supervisor, microphone in hand, paced in front of them.

"We haven't seen conditions like these in almost fifty years." His hoarse voice matched his craggy, tired face. "We had a wet fall and a snowy winter and then the rain just shut off. Libby has had about three-hundredths of an inch of rain since the end of June."

Dan Larson, the forest's fire management officer, joined his colleague on the hot seat. The West Fork Fire had the potential to be as big as the Caribou Fire, which had doubled in size from one day to the next, consuming almost fourteen thousand acres. It had moved eight miles in two and half days.

The big issue—resources.

"We're doing the best we can," Dan added. "We have an incident management team coming in from the Rocky Mountain region tomorrow. We'll be briefing them on the West Fork Fire."

"Can you put it out?" Dean Carmichael yelled out. Others joined in. Some simply nodded. "That's really the question we want answered."

"We're working to contain it. With limited resources we're focused on protecting property."

"We appreciate that." His Colorado Rockies cap in his hands, Dean stood. "But it doesn't answer the question. Over in Kootenai, they're wondering why the fire didn't get put out before it burned down some houses. We're wondering if our houses will be next."

"We can't guarantee anything. We're doing the best we can, like I said."

"Right now, what we want to emphasize is preparation for evacuation." Fresh in a clean, wrinkle-free uniform, his cowboy hat firmly tucked on his head, Emmett entered the fray. "Pre-evac orders mean you should be ready to go in under an hour when the evacuation is ordered."

"Do we need to evacuate now?" Mrs. Washington piped up. An octogenarian who still drove her mauve Cadillac, she would need some extra time just to walk from her house to the garage. "I don't want my Sybil and Huck to be in danger."

Everyone knew Sybil and Huck were her two Siamese cats. They were almost as old as their owner.

"Your homes are not in immediate danger." Emmett scrubbed at his smooth-shaven cheeks with one hand. "But I wouldn't object to you visiting your sister in Florida, Mrs. Washington."

"So the evacuation is coming. You're just pussyfooting around it." Craig Barlow jumped in. "Come on, Sheriff, you don't think this fire can be contained."

"I know everyone is worried. I'm worried. I've got kids and my parents and my brother living here. Family just like you do." Emmett didn't need a microphone. "I'm saying my prayers morning, noon, and night that I don't have to evacuate them. But we have to do what we have to do. My advice is to stay calm, stay in touch with your neighbors, help each other out, and those of you who are on pre-evac notice, keep your phones charged and close by. Pack some bags. Fill any prescriptions you'll need. Pack food for your animals. Be ready to go when that Reverse 911 call comes in. Okay? The Red Cross has opened a shelter at the Assembly of God church. And folks, pray for your firefighters and your first responders."

A smattering of applause echoed through the gym. People stood and their murmurs grew and grew until they reached a crescendo. Looking distracted, Emmett strode toward Tim. "We should get back to the office—"

"Folks, folks, wait, wait. One more thing." Lincoln County Commissioner Keith Carbine flapped both arms. The microphone squealed. People clapped their hands to their ears, but they stopped talking. Everyone froze. "I just wanted to say that the other county commissioners and I are on top of this situation. From our perspective, the coordination between the various agencies has been fantastic. We're in good hands, folks."

"Politicians." Tim snorted. "Like he's done anything to help this situation. We're shorthanded and all he wants to do is get his fifteen minutes of fame and get reelected—"

"Ain't that the truth." Richard Dillon gave Tim and Emmett a thumbs-up as he hopped down from the bleachers and strode by them. "A blowhard if there ever was one."

Emmett tipped his hat at Dillon. "Drive safe, Rich. And don't open that six-pack of Coors before you get to the house, you hear me?"

Dillon chuckled and disappeared through the double doors.

Emmett took Tim's arm and drew him to the other side of the basketball hoop hanging at the end of the court. "Seriously, son, what is wrong with you?"

"Nothing—"

"That guy on the court is our boss." His irritation reverberated as clear as a Montana summer night. "It's one thing to think about trash-talking him. It's another to actually do it in front of citizens."

"Sorry, sorry. You're right." Tim rubbed both temples. His head pounded. His sinuses ached from smoke and dust. He smelled of BO. "It's been a long day."

"What happened with Juliette?"

"What do you mean?"

"Word's floating around the office that you broke up."

"Three fires coming at us from all sides and all people can talk about is my love life?"

"You chewed out poor little Cammie this morning for not putting your phone messages in your box. She wasn't even on duty. That's not you, buddy."

"I'm fine. Just sleep deprived."

"We all are." Emmett slid his hat back on his head. His blue eyes were icy bullets. "Can I make a suggestion?"

It wasn't really a question. "Sure. Please do."

"Go see your friend Pastor Matt."

"We're really busy. Maybe tomorrow—"

"That wasn't a suggestion, actually, so much as an order."

"Yes, Boss."

"And then go home. Get a few hours' sleep. I'll be your alarm."

"I don't need—"

"Again, not a suggestion."

"Yes, sir."

CHAPTER 20

Nothing like getting sent to the principal's office in the middle of an emergency. Ten minutes later Tim knocked on the door of Pastor Matt's double-wide trailer in an older neighborhood on the western city limits of Libby. Matt had painted the ramp and railing since Tim's last visit. The bright blue stood out against the tan trailer.

The door swung open. Matt stood back to let Tim pass.

"Nice legs."

"Thanks." Matt grinned and curtsied. "I got them about a month ago. I'm practicing for next year's Paralympics. I'd like to try out for the Invictus Games too."

When Matt and Tim knew each other in high school, Matt had been a long-distance runner who excelled in several track and field events. Then he went to Afghanistan and got blown up by a roadside bomb that took the lives of three guys in his unit.

"Good for you."

"But you didn't come here to curry favor by complimenting me on my sexy legs." Matt eased into his wheelchair and removed his fancy prostheses. "You look like you've been rode hard and put up wet."

"Thanks. I do nothing but compliment you, and then you turn around and abuse me."

"Come on, Timmy, what's the scoop?" Matt ran his hands over the black crew cut he kept after being medically retired from the Marines, even though it showed off a scar that zigzagged behind his left ear and disappeared around his temple. "I never hear any of the good stuff. I'm stuck here all alone."

Which was a fairy tale, of course. As a youth minister at their church, Matt constantly stayed ahead of youth mission trips, fund-raisers, neighborhood prayer walks, and dozens of other activities designed to draw his charges closer to Jesus and keep them there.

"Emmett suggested I might need a consult with Pastor Matt."

"Or a whop upside the head?"

"Or that."

Matt leaned back. "Is this a one-soda or two-soda consult?"

His way of reminding Tim that he still held a six-pack of Pepsis in one hand. He offered Matt one, grabbed another for himself, and stowed the rest in a fridge covered with candid photos of kids hiking at Glacier National Park, Matt leading the way.

That was the problem with talking to Matt. A guy didn't dare feel sorry for himself. Matt did all the things he'd done before Afghanistan. In fact, he did more and he did them better. He never felt sorry for himself. At least, he never admitted to it.

Tim threw himself on a couch covered with a blue plaid flannel blanket and stuck his long legs on the scarred pine coffee table. He took a long sip of soda and stared at the ceiling. A wave of drowsiness swept over him.

"Make yourself comfy." Matt popped the top of his can. "I'll just sit here and admire the dirt you're leaving on my coffee table."

Tim closed his eyes and studied the inside of his eyelids. "It's Juliette."

"Figures."

"What's that supposed to mean?" Something smacked him in the nose. Startled, he opened his eyes and straightened. A wad of notebook paper fell to the floor. "Hey. No need to get violent."

"How many times in the last year have we had this conversation?" Matt burped and excused himself. "You like her. She likes you. You're God's man. She's a lapsed Christian. You've done everything you can as a friend to help her find her way home. She hasn't done it. What do you think happens next?"

"She got a job offer in Billings."

"I'm sorry."

"She asked me to go with her."

"What did you say?"

"I said no."

"But you wanted to say yes."

"Everything in my gut wanted to say yes."

"That wasn't your gut talking."

Tim set the soda on the table with a bang. "I'm not that kind of guy. I've never been that kind of guy. This is my heart talking, not other parts of my anatomy. I did a stupid thing."

Matt removed his Bible from the table and laid it in the bag attached to his chair. "You fell in love."

"I told myself I could handle it. People think Juliette has it all together. She doesn't. She needs friends. She's got the

Amish girls, but they don't evangelize." Tim ducked his head and studied drops of condensation that darkened the tan of his uniform pants. "I wanted to be her friend. I knew better and I let it happen. It sucks."

"Why are you here?"

"Because Emmett made me come see you."

"Why are you really here?"

"I guess . . . I guess I want someone to tell me it'll be all right." Tim cleared his throat. "I know it's stupid."

"Not stupid, stupid." Matt's lopsided grin took the sting from his words. "Human."

"You're the one person I can count on to tell me the truth. You won't sugarcoat it, but you also won't laugh at me. The worst thing that could ever happen to you happened and you survived. You did more than survive—you thrive."

"You make me sound like a Hallmark card or one of those Wounded Warrior commercials." Matt rubbed his stumps with both hands. "Do you remember Krissy Martell?"

"From tenth-grade biology? The straight-A girl?"

"Yeah, the straight-A girl with the freckles and the cute butt."

"I don't believe I noticed—"

"You did too, liar. Anyway, we reconnected at MU before I dropped out and enlisted. She said she'd wait for me. Sent me care packages, wrote me letters, Skyped with me."

"Was she a believer?"

"Yep. Then I got blown up."

It was obvious where this story was going. "How long did it take her to bail?"

"A couple of months after I got back to the States and started rehab."

"I'm sorry."

"Me too. But the point of this story is that I thought losing my legs was the worst thing that could happen to me. Losing her hurt even more. I was drowning in self-pity and misery and I was hanging on to Krissy like she was my lifeboat. No wonder she bailed. I thought I was a Christian, but all I did was shake my fist at the sky and demand to know why God let this happen. How could He let me suffer like this? Then Krissy, in the nicest way possible, told me she couldn't handle it. She loved me, but she couldn't see herself fitting into my life now."

"Ouch."

"Everything was stripped away. Down to the bone. And that's where I found Jesus. He's my lifeboat. He's my Savior. He's the one I rely on. People let you down; Jesus never will. Sometimes you have to go through the fire to figure that out."

"I get that."

"I don't think you do. My body was ripped apart, but my mind was in worse shape." Matt's voice grew hoarser with each word. "I even went to a Christian psychologist. He had all these pat answers about God wanting me to move from the dark to the light, stuff I already knew. I kept saying, 'I know all that. Intellectually, I know that. How do I *do* it? How do I get there emotionally?' No one could tell me."

"Do you still feel that way?"

"Not most days." He shrugged massive shoulders. "What I was feeling was grief. I had to go through those pesky stages of grief. I had to give up, get on my knees—so to speak—and give it up to the Lord. I gave Him my hurt over Krissy. I gave my desires for a life mate to Him. I gave my insecurities over the parts of me that are missing to Him."

"Just like that?"

"It took time, believe me. I don't have any magic pills for you, my friend."

"What I'm going through doesn't begin to touch what you've been through." Tim grabbed a pillow and smacked his head with it. "I feel like such a loser even complaining to you."

"You're not complaining. You're seeking answers. Answers I wish I had."

"So you didn't get any answers."

"Nope. But I've reached a compromise with Him. I trust He'll do cool things with what's left of me. And no matter what happens, when I get to the New World, I'll get my old, complete body back. In the meantime, He gives me work to do, fulfilling work. He sends me where I'm needed. I choose to go, even if I go alone."

"I don't want to be alone."

"Me neither. We're not alone."

Tim groaned. "I get a stinky, old ex-Marine?"

"No way. I'm getting a dog."

A short-term solution, but still a solution Tim could get on board with. "Yeah, can I help you pick him out?"

"Pick out your own dog."

"Fine."

"Pray for Juliette and let her go."

"If you love her, let her go? Seriously, that's the best you've got?"

"Her parents planted seeds. You planted seeds. Give them time to sprout. Your primary concern, whether you like it or not, is for Juliette's eternal salvation."

"I know." Which irked Tim like the perennial thorn in Paul's side. "I pray for her constantly."

"But are you willing to give her up if that's what it takes, if that's part of God's plan for her?"

The question plummeted through the air and smashed into Tim. A massive ton of boulders, each one marked with words like *selfish, lonely, hungry for affection,* and *unfulfilled.* "It's like you said. Intellectually, I know what the right answer to that question is, but emotionally, it's killing me."

"I know. I'm sorry. But ask God to give you the strength to do what's best for her, not you."

"Easy for you to say."

"No, it's not. You're my friend. I pray for God to give you the desires of your heart." His face reddened, and Matt studied the frayed ends of his denim shorts. "Enough mushy stuff. How 'bout them Broncos?"

The first notes of "Play It Again" blared from Tim's phone.

"Speaking of the lovely wayward lady." Matt wheeled around and headed for the back of the trailer. "I'm gonna take a shower. Talk to Juliette. Then take a nap. You look like regurgitated dog food."

"Gee, thanks," Tim mumbled as he picked up the phone and eyed the photo of Juliette sitting on the back of his truck in shorts and a swimming suit top, eating a slice of watermelon and grinning at him. "Lord, give me strength."

He answered.

"Ignoring my calls is so juvenile." Juliette on the attack was a daunting noise in his ear. "So you don't want to go to Billings with me. It's not that far. Couples have successful long-distance relationships all the time."

"We're not in a relationship." Tim managed to say the words with gentle caring. An enormous feat of self-restraint. "We can't be and you know it. You just don't want to admit it."

"What do you call showing up at my house two or three times a week? What do you call taking me fishing and swimming at the lake? Or watching movies with my family? Like you're part of my family."

"I call it being a friend. Granted, a friend who would like more, but who knows he might not get what he wants."

"You are so bullheaded I could scream."

Tim didn't point out she *was* screaming—at least the pain in his ear thought so. "This isn't about just the differences in our beliefs, although that is the bottom line. It's also about who you are and how you denigrate yourself by flirting with every man who comes within striking distance. How do you think that makes me feel? What does it say about how you feel about yourself?"

"I do not." Genuine disbelief soaked her outraged screech. "I don't flirt with other men."

A long pause filled the line. He waited.

"Much."

"The next time you run into a hot guy of any age, listen to yourself. Better yet, use your phone and record the conversation. Play it back later. Then we'll have this conversation."

"You're jealous, that's all."

"You got that right. I *am* jealous. And I'm ashamed of being jealous. I have no right to be." He leaned his head back and rubbed his throbbing temple. "But I also fear for you. I'm afraid you'll sell yourself short because underneath all that bravado is a little girl who wants to be loved and is afraid she's not worth it. You *are* worth it, and God loves you the way no one else can. Turn to Him and you won't need all that attention from men you hardly know."

"I don't need attention from anyone. I can stand on my own just fine."

"Just once, Juliette, just once, can't you drop the act and be who you really are with me? I'd like to meet the real you, just once."

She hung up.

"That went well."

Matt's solution of getting a dog might be a good one.

Jesus, I know You love me unconditionally. Is it wrong to want more? I'm so selfish. I keep thinking about me instead of her. Keep her safe while she figures this out. Touch her heart. I know You will leave the ninety-nine to search for that one sheep. She is that one sheep: lost, lonely, scared. It breaks my heart. Find her, Lord, so she can find You. Give me the strength to stand back and let You do Your work. To trust You. To walk away if that is Your will for me and for her.

"Please God, don't let it come to that."

He was human, after all.

CHAPTER 21

A cheap date. Guys liked that, didn't they? One beer and woozy. Juliette squinted at the second glass on the picnic table in front of her. Half empty. Or half full, depending on a person's point of view. She swallowed another gulp. This microbrewery stuff was nothing like the keg swill she'd sworn off in high school. It tasted like pee. With this Pioneer Ale, brewed right here at Ballcap Brewery, she tasted wheat and citrus. Her stomach lurched. No matter the beer, a person shouldn't imbibe on an empty stomach.

"Or at all." Tim's snarkiness filled her head. "Shut up."

"When you start talking to yourself, it's probably time to stop drinking." Spencer McDonald reached in front of her and slid the glass to the opposite end of the table. "Haven't you heard? Drinking alone is considered a sign of alcoholism."

"Considering that this is the second beer I've drunk since my freshman year in college, I'm not too worried." *Considering* slurred more than *freshman*, but it was a four-syllable word. Juliette tossed her hair over her shoulder and straightened to her cheerleader posture. "Besides, I wasn't talking to myself."

Spencer laid his crutches against the table and slid onto the bench across from her without waiting for an invitation. The waitress magically appeared and took his order for a club soda with extra lime.

"You don't drink or you don't drink beer?"

"Have you met my mom?"

"No, but I've heard about her. Sorry, stupid question." S-words were hard for an amateur drinker. Juliette slid her beer back front and center. "So why are you here then, if not to get trashed?"

"Feeling at loose ends." He shrugged. "Not ready to go back to the house. In need of company."

"So you come to a bar, 'cuse me, a brewery, to hook up with a chick?" Juliette took a long swallow of beer. She hiccupped. Or maybe it was a burp. "'Cuse me. Have you looked around? There's like four people here and they're all men. For a Saturday night, it's not exactly a happening place."

"I'm not interested in hooking up." He squeezed lime juice into his club soda and stirred it. "Conversation. Sparring. Banter. A little music." He jerked his head toward the three-piece band playing soft rock cover songs on the other side of the patio. "I don't do well with silence these days. And I'm used to running ten miles a day and working out for at least an hour. Without my PT I have trouble sleeping."

Juliette could relate. She'd taken up running in college and even run a few marathons. Anything to sleep. But she couldn't outrun the demons. Getting a job would help. Even if it meant spending her days sucking up to clients who wanted the world to love their antiperspirant or their latest cure for obesity. Sixty hours a week helping clients sell people on the idea that soda could be refreshing even if it wasn't good for them? She knew about insomnia. "Why is that?"

"I duked it out with a ponderosa pine and the tree won." His gaze rested on her beer. "It got me to thinking about things. You know, things. My future. Why do I jump out of planes to fight fires for a living? Why do I go home alone every night? Is that all there is? I sound like a stupid eighties song. Stupid stuff like that. Why are you here?"

"To drink my beer and not be interrogated by anyone."

Interrogated was the wrong choice of words. It came out an unintelligible mess. Juliette downed the rest of the beer and raised her glass in the universal sign of "bring me another."

Spencer pushed the glass back down with a gentle touch. "I think you've had enough."

"I'm not a lightweight."

"I'm pretty sure you are." He shook his head at the waitress, who nodded and headed for the guys arguing over the state of college football in the coming season. "Should I get us some pizza from the food truck?"

Pain twisted like a drill bit in her stomach. Gorge rose in her throat. "Do not talk to me about food."

"Have you eaten?"

More pain, this time sharper. It ran like an electric current from her stomach to her throat. "Who could think about food at a time like this?"

"What time is that?"

"The time when the guy you like gets on his high horse and rides in the opposite direction. He's too high and mighty to compromise on some little difference. He'd rather be alone than be together. He's an idiot."

To her horror, tears threatened.

"What people define as little can differ greatly."

"Let me ask you something. Do I flirt with you?"

"Sure you do."

"Come on, at least take a minute to think about it."

"I'd have to be blind and deaf not to notice it." Spencer managed to infuse kindness into the words. "Why don't you let me take you home?"

"We don't have a home anymore." A wave of exhaustion overwhelmed Juliette. She laid her head on the table and closed her eyes. "The fire took it all."

"I'm sorry for your loss. It must really hurt."

His words hovered in the air above her, warm and comforting. Her throat ached. "So that's why you sat down with me—you figured I was a flirt so I might be into hooking up?"

"No. In fact, I debated whether to sit with you at all." His voice floated around her, softer, with a hint of wondering in it. "I thought you might get the wrong idea. But you seemed so lost and sad, something pushed me over here."

Like decency. Who knew?

A scrabbling sound forced her eyes open. Spencer had his hand on her clutch bag. "Are you robbing me? I only have six dollars and change. My credit cards are maxed out. It's been a while since I worked."

"Of course I'm robbing you." He chuckled. "I'm thinking about giving up smoke jumping to start a second career as a thief. I thought I'd start small with ripping off drunk women."

"I'm not drunk." Juliette closed her eyes again. "It's early. Buy me another round. I've got a job offer. I can pay you back in a few weeks."

"Shawn stops serving at eight, you know that."

"Stupid state law. Why would anybody in his right mind think microbreweries should shut down at eight? It's not even dark yet."

"A question for the Montana legislature. I'm getting your

keys. I'll give them to someone at your house. They can come pick up your truck tomorrow."

"No way. My dad will have a cow. He thinks I'm six. I'm fine. I'm resting my eyes. I'll get myself home in a minute."

"I don't think so." Spencer's hand grasped her arm. "Let's go, *chiquita bonita*."

"Now you speak Spanish?" She didn't move. "Just give me a minute. I don't need help."

"A guy I work with is teaching me Spanish. Here we go." Spencer tugged harder. "You'll like my Tundra. It has a good stereo system. I have Thomas Rhett's new CD."

"No one buys CDs anymore." She scrambled to her feet, swayed, and plopped back on the bench. "I'm fine."

Five minutes later she was enveloped in the warm leather seats of Spencer's silver Tundra. The cab smelled of pine air freshener. She leaned her head back and closed her eyes. At least she'd stopped drinking before the head spins and vomiting started. Thanks to Spencer McDonald, former bad boy turned helper of lightweight drinkers. "I could've driven myself."

"Maybe, but it's ten miles to town and I don't think you want to add DUI to the list of offenses your boyfriend is keeping."

"How did you know Tim gave me tickets the day we met for the second time?"

"I didn't. But no guy likes for his lady to put herself in danger."

Juliette opened her eyes. They were pulling from the parking lot onto Grave Creek Road. "According to him I'm not a lady. Are you a Christian?"

Laughing, Spencer turned down the radio. "I never pegged you as someone who likes to get right to the heavy stuff."

"Tim says we can't be more than friends because he's a

Christian and I'm not." She wiggled so she could face Spencer despite the seat belt. "He's serious about it. He won't even mess around. He uses stuffy words like *unevenly yoked*. Not even Mercy talks like that, and she's Amish."

"So Mercy's a friend of yours. How well do you know her?"

"We've played together since we were little, but that has nothing to do with this."

"My last girlfriend was a Christian."

"Did she mess around?"

"I don't kiss and tell, but in this case, there's nothing to tell." The *click, click* of his turn signal filled the silence for a few seconds. "What's Mercy like?"

"You want to talk about Mercy?" Despite the alcoholic haze, Juliette grasped this clue and hung on to it for a few seconds. Maybe it was safer to talk about Spencer's problems instead of hers. "I knew it, I knew it."

"I'm just curious about Amish folks."

"You grew up around Amish folks, same as me. What's the deal? You like her, don't you?"

"She seems nice."

"You met her a couple of times, and now you have feelings for her. Love at first sight?" She hiccupped. "Sorry. Why would God give us all these feelings if He didn't expect us to act on them?"

"What would Tim say?"

Of course Spencer refused to take the bait. "Men. They always stick together."

"I know what Patty, my ex, said. God gave us those feelings as a gift and we're supposed to treat them like a gift we only share with someone special—our spouse. I respected her for her convictions, but I didn't make it easy for her. I regret that."

"Hmmm." Sleep inundated Juliette. She wanted to tell him something. The thought flitted around inside her head. Something important. "You're not like I thought you were."

"I get that a lot."

If he said anything else, she didn't hear it.

"Juliette. Juliette!"

She bolted upright. Her eyes burned and her head hurt. "Where am I?"

"In my truck." Spencer unbuckled her seat belt and held out his hand. "Let me help you out."

"I'm good." She brushed him off. "Out of my way . . . please."

Of course he did the opposite. He took her arm and helped her onto the sidewalk. He guided her through the gate and up the steps to her aunt's front door. White-hot embarrassment rolled over her in a tsunami. With any luck she would never run into him again in this one-horse, one-stoplight town. "Give me my keys."

He handed them over. One, two, three tries. No dice. The key simply refused to enter the keyhole.

"Let me try." He had the door open in two seconds.

"Show-off."

"What's going on here?" A book in one hand, her dad stood at the door in a T-shirt and shorts with reading glasses perched on the end of his aquiline nose. "Who are you?"

"This is my friend Spence." Juliette's efforts to speak without a slur met with no success. Her father's expression darkened. He had her all figured out, as usual. He was already writing the sermon he would deliver when Spencer drove away. She rushed to fill the space and fend off his familiar righteous indignation. "He gave me a ride."

"Good to meet you, sir." Spencer offered his hand and her

dad shook it, but his expression didn't change. "Here's her keys and her purse. The truck is at Ballcap's. Shawn said not to worry, he won't have it towed."

"Thanks for bringing her home." Dad took the keys and stuck them in his pocket. "I thought we had outgrown this stuff. Apparently I was wrong."

"She's had a hard day, from what I could gather."

"We've all had a hard day. Some of us act like adults about it."

"Don't talk about me like I'm not here." Juliette's head pounded. Her mouth tasted like rotten lettuce. Sleep would fix what ailed her, not a lecture. "I'm going to bed."

"We'll talk tomorrow."

Years of training smacked Juliette in the back of the head. *Spencer did you a favor. You owe him. He was kind. He doesn't expect anything in return.* Gritting her teeth, Juliette stopped at the foot of the stairs and turned. "Thanks, Spence."

"Anytime."

No, it wouldn't happen again. Ever. If her behavior got back to Tim, she'd never convince him they could make it work.

And he might be right.

CHAPTER 22

EUREKA, MONTANA

The garage still smelled of little-boy sweat and dirty feet. Mercy raised the door and let the cooler evening air rush in. Nothing could loosen the feeling of bitter despair that gripped her. She grabbed a lawn chair and set it on the cement driveway, away from her makeshift classroom that reminded her of how life could change on a dime.

Lifting her face to the breeze, she closed her eyes. *Just breathe. Let it go.* The cicadas' monotonous chorus brought with it a calm born of familiarity. It sounded like home. A dog howled that familiar basset hound baying sound. Bullfrogs croaked. Flies buzzed.

Even the sweet, familiar sounds could not erase her sense of guilt. How Caleb must've felt when Mercy said no. Without so much as giving the proposal the thought it deserved. "No" had barreled from her mouth like a bulldozer demolishing a concrete wall. With no thought for Caleb's feelings.

She wasn't the one who had misgivings. He did. Of that, she was certain.

Why did he ask her if his feelings were so lukewarm he couldn't bring himself to show them through a hug or a kiss?

The trees had no answers. Nor did the puny clouds that

scampered across the sky clothed in pinks and purples as the sun dove toward the horizon.

Dusk closed in around her. To sleep would be best, but the fluffy bed with its scented sheets and feather pillows only reminded her that she was not home and would never sleep in her childhood bed again.

"Oh, for Pete's sake, quit feeling sorry for yourself." She stood so suddenly she knocked the folding chair back. "No one likes a whiny girl."

"I should call the CDC. An epidemic seems to have hit Eureka." The low voice came from the shadows cast by massive branches swaying in the streetlights. Spencer McDonald rolled into the driveway on a contraption that allowed him to keep his broken leg bent on a padded seat. "You're the second woman tonight I've heard talking to herself. Is that a thing these days?"

"I didn't know anyone was there." Mercy whirled and set the chair upright. "What happened to your crutches?"

"So you figured it was okay to talk to yourself?" His grin lit up his dark face. His teeth were so white against his tan. "They say you're only nuts if you answer yourself when you talk out loud. Are you answering?"

"Not yet. What are you doing here?" That sounded terribly rude. "I mean, how did you know I'm staying at Grandma Knowles's house?"

"It's okay. I'm not stalking you or anything." He let go of the handles and straightened. "My sister borrowed these wheels from a friend. I went home just now and found it parked in the front hall with a bow on it. She knows I hate being cooped up. I'm used to getting a lot of exercise. Sitting around drives me crazy." He patted the scooter. "She figured the wheels would allow me to get around until I wear myself out. So here I am, about ten blocks from Sis's house."

"That was sweet of Angie. Around here, no one is too far away, I reckon." Compared to Kootenai, Eureka was the big city, but Mercy could ride her bike downtown with little effort. "If I were home, I'd be walking too. But everything seems strange now, different, especially after dark. It's not home."

The basic issue: Eureka was not home.

"You could take a walk with me. I mean you walk, I roll."

Could she? Mercy grappled with the implications. Spencer was an English man. Taking a walk with him alone likely would cause frowns. On the other hand, everything was different now. The world had changed. It was upside down and inside out.

"You can say no. I promise it won't hurt my feelings." His gaze came up and his blue eyes sparked. "But just so you know, I'm harmless. Whatever you may have heard from a certain woman in a red dress, I'm not a bad boy. I hate that term. Life is too complicated to reduce a person to a stupid stereotype." He drew a long breath.

Suddenly, she needed that breath of fresh air that would come from being with someone who was completely and utterly different from her. "I'd be happy to take a walk with you."

"Are you sure?" A surprised grin replaced his gloomy visage. "I don't want you to regret it later."

"I won't."

It was her turn to be surprised. Her mother and father might object to this foray after dark with an Englisher, but for once, she would make her own decision irrespective of their opinions. One day, God willing, she would be married and no longer in a position to make these decisions. Today was not that day.

Spencer flung out his arm in an "after you" flourish.

Mercy tucked her hands behind her back and fell in step next to him. It wasn't too hard to match her stride to his push-off on the scooter. It squeaked under his weight, but the sound wasn't annoying. More like steadying.

Silence ensued for the first block. Did it seem as awkward to him as it did to her? She wracked her brain. He wouldn't care about her scholars or her sisters' argument over cherry versus huckleberry pie. The weather?

"It seems like summer is lasting longer than usual." Spencer spoke first. "A good strong cold front with rain would do a lot toward putting that fire out."

Mercy laughed.

"You find the weather funny?" He laughed with her. "I have plenty more where that came from."

"Did you want to take a walk with me to talk about the weather?"

"You're assuming that me showing up in your driveway was intentional."

"Was it?"

"I suppose I'll go to hell if I lie to a good Christian woman." The scooter quickened. Mercy increased her own speed. He slowed. "What if I did? Would that be so terrible? Juliette said—"

"Juliette was the other woman talking to herself?"

"I don't gossip."

"Neither do I."

"That's good." His arm whipped out and he guided her around a dog's droppings square in the middle of the sidewalk. His arm dropped before she began to breathe again. "For the sake of discussion, let's say it was a mutual friend and move on. After I met you the other night, I kept thinking about you. I don't know why. I thought if I talked to you again, I could figure it out."

"What did Juliette say?"

"She said Amish women don't go out with English men."

"She's right."

"Never?"

"Sometimes during our running around—"

"Rumspringa."

"Yes, our rumspringa, both Plain girls and boys go out with English people. But it's rare that it lasts. They know if it does, they'll have to leave the district and their families. Forever."

"A terrible price to pay for love."

"Most of us choose our faith over love."

"That's not just Plain women who do that." He sighed but didn't continue.

"I haven't known many English women of that kind of faith, but from what Juliette says, Tim puts his faith first over love."

"He's stubborn like that."

"You don't like him?"

"He doesn't like me."

"Why? You just got here."

"I knew him in high school. Or of him. He really only knows me by my reputation, which was exaggerated by our friends' gossip."

No need to dig up decade-old gossip. Tim should know better. People changed. For the better sometimes, sometimes for worse. "So have you decided why you had to see me again? It couldn't be because you saw a challenge, could it?"

"No, no way. I don't know yet, but it wasn't that. Something about you intrigued me. You remind me of someone I used to know. Used to talk to."

He sounded wistful. And lonely. "It's good to have someone you can talk to about important things. Why don't you talk to your friend anymore—the one I remind you of?"

He veered into the grass to avoid a tricycle left on the sidewalk. She veered the other direction. "Because she put her faith first."

"You don't believe?"

"At the time I thought I didn't." Emotion roughened his voice. "I don't know. I couldn't tell her how I felt. When I jump, I see a world only someone—something greater than me—could have created. Then I come down to earth and it's such a mess. I don't get how a good God could let it be so messed up."

"How come you can tell me and not this friend?"

"I don't know. Maybe I worried too much about what she would think of me."

Maybe that's why Caleb couldn't talk to her about his feelings. He didn't want to feel stupid or judged. Maybe. "I wonder if all men are like that."

"Stupid, you mean?"

"It's not stupid; it's human."

"See, I knew those soulful eyes hid a thoughtful heart."

Her soul was something that went to heaven, wasn't it? "What does that mean, exactly?"

"Your heart shows in your eyes. You think about things and you care deeply."

"And it shows in my eyes?"

"Yes."

"We should talk about something else." She stumbled over a crack in the sidewalk caused by the roots of a nearby oak tree. The scooter's squeak increased, then died for a few seconds. "Why did you become a smoke jumper?"

"Fair enough." He seemed to search the empty street ahead of them for the words. "I realized early in my firefighting career that I wanted to be a smoke jumper. I was always intrigued by working with aircraft and I liked the idea of learning a new skill." He snorted.

"What?"

"The truth is smoke jumpers are freethinkers. They have to work in remote places with little or no support. I liked that idea."

Despite all the teachings of yielding oneself to God's will and never standing out, putting faith, family, and community first, Mercy could understand why. As a teacher she worked alone. She created lesson plans. She made decisions about discipline in the classroom. She was in charge. That sounded like pride, but it was true. She loved her friends, but she liked working alone. If a person could be alone with twenty-seven children. "You're a loner?"

"Jumping requires the firefighter to be creative and a problem solver, to think outside the box. I like to think that is who I am down to a *T*. I don't need someone to oversee my work. Tell me what you want done, I'll go do it."

Like Mercy, truth be told. "You want to be the boss of yourself."

"Yep. But smoke jumping taught me some unexpected skills. I learned to trust my supervisor and the guys I work with. We became a team."

"Or a family."

He smiled. That must be how her students felt when she

gave them a pat on the back for spelling a word correctly or doing their times table without stumbling.

"We're self-sufficient as a group. We don't receive a lot of support and we don't need it. We may be out there for as little as two or three days or as much as three weeks. Either way, we have each other's backs and we work like synchronized swimmers."

"Before you wanted to work alone; now you like being part of a team."

"Nobody is more surprised than I am."

"Maybe if you'd been out there with your team, the fire would be out now." Ugly bitterness bubbled up through the cracks in their friendly give-and-take. How could she blame this virtual stranger for her loss? Because she needed someone—anyone—to blame. "Maybe our house and the houses of our friends would still be there."

"That's harsh and not true." His smile died. "You heard Dan Larson. All available resources are being thrown at this fire. They're doing everything they can. You can't control the weather or the fact that people aren't taking care of their properties so we can defend them."

Mercy couldn't help the way she felt. Still, Spencer wasn't the enemy. The fire held that distinction. She took a long breath, inhaling the scent of fading summer and roses past their prime in someone's front yard. "Your team is out there and you're not. Does that bother you?"

"You must've been a reporter in some past life."

"Past life?"

"Never mind. I hate it. I hate not being out there, knocking this fire down. Sitting around doing nothing is worse than walking on a bed of nails."

"Or hot coals?"

He laughed. Another gold star.

"Why did you come back to Eureka now?" It was none of her business. None of this was. But his laugh made her feel as if they'd known each other for years. "Tim made it sound like you hadn't been here in years. Why hadn't you been back to visit before?"

He didn't answer for several long seconds. Maybe she'd gone too far. "My mom asked me to come." He cleared his throat. "She's a drunk."

"I'm sorry."

"I'd moved on. Then she sent me this letter. She's doing her steps and staying sober. She wants me to forgive her."

"Her steps?"

"Alcoholics Anonymous. She has to ask forgiveness."

"Then you have to forgive her. Even if she didn't ask, you'd have to."

"No, I don't." Suddenly, he sounded peeved and miserable. No more gold stars.

"Sorry. It's just that we are taught to forgive from the time we're toddlers. Gott expects it. And you'll feel better. You're carrying it around like a huge tree stump on your shoulders. It'll feel good."

"See, that's what I mean. Soulful. Even if I don't agree."

"Try forgiving her. See how good it feels."

"I'll try." He grabbed her hand and squeezed.

Stunned by his warm, firm touch, Mercy squeezed back. A blush born deep within her bloomed and spread head to toe. Her heart raced like a horse given free rein on an empty back road.

"I'm sorry about your house." His voice deepened and his thumb smoothed the skin on her hand. "I know every firefighter out there is sorry, but knowing you personally reminds me of how much people depend on us to do our jobs."

He let go. Mercy shivered. She did an about-face. "We should head back."

The squeak started again. Seconds later, he rolled alongside her. "Your turn. Tell me about yourself." He slowed his pace, forcing Mercy to do the same. "Why did you become a teacher? Aren't most Amish women your age married?"

"I'm only twenty-two. Pretty average." None of her closest friends were married either. In a small district like Kootenai, choices were limited. Turning down Caleb could have terrible repercussions. She might never marry. Better to never marry than marry the wrong man. No one in the district would disagree with that, not even her parents. Yet they kept gaping at her with wrinkled foreheads and perplexed eyes. "I became a teacher because I love reading, writing, and arithmetic. I love learning. Scholars deserve teachers who do it for love of learning. We may not have a lot of book learning, but what we do have should be good."

"You'll have to quit when you get married?"

She had come to grips with this truth, hadn't she? "Yes. If I marry."

"You don't think you will?"

"I don't know what Gott's will is. I don't know what His plan is. No one does."

"I bet you wish you did."

"It would be helpful."

"What if you could marry and keep teaching?"

"What if you couldn't ever jump again? What would you do then?"

"Turn it around on me, why don't you?" He elbowed her.

She stepped off the sidewalk and slogged through grass for a few steps. "Hey." She giggled, something she hadn't expected to do for a long time. "That was rude."

"I've been told I can be rude. I used to think smoke jumping was it. I'm chomping at the bit to get back out there. I crave the adrenaline high."

"I hear a big *but* in there."

"I want to have a reason to come home after it's over."

"You want to have someone to come home to when it's over."

"Yep."

"I know what you mean."

"I know you do. I see it in those eyes."

"Soulful eyes." She ran her tongue over those strange, insightful words. Did she see his soul in his eyes? Was that an English man's way of sneaking into her head and poking around? Her cheeks were warmer than the humid night air warranted. "It's different for Plain women. We want to be wives and mothers. That is our job in life."

"But it's possible to have more than one job. English women do it all the time."

"We don't believe they do it well."

"I'll let them know."

"We don't judge." She rushed to clarify. "We only wish to keep our faith and our families first in our priorities."

"You just did." He laughed, a deep laugh that invited anyone within hearing to laugh with him. "I'm just giving you a hard time. Each to their own. Many women would tell you they struggle with trying to be superwomen. To have it all isn't what it's cracked up to be, or so I've heard."

"Men don't have to make those choices . . ." Her words tripped over themselves and died a quick death. A horse and buggy stood in front of Grandma Knowles's house. A visitor this late could only be a man who'd come to court.

His long legs sprawled in front of him, hat drawn down, chin lowered toward his chest, Caleb sat in the lawn chair. By all appearances he slept.

Waiting for Mercy.

CHAPTER 23

Some events couldn't be explained away. Sometimes words made them worse. Mercy clasped her hands in front of her to keep them from flapping. She veered away from Spencer, putting as much cement between him and her as she could as quickly as she could. His raised eyebrows and sardonic grin told her he knew exactly what was going on. He moved past her and rolled up the driveway to where an unsuspecting Caleb sat.

"Hey. You're Caleb, right?" He tapped on Caleb's straw hat.

Caleb's head snapped up. He grabbed his hat and glared. "What are you doing here?" His bewildered gaze enveloped Mercy and then whipped back to Spencer. "Oh. I mean, I came . . . never mind." He stood and slapped the hat back on his head of straight, sandy-brown hair. "I'm sorry if I interrupted something."

"You're not interrupting." Mercy's voice sounded high and tight in her ears. "Spencer just happened on me sitting out here and we took a walk around the block. That's all."

"You don't owe me an explanation." With an awkward nod he trudged past Spencer to his buggy. His hands smoothed his horse's sleek neck. The glance he aimed at Mercy held apology. "The garage door was open. The chair sitting there empty.

I figured you were awake. I knocked. Your daed came to the door. He's in there getting us some lemonade. He said tea would just keep us awake. I guess he's having trouble sleeping too."

"Stay. Have your lemonade."

"Yeah, you should stay." Spencer edged toward the sidewalk. "I was just leaving."

"I guess I'm more tired than I thought. I should turn in." His gaze studied Spencer. "It is late and dawn comes early. Church is at Bishop Noah's."

With that pithy observation he hoisted himself into the buggy and drove away.

The *clip-clop* of the horse's hooves punctuated the silence for several seconds.

"I should go too." Spencer moved in her direction. "He's right. It's late."

Despite herself, Mercy stumbled back a step.

Spencer halted. His expression dark, he scratched at his five o'clock shadow. "I don't mean to step on any toes or cross any lines. If I did, I'm sorry. I just wanted . . . to talk to you."

"You're fine. Don't worry about it." The conversation with Spencer had been different than any she'd ever had with a Plain man or any man. Food for thought. "Everything is changing. The Plain aren't much for change, but sometimes it's thrust upon us."

The screen door opened. Carrying two glasses of lemonade, Daed elbowed the door so he could navigate through. "I can't get over the size of that refrigerator . . ."

He stopped so abruptly lemonade sloshed over the sides of the glasses and splashed his dusty work boots. "Where's Caleb and who are you?" He wore his wrinkled, faded work shirt and pants, but his suspenders hung down the back of his pants.

Without his glasses and his straw hat, his face was stripped naked except for his unruly iron-gray beard. He looked like old, worn leather. "What are you doing here in the middle of the night?"

"It's not the middle of the night. I reckon it's about eleven o'clock." Mercy kept her voice soft and respectful. She was in enough trouble. She introduced Spencer. "He's a smoke jumper, but he was injured on the job. He was just telling me about how they fight the fires and the reasons why this fire isn't out yet. Why they couldn't keep it from burning our house down."

"It was nice meeting you, Mr. Yoder." Spencer tipped his Rockies cap at Mercy. "I enjoyed our walk. I'll get out of your hair now and let you get some rest."

Suddenly bereft of words and acutely aware of her father's piercing stare, Mercy nodded.

"No need for formality. It's Jonah." The grudging words didn't change her father's expression. "Good night."

Spencer's scooter brought him rather closer to her than necessary. His head ducked and turned toward her. "Maybe we can do it again sometime." The whisper floated on a breeze suddenly warmer than it had been the moment before.

No way to respond with her father only feet away.

She swallowed and forced herself not to sneak a peek at his retreating figure, not to memorize his broad shoulders or the way his dark curls escaped under the back of his cap.

Instead, she summoned her best smile and traipsed toward her dad. "I could use one of those lemonades if you're offering."

"What are you doing, *Dochder*?" His thunderous expression punctuated his next words: "We may be in the city, but we're still the Plain community of Kootenai. The Ordnung hasn't changed."

"I know that." Her thoughts scattered like raindrops in a stormy gale. "There was nothing untoward about it. He was out walking. I was sitting here when he walked by. He suggested we walk together. I was interested in conversation with a firefighter. I had questions."

The truth, but not the entire truth. God would strike her dead.

"Pull up a chair, Dochder." Daed plopped into the lawn chair. The old leather changed into a hard tree stump. "There's no way I'll sleep now. Or you either, I suspect."

Mercy did as she was told. Seated next to him with a view of the starry night sky peeking through the tree branches, she took the second glass of lemonade and drank. The sweet but tart lukewarm liquid eased the ache in her throat. "I'm sorry if I disappointed you."

"Life is turned upside down. No one knows that better than me." His free hand stroking his beard, he stared up at the firmament. "But this is the time to cling to our beliefs and our way of life."

"I don't understand. I wish I were strong like you."

"I'm not strong." His voice cracked. He took a long draught of lemonade. "I know that in all things Gott works for our gut. It's not for us to question how or why. His plan will be revealed. I'm not a fair-weather believer. Scripture tells us in this life there will be trouble. This trouble is small. We're all alive and we're together, by Gott's grace. We have nothing to complain about."

His conviction made her complaints seem puny and petty. "My head knows what you say is true. It's my heart that has trouble with it."

"You're our born learner. That's why you became a teacher.

Your mind is always working. But sometimes there's no figuring things out." His voice hardened. "Sometimes you have to hush up and buckle down under the weight of your burdens. Accept them."

"I know." Nothing in his lecture told her how to harness the feelings of anger. Anger with God. One couldn't be angry with God. Not and be Plain.

Yet here she sat.

"You won't find what you're seeking for in an Englisch man."

"I'm not trying to find anything with Spencer."

"You're not to see him again."

"I'm not seeing him." She chewed on her lip. "Am I not still free to do as I see fit? I've been baptized, but I'm still single. Still searching."

"The letter of the law." He drew lines in the condensation on his glass. "Your mudder and I want what is best for you. We understood, or we tried to understand, when you broke it off with Caleb—"

"He broke it off with me."

"Because you turned down his proposal."

Kootenai's grapevine worked like spreading, smothering kudzu. "Did you love Mudder the first time you saw her, or did your love grow?"

Such a private thing. Surely her father would rebuff the question as too personal. Or maybe the starlight and the moon would mesmerize him into revealing such a special memory to his daughter. It had been a strange night already—why not one more startling revelation?

He wiggled in his chair, leaned over, and set the glass on the cement, then settled back with his hands over his paunch. "That's a question better asked of your mudder."

Disappointment welled.

"But I will say this, once I saw your mudder at the singing, there was no other."

"Did you know her before?"

"I suppose I did. At school. But a person has to be in that frame of mind. That time of life when you're seeking it."

Looking for love. Perhaps the dark of night was the best time to discuss such a thing with a man like her father, who confined his conversations to weather, wood, and God's will. "That's all I'm doing."

"But you'll not do it with an Englischer."

"I'm not—"

He picked up his glass and stood. "Tomorrow is another day. You have work to do and so do I."

Mercy followed him into the house and into the kitchen where she washed the glasses and put the lemonade in the refrigerator. Wiping her hands on a towel, she turned to find him still standing in the doorway. "What, Daed?"

"Doing Gott's will is what is best for you. Stay away from Spencer McDonald."

With that parting shot he left her.

CHAPTER 24

Two turns through the empty streets of downtown Eureka and sleep still seemed a distant mirage. Anger marinated in adrenaline made Caleb's body hum with a desire he didn't recognize and didn't dare acknowledge. He wanted to hit something. Plain men did not entertain such notions. They were not fighters. They didn't go to war. Not even for love of a good woman. Mercy was a good woman. More complicated than most. Maybe too complicated for a simple woodworker who was happy with a piece of sandpaper in his hand and an occasional Western.

He'd been stupid to take Juliette's advice. Mercy turned him down two months ago. Nothing had changed.

Including the depth of his feelings for her. No matter how he tried to deny them.

He turned onto Third Street. Time to go home, whether he liked it or not. Dawn would come, whether he slept or not. Church attendance would be expected, fire and upheaval or not.

In the middle of the next block, movement caught his gaze. And loud cursing. "Whoa, Snowy, whoa."

He peered into the darkness. The people on this block didn't keep their porch or garage lights on. The closest streetlight glowed at the corner, its beams not stretching this far. "Do you need help?"

"I'm fine." More cuss words.

"You don't sound fine." Stretching his neck, Caleb leaned from the buggy. "Spencer, is that you?"

Spencer sprawled on the sidewalk. His fancy knee scooter lay on its side. "Yep, it's me."

Caleb hopped from the buggy and tied the reins to the closest tree branch. "Let me help you up."

"Why would you do that? A few minutes ago you were madder than a bull separated from all the cows by an enormous electric fence."

"I try not to let my human failings get in the way of being a decent human being." Being the better man had its upside. But Plain men tried to never think of themselves as being a better anything. "You would do the same if it were me." He righted the scooter and held his hand out to Spencer.

With a grunt, the other man allowed Caleb to hoist him to his feet. "Thanks." He swayed and grabbed the scooter handle with one hand. Grimacing, he laid the splinted fingers across his chest. His breathing came in short, painful bursts.

"What happened?"

"It's dark. I was daydreaming and didn't see where the sidewalk buckled. Tree roots, I guess."

"Ouch. Let me give you a ride home."

"No need."

"Your scooter has a bent wheel. You appear to be hurting."

"What's your point?"

"No one has to know you took a tumble, if that's what you're worried about."

"I jumped out of an airplane and managed to hit a tree instead of an open meadow." Spencer's laugh was more of a groan. "I'm not too worried about people thinking I'm clumsy."

Spending time alone with Mercy's suitor didn't rank high on Caleb's list of pastimes. Sometimes a person had to do things he didn't want to do. Frequently. Rooming with Ian hadn't been a picnic. "I'll put your scooter in the buggy."

Without waiting for permission, he followed through. Then he grasped Spencer's arm above the elbow. Despite his tight-lipped attempt to suppress it, Spencer groaned, but he managed to hop to the buggy and climb in.

Caleb grabbed the reins and joined him. "Which way?"

Between panting, Spencer provided directions. Silence ensued, broken only by the horse's *clip-clop* of hooves on asphalt, the rattle of the harness, and the creak of the buggy wheels.

Silence didn't bother Caleb, but this was ridiculous. "How long will it take your leg to mend?"

"Doc says I was lucky. Six weeks to three months." His words didn't match his dark stare. "In a few weeks I go back to see how the bone is healing."

"That's gut."

Now what?

Spencer cleared his throat. "About the scene back there at Mercy's—"

"You don't owe me an explanation."

"I know that. We were only talking, nothing more."

"A Plain woman doesn't walk around town in the dark with an Englisch man."

"We were just talking. She makes good conversation."

That she did. About books and such. He'd never talked to her about feelings. He'd wanted to do it, but he simply didn't know how. His family didn't do it. "Make conversation with an Englisch woman. There are many of those around who'd be happy to talk with you."

"I like Mercy. She's smart and thoughtful and different from most of those women you're talking about. Deeper."

"This conversation is pointless." Caleb pulled in front of the small A-frame house with flower boxes that ran the length of the narrow front porch. In the porch light, peonies, pansies, petunias, and miniature mums elbowed each other for first dibs at sunlight at dawn. He chose his next words carefully. "I'm asking you to let this go. Don't attempt to take her from her family and the only life she's ever known. It would be cruel. It would be wrong."

"I hardly know her. We just met." Spencer eased from the buggy on his good leg. His shoulders hunched. "You're reading way too much into a single walk around the neighborhood."

"I don't think I am." Caleb bounded from the buggy and removed the scooter before Spencer could shuffle to the back. One hand on the buggy, he paused and breathed. Caleb pushed the scooter closer. "Steer clear for her sake. Do the right thing."

"I don't want to do anything that would hurt Mercy." Spencer gripped the handles and bent his injured leg so he could place it on the seat. His knuckles turned white. He hopped slowly past Caleb. "I'll think about what you said. No promises, though. A guy should be able to talk to a girl. Friend to friend."

Which went to show that Spencer McDonald didn't understand the Amish. Caleb climbed into the buggy and headed to the RV.

The Amish didn't want any part of the rest of the world.

The question was, did Mercy?

CHAPTER 25

EUREKA, MONTANA

Heat scorched his face. Flames retracted, then loomed over him, closer and closer, dressed in thick, black, choking smoke. Embers seared the skin on the back of his bare neck and arms.

Spencer struggled to pull his body from a fetal position. His muscles huddled in panicked refusal. The flames enveloped him.

"No, no, no!" Hands on his head, he bolted upright. He fought off sheets damp with sweat.

Pain blew through his leg. He doubled over.

In slow motion, he lifted his head and opened his eyes to a dark, unfamiliar room. Angie's spare bedroom.

No fire.

No smoke.

No burning flesh.

He sucked in air and breathed through the pain in his fingers, his ribs, and his leg. The cut on his forehead throbbed. Bruises up and down the left side of his body ached.

It wasn't so bad. Not like burns hurt. The screams of burn victims reverberated in his head.

The nightmare showed up regularly. It had for years.

Long before he started fighting fires.

It had nothing to do with smoke jumping or his accident.

Why tonight? Spencer gently lifted his leg and set his foot on the floor. Using the sheets, he wiped sweat from his hair, face, bare chest, and arms. He stank of sweat and fear. He lowered his head and closed his eyes.

Tonight, because he'd told Mercy he started smoke jumping because he was interested in aircraft and working independently. True, but the real question had been, why did he become a firefighter?

For that he had to rip bandages from old, unhealed wounds.

Every time he spent time with Marnie, the wound seeped pain. Mercy said he had to forgive her. She was wrong. No one had to do anything.

No focusing on the past. Only moving forward.

He raised his head, grabbed the bedpost, and hoisted himself upright. The pain took his breath away.

Breathe, in and out, in and out. One, two, three, four, in and out, in and out.

After a few seconds, he grabbed a white T-shirt and tugged it on. Then he angled toward the abandoned crutches and scooped them up in midlimp. Tomorrow he'd see about getting the scooter repaired. He swung through the open bedroom door, down the hall, and into the living room.

The fake Tiffany lamp on the end table next to his sister's Amish-style hickory rocking chair bathed the sparsely furnished living room in a soft light. A threadbare sofa, a basket of toys, a Tonka truck, coloring books and crayons, and a Barbie doll decorated the faded but clean beige carpet. A small flat-screen TV hung from the wall.

Angie sat at a folding card table in the corner, her back to him. Her laptop was open and she seemed absorbed in whatever its screen divulged.

"Angie." Hoping not to scare her, he whispered. "Why are you up?"

She jumped three feet. Hand on her ample chest, she swiveled. "It's the middle of the night. You scared me to death, Spence."

"I couldn't sleep."

"You were snoring the last time I walked by your room. Nightmare?"

"You have church tomorrow. Why aren't you sleeping?"

"The McDonalds have one thing in common. We don't sleep." She stretched both arms over her head and yawned. "With three kids, two jobs, and school, I've learned to get by."

She had that right. For different reasons, maybe, but none of them good. "They say staring at electronics makes it worse."

"When the kids are sleeping is the only time I can do my classwork. That's the advantage of doing online classes. They don't care if it's 1:00 a.m." She shut the laptop and stood. "Want some hot tea or cocoa?"

"It's September."

"Warm liquids are supposed to help."

"Not so I noticed. Got any Ambien?" Not that he used sleep aids. The fear of addiction was far greater than the fear of long, empty nights. "Just kidding. What are you studying?"

"I'd like to be a social worker when I grow up." She sighed and pushed straggly magenta hair behind her ear. "But that means doing a practicum and some coursework on a campus somewhere. I need a master's degree. It's hard for me to imagine being able to do that. But with God, all things are possible. I say my prayers and know He'll do whatever is best for me and my babies."

Was allowing her to grow up in the home of an alcoholic prone to blackouts best for her?

"I can see you as a social worker." She would pour herself heart and soul into the job and the people she wanted to help. And the bureaucracy would bleed her dry. "You have the heart for it with the gift of administration."

"That's the nicest thing anyone has ever said to me." Angie removed her purple-framed glasses and wiped her eyes. "Rocky never complimented me. At least not after we got married and I gained thirty pounds."

"Rocky is a—"

"Spencer! I'll do with you what I do with Mom. For every cuss word she has to put a dollar in the jar. When there's fifteen dollars in there, we go to McDonald's for hamburgers and the kids get to play in the fun house."

"They must cheer every time she cusses."

"They know better than to do it in front of me." She sank onto the couch and stuck her bare feet on the pillows at the other end. "Same old nightmare?"

"Yep." He hobbled to the recliner across from the sofa and plopped down so he could put the footrest up and elevate his leg. "Why would it be any different after all these years?"

"Maybe if you confronted her, your subconscious would let it go and you could move past it."

"I thought you said social worker, not psychologist."

She held her glasses up in the air, then rubbed the lenses on her MercyMe T-shirt. "You're avoiding the question. She has to make amends and ask for forgiveness as part of working the steps. Maybe you need to forgive her for what she did.

She doesn't know you know. I'm pretty sure she doesn't even remember doing it."

"That's what blows my mind. How can she not know she started a fire and nearly burned the house down with us in it?"

"It's called a blackout for a reason."

The real reason he became a firefighter. To make sure he was never that scared and vulnerable again. To make sure he could take care of the people he loved. No one would ever do that to him or Angie again.

Especially not Marnie. "Don't leave the kids with her. Please."

"They love her and she loves them. It's way better than a crowded day care. And I pay her—not much, but it's grocery money. The house is paid for, but her SSI doesn't give her enough to live on."

"Do you flinch every time you hear sirens?"

"Not forgiving her is a burden on your shoulders, not hers. She didn't do it on purpose. It was an accident."

"She left the gas burner on. A stack of pot holders caught fire. It spread to some towels and boxes of cereal or whatever. It spread. The entire kitchen was gutted. The living room was . . . It's a wonder she didn't die right there on the couch. That we didn't all die."

"You got me out. You got her out." Angie's voice broke. He shouldn't force her to relive one of the worst nights of their lives. "But not Toby. You did more than a twelve-year-old kid should have to do."

Toby, the stray cat they had adopted only weeks earlier. A scrawny black-and-white kitten who yowled every morning to be let out and then whined to come back in every night. He belonged to Angie more than Spencer. The firefighters found him underneath Angie's smoke-scorched bed.

"I never understood why they didn't take us away from her."

"Because we kept our mouths shut. Better the devil you know than the one you don't." Angie tucked a fat pillow embroidered with *Bless This House* in her arms and laid her cheek on it. "We could've ended up with Dad and his new wife. For all we know she's Godzilla. And he obviously didn't want us. He left us. It was an accident. We knew it was an accident. She fell asleep on the couch—"

"She passed out."

"She fell asleep on the couch. Mom worked all day—"

"And drank all night."

"She provided for us."

"She almost killed us."

"Instead of flinging all this old stuff at me, talk to her. Tell her how you feel. I know that's what any psychologist would tell you." Angie closed her eyes and sighed. "Anyone with half a brain can see it's eating you up. For your sake, have it out with her. You'll stop being angry. She'll stop feeling guilty. You'll both start to heal."

"Not possible." He pushed the recliner back until he lay prone and closed his eyes. "Go to bed, Sissy."

"Now that you're back—"

He opened his eyes. "I'm not back."

"So you're not staying?"

"I have a job in Missoula."

"You have family here."

"Missoula is only a few hours away."

"Yet it's been ten years since you've been home."

"I had my reasons, as you well know." He closed his eyes again. "Go to bed before one of the kids wakes up and wants a drink of water or has to go potty."

The swish of her voluminous skirt alerted him when she got close. Her lips brushed his forehead. "Love you, big brother. I'm glad you're here."

"Love you too."

The *swish-swish* moved away. Her soft words floated on the air. "I'm praying for you."

Having an angel pray for him couldn't hurt.

He might even learn something from her about how it was done.

CHAPTER 26

Who said those who cannot remember the past are condemned to repeat it? The name escaped Juliette. Sunlight pierced her eyes as she stumbled into her aunt's airy, country-style kitchen. The aroma of frying bacon and bread toasting turned her stomach. She'd been a lightweight drinker in college, prone to sudden, unquenchable puking, which was why she learned to turn down the frat boys' offer of murky concoctions early in her career. She always said she was a crazy, happy person without alcohol. Why add to perfection? If they preferred their women plied with alcohol, they could take a flying leap somewhere else. So why the twenty-four ounces of headache the previous night?

"Good morning, sunshine." Mom slid two eggs, two strips of bacon, and two pieces of toast onto a chunky ceramic plate covered with dark-blue flowers. "You missed a good sermon at church this morning. The coffee's hot. Orange juice might be a better choice. It hydrates."

"Daddy told you." Her stomach heaving, she waved off the plate and went to the coffeepot. Aunt Tina's mugs were enormous and perfect. She added milk and extra sugar. "It was two beers."

"He was fit to be tied."

"I'm an adult."

"His thought is that you should act like one."

Juliette slid onto a stool at the quartz-topped island and sipped her coffee. Her mother laid the plate in front of her. Her expression suggested Juliette not argue. She picked up the fork, then laid it down. "Were you and Dad Christians when you got married?"

The smile flitting across Mom's face was the one she displayed when she opened the kids' homemade gifts on her birthday. "We were. You know the story. I grew up in Polson. Your dad was from Kalispell. We met at MU my freshman year in Fellowship of Christian Athletes. I was on a volleyball scholarship. He had a basketball scholarship. We dated all through college and got married right after graduation."

"What if one of you hadn't been a Christian?"

"I guess we wouldn't have met."

"You could've run into each other in the student union or at a football game or someplace you worked."

"I always figured God picked your dad out for me and vice versa. He made it happen."

"You wouldn't have considered marrying Dad if he wasn't a Christian?"

"Does this have to do with you and Tim?"

"Tim's a jerk."

"No, he's not, and you know it."

"I got a job offer."

Her mother shrieked, threw her hands in the air, and rushed across the kitchen. The hug squeezed the air from Juliette. "Where, when, doing what?"

"That's the thing. It's in Billings."

"Billings. That's not so bad. At least it's not in Kansas City or Timbuktu."

"Mom! It's eight hours away. And Tim refuses to consider moving."

"Honey, Tim's right."

"Mom!"

"Sorry, sweetie. I love you and I want you to be happy." More hugging ensued. Mom brushed Juliette's hair from her face and patted her cheek. "I can't tell you how many hours I spend on my knees praying for my children. All of them. I have calluses. I want you to be happy, but more than that, I want to know that your future—your eternal future—is secure. That has nothing to do with Tim."

"It has everything to do with Tim."

"So that's what the drinking was about. Tim loves you, there's no doubt in my mind. The question is, why did you turn away from Jesus? What's keeping you from turning back to Him?"

"I don't want to talk about this."

"Until you do, you'll never be truly happy."

A future filled with unmet goals, unhappiness, and emptiness without Tim unfolded in front of Juliette. "Thanks for the pep talk, Mom."

"I've never understood what happened to you. One day you were running off to youth group with Madison and Olivia and the other girls from church." Her expression perplexed, Mom straightened the silverware next to Juliette's plate. "The next you refused to go. You stopped hanging out with them. You stopped going on the mission trips and working at the pumpkin patch. What happened?"

The feel of Danny's sweaty hands on her bare neck made

Juliette's skin crawl. The smell of his spearmint toothpaste and overpowering Axis aftershave gagged her. The memory crawled from the dark corners of her mind. *No.* She kicked it back into its box, and with it, the whimpers that followed late into the next night and many nights after.

"Juliette, talk to me. Your face is white."

"It's nothing."

"It's not nothing. The expression on your face says it all."

"It was my fault for being stupid."

That sentiment applied to many situations. Trusting a guy new to the youth group was stupid. Taking a walk by the lake after dark was stupid. Wearing that bikini was stupid. Pastor Rick had said modest suits only or T-shirts to cover them. She took her T-shirt off every chance she could. Pastor Rick was too busy tending the bonfire, breaking up ice fights, cooking the hot dogs, roasting the marshmallows, and praying to notice. The guys in her group weren't. Nor was Danny.

Danny with his long blond hair that made him a dead ringer for a surfer. Tanned, a buff body, older than her friends. Danny with the smile that said he liked the way she strutted her stuff.

Liked it so much he was all hands the minute they escaped the bonfire's light. The farther they walked, the closer he moved. His arm, with bulging biceps, locked down around her neck. His fingers pinched her bare belly. His lips bruised hers.

"No. No."

"Baby, you'll like it. I promise."

"Stop. Stop. Please stop."

He didn't stop.

No tender touch, no sweet prelude.

His heavy body anchored her to the ground. Her lungs

couldn't inflate. She had no breath. Panic grew and grew until she screamed.

She opened her mouth, but no sound came out.

She still awoke some nights smothered by his muscle-bound body.

"You're so sweet. You're so beautiful. Thank you."

"Please, please. I . . . can't . . . breathe."

"Do you like me? I like you."

Afterward, he wrote her cell phone number on his hand and then wrote his number on hers in ink. He pressed too hard. It hurt.

Everything hurt.

Laughing and nuzzling her neck, he put his arm around her shoulders and walked her back to the light of the fire. They snuck into the group. Olivia and Madison were singing Chris Tomlin's songs and acting goofy. They were little kids. Juliette never sang another verse of "I Will Lift My Hands."

Danny never came back to youth group.

Juliette never heard from him again and she never told anyone.

She kept smiling. She smiled now. "Do you have some aspirin?"

Her mother brought her a bottle of Tylenol. "Is there something else you want to tell me?"

"I'm good. Thanks, Ma."

"I could pray with you."

"If it makes you feel better."

She sighed and took Juliette's hands in hers and bowed her head. Her face was filled with a peace that made her seem younger and wise and sweet. Juliette swallowed against a lump the size of Montana in her throat and closed her eyes.

The words flowed over her full of grace and forgiveness and a mother's hopes and dreams for her daughter.

Having a mom who cared so much was a gift. Where did that gift come from?

God?

Where were You, God, when I was acting stupid? When I let Danny take my hand for a walk? I thought I liked to live dangerously. I thought I could handle it. You knew better, but You didn't do a thing about it.

Being mad at God, talking to God, that presupposed a belief in God. What kind of God was He? The feel-good God who showered you with blessings like an omnipotent Santa Claus? The peevish Jehovah of the Puritans?

Or Tim's God, who loved all His children and wanted to walk through the trials with them?

Where were You, God, when I needed You?

"Honey, you're crying. Tell me. What's going on?" Her mother's voice climbed an octave. "Let me help you."

Juliette laid her head on her forearm and sobbed. "It's nothing. My stomach hurts so bad."

"How long has it hurt like this?" Mom's hand stroked her hair just like she used to do when Juliette had a tummy ache and went to bed early.

Some things couldn't be fixed so easily. "For about five years."

"Juliette! Why didn't you say anything? We need to take you to the doctor."

"A doctor can't fix it."

The story came out in fits and starts. Pieces more jagged than broken glass, more piercing than arrows, tore at Juliette's throat.

Aunt Tina started into the kitchen. Mother shook her head. She disappeared.

"I'm sorry, Mom, I'm so sorry. I'm so ashamed. It was all my fault. I was so stupid. So, so stupid."

Shaking her head vehemently, Mom dragged her stool closer. Tears ran down her horror-stricken face. "It wasn't your fault, I promise." Her hand rubbed Juliette's back in warm, soothing circles. "I'm sorry you went through that. Why didn't you tell me? Why didn't you report him to the sheriff?"

"I went with him willingly. I did everything Pastor Rick said not to do. Who would believe me? It was my fault."

"It's never a girl's fault. No means no. Where was Rick when all this was happening?"

"Doing his job. Being a youth minister to twenty crazy teenagers."

"And the other chaperones?"

"Around. Eating s'mores and singing stupid songs."

"Why didn't you say anything?"

"I was ashamed."

Mom held her. They cried together. Courtney strolled into the kitchen, stopped in her tracks, and opened her mouth. Mom waved her away. She closed her mouth and went.

"I want to get you some help." Mom snagged two tissues from a box on the table and handed Juliette one. "Let me do that for you, please."

"It was years ago. I'm over it. I'm just hormonal today, that's all. I don't need help."

"You're not over it. You need to deal with it. Out in the open."

"You can't tell anyone." Horror blew through Juliette. Telling someone should've made it better. It didn't. The same thick, heavy blanket of sorrow and shame dragged her down. People couldn't know. They couldn't. "Not Dad, not anyone."

"I can't do that." Her face full of a mother's pain, anger, and empathy, Mom stroked Juliette's hair. Her firm tone didn't bode well. "Your dad needs to know."

"No, he doesn't. Why?"

"It'll help him understand your behavior. So he can pray for your healing. So he can be there for you."

"I don't want him to know." Juliette jerked away. She popped from the chair and paced between the island and the long row of cabinets. "I don't want him to pity me the way you're pitying me right now. I'm not that stupid little girl anymore. I don't need anyone to be there for me."

"You were a fifteen-year-old girl. You were assaulted on a trip where you should've been safe and among friends."

"It was a long time ago. I'm fine."

"You're not fine. I wish Pastor Rick was still around. I'd give him a piece of my mind." Mom smacked her fist against her open palm. Pastor Rick had moved to a larger church in Butte, which was obviously a good thing now. "I trusted him with my baby girl."

"It wasn't his fault."

"And you never saw this guy again?"

"He was a friend of Jeremy's. Jeremy moved to Butte a few weeks later. Danny didn't come to youth group after that. 'Course, neither did I."

"It makes me sick to my stomach."

An even more horrible thought—if that were possible—hit Juliette. "Tim can't ever know."

"You need to tell him, honey. He'll understand."

"How could he?" Juliette didn't understand. How could Tim?

He already hated the way she acted around other men. He would think it was her fault for sure. "He'll understand that I put myself in a situation and now I'm damaged goods?"

"Oh, baby, you're not damaged goods." More waterworks. For both of them. "You're a beautiful, smart, funny woman any man would be blessed to have as a friend and wife and mother of his children."

Juliette blew her nose with a loud honk. She grabbed another tissue and wiped her face. "I don't feel like that."

"I know. That's why I want to get you help."

Juliette had spilled the story in a moment of weakness, and now the past would come crashing down around her. "You can't tell anyone. Promise me you won't tell anyone."

"Baby, I can't do that."

Juliette sank against the counter. Exhaustion blew through her. The kitty cat clock over the stove read 9:43. "Take me to get my truck?"

"So you can go where?"

"I need to get some air. I'll go for a run at the park."

"A run would be good for you, but then I want you home." Mom scooped up her keys from the kitchen counter. "We're not done talking about this. I'll tell Tina we're headed out. She's probably worried sick. Courtney too."

"Don't tell them."

"I won't, honey, but at some point, you have to deal with this or it will eat you alive." She blew Juliette a kiss and swept from the room.

Maybe it already had.

CHAPTER 27

Juliette put the Ranger in park and turned off the engine in front of Nana Knowles's house. Sunday had turned into Monday, but nothing had changed. Her mother knew Juliette's darkest secret. She wanted to help. By now, Dad knew too. They planned and plotted next steps for fixing their oldest daughter. They didn't understand she was irrevocably broken. Which was why Juliette had to escape Aunt Tina's house. So she fled.

Mercy would be teaching, but she had asked Juliette to stop by. So here she was. The garage door stood open. A dozen or so children faced the interior. It had to be warm in there. No fan to stir the air. No breeze.

The *tick-tick* of the engine lulled her. She knew and loved every nook and cranny of this house, from the dusty green eaves to the basement filled with canned goods ranging from green beans to pickled beets to peach jam to cherry pie filling, all grown in Nana's backyard garden and on her trees. Juliette grew up sleeping in an upstairs bedroom in the canopy bed her Aunt Tina had slept in as a child. She played with toys in the attic that had belonged to her dad and Tina. In the fall she and her brothers raked leaves, and Grandpa gave them each two quarters. In winter they shoveled snow and received a dollar for their efforts, along with hot cocoa and Nana's gingerbread cookies.

How sweet it would be to curl up in that bed now and wake up to the smell of Nana's pumpkin pie baking. To have Nana dance with her to Frank Sinatra music. To sit on the rug and listen to Nana tell stories about how Daddy did this or that as a child.

To be innocent and pure and untouched by ugliness.

Those days were gone.

It all seemed a million years ago. Grandpa Knowles's funeral was Juliette's first. Then Nana's two years later. But the emaciated, shrunken lady they laid to rest bore little resemblance to Nana. She'd been round and twinkly and full of sass until Grandpa died. After that she faded away piece by piece, day by day, tear by tear.

Get out.

Lethargy stole her motivation.

Move.

Juliette climbed from the cab and dragged herself to the edge of the garage. Mercy stood in front of a group of her smaller students—her scholars as she called them. They were taking turns reading to her in English. They were adorable with their bowl haircuts, suspenders, and little aprons. Some of the older kids bent over their desks, pencils in hand, lips pursed, writing in composition notebooks. A third group gathered around a portable dry-erase board. They took turns writing multiplication problems on the board and solving them. One by one, they chanted their multiplication tables. Organized chaos.

How did she do it? Mercy was so unassuming in her dress and her manner but so self-assured when it came to teaching. She would never say as much, but she had a calling. Juliette's throat clogged with unshed tears. Everybody needed a calling. A reason to get up in the morning.

Enough with the hormones already.

She swallowed hard and waited for Mercy to notice her.

A second later she did and a smile bloomed. That's when a person received a true picture of Mercy's nature. Her smile could vanquish the worst bad mood. Juliette returned the smile.

"Kinner, we have company. Say good morning to Juliette."

Fourteen heads swiveled. Smiles and giggles followed.

"Good morning, Juliette." Fourteen sweet, high voices chimed in unison.

"Good morning, scholars." Juliette edged between the desks and wooden shelves laden with a dusty Weed Eater, old cans of house paint, oil, and a hodgepodge of tools. "Don't let me stop your studies. I'm here to observe."

"Scholars, why don't you recite your memory verse for this week for our visitor?"

The children who were sitting stood. They turned to face Juliette.

"'Repent ye therefore, and be converted, that your sins may be blotted out, when the times of refreshing shall come from the presence of the Lord.' Acts 3:19."

King James English from the mouths of babes. Juliette clapped in amazement. Did a person clap for verses in an Amish school? She stopped. The kids grinned their appreciation.

"Teacher, can we sing a song for Juliette?" A little girl missing two front teeth lisped the question.

Mercy smiled. "One song and then we'll get back to our studies."

Fourteen childish, high voices lifted in the sweetest rendition of "Jesus Loves Me" Juliette had ever heard. The pounding in her head eased. Her stomach stopped with the somersaults.

"That was beautiful." She clapped again. "Thank you for sharing with me."

"Time to get back to work." Her expression firm but ever kind, Mercy assigned one of the older girls to help the little ones read. Then she and Juliette moved behind her desk where Mercy picked up her coffee mug and sipped. Her eyes were red and surrounded by dark circles.

"You look like death warmed over." Juliette took the cup from her and sipped. "Yuck, you forgot the cream and sugar."

"I needed it black this morning and thank you very much." Mercy rolled her eyes and sighed. "It was a long weekend and I haven't been sleeping well."

"For me too." Juliette hesitated. She handed the cup back to her friend. "I did something stupid."

"I think I did too."

Juliette nodded toward the back of the garage. Mercy led the way. They stepped into the sun just beyond the garage door and stood so Mercy could keep an eye on her students.

"You first." Mercy raised her face to the sun and inhaled. "I'm still half asleep."

"I went to Ballcap's Saturday night. I drank a few beers."

"That was two days ago. You still have bloodshot eyes and dark circles around your eyes." Mercy's words held no judgment. "Why did you do it? Because of Tim?"

"The house. The job. Tim. My life."

"I understand."

"You do?"

Mercy hugged her arms against her chest. "I'm only human. I try so hard to believe the way my mother and father do. But things happen and I find myself doubting. I would never tell anyone that but you—"

"Don't worry. Your secret is safe with me." Juliette studied Mercy's face. She seemed more than tired. "What happened?"

"Spencer McDonald came by Saturday night. He said he was out for a walk and just happened to pass by, but I don't think that's true."

"What did you do?"

"I went for a walk with him. I walked. He had a knee scooter he used."

"It was just a walk." Juliette considered the sudden pink that imbued Mercy's cheeks. "Wasn't it?"

"He's different from any man I've ever known."

"He is different, but you've led a sheltered life." Juliette leaned against the garage corner and contemplated the silky heads of innocent children. Had she ever been that innocent? Had Spencer? "What did you two talk about that has you blushing like a middle school kid?"

"Nothing. Everything. Teaching. Amish beliefs. His beliefs. His mother. Life."

"Whoa. For a first date, that's pretty deep."

"It wasn't a date."

"What was it?"

"I don't know. It felt . . . like friendship."

"Spencer came calling for you. He sought you out at the high school and he sought you out here." Juliette tried to soften her barrage of words. Mercy might be a teacher and a grown woman, but she had little experience with men. "That could be sort of scary. Or if you were me, exciting. But you're not me, so . . ."

"He was nice. Not scary." Mercy chewed on a hangnail, her expression clearly troubled, despite her words. "He said I reminded him of someone. He said I had soulful eyes."

"Holy Toledo."

"Juliette, hush!" Mercy glowered and put her index finger to her lips. "The scholars." Her face crumpled.

Something about her slumped posture set off alarms. "Something else happened, didn't it?"

"We got back to the house and Caleb was sitting in the driveway, waiting."

"Whoops!"

Some of the students swiveled and craned their heads.

"Keep working, scholars." Mercy glowered at Juliette. "Hush."

"Sorry. Mama Mia. What did you do?"

"I tried to explain, but he left. Then Spencer met my daed."

Double whoops. Jonah could bring a boy to his knees with his double-barreled glare. "Did he take a switch to you? Or to Spencer?"

"Of course not." Mercy tsked. "They were polite. But as he passed me on his scooter, he whispered, 'Let's do it again.' Or something like that. Right in front of my dad."

"He's a bad boy."

"He's not. He's been through . . . some bad things."

"His mom's an alcoholic."

"I know. He told me." Mercy sighed. "I feel so bad for Caleb. I hate that I hurt him."

"I knew it. You do have a thing for Caleb." Why did Mercy keep pushing him away? She could be married by now instead of walking the streets with a guy who would only cause her pain and separate her from her family. "You need to tell him you have no intention of taking a walk with Spencer again."

"I don't know if I'll get the chance."

"Make it happen. You're a very smart woman."

Mercy's hug was fierce and so long Juliette fought the desire to collapse into her friend's arms. "A girl needs friends like you," she whispered into Mercy's shoulder. "Nobody better mess with you."

Mercy leaned back and stared. "Are you crying? What's wrong? So you broke your own rule about drinking Saturday night. Today is a new day. You won't do it again."

"It's not that." Juliette didn't have the wherewithal to tell her story again. Not twice in twenty-four hours. It would suck the sweetness from Mercy. She didn't need this ugliness in her life. Especially now with her house gone. Juliette glanced at her phone. "Isn't it lunchtime?"

"I suppose it is."

Mercy trotted to the front of the makeshift classroom. "It's time for lunch and recess. Let's take our lunch boxes into the backyard. Volleyball after you eat, but take your time and eat slowly. I don't want anyone choking on a sandwich because he's in a hurry to play."

An actual problem from the knowing concern shot at Jeremy Plank.

Thirty minutes for lunch. Thirty minutes for play. That's how Mercy intended it, but the children, seated in the grass in the shade of maple and peach trees, their lunch boxes scattered among them, inhaled their lunches in less than fifteen minutes. Gales of childish laughter filled Nana's backyard once again.

A sense of déjà vu assailed Juliette. Grandma and Grandpa never removed the swing set, even after Courtney grew too old or too cool for it. The volleyball net that had been stowed in the garage now split the remaining yard in half. Happy children set free from the confines of desks and books proceeded to play as if they hadn't a care in the world.

No fire threatened to make a second pass at their homes.

No waiting to see what was left of their life in Kootenai.

No separation from friends and family staying in other parts of the Northwest.

No worries.

Children had an amazing ability to live in the moment. They had an innate resilience.

How and when did it become lost?

When someone violated that innocence and threw it away like a piece of junk?

Could it be regained?

It was worth a try.

The PB and J Mercy shared with Juliette, the tart green Granny Smith apple so juicy its sweet nectar ran down her cheek, and the cinnamon spice chewy goodness of a homemade oatmeal-raisin cookie made her stomach forget about its usual pain. Lola wandered across the yard, hopped onto the table, and nosed at Juliette's paper plate.

"How are you adjusting to your digs, sweet thing?" She ran her fingers through silky fur. The kitten purred. "Nana loved cats. Sunflower and Pebbles were her last two, before she died. They liked to sit on this table and sun."

"She was a sweet lady. I remember when she came out to visit in Kootenai and brought us all popcorn balls and candy canes for Christmas."

"She was the best nana ever." Juliette's throat closed. The memories were sweet. If her parents were right, Nana and

Gramps were in a better place. No more tears. No more pain. To believe that would be such a relief. "I've eaten hundreds of grilled hot dogs at this table. I miss her so much."

"I miss my granny too, but I think about her being able to walk with no pain from her arthritis and her heart being strong again, and I know it's selfish to want her back here." Mercy held out the crusts from her sandwich. Doodles loped across the yard from where he'd been begging for food from the kids. He swooped in and took the crusts without pausing. "Don't ever turn your back on this guy. He'll steal your food right off your plate."

"I have a sister who does that." Juliette held out her bread crusts. Doodles sniffed, offered her a pensive stare, then snatched the bread from her fingers. He proceeded to plop at her feet as if exhausted from the effort. "He actually reminds me a lot of Courtney."

"You're so funny. You love your sister and you know it."

"Like I love to pick at a scab."

"Gross!"

They both laughed. Juliette used her fingertips to round up the last cookie crumbs from her paper plate and dropped them on her tongue. Emma approached and touched her denim shorts. "Teacher's friend, do you want to play ring-around-the-rosy with us?" Emma had enough freckles across her nose and cheeks for three kids. Her lavender dress brought out the purple flecks in her sapphire eyes. She was enchanting.

Without answering, Juliette stood and allowed herself to be tugged into the circle of first and second graders.

All-fall-down.

This was a safe place to fall.

"Teacher's friend—"

"It's Juliette."

"Juliette, come play volleyball with us."

So she did. She shucked off her cowboy boots. The grass was cool and soft under her bare feet. Her high school prowess at the game returned quickly. Laughing and breathless, she leaped in the air and spiked the ball.

"No fair, they have a ringer." Mercy's laugh said she didn't really mind. "Take pity on us poor folks."

"Take no prisoners."

Juliette's side won, but nobody really cared.

"It's time to get back to class." Mercy's face glistened with perspiration and happiness. "Gather up your lunch boxes and walk—don't run—back to the garage."

To their credit, not one child argued. Juliette opened her mouth and closed it. She fell into line behind the older kids and marched back to the garage. Mercy winked at her. She grinned and winked back. "That was fun."

"I love lunch and recess."

Mercy whispered the words but Hope grinned. "Teachers aren't supposed to be sad when recess is over."

"Shush."

At the garage door Juliette paused, her boots in one hand. "I should get out of your hair." She couldn't think of where she would go next. Home where her mom would want to talk more was out of the question. The one person she wanted to tell about her morning in Nana's backyard wasn't talking to her. Ever again.

The profound sense of loss knocked her a step back. She swayed.

Mercy took her arm and steadied her. "Why don't you stay? I have an idea."

A preposterous idea. Mercy wanted Juliette to stand in as the teacher.

"I don't know jack about teaching."

"I finished school at the end of eighth grade. You have a college education. My native language is *Deutsch*. Yours is English, which they are expected to learn. You used to keep your dad's books for his horse sales and the mechanic shop. I do basic multiplication and division. You are more qualified to teach than I am."

"To teach Amish kids? Won't your dad have something to say about this? The school board? The bishop?"

"I don't know. It's an experiment, a short one, meant to gain insight, and as such, it will do no harm." Mercy squinted as if trying to see the future. "If they do, I'll beg forgiveness."

The children might beg to differ.

"Please, Juliette. Teach us," Emma and Hope and Josiah clamored. The others joined in. "Please, Juliette."

Or not.

Shoulder against the wall, Juliette tugged on her boots. A woman wearing cowboy boots could do anything. She strode to the front of the classroom. "You asked for it."

Their expectant, shiny, pink-cheeked faces stared at her. Waiting for her to impart wisdom and learning.

She wiped her sweaty hands on her shorts and took a breath. "Let's start with English. How many of you know the words to the song 'Take Me Out to the Ball Game?'"

No one. "Perfect. Here's how it goes."

After that she divided them into teams to play Bible Trivia, a game her parents insisted on playing on snow days. Amazing how well she remembered the stories.

From there, it was time to see who knew their multiplication tables the best among the older kids, while the younger ones drew pictures of their families and labeled each picture in English.

Finally, they had an English spelling bee, divided into age groups, to be fair.

The time passed so quickly, Juliette was surprised when Mercy waved from her seat in the back and pointed at the clock on the desk.

"And that's a wrap!"

Their faces perplexed, the students didn't move.

"It's time to go home. Shoo, go, run like the wind." Juliette stopped short of saying "See you tomorrow," although the words were on the tippy-toes of her tongue. "It's been fun. Thank you for having me."

"You're welcome." They spoke in unison and then they spilled out of their desks and raced for the driveway and freedom.

The familiar memory drifted by. The bell rang and she shot down the hall and out the door to freedom and sunlight and an afternoon ride on one of her dad's horses. Or mucking the stalls or sitting on a stool watching him roll under a Chevy to fix something or other. All greasy and sweaty and busy but still asking her about her day.

"You did great." Mercy trotted behind her desk. "How did it feel?"

"Gut."

Mercy laughed. "Don't get too assimilated. You want to teach them, not vice versa."

"What did you think? Too much competitive stuff? I know you Amish people aren't into competition."

"Have you seen our baseball games?" Mercy straightened desks and chairs as she talked. "They learned from you. That's

important. A variety of teaching methods keeps them interested. We have to have time for written lessons and lectures,
but there's nothing wrong with something fresh and different."

"I thought you were all about tradition, tried and true, dried
and pruned."

"Very funny. Tradition is important to us." Mercy stacked
books on her desk and turned to the chalkboard. She took a
white rag to it, clearing the writing. "But that's beside the
point—you wouldn't be teaching in an Amish school."

"I wouldn't be teaching anywhere."

"Why not?"

"Because my degree is in communications."

Books clutched in her arms, Mercy leaned against her desk.
She wrinkled her nose. "Why? Why did you get that degree?
You never talked about it. Before you left for college, you said
you might get a degree in education or you might go to veterinarian school or—"

"Or I might become a stand-up comedian or compete on
American Idol. I said a lot of things."

"You would be a good teacher. You're good with kids. You're
good with people."

Friends like Mercy were worth more than all the money in
the world. "You give me a lot more credit than I deserve."

"Just think about it, please."

"Why is this so important to you?"

"Because you're unhappy and I don't want you to be unhappy."

"What else?"

"I'm selfish. If you move to Billings, I'll never see you. Eight
hours might as well be eight hundred." She ducked her head.
"Teachers are needed here in this area. In Libby and Eureka

and Kalispell. Or Polson and the other small towns between here and Missoula."

"You have to have a degree in education." Juliette counted off the problems with this scenario on her fingers. "You have to student teach. You have to get certified."

"You're thinking about it." Mercy clapped her hands. If she'd been any younger, she would've jumped up and down. "Let's go to the library Saturday and order the applications online. We can search for the requirements. Maybe having a degree already makes a difference."

"Whoa, whoa. There's a difference between thinking about it and doing it."

"Come inside. Let's get some lemonade and you can tell me what else happened Saturday night. You drank some beer. That's not the whole story, sister."

Mercy pulled the screen door open. Juliette glanced back. From a stinky, dank converted garage classroom to a school classroom. Could it be possible?

A window opened somewhere inside her. A fresh spring breeze fragrant with possibilities lifted the curtains.

She swallowed against the ache in her throat.

A verse also floated on the air. One her mother liked to quote whenever her children complained about something being too hard. With God, all things are possible.

Even forgiving a sin-stained girl like her?

CHAPTER 28

M ost of the time Tim couldn't remember what day it was. He rubbed his eyes, already irritated from smoke and lack of sleep. It didn't really matter, as long as he remembered to go to church on Sunday. It was Monday. No, Tuesday. He spray-painted the big 0 on the driveway of an empty home on Hutton Drive off Bobtail Road. The owners had done the smart thing and hightailed it from an area ravaged by a lightning-started fire fueled by timber, grass, and understory. It had eaten more than ten thousand acres of Kootenai National Forest and another three thousand acres of private property since its birth at the end of August. This was the last house on his route. He tossed the spray paint in the truck, slid in, and headed toward town.

The radio crackled. Cammie was on dispatch and she sounded as frazzled as Tim felt. "Hey, Trudeau, are you out there? What's your twenty?"

"Hutton Drive. Headed your way."

"Can you call me on the phone?"

"Sure."

There wasn't much they didn't put out on the radio, and the hesitation in Cammie's voice said it couldn't be good. Tim made the call via Bluetooth and waited for her to pick up. "What's up?"

"I got a call from Will Dalton up on Whitetail Road." She paused.

Will lived two houses down from Tim's mom's place. "And?"

"He says your mom showed up at her house around lunchtime. He's getting ready to leave so he went over to talk to her, let her know about the evac. She told him she's not leaving. That the sheriff will have to pry her cold, dead fingers off the doorframe."

More like her burned-to-a-crisp fingers. "I moved her to Eureka on Thursday."

"That's what I thought. They all got the Code Red this morning. Sal swept every house by ten o'clock. She must've come back afterward. I thought you'd want to know."

"Why was Will still there?"

"He was working on setting up sprinklers. He doesn't want to leave your mom there."

"Call him back and tell him I'm on my way. He needs to leave. And can you let Emmett know?"

"Will do on both counts."

Spitting gravel, Tim did a u-ey in the middle of the road and hit the gas. The woman was incorrigible. He hit the button on the steering wheel and called her. The phone rang and rang, then went to voice mail. "Mom, call me now. I heard you were back in town. That can't be right. I know I didn't dream driving you to Eureka last week. Are you seriously going to make me do it again?" He disconnected.

Why did she push his buttons like no one else? Why did he have so little patience for her, of all people? Probably because when Mom and Dad split, he wanted to go with Dad. But no one asked him. At least he had those hour-plus drives with Dad between Libby and Eureka every other weekend for a few years before Dad moved to Missoula. Time they spent talking about important stuff like football, cars, and God.

Dad didn't want the divorce. Mom did. Forgiving her had taken a long time. *God, I'm sorry. You expect me to respect my parents, no matter what. I promise to do better.*

If it kills me. And it might.

Five minutes later he pulled into her driveway. Aunt Maddy's '99 Cutlass sat crooked, its front end nose-to-nose with the garage door. Did that mean Leland hadn't come with her?

The front door stood open. Tim pocketed his key and pushed his way in. The smell of Lysol and lavender-scented air freshener bombarded him. His mom's two favorite fragrances. "Mom? Mom!"

He found her in the living room, ensconced in her drab green recliner, her oxygen tank on one side, Snickers, the yappy shih tzu, on her lap, and a large glass of wine on the table on the other side. A *Jeopardy* contestant correctly named the title of Aretha Franklin's first number-one hit.

Even Tim knew that.

Mom frowned. "What are you doing here?"

"I was about to ask you the same thing." Snickers yapped, hopped from the chair, and approached Tim, growling with all the ferocity of a pit bull. "She does know I'm one of the good guys, right?"

"She knows you're mad."

"I distinctly remember driving you and Leland to Eureka a few days ago and telling you to stay put until the all-clear sounded." Her suitcase lay open on the couch. Leland was nowhere in sight. "What happened? Why did you come back?"

"Nothing." She wiped her nose with delicate care not to mess with the tube that decorated the end of it. She tossed the tissue on the end table with a few dozen others. "I decided to come home."

"In Maddy's car? Where's Leland?"

Her lips pursed. Her chin lifted, but the wattle underneath shook. "He left me. He said I was mean and cranky and he left me. He went to his brother's in Kalispell." Fat tears ran down her wrinkled face onto her purple velour jogging suit. Her oxygen tank hissed. "I am not mean and cranky. No more than he is."

"So you two had an argument. Call him, say you're sorry, and all will be forgiven." The argument didn't explain what she was doing back in Libby in the middle of an evac zone. "Tell him to meet you back at Maddy's and you'll kiss and make up."

No guy liked to think about his mother kissing or making up with some old guy, but moms, regardless of their age, deserved to be happy. Everyone wanted a happily ever after. No one wanted to be alone.

Where did that leave Tim? "Does Maddy know you have her car?"

"I left her a note."

"You took her car without asking her?"

"She was asleep. I didn't want to wake her."

"How thoughtful." He closed the suitcase and zipped it up. "Let's go."

"I'm not going."

"You can't stay here. The fire is headed this direction."

Glowering, she grabbed the chair arms with gnarled fingers that ended in long, yellowed fingernails. "I'm staying."

"You're going."

She grabbed the remote, changed the channel, and hit the volume. The theme song to *Judge Judy* blared.

It didn't seem appropriate to sling his own mother over his shoulder and carry her out to the truck like a skinny sack of potatoes. "I'm putting your suitcase in the car." He yelled over a heated discussion between a woman and her ex. "I'll be back for you."

"I'm still your mother. I tell you what to do, not the other way around."

He marched from the house into the warm sun where he laid the suitcase in the truck bed and whirled. Time wasn't on their side. The first notes of "I Shot the Sheriff" wafted from his phone. The office. "What?"

"Not going well, I take it." Cammie's southern drawl was more elongated than usual, which meant she was stressed.

"Another call?"

"I hate to bother you, but I can't raise the sheriff on the radio and he's not answering his phone." Warning bells sounded. Emmett was never incommunicado. "Kimberly has a situation on her hands at his brother's house."

Emmett's brother Paul had his share of challenges, but therapy and a stable drug regimen had smoothed the way for a relatively quiet year. "What's going on with Paul?"

"He's throwing a bunch of appliances and electronics on the lawn and refusing to leave. Sheriff's parents are freaking out and won't leave without him."

"Keep trying to reach the sheriff. I'll head that direction."

Tim did an about-face and triple-timed it into the house. Without a word he found his mother's portable oxygen rig in its sleek, small, black bag and set it in her lap. "Get suited up."

The mutinous glare on her face faded, replaced by unrepentant curiosity. "What happened? Is it a car accident? Is the courthouse on fire? Did my neighbor finally murder that no-good cheating husband of hers?"

"You're not the only one who doesn't want to leave."

"Who is it?" She crept to her feet, one hand on the armrest to balance herself, the other on her bag. "What's going on?"

Her nose for gossip practically sniffing the air, she tottered in purple Keds toward the hallway, oxygen tank trailing after her, while never taking her gaze from his face. "Is it Lois Crabtree? She's a stubborn stink butt if there ever was one. She won't leave without all twenty cats."

"It's Paul Brody."

"Is he off his meds?"

"If I see you calling your lady friends, I'll take your phone."

"I need to change into proper clothes and pack Snickers' food."

"I'll get the food and Snickers' crate." That she still recognized the need to wear clothes was a blessing. "Make it snappy, please. We need to get everyone out of this neighborhood now."

"Keep your pants on. I'm coming."

Nothing like the possibility of juicy gossip to get Eleanor Trudeau's rear in gear. A mere five minutes later, they were on the road with an unhappy dog between them. Another three minutes and Tim rounded the corner onto Bobtail Road. Even at a distance, it was obvious the fracas had escalated. Paul, a stout fifty-year-old, engaged in a tug-of-war with Lou Ellen, his eightysomething mother whose name could be found in the dictionary next to words like *feisty*, *spry*, and *stubborn*. Max stood nearby, both arms flailing in an apparent attempt to get between his wife and his son. Peabody, an overweight beagle, raced around in circles, baying.

The object of their tiff appeared to be a toaster oven.

Tim parked. Snickers banged against her crate and barked as if to support Peabody. Mom held up her phone. Tim swung out his arm and forced the phone down. "No pictures."

"Tim!"

"I'll take the phone."

"You wouldn't."

"Try me."

"Timoth—"

"Stay in the truck." He shoved open his door and ran toward the ruckus. "Stop, stop. That's enough."

Paul jerked the toaster oven above Lou Ellen's head. Yelling, "Don't do it, don't do it," Lou Ellen hopped and batted at the appliance just out of her reach. "Give me that right now or I swear I'll kick you out of this house forever this time."

No one ever listened to him anymore. Tim swooped between the writhing family members, grabbed the oven from Paul's grasp, and backpedaled. "Enough. Enough!"

"He's trying to destroy it." Lou's skinny chest heaved. Her face was red with exertion and her BEST GRANDMA EVER T-shirt was soaked with sweat. "He's trying to destroy every appliance in the house."

"He's off his meds again." Max stated the obvious. "He's gone crazy."

Crazy was not PC these days, but parents living with an adult child diagnosed with bipolar disorder with psychotic features could be forgiven for occasionally losing it themselves.

"They're sending me messages. They're emailing me. They're texting me. They're talking to me. They never shut up." Paul flexed massive biceps and lumbered closer. Tim eased back. Paul swiped tears from his face with both oversized paws. "They're telling me to do things . . . things I don't want to do."

His words ran together so rapid-fire they were difficult to understand.

Tim edged between Paul and his parents. "Are they telling you to hurt yourself or someone else?"

His shoulders sagged. "I have to destroy everything. The laptops, the TV, everything. You gotta help me."

"I know you feel that way, but—"

Paul grabbed the toaster oven and smashed it to the ground. His hands went to his oversized ears. He sank to his knees and leaned forward until his whole body lay flat in the grass. "Shut up, shut up, shut up!"

"It's okay, Paulie, it's okay. We won't let you hurt anybody, honey. I promise." Lou's voice quivered as she knelt and patted his head with shaking hands. Peabody stopped baying and licked Paul's face. "Nobody is hurting you. Mom and Dad are right here beside you."

Tim took Max aside. "I'd say call an ambulance, but at this point, we need to get out of here now. There's no time. Do you have your stuff packed?"

Max shook his head. "He dumped the suitcases on the ground. He was sure we'd hidden electronic devices in them."

"Grab what you can. Do you know where his meds are?"

"We found the bottles in the kitchen trash. I think he put the pills down the garbage disposal."

Not an unusual occurrence, but the timing sucked. "Where are you going?"

"To Daphne's in Eureka."

"I hate to impose, but can you take my mom and her dog with you and drop her off at Maddy Gfeller's? Call the clinic and tell them we're on our way in."

"We should go with Paul. He's our son."

"Let me do this for you. It'll be easier for him and for you if he doesn't have to do it in front of you." This wasn't their first rodeo or Tim's. "You know how bad he feels when he comes out of one of his episodes."

It took another fifteen minutes to get Paul up off the ground and into the truck. He screamed obscenities and pounded on the dashboard. Tim jammed his foot on the accelerator and raced to Libby's only mental health clinic that provided limited in-patient services.

It took a sweet nurse with the face of the Madonna twenty minutes to convince Paul he should spend some time "resting." He climbed into a bed, dirty clothes and boots, and closed his eyes.

"He's coming down." The nurse handed a clipboard stuffed with papers to Tim. "You can start on these. Is his family on the way?"

"I called Sheriff Brody and left a message."

Tim perused the papers. Most of it was beyond his small store of knowledge. The staff here knew more than he did about their frequent flier. Paul was diagnosed in high school after a series of increasingly bizarre incidents that got him suspended four times. He managed two semesters of college before he returned home to hold a job at his father's hardware store for as long as he took his medication.

"How is he?"

Tim glanced up at his boss's voice. His face gray with fatigue, Emmett trudged down the hallway.

"They gave him something to help him sleep. His doctor is on his way."

"Dr. Rollins is a good guy. Nice of him to come to Libby ahead of schedule."

"The nature of the beast, I reckon." Tim held out the clipboard. "Have a seat. Did a Hummer run over you?"

"I made the mistake of going by Colleen's to make sure she and the kids were getting out." He plopped into the navy padded chair next to Tim and stared at the clipboard as if it were a coral snake. "She had a meltdown."

"About the evac?"

"No, they were packed and ready to roll out to my in-laws in Missoula. About the divorce settlement. I feel like a country music song. I'm going through the big D and I don't mean Dallas." He slapped his cowboy hat on his lap and ran his hands through thinning auburn hair. "She got the house, the Suburban, child support, maintenance, and the kids. The carcass has been picked clean. What else does she want?"

"Your soul to rot in hell?" Tim's attempt to inject levity into the conversation met with an eye roll. "I imagine she wants you to feel as bad as she does."

"Why does she feel bad? She asked for the divorce. I never wanted it."

"You're asking me to figure out how women think, and we both know that ain't happening."

They sat in silent tribute to that truth for several seconds.

"We were high school sweethearts. Did I ever tell you that?"

More than once. Tim simply nodded.

"It's such a cliché. She was homecoming queen. I was QB1." No bitterness marred the words. Only nostalgia and lost wonder. "I thought we would grow old together. But she has other plans. She fell out of love with me. Maybe it's my fault for never being there. Maybe I didn't try hard enough. Maybe I took love for granted. Don't you ever do that. If you end up with Juliette or some other woman, give her all of you all the time. Don't let your job come before your family."

"You realize as my boss you're on the losing end of that equation?"

"As your boss I'm telling you to listen to the voice of experience. I see how the air in the room explodes when the two of you are together. Don't ever lose that feeling. Hang on to it. When it's gone, there's no getting it back."

"I'm not sure I'll get the chance, but if I do, I'll remember it."

"At least I got to hug the kids before they left. Even Zoe, and she's not the huggy type." His tone bittersweet, Emmett turned his hat round and round. "Colleen hasn't tried to turn them against me. I'll give her that."

"Thank God."

"You don't think you can lead Juliette back to church?"

Tim told his boss about the job offer in Billings. "She had the audacity to suggest I go with her."

"Don't feel obligated to stay here on my account."

"You're a handsome man, but Juliette is gorgeous." Tim summoned a smile to go with the small joke. "I can't go with her, because I can't be with her. Not unless her heart changes."

Emmett's growling chuckle rumbled and then died. He leaned his head against the wall and closed his eyes. His enormous hands laid across his paunch. "I've known Juliette since she had training wheels on her little pink bicycle with the basket on the front and the tassels on the handles."

"I wish I'd known her then. Maybe I'd have her figured out by now."

"Something happened to her."

"Yeah, she grew up."

"No, something happened that changed her. She was a sweet daddy's girl with a breezy smile who'd do anything for anybody. Then one day she turned into a woman flaunting herself to any man who gives her a second gander. That's not normal."

That Emmett had noticed Juliette's propensity to flirt with her body made Tim's face burn. "Maybe she just grew up."

"I've seen that kind of hurt before." Emmett opened his eyes. He swiveled until he stared directly at Tim. "She's got a wound festering inside her. Get her to talk about it and maybe you can help her figure out why she's so mad at God."

"She says she doesn't believe in God."

"She does. That's why she's so mad at Him."

No one judged character better than Emmett, and he'd seen more than his share of tragedy and evil in his years as Lincoln County sheriff. "I'll work on figuring out what happened to her."

Emmett aged before Tim's eyes. "You're not going to like what you find. I'm telling you that now. Don't flinch. She's blaming herself for whatever happened. Don't you do it too."

"I would never." Tim wavered for a second. "You said you'd seen that hurt before. Who did you see?"

"A twelve-year-old girl who'd been molested by her grandpa."

Tim's breakfast rose in his throat. He swallowed.

"I have the community meeting at six." Emmett settled the clipboard on his lap and grabbed the pen. "I want to sit with Paulie for a while. Can you cover things until then?"

"Absolutely." Tim stood and started toward the door.

"Hey, Tim."

He paused and turned. Emmett cleared his throat. His Adam's apple bobbed. "Thanks for helping out with Paulie. And what I said about Colleen, I'd appreciate it if you would keep that rant—"

"No worries. We all need to vent. Even superheroes like you."

The superhero bit lightened Emmett's expression a fraction. "Get out of here."

"Going, Boss."

Every time he wanted to wallow in his own problems, Tim received an express reminder from God. Others had heavier crosses to bear. Emmett would never see his brother as a cross. He was family.

God, please lighten Emmett's load a little, if You can. And smack me upside the head the next time I complain.

CHAPTER 29

Doctors should prescribe work for what ailed a man. Caleb leaned into the razor-sharp draw knife and peeled more outer bark from the lodgepole pine log. God, in His goodness, had provided an empty warehouse for Arthur Duncan to set up shop until they could get back to work at Montana Furniture in West Kootenai. Caleb's boss's company had hundreds of orders pending from customers and more than a dozen retail outlets across the country. With fall and then the holiday season closing in, Arthur had hauled as much equipment and wood inventory into Eureka as possible during that small window of opportunity.

Tuesday appeared as a perfect fall day for working in the shade of a maple tree outside the warehouse on the outskirts of Eureka. A breeze startled the leaves occasionally and two robins kept Caleb company with their sporadic chatter. A long afternoon stretched in utter peace before him. He could almost forget about the fire.

And Mercy.

The beautiful log came from a tree harvested from the Kootenai National Forest for its straightness and its strength-to-weight ratio. The standing dead tree hadn't fallen, nor had it died. Arthur never used green wood because it would warp, and they never harvested live trees from the forest. Taking the dead trees reduced the threat of wildfire, although it hadn't seemed to help much this year. They didn't even use heavy equipment for fear of scarring the living trees. This log was perfect for the children's table Caleb planned to make for his host's four offspring. Humming, he laid the draw knife aside and examined the log. It had a perfect skip-peeled texture created by leaving a layer of inner bark.

Time to start on the joints. Once the table had been assembled using the hole-and-peg-style joints, he would do the stain and lacquer. Woodworking was labor and thought intensive. That's what made it the perfect prescription for not thinking about his problems.

Like Mercy.

A buggy pulled into the circle drive and parked several yards from where he worked. So much for peace and quiet.

Jonah Yoder climbed down and ambled across the yard. "Afternoon."

Returning to his work, Caleb nodded.

"You left sudden-like the other night."

"It was late. I was tired. I figured you were too."

"My daughter doesn't use the gut sense Gott gave her."

Mercy not only had good sense she also was smart in a way that many people were not. She had more book learning than most Plain folks. She was self-taught through reading. Plain people didn't put store by school learning but respected those who did. Mercy was a thinker. Log over his shoulder, Caleb moved toward the warehouse. Jonah followed him inside.

"Your dochder thinks harder than most."

"Agreed."

Caleb deposited the log on a long table with several others. He picked up a piece of sandpaper and went to work on a chair that sat nearby, waiting to be varnished. "Did you have something to say to me?"

"You saw this man Spencer with her?"

"I did."

"I'm concerned for her well-being."

"I spoke to him."

Jonah's thick gray eyebrows drew together. His expression lightened. "You did? When?"

"Right after I saw them together." Caleb bent into his work, his gaze on the knotty grains of the wood. "We spoke of what is best for a Plain woman. Spencer McDonald is from Eureka. He of all people knows better than to play with fire."

"It's a sin to worry. Yet I find myself in a tug-of-war with my thoughts over this. I know I have no right to ask for your help."

"You know what happened?"

"Only what my fraa tells me."

Apparently that was enough. From the discomfort on Jonah's face, the man wanted to be anywhere in the world but in this shop discussing his daughter's well-being with the man she'd turned down. Yet here he was. He loved her that much.

Caleb abandoned the sandpaper and locked gazes with Mercy's father. "Regardless of what happened in the past, I also am concerned for Mercy as a member of this Gmay. As we should all be concerned for one another. I made it clear to Spencer that we cannot stray from our faith with an Englischer. What is at stake if we do."

"Do you think he'll leave her alone?"

"He understands the consequences, but he has an Englischer's perspective on the world."

His scowl fierce, Jonah nodded. He rapped on the table twice. "Come to dinner with us tonight. My fraa is making fried chicken and cherry pie."

In other words, wrest Mercy's attention from a man who might tempt her into the world. "I have an invitation from Arthur's fraa."

The temptation to cancel was strong, but he would find another time and another way to reach out to Mercy.

"Her eternal salvation is at stake." If Jonah kept pulling at his beard like that, he would soon have no hair on his chin. "Her life with her family and community."

"I know, but the choice is hers alone. She must make it."

Jonah rocked on his heels for several seconds. He wanted to say more, that was obvious. His gaze contemplated the canvas-covered furniture along one wall. Finally he sighed. "Another time then."

"Jah, another time."

Jonah left as quickly as he'd arrived.

To have a father who cared so much he would overcome his natural reticence to speak to Caleb about such personal, private matters would be a gift. Caleb shooed away envy the color of a sour Granny Smith apple. His own father was such a faint memory.

Caleb jogged out to the phone shack by the road. He pulled the letter from the pocket made by the broad flap of his pants and punched in the number he'd written on the envelope. Six rings later the machine kicked in with a message. He closed his eyes and tried to order his thoughts. At the sound of the beep, he drew a breath. "Mudder, it's me, Caleb." As if she wouldn't recognize his voice. "I received your letter. I'm glad all is well.

My cabin burned. I plan to rebuild. Maybe you can come for a visit in the spring. I have to go. *Faeriwell*."

He laid the receiver in its cradle. His sight blurred. It could be hours or days before someone in his family remembered to traipse to the phone shack to check messages. Then they would go about their business as usual.

So would Caleb. God had led him to Mercy. Caleb would set aside his anger, his hurt feelings, his jealousy, and step up.

Mercy's life as a Plain woman was at stake. Even more important, her eternal salvation was in question. In the end God would decide her fate. In the meantime Caleb had a duty to use every means to guide her in the right direction.

Even if that meant being rejected again.

CHAPTER 30

Mercy's nose led her through the house to the kitchen where a cherry pie sat on the windowsill cooling. Her mouth watered and her stomach rumbled after a long day in the stuffy, stinky garage-slash-classroom. The scholars wanted Juliette to come back, and so did Mercy. Her presence on Monday had been a welcome addition. But teaching in an Amish school didn't work that way. It was a Plain person's job.

Her mother stood at the stove stirring sliced potatoes and onions in a skillet. More mouthwatering aromas enveloped Mercy. She opened her mouth to sing her mother's culinary praises, but Bishop Noah Duncan, Deacon Tobias Eicher, and Minister Lucas Zimmerman sat around the table with her father. All four nursed glasses of cold tea. A plate of peanut butter cookies occupied the space in front of them on the table. All four stared at her as she entered the room. She closed her mouth.

"Dochder, we have company for supper." Father managed to mingle forced joviality and faint warning. "They're visiting all the families since we're scattered across the valley."

"It seemed a good idea to make sure all is going well. The Gmay is flung far and wide, but our faith continues to hold us close." His earthy-brown eyes cool, Noah's gaze pierced to the bone. Unlike Father, he didn't smile. "We were glad to hear classes resumed despite the setback."

Setback was one word for what happened to Kootenai and their home. Not the one Mercy would have chosen. "We thought it was important for the kinner to have that stability at a time when everything else is turned upside down." She went to the counter and poured herself a glass of water. Hoping to erase the bitter taste in her mouth, she sipped and swallowed. "But it's hard for the scholars to concentrate when they don't know when they're going home or what they're going home to. Still, they try."

"Gott's plan will unfold in His time." Noah set his half-empty glass on the table with a firm *clink*. He clasped his hands together and steepled long, thin fingers. Noah had been chosen by lot as bishop four years earlier at the ripe old age of thirty. Since then his once-skinny frame had filled out. His cheeks were round and his paunch substantial. It was as if his body grew into the job. "That's true of all things in life, of course. I remind myself of that whenever I find myself questioning my circumstances. I would hope you'd remind the kinner of that."

"I do."

The silence grew as if the men expected her to expand on her response. They all had children of their own. Surely they had an inkling of what it was like for small children to be ripped from their homes and rushed through the countryside to sleep in unfamiliar beds in unfamiliar houses and not know when they would be able to go home or to what.

"We also wanted to let you know the emergency fund will be available for rebuilding as soon as the authorities let us return."

Tobias filled the silence. Although his remark was directed at Father, Mercy's heartache eased at his words. The community took care of its own. "Offerings to help with removing the debris and constructing the new house are pouring in from other communities as far away as Lewistown, St. Ignatius, and Gold Creek."

"Gott is gut." Although his face was stoic, Father gulped down tea like a man who'd spent a week in the desert. "He will provide."

"The women are gathering supplies and foodstuff." Lucas swiveled and directed this to Mother, who busied herself plucking hot rolls from a pan and dropping them in a basket. "They'll be ready to help with meals as soon as we get the all-clear."

When would that be? No one said.

"Mudder, can I help you with something?" She turned so the men couldn't see the questions on her face. They were blessed to have Plain friends across the state. "Shall I set the table?"

"We'll eat in the big room." Tongs in hand, Mother turned from the stove. "The fried chicken is almost done. You can mash the potatoes and put the gravy in a serving bowl."

She spoke of food, but her gaze beseeched something else. Restraint. Obedience. Humility. All of the above. Mercy sighed. Mother knew her too well.

"Before we eat, I'd like to take a few moments to speak of another matter." Noah's voice deepened as if weighty matters weighed it down. "Something has been brought to our attention that involves you, Mercy."

Mother dropped the tongs. They clattered on the laminate wood floor. "Sorry, sorry."

"Sit for a moment, both of you." Noah straightened and

moved the tea glass and cookies to the middle of the table. "Let's talk before we eat. Then we can enjoy our meal with lighter hearts."

He brought with him a heavy heart. Mercy's own heart sped up. Sweat dampened her palms. She breathed. She'd done nothing wrong. Why did she feel guilty?

She eased into the chair next to her father, farthest across from three elders chosen by lot to lead their flock. Her mother took a seat on the other side of Father. Silence reigned for several seconds.

"A story has found its way to us." His forehead wrinkled under prematurely graying hair, Noah smoothed his thin beard. "Understand that this was not gossip. We would not tolerate gossip. It was concern and a desire for counsel that brought the matter to our attention. And concern for our scholars."

Her scholars? "I don't understand—"

"Mercy." Her father held up his hand. His hazel eyes held warning. "Do not interrupt."

She bowed her head and waited.

"Is it true you allowed an Englischer to substitute for you in the classroom?"

Mercy glanced at her father. His expression grim, he nodded.

"Not substitute, really. I was there the whole time. I offered— suggested—that Juliette try it out yesterday afternoon to see how she felt about teaching."

"Our kinner are not an experiment." Lucas's expression was somber but his tone kind. "I've known the Knowleses since Juliette was a *bopli* in diapers. They are gut people, gut neighbors. Juliette is your friend. But she has been away and only returned recently. She returned changed."

"I know. I only thought to help her—"

"Our kinner don't attend public school for a reason." Tobias added his weight to the one-two-three punch. "We don't want them exposed to the fallen ways of the world, especially those of the big city, of the so-called higher learning of a university."

Missoula was not a large town by most standards, nor a hotbed of iniquity from what Mercy had garnered from Juliette's stories. More importantly, Juliette had been and continued to be a good friend to Mercy. "Juliette is still a gut person—"

"Juliette was seen leaving a tavern unsteady on her feet and apparently under the influence of alcohol this past weekend." Noah's face turned ruddy and his cheeks puffed out. "She left in the company of a man."

Eureka was a small town. Nothing escaped the notice of its residents. Not unfaithfulness, drunkenness, accidents, disloyalty, deceit, nothing. If only uplifting incidents of kindness and joy spread along the grapevine so quickly. "Her house burned down—"

"As did yours."

"I know, but—"

"Enough, Dochder. This issue was of such great importance all three of your elders felt it necessary to visit us together." Father's voice held a note of disappointment she'd never heard before—at least not directed at her. "Take heed of their words and their concerns. They'll be the same concerns of every parent who has kinner in your classroom, including your mudder and me."

"Did Hope or Job say something? They love her. She made learning fun."

"I'm not concerned with them having fun." Father didn't raise his voice, but it held determination. "I want them to be guided on a path of righteous and clean living. Juliette and her family are our friends, but we still must use caution when Englisch influence might be hurtful to the kinner."

Mercy swallowed against hot tears. It was unfair. Were they not also expected to show kindness and compassion toward their fellow human beings, whether believer or unbeliever? Juliette languished somewhere in the middle and she needed special care in order to bring her closer to God, not cast her farther away.

"Do you understand this concern?" Noah's voice softened. "Or do we need to arrange counseling sessions? I don't want to have to remove you from your post and appoint another teacher."

Joy became a speck in the distant past. She'd arranged her life around teaching. She'd chosen it over the possibility of marriage to Caleb. "Nee, nee, please don't do that. I love to teach."

"You'll consult with us before you make an important decision like this in the future?"

"I will." She managed a whisper devoid of any stubborn denial or anger. "It won't happen again."

Tobias picked up a cookie and nibbled while Lucas took a swig of tea. Mercy breathed and stood. She still had to help with supper and the cleanup before she could escape. She would not cry. She would not sniffle.

"And then there's the matter of an evening stroll in the company of a stranger, an Englisch man." Tobias brushed crumbs from his beard and fixed her with a stern glare. "The same Englisch man seen with Juliette earlier in the evening."

Mercy sat.

Mother's intake of air was audible. Had Father not told her about Spencer's visit? Surely they'd discussed it. How had the elders found out? Not that it was a secret. It had been innocent and, as such, not something she'd tried to hide.

Mercy gripped her hands in her lap and raised her gaze to meet Tobias's. "Spencer McDonald, you mean."

"So I've been told that's his name. I haven't met him myself." Noah leaned forward in his chair. His gaze drilled her. "I know that being in Eureka makes everything seem catawampus, but the Ordnung hasn't changed. Our faith hasn't changed. We're to hold ourselves apart from the world, especially when that world is so distant from what we believe."

"It was only a walk." Mercy bit back more words. Her father's ominous stare forbade her to argue with their bishop.

"A walk with Spencer McDonald, who spent part of his evening in a tavern with Juliette Knowles. These are the people you want to associate with in the evening and teach our kinner during the day?"

"They knew each other in high school and I can tell you Spencer hadn't been drinking alcohol."

"Be that as it may, your outing with him is cause for concern."

"May I ask why?"

"Isn't it obvious?" Lucas's scorn burned through his words. He of the three was the most difficult to like. The most ponderous in speech and thought. The most unwavering in judgment. "You're a young, unmarried Plain woman. You're the teacher of our kinner. He's an Englisch man, a worldly man who frequents taverns and comes to Eureka after years away to visit a mudder who is an alcoholic."

"He's a smoke jumper with knowledge of fires and how they are fought. He offered insight—"

"That should be shared with your elders, not with you."

What Lucas meant to say was with the men of her district.

Spencer sought her out, not vice versa. She should've said no. She'd convinced herself a walk would have no consequences. She'd been wrong. "I understand."

"I've talked with Lucas and Tobias about this at length." Noah rubbed his forehead. He winced as if in pain. "Again, you teach the scholars. The kinner learn from the example you set. You must always be aware of this."

"I'm sorry."

"You recognize the truth of what we're saying?"

"Jah."

"Gut. I trust it won't happen again." Noah tapped on the table in a one-two-three rhythm. "I told Tobias and Lucas I believed counseling would be all that was necessary. You've always been gut about following the Ordnung. There were no problems even in your rumspringa. I expect this conversation to be the end of it."

Her rumspringa had been quite average. A stretching of her wings with English clothes, a few movies, talking on Juliette's phone when she came home from college in the summer, an occasional foray into makeup and costume jewelry, but none of the more worrisome—for parents—experiments such as dating an English boy or driving a car or drinking alcohol at keggers on some unsuspecting English parents' property.

She'd never felt the need or the interest. She nodded. "I understand."

"Gut." Noah pushed back his chair and stood. "I'm so hungry I could eat a cow."

"Chicken will have to do." Flapping her dish towel, Mother laughed in a high, nervous cackle. "I hope you have room for mashed potatoes and gravy. And corn, we have lots of corn."

"We'll get out of your way so you can prepare to serve it."

Father's meaningful stare told Mercy more discussion would follow.

She waited until they sauntered from the room, already discussing the fire and when families might be able to return to Kootenai. She turned to her mother. "I'm sorry."

"Surely you knew better." Mother's cheeks darkened to a dusty rose. "I used to worry about the path Leesa might take, but never you. I knew you would be faithful in your efforts to do what is right."

"I never thought helping a friend would be seen as wrong. You've known Juliette since she was a bopli."

"And I've watched her struggle." Mudder sighed and shoved a loose strand of silver-blonde hair under her kapp. "I pray for her just as I pray for you. Your rebellion is different from what I see in other young Plain boys and girls. It's more muted. More of an undercurrent. More in your head than in your heart. You think too much. You mull and stew and pick apart our faith and our rules. You read too many books that take you into the world even when physically we keep you close to us. It causes me pain to watch you struggle."

Regret blew through Mercy. Her mother saw much more than she should. "I'm not rebellious. I have a need to think things through, to study on them."

"Which is why Gott made you a teacher."

"I'm sorry you have suffered for my actions." Mercy picked up a pitcher and poured water into glasses for her brothers and sisters. "I seem to be floundering. I thought it would get better as I got older. I still wonder if I've made the right choices recently. Choosing teaching over the possibility of marriage."

"Yet you take a walk with an Englisch man instead of the

Plain man who would take you back despite your refusal of his offer of marriage."

"I don't know that Caleb will take me back." Because Caleb never seemed to speak his mind. Instead, he expected her to interpret his actions. "He doesn't talk much and now he's angry because Spencer was here. I didn't invite Spencer to come. He simply showed up."

"And you didn't send him away." Mudder settled fried chicken legs, breasts, and thighs onto a thick ceramic platter. Her distant expression spoke of memories recaptured. "Your daed and I courted for two years. For me, love grew over time, but I longed to see him more and spend more time with him, getting to know him. Men aren't always able to speak about their feelings. Your daed doesn't say much, but I know from the way he acts that he cares."

Criticism played hide-and-seek in her mother's words. "I was surprised by the proposal because he never indicated he felt . . . like that."

Not even a simple kiss. How could she tell her own mother of her concern over this lack of physical affection? She didn't dare. Did the physical grow out of a love nurtured over time? Maybe she hadn't given Caleb a fair chance. The air crackled between Spencer and her. They'd only known each other a few short days. Confusion enveloped her. "It didn't feel right."

Her mother dumped mashed potatoes into a big bowl and scraped the edges of the pan with more vigor than necessary. "You must trust your feelings, then. Better to wait than to be married to the wrong man."

"How can I trust my feelings when they always seem to get me in trouble?"

"Remember what you've been taught since you were little.

Pray. I have prayed for you since before you were born."
Mudder picked up the platter of chicken. "Come, let's do the
other thing we are called to do."

Serve the men.

Mercy grabbed the bowl of corn and the potatoes. An acute
sense of relief swept over her. She had made the right decision
once. She could do it again.

Caleb with his pale-blue eyes that held a hint of sadness
and smoldering heat never expressed. His love of books and all
things cowboy. His firm command of his faith and a mysteri-
ous past. The way he said her name lingered in her ears long
after he left her sight. His aggravating silence filled with unsaid
words and unspoken feelings.

Leesa peeked her head in. "The table is set. The men are
getting restless."

"We're coming. Bring the rolls and the salad. We'll come
back for the water."

Leesa did as she was told, but curiosity shone on her face.
"Why is Daed mad?"

"He's not mad." Mother's response sounded halfhearted.
"Only disappointed."

"I got my hands spanked." Mercy summoned a smile. "But
we're fine. Noah says money is available for the rebuilding."

No need to share the negative when there were positives to
be had. "And our friends from the other Gmays are preparing
to help us rebuild."

They chattered about the future as they served the meal, the
elders looking on with good-natured impatience.

A future that loomed differently than it had only the day
before.

CHAPTER 31

Supper under the watchful, assessing gaze of a bishop didn't lend itself to good digestion. Mercy parked her bike next to two others in front of the ice cream shop on Dewey Street in downtown Eureka. Her stomach grumbled. Most of the chicken and fixings on her plate had been scraped into the trash can under her mother's disapproving gaze. Cleanup had been unusually quiet. No one objected when she donned her sneakers and announced she wanted to take a bike ride.

Evenings like this she missed Nora and Christine the most. She needed their counsel. ASAP. Juliette's crazy perspective always made her smile too. But Juliette couldn't know that her foray into substitute teaching had been called into question. Ever. Mercy would have to settle for a banana split instead of a girl huddle.

She pushed through the double glass doors into the store painted in green, pink, and blue pastels. The bell tinkled a cheery tune and AC-cooled air washed over her warm face. Her spirits lifted. Noah had spoken his piece. Her father had done the same. It was behind her.

Except for one small detail. She wasn't sorry.

One big, fat detail.

Mercy tried to wring one ounce of sorry from her less-than-contrite heart. She couldn't. The walk with Spencer had been interesting. Thought-provoking even. Learning how others saw the world wasn't necessarily dangerous. It stretched the mind. It helped a person know what she believed and why.

A scary thought for people who held themselves apart from the world so as not to be sucked into it. Mercy edged between Formica-topped tables full of high school kids eating ice cream and thumbing texts on their phones. She waited in line behind an older couple grumbling about teenagers and their endless selfies.

As for Juliette, she needed help. Why she stumbled remained a mystery. Despite the determined happy-go-lucky bravado plastered all over her face, pain occasionally made a mad dash across her expressive features. She had a good heart, but some wound festered inside her. A thorn in her side that couldn't be relieved. Just like Paul's.

Gott, am I wrong to help a friend?

She moved to the front of the line and returned the cashier's smile before perusing two dozen barrels of creamy, heavenly flavors of deliciousness. Banana split or hot fudge sundae or milk shake or a bowl of her favorite flavors? She reveled in the possibilities. When it came to ice cream, choices were good.

"Decisions, decisions."

Mercy turned at the familiar bass. Her heart did a strange *kerplunk*. His smile tentative, Caleb stood behind her. His faded blue shirt and his black pants were dirty, but he still made her heartbeat stumble a step or two. His smile grew less tentative, more inviting.

His pale-blue eyes were so different from Spencer's deep sapphire that saw right through her. Caleb's eyes held her with bridled feelings as if he were on the brink but holding back. If he ever let go, an explosion surely would follow. To be there that day would be a gift. One she might never receive.

"I know it's tough, but you probably should decide soon." He chuckled but the two kids behind him weren't smiling. "The line's getting longer."

"I'm having a banana split. I've decided." Decisions regarding ice cream were easy. What to do with this man standing behind her, not so easy. "And you?"

"One scoop of Mississippi Mud, one scoop of peanut butter chocolate, and one scoop of Oreo chocolate ice cream."

"I guess you like chocolate." She returned his grin. "That might be the most chocolate I've ever heard a person order."

"You don't know my sister. She can eat a half gallon of chocolate chocolate chip by herself."

Caleb never talked about his family. After two years, he was still an enigma. Mercy liked that word. A mystery. Before she could take the piece of paper from the cashier, Caleb swiped it and handed both to the cashier with a twenty-dollar bill. After all his anger on Saturday night, now he was determined to be nice. More confusion.

"You don't have to do that." Her salary from teaching was small, but she'd saved most of it. There weren't many ways to spend money in Kootenai. She held up her ten. "I have my own money."

"Let a friend treat you."

A friend? Their relationship had a new name. "Danki. Which sister? I know you have three."

He took his receipt and they moved to the end of the railing where the worker was preparing her banana split. "Emma, the one that's nineteen. Rosie is the pie-eater. Karen prefers cake."

"You hardly ever talk about them."

"I know I don't talk as much as you would like."

"Not everyone talks nonstop." She picked up her banana split and studied the people around them. Most of the tables were occupied. "It's busy tonight."

"Sit with me, why don't you?"

Did he feel obligated or did he really want to sit with her? After everything they'd been through, he'd probably prefer to sit anywhere but with her. Mercy groaned inwardly. "Lead the way."

Caleb took his bowl, grabbed some napkins, and moved to a table near the back, away from the throng of football players discussing their opponents in the upcoming season. Mercy followed with her oversized banana split. It was big enough for three people.

He pulled her chair out for her and then sat. Maybe Mother was right. A woman had to take her time and learn to draw a man out. Gradually over time until feelings surfaced. "Why don't you talk about your family?"

Caleb took his time wiping his face with a napkin. It seemed he wouldn't answer. Finally, he met her gaze. "There's not much to tell. My daed died when I was eight years old. Karen was a tiny mite. Mudder has never remarried even though everyone thought she should. *Onkel* John ran the farm until Mark took over last year when he retired."

"I'm sorry."

"I don't need any pity."

"It's not pity." The words stung. "It's sympathy. It's a hard row to hoe."

"Sorry, that's why I don't like to talk about it. It was hard for my mudder. She worked nonstop to make a life for us. She had five kinner ages ten and under."

Mercy took a bite of ice cream and banana to fortify herself. They'd started down this road. No stopping now. She swallowed and stared him straight in the eye. "What happened to your daed?"

Caleb stared in return. His blue eyes swam with emotion. "He fell in a manure pit and drowned. Him and his brother Isaac."

His words were matter-of-fact, even as his face reflected her thoughts. A horrific death. Mercy struggled to swallow. The next breath didn't want to come. "Gott's will is sometimes hard to fathom."

"It was a long time ago. Mudder never questioned. She went on as if nothing had changed." Caleb's gaze skipped to the window, but his expression said he was thousands of miles and years away. "My groossmammi and groossdaadi moved in with us. They had just lost two *suhs,* but they never whispered a word of unbelief. They never cried, not even at the funeral."

That pattern was repeated in Amish communities across the country. Plain children learned early that they were simply passing through this world. Pain and heartache were to be expected. God's will was not to be questioned. "And you?"

His expression inscrutable, Caleb perused his melting ice cream as if he didn't know how it got there and picked up his spoon. "In everything they did, they showed me what unshakable belief is. They lived their faith. I try to do the same."

Shame swelled in Mercy. After natural disasters, people often spoke of how the loss of property meant nothing. Only loved ones mattered. They were right, of course. Why did she find it so hard to accept? She was small. So small. *Gott, please forgive me.* "I'm sorry about the other night."

"You have no reason to be sorry. You owe me nothing."

His lopsided smile belied his words. No matter what had happened between them, the thought that she'd hurt his feelings ate at her. He cared deeply for her. Otherwise he wouldn't have proposed. Those feelings didn't disappear overnight. What about her feelings? The days leading up to that proposal had been happy ones. She enjoyed his company. She liked the way his gaze rippled over her as if coming back for seconds or thirds of his favorite dessert. The touch of his hand on her arm when he helped her into the buggy sent a ripple of pleasure through her. Every touch made her long to go deeper. He had been the one to hesitate.

Why? If only she could see into his heart. See what kept him from taking that step and showing her his love in those special ways of a man and woman. "I'm sorry I hurt your feelings."

"Hurt my feelings?" He pushed the bowl away and dropped the spoon on the table with a *clunk*. "Is that what you think you did?" He leaned closer. "I asked you to marry me because I love you."

"I understand that. At least I think I do."

"You don't feel the same way about me. *I* understand *that*."

"You didn't give me a chance to explain."

"Explain what?"

"We can't talk about this here." Mercy swallowed against sudden tears. How could she talk about her desire for more affection in a soda shop filled with giggling teenagers and elderly couples sharing a bowl of vanilla ice cream? "Could we please just eat our ice cream and enjoy this moment?"

After a long pause, Caleb nodded. He picked up his spoon and attacked the chocolate peanut butter ice cream with all the vigor of a starving man. "I had this feeling when I was in Indiana. I was restless and I couldn't figure out why."

Maybe he did understand. "What did you do?"

"I picked up and moved to Kootenai, Montana."

Mercy focused on dainty bites of banana, vanilla ice cream, and whipped cream. The coolness soothed her aching throat. "I never thought my family would be starting over at a time like this. Our home is gone. But you know how it feels. Your cabin is gone. I don't understand it."

"Jah, these are unsettling times." He pushed his bowl toward her. "Ice cream helps. Would you like to try mine?"

He did indeed understand.

"I think you're angling for a bite of my banana split."

"The whipped cream and cherry, actually."

She couldn't help but laugh at the childish entreaty in his voice. "I get a bite of all three kinds of ice cream in return for you getting all three cherries and a dollop of whipped cream."

"Seems like a fair trade." He helped himself to a generous bite of whipped cream and two cherries. He concentrated on savoring the mingled flavors for a few seconds. "I came to Montana to seek a fresh start."

"Did you find it?"

His spoon hovered in the air as his gaze, full of heat and light, sought and captured hers. "I thought so, but now I don't know."

She shivered. "What if I said you shouldn't give up so easily?"

"I'd say, I'm still here, aren't I?"

The scent of hope lingered in the air.

CHAPTER 32

EUREKA, MONTANA

Good food was the oldest trick in the book when it came to feminine wiles. Lasagna, salad with Italian vinaigrette, garlic bread sticks, fresh green beans with chunks of bacon and onion, and a chocolate sheet cake for dessert. Spencer leaned back in his chair and considered loosening the belt on his jeans. Marnie was up to something. Her cooking skills had improved since his teenage years when he'd scavenged for mac and cheese in a box or ramen noodles in barren kitchen cabinets.

Mikey, strapped into a booster seat at the other end of the table, belched. His face and hands were covered with frosting. Kylie giggled. Angie shook her finger at the toddler. "What do you say?"

"'Cuse me."

"Good job." Angie took a sip of her iced tea and settled the glass next to her empty plate. She tucked a light blanket around Janie, who slept in her carrier on the adjacent chair. "Thanks for cooking, Mom. The food was really good."

Marnie bowed her head in acceptance of the praise. "Spencer, another piece of cake? More tea?"

He patted his flat belly. "No way. If I keep eating like this, I'll never meet my PT regs when I do go back to work."

"You're all muscle. You always were a good athlete." Marnie stood and began clearing the plates. "Both your dad and me played sports in high school, but he was the one who excelled."

Excelled at running away. No point in digging up old graves. "I like working out. It makes sleeping easier."

"I'll help with dishes before I go back to the house." Angie grabbed a wipe and mopped Mikey's face and hands. He squawked in protest. "Hush, child. I really appreciate you letting them spend the night so I can study for my test."

"I could watch them." Spencer bit back the rest of the thought. Better he should babysit them than a recovering alcoholic. "I don't mind and they could sleep in their own beds."

"I like having them here," Marnie objected. "We'll watch a movie and eat popcorn. They love that."

"If they're at the house they'll want my attention. No candy, Mom, and make sure they brush their teeth. Lights out by eight." Angie scooped up the salad bowl and headed for the kitchen. "Spencer, it wouldn't hurt for you to help with the dishes."

Angie had changed. She'd found her take-charge gene. Sitting around with his leg up for over a week now had him well on his way to the loony bin. Even with the kids to entertain him. Spencer hoisted himself to his feet and began stacking dirty plates and laying silverware on top of them.

"You don't need to do that." Marnie tried to shoo him away. "You're convalescing."

"His leg is broken, not the rest of him," Angie yelled from the kitchen. "Don't spoil him."

Not likely after all these years. "She's right. Why should she do all the cleanup?"

"You can help in a minute. I want to talk to you. How about some coffee? I made a fresh pot." Marnie unbuckled Mikey and settled him on the floor. Cake crumbs tumbling to the floor in his wake, he scooted after Kylie, who made a beeline for the living room. "I'll turn on the movie in a minute, bubba."

So far conversation had been limited to the kids' antics during the day, the number of dirty diapers Marnie had changed while Angie was at work, and whether rain would finally come and douse the flames in Kootenai National Forest. "Sure, coffee would be good."

She disappeared into the kitchen and returned a few minutes later with two oversized earthenware mugs filled halfway with coffee. She'd added a generous dollop of milk without asking. Spencer took his coffee black, but there was no way she would know that.

"There's something I need to tell you."

This should be good. Thankful the words hadn't escaped his mouth, Spencer eased back into the chair with his mug in his hand. "What about?"

"I'm getting married."

Thoughts rushed at him. Because that worked out so well the first time. Why tell him? Her life since his departure was a complete blank. By his choice. Why should he care? Why did his throat tighten and his fists clench? He stared into the murky coffee. "That's your business, not mine."

"The proper response is congratulations," Angie hollered from the kitchen. She had big ears and a big mouth.

"Congratulations." The words sounded begrudging in his own ears. "But why tell me now?"

"One of the reasons I was eager for you to come back was so you could meet Jacob. Jacob Johnson. He's a great guy. He's a carpenter. The kids love him. Angie likes him. He goes to our church. I'd like you to be here for the ceremony."

"Why?"

"Spencer." Angie's voice carried a warning. "Just listen and try not to be so you."

When had she started being such a pain?

"Because you're my son and Jacob will be part of our family."

"It's been years since we were a family, if we ever were. You think you can say 'Hey, sorry about all those years' and 'Hey, let's be one big happy family' now?" Spencer crossed his arms over his chest and gritted his teeth. His heart thumped. The sound of blood pumping rushed in his ears. "It doesn't work that way. What you do with your life doesn't concern me. It hasn't for years."

"I know it's not that easy, but I'm no spring chicken and life is short." Her lined face pensive, she stirred sugar into her coffee. "I blew every shot I ever had at happiness, at a family life. God's giving me one more chance in my old age. I was hoping you could be happy for me. That you could be a part of that. We could be a family again, if you give me another chance."

Yeah, and she had some oceanfront property in Wyoming she wanted to sell him too.

Spencer grabbed his crutches, pushed back his chair, and stood. "I gotta go. Thanks for the food."

"Spencer."

He shoved through the door and out into the humid evening air. The sun hovered on the horizon. He faced it and let the sun burn away the shame and anger. Pretty Patty would say forgiveness would help him heal as much as his mother.

Pretty Patty was a sweet woman whose parents had been married for forty years, lived in the same house she grew up in, and gave her and her three siblings an idyllic childhood complete with a two-story house, two-car garage, Girl Scouts, Little

League, church on Sunday, and a swimming pool in the back-yard for birthday parties.

He hobbled the two blocks to Angie's duplex and let himself in. After spending a few hours with two women and three small children, the silence served as a balm. His headache ratcheted back from bongos to snare drums.

Maybe he could sleep, finally. Sleep would be a nice release.

He tugged off his sneaks and socks and threw himself on the guest bed without changing. A slew of sleepless nights had caught up with him. His eyes closed and the light dimmed.

Sirens screamed nearby.

He jerked awake. The same old nightmare. He opened his eyes to a dark room.

The angry wail of sirens didn't stop.

They came closer and closer. Louder and louder.

The angry wails sent chills scrambling up his spine and across his shoulders. His muscles bunched. They wanted to run, to hide, to jump through a window.

Not a nightmare. He bolted upright.

"Spencer! Spencer!" Angie's scream and pounding mingled with the sirens. "Get up, hurry, get up."

He threw off the sheet. Angie jerked open the door. "Mom's house is on fire!"

CHAPTER 33

Flames lit up the night. Black smoke rolled over the rooftops of dilapidated houses made of wood and stucco. Their faces groggy with sleep, neighbors in pajamas and housecoats stumbled from their homes. Spencer's heart pummeled his chest. Panting, he hobbled toward Marnie's house. Rocks and twigs bit into the soles of his feet. He cursed under his breath and heaved himself forward on crutches that only got in his way.

Her sobs intermingled with words of fervent prayer, Angie raced ahead. Her bare feet slapped on the pavement. Her magenta hair flew behind her.

This isn't happening. This isn't happening.

God, how could You let this happen again?

Fleeting images ricocheted in his head. A twelve-year-old boy in shorts and a dirty, ragged T-shirt pulled a sobbing little girl with bony wrists and tangled hair in her face from the closet where she cowered under a faded blanket. He dragged her from her bedroom, down a smoke-filled hallway, and through hungry flames that licked at his feet and burned his lungs.

The sound of Angie screaming her kitten's name still echoed in his dreams on long nights filled with more thick smoke and fire that never burned itself out.

Fire trucks screeched to a halt in front of Marnie's house. Volunteer firefighters poured out and began rolling out hoses. Smoke billowed from broken windows. The smell of burnt rubber and shingles permeated the air. Flames licked the sky above the roof.

How long had it taken the firefighters to jump from their beds, drive to the station, and haul butt to this location?

Too long.

Cursing a body that refused to cooperate, Spencer struggled forward. Sweat rolled into his burning eyes. His stomach lurched. His vision darkened. Purple dots danced in the darkness.

Breathe, breathe, breathe.

He searched the milling crowd and the cluster of firefighters. *God, God, God.*

There.

Marnie knelt on the crumbling sidewalk outside the picket fence that surrounded her yard. Janie nestled in one arm, she snuggled Mikey and Kylie close with her other arm. Kylie sobbed, but Mikey was intent on escaping his grandmother's arm. He wanted a ride in the fire truck.

"Is she hurt? What did you do? What did you do?" Angie bolted toward them. She dropped to her knees and tugged the screaming baby from Marnie's arms. "Were you smoking? Did you leave the stove on? What was it this time?"

"No, no, no!" Alarm and disbelief warred on Marnie's face. "I didn't do anything, I promise—"

"Just like last time. What was I thinking? Spencer was right." Angie grabbed Kylie with her free hand. Her head sank into the little girl's hair. She sobbed. "I believed in you. I forgave you. I trusted you."

"I don't know what you're talking about." Marnie's soot-stained face crumpled. "The babies were asleep. I was asleep. The smoke alarms blared. Scared the poop out of me. I got the babies up and out of the house. That's all I know."

"It was your fault, just like the first time."

"I didn't start that first fire either. I was asleep on the couch . . ." Confusion colored her face. Slowly, horror dawned. "It wasn't my fault."

"You almost killed us."

All these years Angie had refused to engage, refused to lay blame. Ever the peacemaker. The dam had broken and fear released all the pent-up rage of a young girl, suddenly homeless in the middle of the night with a dead cat under her bed.

"Hey, hey, slow down, Sis." Spencer wobbled on his crutches. The desire to comfort and protect his sister, once an everyday occurrence, returned tenfold. "Everybody's okay. The kids are fine. Let me talk to the firefighters and see what happened."

He wasn't twelve anymore. Angie had children of her own now. She needed to hold it together. Marnie wasn't a drunk anymore.

They had all changed. Life was like that. A free fall. Sometimes the wind shifted and knocked people into the nearest big tree. Their only choice was to pick themselves up, brush themselves off, and keep going.

"It's okay, Mommy." Kylie patted Angie's hair. "We didn't get hurt. Grandma carried us out."

"She got my Transformers." Mikey clutched the toy to his tiny chest. "Can I ride in the fire truck?"

"Not this time, little man." Spencer patted his silky hair with a shaking hand. "I'll be right back."

Bob Davidson had charge of the scene. Spencer's fellow classmate at Eureka High had shared his affinity for all sports.

At Spencer's approach he lowered his radio and offered a reassuring smile. "We've got this. We don't need a hotshot smoke jumper's help."

Amazing how people in this town kept track of folks. "How bad is it?"

"It likely started in the laundry room. Kitchen, dining room, and living room are gone. It's pretty much under control. There will be water and smoke damage to the bedrooms, though." A touch of regret played across the man's face. "We're volunteers. It takes a while for us to get here. A regular fire crew centrally located probably could've put the fire out before it did so much damage. Plus there just aren't enough of us."

"You guys are doing your best. I appreciate you volunteering your time." With any luck, Marnie was smart enough to keep her homeowner's insurance up-to-date. "Any idea on the cause?"

"Too early to tell, but if I had to guess, it's probably gonna be electrical."

Davidson's radio squawked. He keyed it and responded. Spencer stared at the house. Blackened windows, broken glass, rolling smoke, but the firefighters were making quick progress on the flames. The familiar smells of burnt wood, rubber, and wet debris sent the desire to get back to work spiraling through him.

He did not belong on the sidelines. He had a mission in life, fighting this beast on all fronts.

"We've seen a lot of fires in these old houses recently." Davidson clapped him on the back. "The wiring is shot. Your mother will need another place to stay for a while, but it's not a total loss. She's blessed."

Blessed that no one was hurt.

"Thanks."

"No thanks necessary. If you ever decide to come back to Eureka for good, we could use an experienced firefighter on the crew."

That would never happen. But it was nice that someone saw him for what he was now and not what he'd been all those years ago. "I'll keep that in mind. Thanks for taking on such a tough job for no pay."

"My chance to live dangerously." Davidson grinned and headed toward the house. "But we really could use some help," he called over his shoulder. "All the young folks flee this town and don't come back. That leaves mostly old farts to do the heavy lifting. I'm the exception to that rule."

Davidson, who was an accountant, had stayed around to marry the homecoming queen and go to work in her dad's firm. At least that was the word on the grapevine known as Angie Rockford. "We'll be at my sister's two blocks down if you need to talk to Marnie."

"Got it."

Spencer swung back to the curb where Angie and Marnie now sat, the kids on their laps. Half a dozen neighbors had congregated around them, offering comfort, advice, and a place to stay.

The upside of living in a small town.

Spencer squeezed between an elderly couple in the middle of explaining how to get the smell of smoke out of drapes. A lady in a pink bathrobe and flip-flops offered to let Marnie spend the night on her couch.

"Let's go back to Angie's."

Angie wiped her sodden face and stood. "What did they say?"

"Likely an electrical fire caused by old wiring in the laundry room."

"Janie's been spitting up all day. Mikey wet the bed during his nap." Marnie's turn to cry. "I put a load of bedding, towels, bibs, and baby clothes in the dryer before I went to bed. It's all my fault."

"No, it's not." Angie squatted and hugged her. "Mom, I'm so sorry, so sorry."

Marnie's shoulders slumped. Janie whimpered. "It's okay, baby. I deserved it and more."

The waterworks were unnecessary. A nearby fire hydrant provided all the water the firefighters needed. And too many bystanders stood listening to them air their dirty laundry. "Not here, guys."

"Right." Angie thanked everyone for their kind words, advice, and offers of food and housing. She handed Janie, who had her thumb in her mouth, to Marnie and hoisted Mikey to her hip. "Let's go home."

"Are you sure you want me there?" Marnie stared up at her daughter. "I can stay with my neighbors if you're worried—"

"I was crazy with fear. I know you would never hurt the kids." Angie held out her free hand. "You'll stay with me until we figure out what to do with your house."

She glanced back at Spencer. "Are you coming?"

He stared at their entwined fingers. His sister's capacity to forgive and forget was unending. The love—and the peace—on their faces seemed so inviting.

"Come on, Uncle Spencer." Kylie slipped her small hand into his. "Let's go. I'm tired."

"Me too. That sounds good." He let the little child lead him home.

CHAPTER 34

LIBBY, MONTANA

Maybe he wouldn't be there. Maybe Juliette could get back in her Ranger parked in front of Pastor Matt's house in Libby and drive an hour and twenty minutes back to Eureka, no harm done. It had been four days since she told her mother about the assault. Four days of her mother's troubled gaze following her around the house. Four days of dropped hints. Four days of her dad's anxious looks. Waiting. Waiting for her to reach out. Her hands were tied as surely as if her attacker had used rope and double knotted it. The memories were like a sock stuffed in her mouth, choking her. Something had to give. She needed the key to open the cell containing her old, soul-searing memories before her inside rotted.

Don't be an idiot. Knock.

She knocked. Nothing happened. Heaving a sigh of relief, she headed back down the ramp painted a stylish cerulean blue. Creaking told her the trailer door had opened. Gritting her teeth, Juliette pivoted. A broad-shouldered, tanned man in a wheelchair smiled up at her. Tim had told her the story about how Pastor Matt lost his legs in Afghanistan, but he hadn't mentioned that his old friend from Libby High School was an attractive guy with a black crew cut and huge brown eyes that no doubt missed nothing when his youth group kids were thinking about misbehaving.

"I'm Juliette Knowles." She stuck her hand out.

"I know." He had a firm handshake. "To what do I owe the pleasure?"

"Can we talk?"

His gaze enveloped hers for several long seconds. His expression wary, he cocked his head. "It's a nice morning. Let's sit out at the picnic table."

He was smart. A youth pastor never counseled in a room alone.

She allowed him to pass and followed him out to a rough-hewn picnic table, weathered gray, sitting to the left of his double-wide in the shade of a stand of birch trees. The bench had been removed on one side. He wheeled up to the table, withdrew his Bible from a pouch hanging from one arm, and laid it in front of him.

Juliette plopped her sweating soda cup on the table and sat. What was she doing here? Besides drowning in a sea of remorse, guilt, and shame. She needed someone to throw her a life preserver. The words stuck in her throat.

The silence stretched. The breeze rustled the leaves in the trees. Such a peaceful sound. Maybe they could sit here and not talk until the lump dissolved in her throat. Until the pain in her gut subsided. Until the sin washed away.

"Whenever you're ready, Juliette." He opened his Bible to the book of Psalms and studied the pages with earnest intent.

The kindness in his voice undid her.

She bit her lip and concentrated on the way wispy clouds clothed the sun and then moved on without a backward glance. "I don't know what to do."

"I'm not sure what we're talking about. It's obvious you're in pain." His eyes dark with unexpected compassion, Matt leaned forward in his chair, his hands splayed across the open Bible. "Tim's my friend, so I want to be careful about how I handle this."

"I didn't come to see Tim's friend. I came to see the youth minister."

"Okay." His eyebrows lifted, but his smile offered encouragement. "How can I help?"

"What I tell you is confidential, right?"

"I'm not a priest, but I don't break confidences. Unless you're about to tell me you plan to hurt yourself or others."

"Something happened to me." To her everlasting mortification, tears welled. She breathed. She'd spent years not crying about this. Why did it suddenly haunt her every breath? "While I was at a youth group retreat at Lake Koocanusa. It was a long time ago."

"Not so long ago." His voice softened. "Do you want to tell me about it?"

"I'm not sure I can."

He was a man. A man of God. A minister. But still a man.

What was she thinking coming here? How could she tell him something she couldn't bear to tell the man she loved?

They sat in silence again. Cars rolled past on the street. A man stuck his arm out the passenger-side window of a pickup and waved his hello. Matt smiled and saluted.

Birds chirped. A dog barked. Cicadas serenaded them.

Life went on.

It seemed so unfair.

"I want to know why God let it happen. All this garbage about God's got this. God is good. God works everything for our good. God has a plan for us. For me." She stopped and gritted her teeth. *I will not cry like a big baby.* "Really? I'm not seeing it. Now Tim doesn't want me because I don't get it. I don't get the fairy tale."

"I take it you haven't talked to him about why you have a hard time believing."

"How can I? He'll know what I did . . . that I'm . . ."

"The truth is you don't blame God." He laced his fingers together, his knuckles white, but his tone was ever so gentle. "You blame yourself."

"Look at me. I'm all about flaunting it. I didn't learn anything from my mistake. I was stupid. I had on this bikini. I left the others at night and took a walk with a guy I hardly knew—"

"I can assure you that I don't have all the answers. I wish I did." Matt leaned back and rubbed his hands over both stumps. "But I can tell you this: What happened to you wasn't your fault. The man who did it. That's on him. We're responsible for our actions when we hurt other people. You did nothing to deserve an assault. It doesn't matter what you were wearing or what error in judgment you made. This guy assaulted you. You've let this eat at your self-esteem for years now. You need help changing that pattern of thinking, that monologue in your head. Let's get you some help with that."

The words flowed around Juliette in a steady stream, but the memories ran roughshod over them. His white teeth. The scar on his chin. The rough feel of his unshaven skin. His smell of spearmint toothpaste. His uneven breathing in her ear. The sound of his voice filled with a sort of victory. The roughness of his hands on her body.

"I didn't stop him."

"Could you have?"

The feel of his arm like an iron bar around her neck suffocated her again. The weight of his body anchored her against the ground. Rocks bit into her shoulder blades. She couldn't get a breath. "No."

"I can't begin to imagine what you went through." His voice went hoarse. "I'm so sorry, Juliette, for your pain and suffering."

The kindness of his words served as that life preserver pulling her back from choppy, storm-whipped waves. "Thank you."

He cleared his throat. His gaze meandered to the tree branches wavering in the breeze. "Getting my legs blown off taught me some hard lessons. When God said there will be trouble in our lives, He wasn't kidding. But He didn't make it happen. He wasn't trying to teach me a lesson. We live in a broken world. Sin invades every part of this place. War, violence, abuse, poverty, sickness—it's a tough gig."

"So what good is He?"

"He's everything good. He promises to walk through it with us. He cares for us. He loves us. And He will take us home where we'll have complete healing. We will have joy. No more tears, no more pain. We can cling to Him for grace and mercy."

"I wish I could believe that."

"You're on the right track."

"How do you know?"

"You're here now, talking to me. You care so much about Tim you were willing to come here and talk to a man you don't even know about the worst day of your life. That's some serious love."

He was right. She loved Tim Trudeau. She wanted to let go of the past. If only she could figure out how. "What now?"

"You're not going to like it."

"I haven't liked it so far, so that doesn't surprise me."

"Forgiveness. For the guy who did it, which really stinks, I know. Forgive yourself."

"Seriously?"

"You'd be surprised how much lighter you'll feel. Forgiveness sets you free. It takes that burden off your shoulders so you can move on. Forgiving yourself may actually be harder, but if you're like me, it's all about baby steps."

"You forgave ISIS or whoever it was that blew up your truck?"

"Yep. More or less." He laughed, a soft, comforting sound. "In the interest of full disclosure, there are nights when I have to start all over again. But I keep at it. It's the only way I can move forward. That and the kids. They remind me of what is good in my life."

Like Courtney. Like Mercy's scholars. Like Tim. He wasn't a kid, but he was the good in her life. "What now?"

"Talking to me is good, but I honestly hope you'll consider professional help."

"That's what my mom said."

"Your mom is a wise lady. You also need to tell Tim."

How would that conversation go? Tim's face misshapen with horror and distaste? "Not yet. Promise me you won't tell him."

"That would never happen, but you can't have a true relationship with any man—especially a man like Tim—without sharing every part of your life with him. And Tim is a good, good man. He will help you heal. I think you know that."

"I should go." Before she started bawling. "I need to get back to Eureka."

"Would you mind if I pray for you first?"

She took a deep breath and heaved a sigh. "Lord knows I could use all the help I can get."

"Yes, He does."

She closed her eyes and let the words wash over her.

CHAPTER 35

Life went on. The number of people shopping in the Kalispell Walmart on a Saturday morning a week and a half since the evacuation of West Kootenai proved that. Spencer leaned on the cart, which Angie had rubbed down with an antibacterial wipe and dried with a paper towel at the entrance before allowing him to touch it. They were on a mission to replace the kids' clothes lost in the fire and get cleaning supplies, disposable diapers, wipes, dog food, and more groceries. For small children her little ones ate like horses. The underlying mission was to get out of the house before they drove each other crazy.

An insurance adjuster had inspected the house and made his report. Until the check came, they were on hold in Angie's tiny duplex. His sister wandered through the little girls' clothing section, picking up first one shirt, then another, and then another from the clearance rack, as if it was the most important decision she would make in her life.

She held up a white-and-green T-shirt that read GIRL POWER and featured a superheroine of some kind reading a book. "Do you think this will fit Kylie? She's growing so fast, it's hard to keep up." She squinted and pursed her generous lips. "Do you think she'll like it?"

He shrugged. "What I know about little girls' clothes would fit on the head of pin."

"You need a wife."

"Is Rocky paying child support?"

"You're mean."

"It's not my intention to be mean." He took the T-shirt from her and laid it in the basket. "I'm just asking because if he's not, you can take him to court. Get a lawyer and go after him."

"Jacob had a talk with him. Rocky's paying. Not enough when you have to feed and clothe three kids, but it's what he can afford and it's better than nothing."

"Better than nothing isn't the standard that should be used when it comes to stepping up and taking responsibility for children."

Had their father stepped up? It seemed likely since they'd never been homeless and Marnie rarely held a job more than a year at a time.

"I don't want to fight with Rocky. It's not good for the kids." Angie threw a package of little girl socks in the basket. "I don't even want to talk to him. I work. Mom watches the kids, which saves me a ton of money. I couldn't afford to put them in day care. We're doing fine. Better than we were when he was around, actually."

The words came like a blow to his gut. "Was he hurting you?"

She frowned over a pile of little boy shorts on a table full of end-of-summer sales. "Not the way you mean. But that old saying about sticks and stones is totally wrong. Words hurt. A lot."

"I'm sorry."

"Me too." She added Hulk pajamas to the basket. Sudden

tears brimmed in her eyes. "I never wanted to be a divorce statistic. I prayed to stay married. I talked to Pastor Ruben several times. He prayed with me. I tried to get Rocky to come to counseling with me. He refused. I didn't want the kids to grow up without a father the way we did."

Spencer gave her shoulder an awkward pat. "It really irks me that you can't catch a break."

"I have three great, healthy kids. My mom loves them and cares for them." She sniffed and smiled. "I have a good job. And a second one that helps pay the bills. And you're here."

"Aww. You're way too forgiving."

"Seventy times seven."

Basically Mercy's take on forgiveness. The women were ganging up on him. "What would Jesus say about a cheating husband?"

"To the wife? To forgive. To the husband, to go and sin no more." Her smile turned grim. "But we both know that isn't going to happen, so I'm getting on with my life, knowing God sees me and knows my circumstances."

And teaching her big brother a lesson at the same time. Angie must be sick of making lemonade from the lemons life hurled at her like baseballs thrown by a big-league southpaw pitcher. Yet she always managed a smile.

Waving the list in her hand, she pointed in the opposite direction and strode past him. "Onward and upward. Diapers and wipes."

"Lead the way, Sis. I'd follow you anywhere."

Her giggle made him smile.

He turned the basket around in a less-than-graceful U-turn and followed. Then he saw Mercy. The last person he expected to see in the middle of the boys' underwear section at Walmart.

He halted. "I'll catch up with you in a minute," he called after Angie.

She waved and kept going.

At the sound of his voice, Mercy turned. Her first reaction was to smile. That was good. Followed by a frown. Not so good.

He left the basket and wound his way through the overstuffed racks. "What are you doing here?"

Her hands fluttered. Packages of little boy underwear fell to the floor. "*Ach.*" She disappeared behind the table. Fumbling sounds. More packages slid off the table. "So sorry."

Seconds ticked by. He peeked over the table. She bent over, head down, the packages in her arms. Not moving.

"Mercy?"

She looked up. Chagrin bloomed in her face. "Here."

"I know. Are you getting up? Do you need help?"

Her flushed face turned a deeper shade of scarlet. Like a beet. Almost purple. "No. Thank you."

"What's wrong?"

"Nothing."

He traipsed around the table, leaned on his crutches, and offered her his hand. "Let me help you."

"I don't need your help."

Something in her expression registered. Fear. Shame. Embarrassment. The desire to flee. "Did I do something wrong?"

"No. Not you. Me."

"You don't want to be seen with me?"

"It's not that. I'm just clumsy."

"You're a terrible liar."

She stood and her gaze strayed around the store. She looked like a hunted rabbit in search of a hiding place the fox couldn't find.

"It's okay. It's a big store. You tell me where you're headed next and I'll go to the other side."

"You don't have to do that." She stuck the packages on the table and grabbed her basket. "I'm almost done."

Her basket overflowed with sewing stuff, toilet paper, dish soap, clothes soap, bundles of material, and assorted other household goods. Amish folks didn't come to a place like Kalispell very often. It was too far. When they did, they stocked up. "How'd you get here? Did you hire a driver?"

The frown disappeared. Her lips twitched. "No, I hitched a ride."

His horror must've shown on his face. She laughed. Her laugh made him laugh. The mom pushing a double stroller and arguing with her son over the toy she refused to buy him must've thought they were two goofs. Mercy laughed so hard tears teetered in her eyes.

Apparently she'd decided to ignore whatever was worrying her. As soft as Mercy appeared, she had a nice backbone of steel.

"Did you catch a ride on an eighteen-wheeler?"

"No. With Juliette."

"Where is she?"

"Searching through the big bargain barrel of five-dollar movies for something the whole family can watch." Mercy seemed perplexed at the idea. "It seems like a hard choice. She's been there for a while. She said she would come find me after she finishes her list. She has her own basket."

Her face flushed. She stopped. "Sorry. I don't usually babble so much."

"It's okay. I like to listen to your voice. You have a different way of talking. All you Plain folks do, but especially you."

"Because English isn't our first language?"

Maybe. Mostly he liked the softness of her voice. It matched her fresh face and simple dress.

She edged toward the aisle. "I should find Juliette."

How could he make this chance meeting last a little longer? After the fire and being squashed into Angie's tiny home with two women and three children, it seemed like a gift. Plus, he needed to find out what was bugging her. "Can I buy you a sub sandwich?"

Her expression wary, she chewed her lip. "Why would you do that?"

"Because I'm nice and you're nice."

She didn't seem convinced. "We can be nice together?"

"Are you scared of me or something?"

"I'm not scared of anything." Despite the bravado in her words, Mercy's wariness deepened.

"Are you afraid of someone else?"

"I only want to do the right thing."

"Did someone tell you that talking to me was wrong?"

"Something like that."

"All English men or just me?"

"We can't be . . ." The flush spread across her cheeks and neck. "We shouldn't be alone."

"We're not. We're in the middle of Walmart. The busiest store in Kalispell."

"I am hungry." She chewed her lip some more. "But I'll buy my own sandwich."

"Fine. I'll lead the way."

Spencer texted Angie his whereabouts. She asked for a ham and swiss cheese on a multigrain bun with all the fixings. He led the way to the sub sandwich shop at the front of the store.

Her last text read: Enjoy your date.

It wasn't a date. A guy could be friends with a girl. Pretty Patty had taught him that. No matter what happened, he was definitely paying. A gentleman always paid. He might not be a gentleman, but he knew how to treat a lady.

Mercy was definitely a lady. Juliette said he should leave her alone, but somehow he couldn't. He felt as if he missed her and he hardly knew her. Which made no sense.

She always appeared to be about to flee. Like a prisoner in a cell. She simply needed someone to turn the key and open the door.

Maybe Spencer was that someone.

. . .

Mercy's heart did belly flops. *It's only a sandwich.* A long line of customers waited at the sub sandwich shop. Spencer parked his cart in the wide aisle outside the shop and pulled his crutches from it. She parked next to him and followed him to the line. So much for a quick in and out. Why hadn't she said no?

God only knew. *You do know, don't You, Gott?*

What were the chances of their meeting in a Walmart in another city? Coincidences didn't happen. If some reason existed for this chance meeting, what was it? A test to see if she would stay true to her promise? She'd promised not to take any more walks with Spencer.

Splitting hairs. She'd agreed not to talk to him.

Yet here she stood.

She wanted to talk to Spencer. Her mother would say he was the green grass on the other side of the fence.

She might be right.

"Cat got your tongue?"

Spencer stared at her with a strange expression, the same odd look he'd had when their gazes met over stacks of boys' underwear.

"No. My tongue is fine."

"Are you regretting saying yes?"

"Maybe."

"What did they say about me? Am I a bad influence?"

"They saw you coming out of a tavern with Juliette the night we went for a walk."

An entire week had passed since that night. She hadn't seen him again. Caleb, she'd seen once.

"I was helping out a friend in need."

"I told them you hadn't been drinking." She hesitated, longing for a facility with English words. To be able to wield language the way her favorite authors did. "It's not you specifically. I'm a young, single Plain woman. I shouldn't be gallivanting about after dark with an Englisch man."

"I don't understand why it makes a difference, English or Plain."

"Our rules are intended to keep us apart from a fallen world. So we don't fall into the sinful ways of the world."

Spencer's eyes narrowed. His jaw worked. Had she made him mad? "I'm sorry—"

He shushed her. "I'm thinking. I don't do that very often and it hurts." His forehead and nose wrinkled and his mouth opened. A person might think he had a terrible toothache. She giggled. He smiled. That knock-your-kapp-off smile.

"Many years ago my sister used to drag me to Sunday school once upon a blue moon. She blabbered on about stuff. I think a few things stuck." He leaned against his crutches and moved up a few inches as the line shrank. "I'm pretty sure the basic premise is that everyone in this fallen world is sinful. Everyone falls short. How can you guys set yourselves off like your sin doesn't make you stink too?"

"Oh, we stink." She shook her head and giggled again. "It's not that. But we try a lot harder to avoid sin than the rest of the world seems to be trying. We have a set of rules to help us."

"And right now, you're breaking one of those rules?"

"I am."

"How come?"

"I'm not sure." Which scared her to no end. "Because you asked nicely and because I keep thinking about how our house burned down and everything is gone. We've tried so hard to follow Gott's Word and bend to His will. Is it His will for us to lose everything?"

"Do you believe God is good?" His sapphire eyes were filled with piercing light. He really wanted to know.

Mercy searched for the right words. All those years of being sure, gone in billowing flame and smoke. "I do. I think I do. I did."

"Not the same thing." He hopped forward again. "I believe it's important to knock around in this world, to see what's out there. To test the limits. That's how you know you're alive. I figure the fire is another way of testing your faith."

"Gott doesn't make bad things happen. I just wonder why He doesn't stop them. He can. He can do anything. We believe He has a plan for us. What kind of plan is this?"

"I'm right there with you." Spencer stared at the chopped vegetables and toppings as if the answers they sought might be found between the pickles and the tomatoes. "What kind of plan makes my mom an alcoholic and my dad a loser who leaves his kids with a drunk?"

Hard questions. She had no answers.

He ordered two sandwiches and then pointed at Mercy. "Put hers on my bill."

"No, no, I can get my own."

The cashier shrugged and kept making sandwiches. When the bill went to Spencer, it had all three sandwiches, three bags of chips, and three sodas on it.

"That wasn't the deal."

"It wasn't the plan?" He grinned and cocked his head toward the only empty booth. "Can you bring the food? Maybe it was God's plan. Did you ever think of that?"

Mercy glanced around. Not a familiar soul in sight, but that didn't mean anything. God saw and God knew. Maybe she could plead temporary insanity or a brain tumor or a sudden fever that turned her into a raving lunatic long enough to have a sandwich with a nice man who made her laugh.

She grabbed the tray and headed to the booth where she eased it to the table and plopped down across from Spencer. At least they were away from the swarm of people out in the store. Surely no one would see them here.

"There you are." Angie barreled toward them. Juliette stalked through the high round tables behind her. "Look who I found searching all over for you, Mercy."

Juliette's eyebrows were on permanent high alert. She shot Mercy a grim frown. "I figured you were getting a sandwich to go."

"Are you in a hurry?" The seventy-minute drive from Eureka to Kalispell had been the quietest time Mercy had ever spent with Juliette. The other woman, normally bouncing off the ceiling and singing at the top of her lungs, mumbled responses to questions or didn't respond at all. "I can get a bag for this. Do you want a sandwich? I'll get you one."

Juliette shook her head and scooted onto the seat next to Mercy while Angie did the same on Spencer's side of the table. "Just eat. Do you have everything on your list?"

"I still need a couple of things for the girls. Aren't you going to say hi to Spencer?"

Juliette's scowl answered that question.

"Somebody got up on the wrong side of the bed." Spencer pushed his soda toward her. "Have a drink. Maybe you need some caffeine. I don't have cooties, I promise."

Without a word Juliette pushed it back. Instead, she plucked barbecue chips from Mercy's bag and began breaking them into smaller pieces.

"We need to get back." Angie took a bite of her ham and cheese sandwich, chewed, and swallowed. "I have to work a shift tonight."

"I don't like you working at a convenience store." Spencer growled deep in his throat. He sounded like the mountain lion that had been peeking at them from the trees when they hiked on their favorite Cabinet Mountain trails. "I really wish you would quit."

"Are you planning to pay my utility bills and my tuition?" Her tone tart, she took another big bite of sandwich and sighed.

"I have some savings—"

"No way." She spoke through a mouthful of bread. She shook her finger at him and covered her mouth with her other hand. "Nope."

He had a generous nature.

So did Caleb.

The thought struck her with the sting of the sapling branches Father used to spank her and the others in the woodshed when their transgressions warranted it. With Mercy such forays to the shed were rarely necessary. And all the more ingrained in her brain.

Her appetite gone, she swept the other half of her sandwich into its wrap and handed it to Juliette. "Could you carry this? I'll bring the soda and chips. We can share."

Juliette didn't argue. Spencer wanted to, if his frown was any indication, but he didn't.

"Thank you for the sandwich." She didn't try to explain her abrupt departure. "Have a safe trip home."

"It's just up the road." He tilted his head. The hurting face had returned. Thinking really did pain him. "It was really nice seeing you again."

Angie popped up and slid into the spot Mercy and Juliette had vacated. "Come by the church. We have a ton of canned goods, bottled water, and clothes people have donated. If you need anything at all, come see us. That's what we're there for."

She paused. She had that hurting head look too. It must run in the family. "We'd love to see you at church tomorrow. I know you have your own services, but since you're spread out all over the place, you're welcome to worship with us."

"Thank you." Mercy could only imagine the reaction her parents would have to such a suggestion. "It's nice of you. It's our week off, so mostly folks will visit with each other."

As she walked away Mercy could feel Spencer's gaze burrowing into her back. The urge to turn around and stare sat on her shoulders and whispered in her ears. She brushed it away. *Keep walking, girl, keep walking.*

Fifteen minutes later they were in Juliette's truck headed for Highway 93. Juliette still hadn't said a word.

"Are you mad at me about something?" Mercy turned off the radio and scooched around in her seat belt to get a better read on her friend. "You've been crankier than a baby with colic."

Juliette grabbed the Sprite and took a long draw on the straw. Her natural buoyance had been depleted by some unseen pinprick. Her eyes were red rimmed and her nose was running.

"What is wrong? Are you sick? Please talk to me, Juliette."

"I'm not mad at you. I'm not sick." Her voice cracked. "Not everything is about you."

Mercy sank against the seat and stared straight ahead. Never were truer words spoken. Did she appear that self-absorbed and full of herself to others? "I'm sorry."

"You don't have anything to be sorry for. That's what I'm telling you."

"Then what is this about?"

"I can't tell you."

"Is it Tim?"

"No. It's me."

Juliette always drove fast, but today it felt as if the truck flew down the road. Air zoomed past the windows. The AC made Mercy shiver, but so did the speed. "Could you slow down a little?"

"Sure."

But she didn't. Finding words to help was difficult, not knowing the problem. The remainder of the ride passed in silence. They pulled up in front of Grandma Knowles's house in record time.

Juliette put the truck in park and turned off the engine. She didn't speak.

"I'm worried about you." Mercy spoke into the silence because it scared her more than the sin of worry. "Please let me help you."

"You can't, but it's nice to know you want to." Her hands still on the wheel, Juliette laid her head against it. The seconds ticked by. A muffled sigh followed. She raised her head. "I'll be fine. But you can do me one favor."

"Of course. Anything."

"Stay away from Spencer."

"Why?"

"Because he's wrong for you. And you're wrong for him. You're both seeking something and you won't find it in each other." She looked at Mercy for the first time. "I don't know much, but I know that."

"It's not like that. We're just two people trying to figure things out. We're bouncing ideas off each other. That's it."

"That's how it starts. You can't trust a man like Spencer. He means well, but he's messed up—too messed up to help himself. I've been out there." Juliette leaned across the seat and grabbed Mercy's hand. "I thought I wanted to be out there, but I found out everything I need is here. Don't give me another thing to worry about, okay? I've got enough stuff on my plate." She squeezed Mercy's hand and let go.

Mercy pushed her door open and slid out. The last person she expected to give her such advice would be Juliette.

Which made it all the more powerful.

"Are you sure you're all right?"

"I'll be fine. Do you need help getting your bags in?"

"I'm good."

"You are. Stay that way, please."

Mercy removed her bags and set them on the sidewalk. Juliette drove away.

Juliette's words reverberated in the late-afternoon air.

Stay that way.

CHAPTER 36

EUREKA, MONTANA

Now or never. Pastor Matt's words pulsing inside her head, Juliette pushed through the back door of her aunt Tina's house, kicked off her flip-flops, and dumped the sack of groceries on the granite-top island in the middle of the kitchen. The rope that kept Juliette from reaching out slid away. The massive knot dissolved. She could breathe again.

Serving spoon in hand, her mother turned from the stove and smiled. "Oh, good, you're here. Your dad just brought in the burgers from the grill. I've got tots in the oven and Courtney made a big salad."

Get help. Get help. You need help. Accept help. "I need help."

"Sure. I'll send Courtney to get the rest of the bags. She's around here somewhere."

"No, Mom, I mean I need help." She swallowed back tears that had threatened in every aisle of Walmart. At one point she'd ducked into the bathroom to get her act together. Ridiculous. "Professional help."

The spoon hit the counter. Mom tossed aside her apron and trotted around the island. Her tight hug allowed Juliette to bury her head on her mother's shoulder and close her eyes tightly. Still the images came unbidden and unwanted.

Her stomach rocked. She raced to the kitchen sink and heaved. Bitter acid burned her mouth. It tasted like fear and regret and anger and disgust and decimated innocence.

Mom's hands rubbed her back in a comforting swirl. "Please, God, take away my Jules's pain. Make her whole again. Heal her. Take her right hand and walk with her through this valley. Lord, I pray, take away the ability of those memories to hurt her. Let her see them in her mind's eye and then discard them, knowing they can no longer hurt her. Bless her and keep her safe."

Peace. It sounded so good and so distant. What would it feel like not to have this push-and-pull in her gut all day and all night?

Wiping at her face, she tugged away from her mom just in time to see Dad standing in the doorway. Tears rolled down his craggy face. "Baby, I'm so sorry."

"It's okay, Daddy, I'm fine."

"You're not fine, but you will be." She met him halfway and he enveloped her in a hug that nearly broke her ribs. "I know someone in Kalispell who specializes in this kind of stuff. She's waiting for your call when you're ready."

"I'm ready."

He grabbed a napkin from the island, sopped up tears, and blew his nose in a loud honk. "I came in here to tell you there's someone asking for you out front."

She didn't have many friends in Eureka. She'd just dropped Mercy off at Nana's. Poor Mercy who tried so hard to be a good friend. "I don't feel like talking to anyone right now."

"I think you'll want to talk to him. If you don't, I imagine he'll sit out there all night."

Tim.

Taking her time, Juliette stepped into the guest bathroom in the hall, washed her face, brushed her teeth, fixed her makeup, and combed her hair. A face she barely recognized stared back at her from the mirror. Dark circles clung around her eyes and faint lines had begun to form around her mouth. She sucked in air and squared her shoulders. "You can do this."

She pinched her cheeks to bring the pink back and added a dab of red gloss to her lips. "Here we go."

Tim leaned against his truck, his back to the house. She let the screen door slam. He turned. No smile. No greeting. He simply waited. She marched down the steps and stopped with the truck bed between them. "Long time no see."

"It's been a few days." He shoved his cowboy hat back on his head and leaned both arms on the truck. He pointed at two fishing poles and a cooler. "You interested in doing some fishing?"

She studied his face and then the sky behind him.

The first time he suggested they do something together had involved fishing in the Kootenai River with some of his deputy friends. She caught six trout to his two. They fried a whole mess of fish over a campfire and served them with roasted corn on the cob, buttered Texas toast, watermelon, ice-cold diet Pepsi, store-bought chocolate chip macadamia nut cookies, and lots of laughter.

His friends were nice and grown up. After a while, she and Tim crept away. They hung their bare feet in the cold water, listened to the coyotes howl, and told whopper fish stories. Then he took her home and dropped her off at the front door with a chaste kiss on the cheek.

In her lengthy book, the best first date ever—even if he wouldn't admit it was a date. "Sure."

"Get in."

The first five or six miles were spent catching up on the evacs in Libby, his mom's crazy antics, and her foray into teaching at an Amish school.

He shoved the sun visor down and adjusted it against the early evening sun. "So nothing else going on?"

"Just waiting for the all-clear so we can get back to Kootenai. We want to see what we can salvage, start removing the debris. Dad is going to rent an RV—"

"I meant with you."

The sharp tone was so unlike him.

"What's going on? What made you decide to talk to me today after breaking up with me at the Front Street Grill?"

He turned onto Highway 37 toward Rexford. "Have you been to Libby lately?"

Sudden fury and a sense of betrayal burned through Juliette. "He had no right to tell you. He said he would keep our conversation in confidence."

"Matt didn't tell me. Dan Whitely drove by and saw him talking to a pretty woman with long blonde hair. Didn't recognize her."

The man who waved. Of course he knew Tim. "Is there some law against that?"

"No, but I've spent the better part of the last few days trying to imagine why my . . . why you would be talking to my good friend Matt. And why you didn't tell me about it. He refused to talk about it at all."

"Maybe it's none of your business. You bailed on me, remember?"

"You took a job in Billings. You bailed on me." He groaned and pounded on the steering wheel. "I don't want to fight with you."

The kindest, gentlest man in the world was beating up his truck because of her. "I don't want to fight either. By the way, I'm not taking the job in Billings. I haven't called them yet, but I plan to."

"Tell me it isn't because of me." He glanced her way and back at the windshield. "I don't want to be that guy who stands in the way of a woman's happiness."

"You really think a job shilling toothpaste or eyeliner will make me happy? It isn't about you." She sought the words with care. "I need to stick close to home right now, close to my family."

He pulled onto the road that split tiny Rexford and passed the store. People waved. Juliette rolled her window down and waved back. Inhaling the scent of pine and fresh dirt, she kept her gaze on the turquoise lake that sparkled in the distance.

Neither of them spoke again until he eased onto the dirt road that led to Rexford Bench. The campground was busy, but he managed to find a parking space away from a family gathering that looked like a massive reunion.

He got out without a word. Juliette did the same. He grabbed the ice chest. She took the fishing rods. The silence continued as they walked the path that led to a rocky outlet nestled among towering ponderosa pines where they could see the hoodoo sandstone formations in the distance. One of Juliette's favorite spots. An osprey floated, dipped, and dove, hunting for kokanee. With any luck they'd see a bald eagle fishing for its supper.

Juliette picked the biggest boulder close to the water that lapped in a soothing rhythm against the shore. Her heartbeat slowed. The knots in her stomach loosened. "This is perfect."

"There's a tub of night crawlers in the cooler." His expression still somber, Tim took one of the rods. "Whoever catches the first fish, the other one has to do the cleaning."

"Even better."

No banter today. No tales of forty-pound catfish.

Not every moment of life could sparkle and shine.

Sometimes all a person needed was the comfort of a close friend's presence.

She loaded her hook with a squirming earthworm and let it sail. The smell of earth, fresh water, and rotting leaves engulfed her. The breeze touched her face. She leaned into the sun and let the rays warm the cold, dark corners of her mind.

Her legs turned to mush under her. She dropped the rod and knelt. The story clamored for release. Her throat was too clogged with tears to speak.

Tim dropped his rod and scrambled over the rocks to her. "You know there's nothing you can't tell me, Jules, nothing." He plopped down next to her and folded her against his chest. "No matter what happened to you, I will always, always love you. Nothing you did in the past will make a difference. That's a promise. You can take it to the bank."

Razor-sharp pain cut a jagged line in her stomach. She doubled over and clutched her gut. "I was raped when I was fifteen at a youth group retreat right here at Lake Koocanusa. My friends were eating hot dogs and s'mores while I was being assaulted in the forest."

The words leaped into the air and fell to their death in the deep, clear water.

Gone. Over. Done.

"I'm so sorry. I can't imagine how horrible this must have been and still is for you. I want to take it away somehow. I feel like I just got stabbed in the gut." Tim's hand stroked her hair.

She raised her head. His hands were gentle when they moved to stroke her cheek, but ferocious storm clouds gathered in his eyes and hardened the lines around his mouth. "I hate this."

"Just don't be mad at me." Her voice quivered. She fought to control it. "I couldn't stand it if you were mad at me."

His expression softened. He took her hands in his and squeezed. "Why would I be mad at you?"

"Because it was my fault. I was stupid and I did exactly what you said I do. I flirted."

He flinched. "I didn't know this happened. I would never blame you for this."

"There's something wrong with me."

"I love you just the way you are."

He put his arm around her. They didn't move. The sun and the water and the chorus of frogs croaking worked their healing balm.

"I've felt so guilty about it for so long, I don't know how to stop."

"I'm no expert." He cleared his throat and kissed the top of her hair. "But I know it's not your fault. You have nothing to feel guilty about. I wish I knew how to make it better. I feel so inadequate."

"You don't have to do anything." His presence and his touch were enough in this moment. Knowing he would support her meant she could get through the next moment and the one after it. "Just knowing you're here helps."

An eagle made his appearance. His enormous wings spread wide, he soared high above the lake, searching, hunting, mingling his beauty with the blue sky that provided a spectacular backdrop to his regal aerial performance. Tim pointed. Juliette nodded. Then she told him her story.

His face turned to stone. His fists balled. His breathing turned harsh. Juliette leaned into his chest and listened to his heart race. Still, he didn't speak.

She straightened and wiped at her face with her sleeve. "Well?"

"I hate that this happened to you." His voice was hoarse. "I hate that you carried it around all these years. That you bore the memories alone. I hate that you waited so long to tell me."

"I was afraid of losing you."

"Then you don't know me."

"I know you are the nicest, kindest, sweetest man alive."

"Not right now, I'm not. Right now, I want to hit something."

"Could you maybe just hold me first?"

"I can do that." His voice broke. "For as long as you need. Forever."

. . .

Fury could be clean. It could burn away the dregs of hurt and pain. Or it could be corrosive. Tim's boiled up in his chest until his bones and sinew hurt. His hands ached from balling them in fists. The desire to hit something—preferably the man who assaulted Juliette—enveloped him.

What kind of man did that make him? Returning violence for violence?

He groaned. Juliette stirred. The shaking had finally abated, but her face and his shirt were sodden with tears. "What are you thinking?"

"I'm thinking I give you such a hard time about not being a believer and this happens and I discover my faith is more about lip service than actually walking the walk."

"I don't believe that. You're the best Christian man I know, besides Daddy."

"I want to find the guy and kill him."

"I've had the same fantasy many times." Juliette's laugh was bitter. "What would your friend Dr. King say about that?"

"I reckon the reverend would say God will forgive us our humanness. Then he'd go on to remind us of his hard-and-fast rules on nonviolence. He'd say to fight evil, not the evildoer. He'd say the evildoer is a victim too."

"That doesn't give me much comfort." She dug a tissue from her jeans pocket and blew her nose. "I can't see a guy who takes advantage of a situation like that at a church youth retreat as a victim. I don't think I want to."

"Me neither. But Dr. King says we not only refuse to shoot our opponent, but also refuse to hate him. The center of his philosophy was brotherly love. The power of God working within us. The most powerful weapon we have is love."

"So I'm supposed to love the man who sexually assaulted me?" Her snort turned into a sob. "I can barely think of him at all, let alone forgive him."

"It's a tall order." Tim tightened his arms around her. The desire to hold her so close that no one could ever hurt her again washed over him. He couldn't get close enough. To share her skin, her hurt, her pain—only then would he be close enough. "I know I'm not there."

"And you wonder why I have trouble with God."

"There are days when He's not happy with me either, I promise."

"Matt says the only way to heal is to forgive him."

"I hate it when he's right." Tim tried for a laugh, but it came out strangled and sad. "God forgives us His Son's death. I can't imagine how that felt." He worked to keep his emotions at bay. "Dr. King says the aftermath of violence that isn't forgiven is bitterness."

"Is that why my stomach hurts all the time?"

Tim kissed her forehead and snuggled her closer. "I think so. We'll work on soothing your heart and your stomach."

"You promise? I can't bear to think of facing this without you."

The entreaty in her voice lit fires Tim hadn't known existed in his heart. "I promise."

The water lapping the shore filled the silence. Tim closed his eyes. Juliette's body relaxed against his chest. Healing floated on the quiet.

"Tim."

"I'm here."

"I love you."

"I love you too."

What came next was up to God.

CHAPTER 37

EUREKA, MONTANA

Having some place to simply be in a small town like Eureka could be challenging. A guy could only spend so much time in Walmart eating sub sandwiches with interesting Amish women. Spencer slid from his truck, grabbed his crutches from the back, and swung across the parking lot toward the church. The Type 2 Incident Command Team had a public information officer staffing the location. Media stopped by, as did citizens wanting to know the latest. It gave him an excuse to get out of the house. Three adults and three kids in a three-bedroom duplex with one bathroom and a miniscule backyard resulted in its share of squabbles.

And frowns laden with questions. He still hadn't given his mother an answer regarding the wedding. Nor had he met the groom.

She seemed to labor under the illusion that Spencer planned to stay in Eureka. He did not, would not, could not. He sounded like a children's book. He would not eat green eggs and ham and he would not stay in Eureka.

Hence the trips to Walmart, the grocery store, and the park. Next up, taking the kids on their first fishing trip.

But not today.

Many of the Kootenai refugees needed an escape too. Jonah Yoder, Caleb Hostetler—who didn't look any friendlier than he had that night of the fiasco with the scooter—and Noah Duncan, the Amish bishop, stood around gabbing and drinking coffee.

No Mercy. She wouldn't be here. She had to teach. Maybe she needed an assistant. He shut that thought down. Why did he always gravitate toward the unavailable women? Images of her wary smile and uncertainty at the Walmart ran circles in his head as he approached the PIO, Jeremy Johnson. His presence in her life caused her nothing but trouble.

She reminded him of someone.

Shaking off the commentary on an endless loop in his head, he shook Jeremy's hand and asked the same question on everyone's mind. "Is it contained?"

"We're throwing everything we've got at it." Jeremy grimaced. He was a fresh-faced new college graduate who still had pimples on his nose and a feathery mustache that might have been drawn on with a black pen. "We're constructing a containment line as wide as a football field to protect the remaining structures in Kootenai, but it's still dangerous in there. They're concerned the fire might circle back around."

Still.

"How much longer—?"

Jeremy's phone rang. He held up a hand and palmed the phone to his ear. He mostly listened, and as he did, his smile disappeared. He disconnected and stared at his slick leather loafers.

"Are you okay? Did something happen?" Spencer glanced around for a chair. The guy needed to sit. "Can I get you a glass of water?"

"I'm fine. It's just bad news, man." He sighed and the professional, all-business PR persona made a ragged appearance. "Do you know a jumper named Chase Wilson?"

"Sure I do. He's the newbie on my team." Spencer stopped. The familiar, ugly suspicion that life was about to deal him another blow made his stomach drop. "Why? How do you know Chase?"

"I don't." Jeremy's shoulders hunched. He ducked his head. "We just got word. Your team jumped into the Gibralter Fire yesterday. He was digging the containment line when a tree fell on him."

Chase's incessant foot tapping and leg wiggling had been stilled by a ponderosa pine or a stately Douglas fir.

The newbie would no longer prepare the coffee or experiment with Spam sushi.

"He was just getting started." The stilted words were stupid.

"Yeah, Boss said he was twenty-four."

It had only been a week since a hotshot crew member was killed in the Florence Fire in Lolo National Forest south of Missoula. He was part of an elite firefighting crew trained to fight wildfires at close range with hand tools. "He knew the risks." More stupid words. "He loved what he was doing."

He didn't love packing the chutes or repairing them on a sewing machine at the base. He called it women's work, which only made Spencer and the other guys give him more "women's" work to do.

His coffee tasted like burnt plaster.

Spencer pivoted on his crutches. The room stifled him. His lungs begged for air. Weaving between clusters of volunteers sorting clothes and groups of citizens digesting the latest news, he headed for the door.

Tim Trudeau followed him out. "Hey, Spencer, I just heard the news. I'm truly sorry."

"I appreciate that." He kept moving.

"Spencer, wait."

"I really have to go."

"Some of us are talking about having a memorial service to honor the firefighters who've given their lives battling these fires." Tim chopped short his long strides to stay even with Spencer's uneven pace. "We were thinking it might help the folks who are grieving over their lost homes too. It gives people some perspective on what it takes to get through this."

It was a nice idea, but why tell Spencer? "Sure. Makes sense."

"We thought we'd do it tomorrow. At the high school. It's neutral territory. No denomination."

"I'll be there." Even if he couldn't understand any of it. Send guys out there to fight an out-of-control inferno and then let a tree crush them. "Angie will be here later. Just let her know what time."

"Would you be willing to say something?"

"I don't do public speaking." His heart did that uncomfortable double whammy against his breastbone. "Get someone else."

"Wilson was your buddy. You jump. You know the risks and the rewards. The folks could use your leadership right now."

"I'm no leader."

"You didn't used to be, but from what I hear, you've turned your life around." Tim's expression darkened. "Why not step up and do the right thing here?"

"Can I think about it?"

"Yeah, sure. And I really am sorry."

Spencer stumbled outside. He leaned against the wall, letting it hold him up. Now would be a great time for a vice like smoking or drinking. A bowl of ice cream just wasn't the same. A place to scream until his throat hurt would be a good option.

Or a woman willing to let him lose himself in her.

That woman didn't exist.

He'd never allowed himself to get that close. His gut hurt from the desire to hold and be held.

Get over yourself.

He gritted his teeth and straightened. His phone rang.

Dan Martinez.

"Hey, Danny boy."

"You heard?" Dan's words faded in and out. The reception was terrible. He sounded like he was on the moon.

"I heard. Are you still in the park?"

"I gave him CPR, man. I carried him out." The man's voice cracked. "He was dead the second the tree hit him."

"He went down with his boots on."

"Yeah, man, he did." Dan coughed and swore. "Just wanted to make sure you knew. For some unknown reason the guy respected you. He talked about you nonstop after you left. We told him to shut up, but he never did."

"Did he make the Spam sushi?"

"Yeah, it wasn't half bad."

They were silent for a three-count.

"Are you going back in?"

"I want to, but they won't let me. The team is done. They're coming out. We have to get back to base before we get called out again. It's a moving target."

The worst wildfire season in the history of the state. "Be safe."

"Get your butt back here as soon as you can."

"Roger that."

The phone went dead.

Spencer smacked a crutch against the building. Only the fear that it would break and leave him to hop to the truck on one crutch kept him from doing it again.

Nothing, not even the love of a good woman—or his family—could stop him from returning to the job. It was what he did. And who he was.

Someone had to pay the price for people usurping nature's territory in the mountains.

Fighting back would be his homage to a kid who loved playing with fire and didn't live long enough to show it who was boss.

As soon as his leg healed, Spencer would straddle the beast again.

CHAPTER 38

Despite the short notice, a slew of folks from Rexford, Eureka, and Libby had turned out for the memorial service on Sunday afternoon. Tim peeked from behind the thick blue curtains on Eureka High School's auditorium stage. Every seat was full and people were still streaming in. Standing room only. It would be ironic if the fire marshal had to shut them down because the crowd was over the facility's legal occupancy. His stomach roiled. He popped an antacid. Emmett sidled alongside him and peered out. "Big crowd. Even the Amish folks came. Are you ready for this?"

"How did I get roped into serving as master of ceremonies?"

"It was your idea to do this whole shebang." Emmett slapped him on the back. "And a good one too."

"So why do I feel like I'm about to hurl?" His claim to fame in high school had been barfing all over Juliette's tray in the cafeteria. It had taken years to live it down. He couldn't do it again.

"They need to grieve and they need to start healing," he said, more for himself than Emmett. His boss already knew why the service was necessary. "A community coming together to grieve will rebuild together."

"Don't tell me, tell them." Emmett straightened Tim's tie. For a second, time stood still and a glimpse of what life would've been like with a father shimmered like a mirage in the distance. Then it was gone, a wispy bit of smoke that evaporated before Tim could grab on to it. Emmett grinned. "You'll be fine. The Holy Spirit lives and breathes in you, kid."

"From your lips to God's ears."

Tim took another gander at the crowd. Juliette sat half a dozen rows back with her whole family. Sweet Juliette carrying around a boulder of shame, regret, and guilt on her shoulders all these years. The sound of her tearful voice begging him not to be mad at her haunted his dreams. He longed for a way to reach back in time to rip to shreds the guy who took her innocence and joy. How could Tim ask her to forgive if he couldn't?

Now wasn't the time to ponder such questions.

"All three pastors are here and Dan." Emmett's way of telling him it was time to pony up and get the show on the road.

The incident commander would talk about the status of the fire and the number of personnel working them so folks would know how many people were putting themselves in harm's way to end the threat to their homes. One pastor from each community would speak. While Eureka wasn't in danger from the fires, the small town had welcomed many family and friends from the other two communities into its midst during the threat.

Spencer, so far, was a no-show. The guy was hard to read. His sister said he would be here. Yet he wasn't. Maybe if Tim had been more welcoming from the start, Spencer would've felt safe speaking in front of his hometown crowd. If Tim hadn't been so judgmental, the guy might believe he would be supported in his time of grief.

Sorry, God. I'm a work in progress.

Don't apologize to Me, apologize to him.

Tim sighed and glanced at his wristwatch. "Seven o'clock straight up."

"No sense keeping these folks waiting." Emmett gave him a nudge. "God be with you, son."

Tim handed his hat to his boss. He patted his forehead with a tissue and stuck it in his uniform's pants pocket. He took a step. His phone chirped. He glanced at the screen. A text from his mother.

> Call me.
> Busy.
> 911.

He gritted his teeth. "It's my mother. She says it's an emergency."

Emmett grinned. "Two seconds."

Just about what it would take to solve any emergency Mom could manufacture. He hit her name on favorites. "Mom, I'm about to go onstage—"

"Leland and I eloped to Vegas."

After a second the words registered. "Leland came back to you?"

"He brought me a two-pound box of Brach's chocolates, two dozen red roses, a big, fat diamond ring, and two tickets to Vegas." Her smoker's laugh cackled in Tim's ear. "He said we're not getting any younger so we better tie the knot and get it over with."

"He's a sweet talker."

"Isn't he? We're on the hunt for one of those Elvis chapels. He's booked a suite at the MGM Grand. We're going to see Celine Dion after."

"That's great news. Congratulations."

"You really mean that? You're not mad?"

"Of course not. Believe it or not, I want you to be happy." His sisters would be happy too. Mom would be Leland's problem now. "Take pictures. The girls will want to see them."

"They'll be pea green with envy when they see the ring."

Not so much. "Be careful and enjoy yourself. Call me when you get back."

"Son, wait." Her voice quivered. In Tim's entire life, he'd never known her to cry. "I want to thank you for being so patient with me. You're a good son. I love you."

The phone almost slipped from his fingers. The small miracle bowled him over. Anything was possible.

"Tim, are you there?"

"I'm here, Mom. I love you too."

"I'll bring you a shot glass."

Just what he needed.

She was gone.

Emmett gestured toward the stage. "Go, go, go."

He went. His boots clacked on the hardwood stage. He strode to the podium. The spotlights blinded him. Programs used as fans went *whap, whap,* breaking the silence. Children whispered. Adults shushed them.

Leaning down, he spoke into the microphone. "Good evening." It was too short or he was too tall. He adjusted it with both hands. It squawked. He jumped and let go.

A titter of laughter rose and then died.

God, help me do this right.

His eyes adjusted. He stared out at the vast sea of faces, waiting, expectant, uncertain, curious, unhappy, wondering.

"We're here tonight to honor our fallen firefighters, to pray for those who still fight these monsters, and to pray for the strength and stamina we'll need in order to rebuild in the coming days. I'm not sure what the best way is to do this. I just know that there's power in prayer. Scripture says where two or three are gathered in the Lord's name, there He is with them. So let's start by bowing our heads and give our hearts and this night to our Creator."

The words flowed with no effort. Adoration. Confession. Thanksgiving. Supplication.

"Heavenly Father, you are the Great I Am. You are all powerful. You reign supreme. You give us what we need. You are the Great Physician. You hold our hands. You are our rock. We confess that we are weak. We worry. We don't turn to You in our need. We try to do everything on our own. We want to control our situations instead of turning to You. We mess up over and over, and yet we still think we know better than You do.

"Still, You deliver us from our oppressors. You heal our wounds. You break our chains. You forgive us when we don't deserve it. You carry us through the pain. Lord, we lift up to You the grieving families of Chase Wilson and Garrett Milano. We ask that You let them feel Your presence. Hold them in Your arms. Heal their broken hearts. We know we'll never understand why these things happen, but we also know You have a plan on such an enormous, broad landscape that we can't see its vast scope.

"We live in a fallen world where evil is rampant, but You

are still good and You will be victorious. You will erase every pain and dry every tear. On that we can hang our hats and our hearts. We pray for the firefighters, law enforcement officers, and first responders who are out there as we speak fighting these massive fires. Keep them safe, Lord, watch over them. Bring them home safely to their families.

"Lord, we pray You will soothe the pain of the folks in this room who have lost their homes and property to wildfires. We thank You that no lives were lost, but we know how their hearts grieve for those special mementos that can't be replaced. Knit us together as one big community so we can support each other and work together to build new homes, better homes. Bless our efforts and fill every room of every house with Your Holy Spirit.

"Lord, we are so thankful for the abundant blessings You have rained down on us. Let us never forget how blessed we are. Let us never forget the sacrifice You made for us when You gave Your only begotten Son to die for us on the cross for our sins. Let us never forget how His sacrifice erased our sins. Let us never forget how great and endless Your grace and mercy are.

"In Jesus' holy, holy name.

"Amen."

The power of that word, whether it was in a church filled with wooden benches, at a Sunday supper table, or in an auditorium filled with grieving folks, never ceased to amaze Tim.

Heads remained bowed. A sweet stillness swept over the auditorium. Silence reigned.

The auditorium doors swung open and Spencer McDonald slipped inside. His crutches thudded against the laminate wood. His head up, he stared straight ahead as he swung down the aisle toward the stage.

"We have with us this evening someone who knew fallen firefighter Chase Wilson. I'd like to ask Spencer McDonald to share with us his recollection of Chase."

Spencer took his time hobbling onto the stage. The crowd maintained a respectful silence while he made his way to the podium. He handed his crutches to Tim, nodded, and said, "Thanks. Sorry I'm late."

"You're not late. You're right on time."

Something in his face said he, too, had the urge to vomit. Tim laid his hand on Spencer's shoulder and squeezed. "I'm sorry for your loss."

Spencer nodded.

Tim prayed as he returned behind the flowing curtains. *Give this man peace, Lord. Give him comfort. Give him words.*

. . .

Spencer faced the crowd. They might as well be a firing squad. His heart pounded so hard they could probably hear it in the first five rows. Sweat soaked his armpits. His hands were slick. A piercing pain like a sharp arrow reverberated between his temples. Tim's words had propelled him from his safe place listening behind the double doors. The deputy's prayer had moved Spencer from angry cynicism to the certainty that he couldn't continue to avoid an arbitrary line he'd erected during years of hurt and pain. His mom's drinking. His dad's flight from responsibility. The fire. He cleared his throat.

God, I'm not a praying man. You know that. So I don't have the right to ask You for anything. But I hear You're merciful and You show grace. I could use both now. Forgive me for being such an unforgiving jerk. I'm still here. Chase isn't. I think You got that backward. Show me what to do now.

The silence seemed less threatening. More a comfortable cloak of people waiting while a hurting friend marshaled his thoughts.

"I'm not much of a public speaker." His voice croaked like an old bullfrog. He cleared it again. "So I hope you'll bear with me. You'd think a guy who jumps out of a plane and fights wildfires for a living wouldn't be such a fraidy-cat when it comes to talking in front of people."

Soft laughter rippled through the crowd. His vision cleared and faces began to appear. Juliette. Angie. Marnie. The Knowleses. The other Eureka families he'd known growing up. The volunteer firefighters who saved his mom's house from annihilation.

Mercy. Her sweet, kind face filled with empathy encouraged him.

Small communities were family. With all their foibles. The gossip. The nosy neighbors. The lack of anything better to do. The caring. The meals when a person was sick. The caring for the pets when a family was gone on a trip. The hugs when a loved one died.

A restless murmur ran through the auditorium. Someone sneezed. A child giggled.

"I can tell you that Chase Wilson was no fraidy-cat. He was the youngest guy on our crew. The newest. He brought three years of experience as a helicopter rappeller to the table plus three years on a line crew. He was the only guy who could beat my mile and a half in under eight minutes."

Spencer went on to describe Chase's aversion to sewing machines and how they teased him about his cooking prowess when it came to all things Spam. "Chase was a newlywed. Six months in. We teased him about that too. What girl would marry an ugly guy like him?

"Truth is, some of us were jealous. He was a good guy with a good sense of humor. He was all in with whatever he did. He didn't hold back. He and his wife, Megan, just found out she's expecting."

Spencer stepped back from the podium for a second. *Breathe, breathe, breathe.* Hot tears choked him. *No, sir, buddy. Not here. Not now.* He gritted his teeth and stepped up once more.

"I think the thing Chase would want you to know is that he'd do it again. He was out there doing a job he loved. We all love our jobs. And we never forget that we're fighting fires for people like you. I know you're scared and you're frustrated and you're worried. When I jump out of that plane, my plan is to do everything I can safely do to make sure you have homes to return to. Don't ever forget that. And don't forget Chase. Remember him always."

He grabbed the podium with one hand and turned. Tim met him with his crutches.

"You did good by him," the other man whispered.

No words came in response. He'd used them all up.

Tim stayed to introduce a minister from Libby. A young guy who looked like a vet who offered his condolences to Spencer before walking out on two sleek prostheses.

Adrenaline still pumped through Spencer, but every muscle ached with exhaustion. His fingers, clenched on the crutch handles, hurt. He stopped to listen.

Matt Rohrer spoke with intensity about Bible verses that said in life there would be trouble, but not to worry because God had overcome those troubles.

Good thing, because Spencer had no idea how to begin to do that.

He turned to go. Tim fell into step next to him. "If you ever need to talk, I'm available." Tim ducked his head, his expression diffident. "We could grab a cup of coffee sometime."

An unexpected invitation from a guy who couldn't hide his disdain only two weeks earlier. "I don't know that I'll be around here much longer."

"I figured you'd stay around to help your mom fix up her house. And then I heard she and Jacob Johnson are getting hitched in April."

Small towns. "Yeah, I haven't decided. With my bum leg I don't know how much help I'll be."

"Me and my friends are available to help when we're not working."

"That's nice of you. Thanks."

"Take care." Tim halted. "God bless you."

The big guy didn't sling the words out there like a trite platitude. He really meant it. Less than two weeks ago he'd been certain Spencer was trouble. "Why are you being so nice to me? You don't even like me."

"I'm just stupid sometimes. God knows how much I've changed since high school. We all have. We all had family issues in high school. Most of us have them now. I did and I still do. I know you did and I never cut you any slack over it. I'm sorry about that."

"You never did anything to me."

"Except judge you, and there's no excuse for that."

It was Spencer's turn to stare at the floor. "Thanks. I appreciate that."

"I hope you'll stay around until you heal up. Eureka's not so bad."

Not so bad at all. "I haven't decided anything for sure."

"At least stay for the speechifying. Pastor David from Kootenai Community Church is a powerful speaker."

Spencer wavered. What could it hurt? It would be the most church he'd attended in years. Maybe he would get credit for three services with three preachers. Pretty Patty's pleased expression appeared in his mind's eye. "Sure. Why not?"

. . .

Mercy squeezed past her brothers and cut left in the aisle against the flow of people exiting the auditorium. They were eager to get to the gym where women's groups from four or five Eureka churches had set up tables of coffee, juice, iced tea, and all kinds of desserts. She couldn't go there until she said something to Spencer. The pain in his voice as he eulogized his friend and fellow firefighter had touched a chord deep in her heart. Such angst. She'd thought only of herself and not of the sacrifices made by others. So selfish. A house could be replaced. A friend could not.

"Mercy! Where are you going?" Leesa's high voice carried over the buzz of hundreds of conversations reverberating against the auditorium walls. "You'll get left behind."

"I'll be right back. I have to tell someone something."

Leesa shrugged. "It's your funeral."

So to speak. If the elders saw her talking to Spencer in public, there would be a price to pay. Her heart warred with her brain. Words of consolation. Quick words.

She dodged a mother with a toddler on each hip and squeezed past a wizened old man with a walker. The door to the backstage stairs opened. Sheriff Brody tipped his hat at her and said howdy, followed by the minister from Kootenai Community Church and Pastor Matt. No Spencer. She let the men pass and then slipped in.

Spencer leaned against a wall, his crutches propped next to him, talking to Tim. The sheriff's deputy's hands moved as he spoke, punctuating his words. Mercy hesitated. She shouldn't be back here. Her emotions had bested her once again. She backed away. Tim looked up. "Mercy, I'm so glad you and your family could come. It was nice to see friendly faces in the audience. Did you need something?"

"No, no, I just . . . I . . . nothing. I took a wrong turn."

The biggest yet wimpiest lie she'd ever told.

Tim glanced at Spencer and then back at Mercy. He shoved his hat on his head and nodded. "Good talking to you, Spence. I need to find Juliette. I promised to split a piece of her aunt Tina's huckleberry pie with her."

As he brushed past Mercy, he fixed her with a somber but kind stare. "Take care. Don't take too long or all the pie will be gone."

"My mom brought snickerdoodles."

Patting his belly, Tim groaned and disappeared through the door. Mercy turned to Spencer.

"I came to tell you I'm sorry for your loss."

"Thank you." He swiped at his face with his sleeve. "I'm sorry I got you in trouble."

"It's okay. I'm a big girl and I'm responsible for my actions."

Spencer shook his head. "My sister says I should leave you alone. So does your friend Caleb. And Juliette."

"They mean well. They don't think an Englisch man and a Plain woman can be friends."

"But they can?"

"I don't think God intended for rules to prevent human beings from offering condolences to friends." Not a heretical thought, surely. "I wonder if God meant for us to offer comfort in times of loss, regardless of what we believe."

"You're a smart woman, Mercy Yoder." Spencer studied a spot on the wall over her shoulder. He moved as if his leg hurt—or maybe it was his heart. "I've been lucky to know more than one in my life."

"The woman I remind you of?"

"Yeah. Patty had your same heart for God and she saw things in me that I didn't know were there."

"Maybe you should go see her again."

Longing mixed with uncertainty spread across his face. "You think she'd take me back?"

"She saw something in you the first time. If she's the woman you say she is, she's never stopped praying for you. The question is, have you let God into your heart? That's what she'll want to know."

He ducked his head and studied his injured leg. "I'm working on it, actually."

"That's all she'll need to know."

"You sound pretty sure of yourself."

"If I were in her shoes, that's how I'd feel." Mercy leaned against the wall across from him. They were far too close in the way they saw the world. The way their thoughts mingled was scary. They'd only talked a few times, yet here they were conversing as if they'd known each other for years. "You're blessed to be loved by a woman who cares about your salvation."

"I get the impression that there's a guy who's concerned about yours as well."

What did he know about Caleb? "What did Juliette tell you?"

"She didn't. Caleb gave me a ride home that night after we took a walk. The guy's got it bad for you."

He had a funny way of showing it. She shouldn't be talking about him to an English man. "That's private."

Spencer laughed. "It's okay to talk about my love life but not yours?"

"Single Plain women don't have love lives."

"You need to go find Caleb and get one."

"You need to go find Patty and get one."

He straightened and held out his hand. "It's been good knowing you, Amish girl."

"Thank you. Same here." She took his hand and shook hard. "Have a good life."

"You too."

He went first. The door shut with a slight *thud*, leaving her in the semidarkness of the tiny alcove. She wanted a good life.

She wanted it with Caleb.

Time to go find out if he wanted the same thing.

. . .

Caleb shifted in the front-row auditorium seat. Seconds ticked away. He should go. Yet he waited. With the promise of food and drink, the auditorium emptied quickly. The pastors left. Sheriff Brody left. Tim stopped to say hello and then moved on in search of Juliette's company and pie. Still, Caleb waited.

A door thumped and the curtains that hid the backstage entrance fluttered.

Spencer swung down the aisle on his crutches. He halted. "Caleb. You're missing out on a spectacular spread of pies in the gym, or so I'm told."

"I'm sorry for your loss."

"Thank you." He moved closer. Dark swaths circled his eyes like purple bruises. He no longer wore a bandage over the cut on his forehead. The stitches likely would leave a scar. "But you weren't waiting here to tell me that."

"Where is she?"

"She came to express her condolences, that's all." Sympathy softened Spencer's expression. "We're just friends."

"Sure."

"She's worth fighting for."

"I also know that, but it's not my . . . feelings that should be your concern." As much as Caleb had to keep telling himself this. "It's her faith that's at risk."

"It's not at risk. She's firmly planted in her faith. Don't take my word for it. Ask Mercy for yourself."

"I will ask her."

"Ask me what?" Mercy pushed through the alcove door. Her flushed face only made her prettier. Spencer resumed his hobble up the aisle.

Mercy strode toward Caleb. She put her hands on her hips and stared. "What did he tell you?"

"He didn't have to tell me anything." Caleb rose. Anger mingled with embarrassment. Why did he keep doing this to himself? "I thought maybe we could continue that conversation we had at the soda shop. Maybe take a ride. Start over fresh. Leesa said you went backstage. I couldn't for the life of me imagine why."

Because I'm not the brightest guy on the planet. He needed to have his head examined. Being turned down once wasn't enough.

"I'm so sorry." Mercy's face flushed scarlet. "I didn't know you were waiting."

"Would it have mattered?"

"What are you talking about? I told Spencer I was sorry for his loss. I told him he should go find an old friend of his. And then I was coming to find you."

He brushed past her and trudged up the aisle. "Sure you were."

"Caleb, wait. I only wanted to offer the condolences of a friend. He seemed so sad."

Caleb whirled. "You are a Plain woman. He is an Englisch man. It's not proper for you to be alone with him. To speak to him in private."

"I didn't intend for it to be in private."

"Any more than you intended to walk with him the other night." He trod closer. Too close. He could see unshed tears teetering in her eyes. They were huge and filled with confusion and uncertainty. "I won't vie for you. If you have eyes for another, so be it. I'm a simple man with little to offer. I know that. I don't compete. It's not what we do."

"I don't have eyes for another. I'm sorry."

"You said that already."

"And I meant it. I'm not asking anyone to compete." Her voice grew steadier with each word. "If you don't trust me, then we have a much bigger problem than I first thought."

"How can I trust you when I keep seeing you with another man—an Englisch man?" He shoved his hat on his head and walked away.

"That's the most emotion you've ever shown in the time I've known you."

Lest he show more emotion than he should, Caleb kept walking.

"How was I supposed to know you really cared? You were lukewarm at best, cold at worst."

He halted. Showing emotion only caused trouble. It left him open to more hurt and embarrassment.

"Why didn't you ever kiss me?"

Heat burned his face hotter than any flames. His boots weighed a thousand pounds. *Turn around.*

He forced himself to turn. "What?"

"It's a simple question. You wanted to marry me, but you couldn't bring yourself to hold my hand, let alone kiss me. I may not have much experience with these things, but I know physical affection is part of what binds a *mann* and a *fraa* together."

"I'm not gut at it."

The words hung in the air like thick, dark, black clouds.

Mercy's eyes widened. Her eyebrows shot up. Her mouth dropped open. "How do you know?"

A road no man wanted to tread twice. "I had a special friend in Indiana."

Her face reddened. "You don't have to tell me—"

"I want to tell you. It's not you who is lacking. It's me." He walked back down the aisle and sank into a seat on the front row. "Sit with me. Please."

She sat next to him.

He contemplated the stage. "I was eighteen. I thought I knew what I was doing. I thought we were in love. That she loved me like I loved her."

He managed a surreptitious side-glance. Mercy studied her hands, folded in her lap. He marched forward through the painful dense forest of memories. "She broke up with me. Six months later, she married another man."

"I'm sorry you were hurt."

"I promised myself I would do it better next time. I would slow down and not scare the next woman away. I figured I must not be very gut at it. She never said, so how was I to know?"

"You didn't scare me away, but you never made me feel like you really wanted me like that, either. Like a mann wants a fraa." Her voice was small and embarrassed. "I couldn't imagine why you wanted to marry me if you couldn't bring yourself to kiss me."

"Believe me, I wanted to."

"And then I turned you down and you were hurt all over again."

"It's all right. I'll live." Her hand slipped across the arm of the seat. Her fingers touched his. He grasped them. His heart hammered in his chest. "What about Spencer?"

"Spencer is in love with another. You have nothing to worry about there."

"Maybe we can start again."

"Or pick up from where we left off?" She leaned closer. She smelled of snickerdoodles. Cinnamon and sugar. Sweet and spicy. "Have a do-over."

"I'd like that."

The air crackled between them. He leaned closer. Her hazel eyes swam with emotion. They met in the middle. A soft, sweet kiss that grew and deepened. Months of pent-up feelings exploded.

They both jumped back. Mercy's smile illuminated the entire auditorium. "I don't have any experience, but you're wrong about being bad at it. I'm sure of that."

CHAPTER 39

WEST KOOTENAI, MONTANA

An eerie silence like that of a deserted cemetery reigned. Mercy stood with one hand clasped in Hope's and the other in Job's as they stared at the remains of their home. Knowing that their home had been destroyed and seeing its remnants were two different animals. Almost a month had passed since the fire destroyed their past. Now the time had come to shut the door on what had been lost and move forward. Or so her father said.

Her family made a meandering line that began with Father and Mother, who held a wiggling Levi in her arms, and made its way through the rest of their children. Tears ran down Leesa's face. Abraham, a replica of their father, stared at the enormous pile of debris and ashes with the granite face of a man attending his own funeral. Moses had one hand on Seth's shoulder. None of her brothers showed emotion. How did they do that? They knew what was expected and they did it. To be so obedient.

Full of emotions that fell into each other like clothes wound together and ripped apart in the wringer wash machine, she had to shake them out, hang them up to remove the wrinkles, and try to make them presentable.

Their home had been reduced to a heap of rubble. The cargo trailer's sides were melted. As if fire wasn't enough, it seemed a tornado had ripped through the property, leaving nothing recognizable in its wake. Except the lean-to where they stored their buggies. It still stood, only forty feet from the house.

Father bowed his head. Everyone followed suit.

A sob broke the silence. Glad for a reason to take her gaze from the destruction, Mercy knelt, ignoring the snowy-white ashes that coated her apron, and hugged Hope. "We'll rebuild. We'll be fine."

"Where are Nickel and Dime?" His lower lip protruding, Job turned to Father. "Where is the chicken coop? Where are the chickens?"

"Down the mountain." Father wiped his face with his bandana. "Critters are smart. Don't you worry about them. Don't worry about anything. The trees will grow again. The grass will turn green. We'll fish and hunt and grow our food just as we always have. We have much to be thankful for."

They were all safe. No lives lost. Stuff could be replaced. Life went on. Mercy dug deep for the teachings that had been the bedrock of her faith since the day she was old enough to understand the words spoken by her parents and the church elders.

"No lives were lost." He spoke as if Mercy said the words aloud. "Your mudder and I rejoice that we're all still together. We have each other. Our neighbors have their houses. We rejoice for them. We rejoice because we have friends and neighbors who will help us."

He let go of Mother's hand and trudged through the ashes to where Mercy hugged Hope and Job. His hand squeezed her shoulder. He patted Job's hatless head. "Already Noah and the others are talking about a mobile home we can borrow to live in while we rebuild. We'll start today, now, by removing the debris. They'll be here soon to help."

His head lifted, shoulders squared, Father strode to the wagon Abraham had driven behind the buggy. He pulled a grocery bag from the back and began to hand out work gloves. Even Job received his own small pair.

"Together, we'll rebuild. This is Gott's plan for us. It's our job to make the best of it."

Mercy accepted the tan cloth and leather gloves. They felt heavy in her hands. So heavy she might drop them. The ache in her throat spread across her chest and invaded her heart. "May I go to the school first?"

To her amazement the words came out devoid of her deep sadness. The children didn't need to see her weakness. If Father and Mother could be strong, so could she. *Please, Gott, let me hang on a few more minutes. Falling apart is not acceptable. Please, please let me go.*

"The school is fine."

"I want to see about the smoke damage. Caleb said painting would be necessary. And airing it out. The sooner we start, the sooner we get things back to normal."

Whatever that meant. She wanted to see it with her own eyes. Families who still had their homes were returning to Kootenai today. That meant school needed to resume here as well. A truck was needed to convey the desks back to their home.

And their teacher needed to live here as well. As soon as possible.

Caleb might help with that. Hope and love would spring from these ashes like the plants that would unfurl their green leaves come spring. No matter how often the flames came, life renewed itself on these mountains and in this forest.

Her father's gaze bounced to her mother. Some unspoken words passed between them. "Jah. But come back directly. I want the family together today."

Ten minutes later she pulled up to the school. Not a single scorched board. She sat in the buggy, not moving, and stared at the log cabin–style building. It still stood.

Caleb and her father had said it did. Yet confirmation had been needed.

Life did, indeed, go on.

The grass shone a brilliant green against the dark earth. The leaves had begun to turn vivid orange and red on the maple trees by the front door. The cool breeze rustled in the leaves, an autumn sound incongruous with the scent of decay and darkness that hung in the air.

The breeze nudged the wooden-plank seat on the swing set that still held a place of honor a few yards away from the building. The squeak of the chains sent memories frolicking. Little boys jumped from the swings and took flight. Children shrieked with laughter as they raced around the makeshift baseball field. Life would go on here.

Still, she sat.

Seeds of a different sort were planted here. Seeds of learning. Not just reading, writing, and arithmetic. Seeds of thought. Of knowledge.

Perhaps they weren't as important as the other kinds of seeds her father and mother valued. But Mercy pressed close to this learning because it brought her some modicum of understanding.

And even if she didn't understand, faith was all about trusting. Trusting that which she could not see. Trusting in God's goodness and His grace.

Gritting her teeth, she hopped from the buggy and approached the building. She touched the smooth solidness of the door and ran her fingers over the rough-hewn logs. It wasn't an apparition. It wouldn't disappear from her life. Not today or tomorrow.

Inside, sunlight poured through the windows, the beams highlighting dust and smoke that still lingered in the air. The smell of burnt dreams could not be escaped. It clung to the wood along with particles of lost dreams.

The smell of a campfire would never be enticing again.

"I thought that was you."

She turned to find Caleb standing in the doorway. A powerful wave of déjà vu swept over her. Only a month ago he'd been a past mistake who'd stood in that door and announced the approaching fire.

Now he was her way forward.

Tragedy had a way of stripping the veneer from a person until normally hidden emotion escaped through the wounds, through the sweat, through the blood, that seeped out.

"I had to see."

"I knew you would be here." Despite the autumn temperatures, his shirt was soaked with sweat and filthy. "We'll need to paint."

No mention of the tender words spoken in the auditorium or the kiss. "Getting the windows open will help too."

"Wait, in case we get rain."

Rain would be a lovely, welcome respite. "Your cabin?"

"We've started removing the debris." He put his hand on his back as if reminded of the ache caused by such hard work. "Tobias and Aaron and Henry helped, but we stopped."

"Why?"

"We're headed to your place to help Jonah."

"You don't want to get yours done?"

"I want to take time to think about what needs to be built there." His eyes were red rimmed from irritating soot and ash, but he smiled. "It won't be a cabin this time."

Despite the images of devastation that pressed on her from every quarter, Mercy smiled. "No? What will it be?"

"It will need three or four bedrooms and a big kitchen and a stone fireplace."

"For s'mores?"

He grinned. "And warmth while we play checkers on long, cold winter nights."

We? "It sounds lovely."

"There's so much work to be done. I have to go." He moved toward her. Again, she met him halfway. Wasn't that what love meant? Another kiss. Despite the urgency in his voice, he took his time, his hands moving from her cheeks to her shoulders, running down her arms, and then to her waist, leaving her breathless, weak-kneed, and longing for more. "See you at your house."

And he was gone.

For a man who'd hesitated for so long, he seemed to be making up for lost time. Mercy put her hand to her warm lips. Not that she was complaining. She scurried from the schoolhouse. She, too, had much work to do. S'mores, kisses, and checkers in front of the fireplace beckoned to her in the distance.

Her future beckoned.

CHAPTER 40

A guy never got too old for story time. Spencer stood in the doorway and watched while Marnie read *Three Billy Goats Gruff* to Kylie and Mikey. All three were crisscross-applesauce on the braided rug in front of the couch. The coffee table had been moved and sheets draped over two kitchen chairs at each end between the couch and table. Thus creating the perfect tent.

Janie, who lay on her back on a blanket, gurgled and batted at toys that hung overhead. Marnie read most of the story, but the kids chimed in at just the right moment when the line "Who's that trip-trapping across my bridge?" appeared. Their voices deepened and they all laughed as if it were the funniest thing since they discovered farting in the bathtub.

In the days since the memorial service, the cut on his forehead had healed. He removed the splints on his fingers without the approval of a doctor. His leg no longer hurt. His heart also seemed on the mend. Mercy's advice to forgive his mother and return to the woman he loved pursued him no matter how hard he tried to forget it. Should he dive for cover under the couch or run until he hit the Mexican border? Maybe farther.

Or he could take her advice and get over himself. Tim's

prayer still rang in his ears. His sins were forgiven. So were Marnie's. All he had to do was accept it and let go of the past.

A tall order.

The story came to an end and Marnie closed the book. "Okay, wee-wuggums, it's time for graham crackers and milk." She crawled from the tent on her hands and knees. "And then what time is it?"

"Nap time!" Mikey yelled.

"Yep!" She glanced his way. Spencer waved. Marnie offered a self-conscious smile. "Nap time for Mikey and quiet time for Kylie."

"Sounds good to me. Snacks and naps." Spencer leaned down to receive two advancing whirlwinds who discovered his presence at the same time as their grammy. "Two things no one should ever give up. You'll remember I said that when you're out in the world adulting and wondering what you got yourself into."

"Do you want milk?" Mikey tugged on his arm. "Snacks, snacks."

"In a minute. You go sit at the table." He nudged the tiny dynamo toward the kitchen. "I need to talk to Grammy for a minute."

"Let me set them up with their snacks." The careful politeness of the past week resurfaced. She picked up Janie and held her out. "Hang out with your niece until I come back."

He settled his crutches against the wall and took the baby. They'd become fast friends over the last month. Her familiar scent of formula and baby stuff made him smile. "What's up, cutie pie?"

Marnie left him holding the bag, so to speak. Janie had wispy blonde hair on top of her head but not much on the sides.

Her eyes were blue and her skin milky white. She fit nicely in the crook of one arm. "Have I mentioned that your momma will have to fend off the boys with a stick when you get older?"

Janie didn't seem to make much of that observation. He wiped at some drool on her chin. She grabbed his finger and gummed it. Her fingers were so tiny.

So perfect. So unblemished.

"I don't know how God came up with this design, but He knew what He was doing."

Janie's rosebud lips widened. She yawned.

"Am I boring you?"

No response. Her eyes closed.

"Guess so."

He settled into the glider rocker and waited. Contentment, so long a stranger in his life, stole over him. For once, he didn't fight it or question it.

Marnie returned minutes later with a milk mustache and a handful of graham crackers. "Want one?"

He shook his head. "I'm sorry."

"You're sorry?"

"You apologized for not being a better mother when I was a kid." Ignoring the urge to remind her of what an understatement that was, he stared at Janie's petite sleeping face. "I blew it off. I shouldn't have done that."

"I don't blame you. It's a lot to forgive." She nibbled at a cracker. "I probably don't remember half the stuff I did or didn't do in those days. I know I missed your high school graduation. I wasn't there when Kylie was born. I barely remember when Mikey was born. And from Angie's reaction to the fire the other night, I apparently started a fire and put both of you in terrible danger . . ."

Her face lined with regret and resignation, she stared at the window over his shoulder. Tears trickled down her cheeks and dripped on her red Bon Jovi concert T-shirt. "How is it possible that I don't remember that night?"

"You were out of it."

"All these years I kept telling myself it wasn't that bad. You guys didn't have it that bad. At least I stayed. I tried to bury the fact that your dad left because of me. It was my fault you grew up without a father." She dumped the crackers on the table, grabbed a tissue, and scrubbed her face. "And then to find out I almost killed you. No wonder you refused to come back. I can't imagine how Angie has been able to stand to be around me, let alone let me close to those kids."

Spencer grappled with conflicting emotion. She was right. Spot-on. Everything she said rang true. Yet watching her beat herself up was agonizing. For the first time in his life, those years appeared before him through her eyes. "Angie is better at forgiving than I am. She's a better person than I am."

"It's more like she suppressed it all and it all came bursting out and exploded in my face."

"For which she immediately felt terrible because that's who Angie is."

"She's a believer. She doesn't just talk the talk, she walks the walk." Marnie wadded up the tissue and stuck it in her pocket. "I feel terrible because I'm responsible for your lack of faith on top of everything else."

"I'm a big boy. It's on me if I choose not to go to church."

"I hate to think you don't have God or a good woman in your life. A man needs both."

Pretty Patty's sweet face floated through his mind. A man had to take responsibility for his actions. And just because he didn't go to church didn't mean he didn't believe in God. He'd just preferred to run his own life.

Patty's husky voice whispered in his ear. *"How's that working out for you, big man?"* A shiver, almost like fever, ran through him. Not good, not good at all. He was tired of going it alone. "If I don't, it's my own fault."

"But I didn't set the example. I didn't establish a foundation. I never prayed. I never read the Bible." Marnie grabbed her hair and wound it into a knot. A sudden memory surfaced of those hands braiding Angie's hair the day she started first grade. It did happen. There had been normal days. "You never had good role models for relationships or marriage."

"At least you taught me what not to do." He tried out a laugh. It sounded more like a half sob. He heaved a breath. "It's not like Dad did much better."

"It's my fault he left. He's not to blame for my sins."

"A stronger man would've stayed. He would've helped you quit." Spencer counted to ten silently. Too many years of keeping all this stuff bottled up. It was like prying stones from rock-hard frozen ground. "He could've been a parent to Angie and me when you weren't."

"All true and that's on him." Her voice quivered as she rubbed at reddened eyes. "You kids probably don't remember, but your dad did his share of drinking. That's what we had in common. It's how we met. Not a foundation for having a family. But he managed to hold a job and confine his drinking to the weekends. I couldn't."

"Like you said, addiction is a disease." Spencer's thoughts played ring-around-the-rosy with the question he hadn't asked in ten years. He shifted the sleeping baby to his other arm, careful not to jostle her. "Do you ever hear from him?"

"Once in a blue moon."

"So you don't know where he is?"

"Last time I talked to him was when Janie was born. He was in Seattle. He and his wife. I thought since he was close he might want to come and meet his grandkids."

"But he didn't."

"He didn't say that." She winced and rubbed the bridge of her nose. "In fact, I think if he could see them without running into me, he might do it."

The next question stuck in Spencer's throat. He swallowed. "Does he ever ask about me or Angie?"

Her bright smile was reminiscent of the one she gave them in the old days when they wanted supper and there was no food in the house. "Sure, sure he does."

And there really was a Santa Claus. "Anyway, I just wanted to say I hope you'll accept my apology for being such a hardhead."

"You don't know how much that means to me." Marnie slipped over to his chair. She leaned down and kissed the top of his head the way she used to do when he was under four feet tall and leaving for school in the morning. He breathed in her scent of Ivory soap and Jergens lotion. The memories were there. Hidden under mounds of ugly emotional debris. "Forgiving is one thing. Learning to trust is another. I don't expect Rome to be built in a day. I'm hoping you consider meeting Jacob."

"Can I get back to you on that?"

She backed away and swiped at her face with both wrinkled hands. "Sure you can, honey."

Honey. The memory of that slurred voice calling him late at night into a darkened, smoky living room, TV flickering the only light, asking him to bring her some ice loomed. He fought it back into its box. "Can you do me a favor? Call me Spencer."

"Absolutely. I don't mean to—"

"Just starting fresh."

"Right." She scooped up the crackers. "I need to check on the kiddos. They like to dunk the crackers. They tend to make a mess."

"Have you received the check yet?"

"Came today. We're ready to get to work."

"Who's we?"

She beamed. "Jacob is good at fixing things. We'll start demoing on Tuesday. My friend will watch the kids. You should come. Demoing is the fun part. Maybe you can work out some of your aggressions and help at the same time." Her smile faded. "If you want, that is, and you don't have—"

"I'll think about it, Marnie."

"Could you do me a favor?"

"Okay."

"Call me Mom."

Full circle. He stood, handed over sleeping beauty, and hot-footed it from the living room before he did something stupid like cry.

God, I'm trying. Marnie—Mom—isn't the only one who needs grace. I don't deserve it, but a pretty lady once told me You have more than enough to go around. Help me to forgive and forgive me.

Thanks. I mean, amen.

CHAPTER 41

In the days since they'd been allowed back into West Kootenai, help had come in waves. Waves of friendship, hard work, and loving support. Caleb gulped down a huge swallow of water and let the dipper hang from its rope attached to the Igloo. It sat on one of nearly two dozen picnic tables arranged in the field in front of what used to be the Yoders' front yard. The spread of food could surely feed the towns of Kootenai, Rexford, and Libby combined. And Eureka thrown in for good measure. Ham, chicken, roast beef, and peanut butter spread sandwiches on homemade bread. Bushel baskets of apples, oranges, plums, and peaches. Pasta salads, green salads, gelatin salads, pickles, green tomato relish, potato chips, cookies, cakes, pies. And everything needed to serve the food.

A turnkey production by the most efficient catering service the English world would rarely, if ever, see.

Women from as far away as St. Ignatius and Lewistown bustled back and forth between coolers and boxes behind the tables, replenishing food as the workers, at least fifty of them, took turns filling their plates.

The weather cooperated by offering a gorgeous October day.

Temperatures that morning began at a crisp forty-five degrees. The sun warmed their faces and offered a soft breeze of encouragement.

Meanwhile, the enormous task of removing debris and depositing it in mobile Dumpsters had begun. Jonah, wearing long sleeves, boots, a hat, and a mask, led the charge. The difference was already apparent. The walls of the cement basement would soon be revealed.

Caleb's back ached and his shoulders hurt, but it felt good. He wiped his face with his sleeve and turned to head back to the detritus that had been the Yoder home. A platter of sandwiches in her hands, Mercy stepped into his path.

"Did you get enough to eat?"

"When a sweet woman offers me food, I can't help but accept." The image of her standing in their kitchen someday offering him a platter of eggs and bacon seemed so real he could smell the bread toasting. He took a sandwich. He'd been down this road before. How did he know she wouldn't say no again? He glanced around. "I'd like another kiss for dessert."

Her cheeks turned pink. "Rain check?"

"I'll hold you to that." Why had it been so hard to say and do these things before? Now that he'd kissed her, all he could think about was kissing her again and again. Any residual bitterness from past lives and love dried up and blew away in the brisk October breeze.

"It's nice of you to come here first when your own cabin needs work." She ducked her head and placed the platter on the table. "So many people have come. It's amazing. Gott is gut."

"So gut." Good to give Caleb another chance with this woman. Everything else paled in comparison. "I've had another letter from my mudder."

Mercy took a step closer. "What did she say?"

"She said they'll come out for a visit in the spring after I've had a chance to rebuild." He heaved a breath. "I was thinking it would be a gut time for her to meet you and your mudder and daed."

"A really gut time." Mercy was so pretty when she blushed like that. "Your house should be done by then."

Their house.

. . .

Mercy's back ached and her shoulders hurt, but the creepy crawlies were gone from her brain. The harder she worked, the better she felt. She stretched on her tippy-toes and then relaxed against the picnic table. Come what may, she was ready. Everything about the morning—the fresh autumn air, the chatter of friends and family from communities across northwest Montana, the hard work—spoke of optimistic new beginnings.

The feeling of hope had arrived like the prodigal son returning to the fold.

Juliette plopped down next to her. "How are you?"

"Wunderbarr, actually. How about you?" She took the saucer-sized oatmeal-raisin cookie offered by her friend. "Now that the school is clean and neat and open and I have my books back, I feel better."

"Good." Juliette leaned closer and eyeballed her. "You look really wunderbarr. Come on, girl, tell me what's got you blushing like a girl with new undies from Victoria's Secret?"

"Juliette!"

"I'm sorry. I forgot. Proper Amish girls don't wear fancy panties or any panties at all, maybe. Do you wear panties?"

"We do. Ach, stop it. We don't talk about our drawers."

"Yet you just did." Juliette grinned and took a big bite of cookie. She chewed with great satisfaction. "I take it Leesa baked these cookies."

"Now you're insulting my baking." Mercy rolled her eyes and shook her head, even though it was true. Leesa had always been the better cook. "Why exactly are we friends?"

"Because you know I'll always tell you the truth." Juliette laid the cookie on a napkin and pointed toward the road. "And the truth is, life is about to get much more interesting."

"I don't need my life to be more interesting." In the midst of terrible destruction, her new life was unfolding. She needed nothing else in this world, except to work next to Caleb, rebuilding their little piece of God's gift to them.

She leaned forward and put her hand to her forehead against the sun. Tim's truck pulled in next to a dozen others on the road. The sun made her squint. "Who is that with Tim?"

"That would be Spencer." Juliette dusted crumbs from her hands and stuck her cowboy hat on her head. "I do believe you have company."

"If I have company, so do you."

Mercy hopped up. Juliette grabbed her hand. "Wait. I have to tell you something."

Mercy paused. Juliette sounded so unlike herself. Uncertain. She was never uncertain. "What is it?"

"I'm thinking about teaching."

Hallelujah. She sat back down. "That's wunderbarr!"

"You think so? Really?" Juliette's face scrunched up in a half frown, half smile. "Am I crazy? I'd have to go back and take education courses and student teach and it means more school loans and being away from home again, but I know how badly teachers are needed around here and I really want to stay close to . . . home and—"

"Stop." Mercy threw her arms around her friend and hugged her hard. "You can do anything you set your mind to. That's what makes you . . . you."

"Thanks." Juliette hid her face on Mercy's shoulder for a second. Then her head came back up. "Spencer's headed this way."

"Nothing unusual about that. He's a friend."

"Uh-huh." Juliette waved and stalked off toward Tim and his truck.

Why did no one believe her when it came to Spencer? Mercy scooped up half a dozen dirty paper plates and stuffed them in an oversized trash bag.

"Hey, Mercy."

"Hey." She dumped the trash, tied up the full bag, and lifted it out.

"Let me help you with that." Spencer loomed over her. "It's heavy."

"And you're on crutches."

"But not helpless." He followed her out to the pile of debris by the road where they were stacking the trash bags. The men would take them to the Dumpster later. "I couldn't leave without saying good-bye."

"Did you talk to your mom?" She hoisted the bag into the growing stack and turned to face him. "Did you find it in your heart to forgive her?"

"I did. Because of you." He shook his head. "You're not like any woman I've ever known. Except maybe one. This time I've had, talking to you, has helped me get my head on straight better than time with any shrink. I just wanted to say thank you."

"You don't owe me any thanks." Glancing around at the beehive of activity, Mercy dusted her hands off and started walking. Any second they would notice her conversation with Spencer and she'd be in hot water all over again. She couldn't allow that to matter. Spencer had come into her life so suddenly, and now he would be gone just as quickly. "Talking to you helped me figure out some things too. I was feeling sorry for myself instead of seeing all the blessings in my life. And, by the way, you were right about Caleb. So we're even. I hope you find what you need."

"Me too. I mean, I plan to. I know just where to start, soon as the repairs on my mom's house are finished."

In easy silence, they walked on together. Concern written all over her face, Juliette met them halfway. "Tim said you wanted to help." She squeezed between Mercy and Spencer. "I thought maybe you'd be helping your mother. I drove by the other day and it seemed like a bunch of people were working."

Mercy shared a smile with Spencer. Juliette was so cute in her worry, and so off base.

"The insurance money will make it possible to rebuild completely. She'll have a better house than before with the new kitchen and new appliances." Spencer picked up the conversation as if he had no idea why Juliette had intervened. "I kicked in for a new washer and dryer. We finished demoing. They're working on framing the new rooms today. I have to get back soon."

"My parents have dipped into their retirement savings until their insurance check arrives." Juliette squeezed Mercy's hand and let it drop. "We need to get the house boxed in before winter gets here."

Everybody was in that same boat. The community workforce

would pick up and move to the Knowleses' property once they had the Yoders' house boxed in. They were making the rounds.

"Have you talked to FEMA? They're helping the people affected by the hurricane in Texas. They've got temporary buildings and money for rebuilding." Spencer hunched over his crutches and winced as if something hurt. "We've got firefighters down there helping too."

"Too much bureaucracy and red tape. Besides, we like to take care of ourselves," Juliette replied, but her attention seemed elsewhere. Tim was talking to her dad. "As long as we're able to do that, we figure others need the government's help more."

Mercy nudged Juliette with her elbow. Something was up with her friend. "And we Plain folks have our own emergency fund. We pay for our own schools, medical bills, everything we need. We don't expect to be rescued. No one owes us anything."

When it came to rebuilding or to love.

"That's admirable."

"We don't think so. It's just the right thing to do."

"I guess I should see if there's something a gimpy guy on two crutches can help with." He paused. "Take care."

Juliette groaned. "Just go."

"Juliette!"

"It's okay." Spencer smiled, but his eyes filled in the rest of his message. He would never forget her, nor she him. "See you around, Mercy. Juliette."

"Not if we see you first." Juliette growled like Doodles when he tussled with Lola over a rag toy. "Good riddance."

Mercy waited until he was out of earshot to turn to Juliette. "You didn't need to be so mean."

"You're too nice. Go find Caleb. Tell him you'll marry him and stop hem-hawing around."

"You have no idea what you're talking about. Caleb and I are good. More than good. So take care of your own business." Mercy shook her finger at Juliette. "Stop avoiding Tim. Tell him you're planning to return to church and then do it. Tim's not the only one waiting on you. Gott is waiting."

"Well, be that way." An expression of infinite uncertainty on her face, Juliette flounced away.

. . .

Having her own advice blow up in her face was no fun. Pondering her next move, Juliette sauntered through clusters of workers who looked like coal miners with black soot all over their faces and clothes. Spencer paused to talk to Tim and then walked away. She waited until he was out of earshot, then moved in.

"What did you say to Spencer?" Tim's eyebrows were getting a workout. "He said he was hitching a ride back to Eureka with Emmett."

"I told him he should go work on his mother's house and leave Mercy alone. Not in those exact words, but like that."

"That's not very nice." Tim followed the other man's progress for a few seconds, then turned to Juliette. "The guy's trying to get his act together. Give him a break."

"Caleb is totally into her and she's blowing it because of a guy who has the hots for a girl in a long dress and apron."

"You do have a mouth on you, girl." Tim grabbed her hat and shoved it down on her forehead. "What is it exactly that drives me nuts about you?"

"Do you have a couple of minutes for me before we dive into the mess?"

"Always."

Her throat constricted. Despite the breeze, perspiration dampened her face. She breathed and lifted her anxiety to the sky. Whatever happened, happened. She had no control. Never had. Dr. Kenyon said people were afraid of letting go of control and giving it over to God.

Dad would line up a Christian counselor. But Dr. Kenyon was nice and she didn't judge. Or cough up platitudes. "Let's walk down the road. I saw some little green leaves popping through the dirt down by the creek."

How many people watched them walk away?

It didn't matter. Mom and Dad would be glad. So would Courtney. Her sister asked all kinds of questions and popped up to give her hugs and kisses at the strangest moments—in the middle of an MU game on TV or Monopoly night or when she was sound asleep in the double bed in Aunt T's house.

After a while Tim took her hand like it was the most natural thing in the world.

The creek burbled in the distance. A hawk soared overhead. Patches of green trees mingled with burnt sticks that crunched under their feet.

"Are you planning to talk, or are we just stretching our legs?"

She let go of his hand and turned to watch the tiny waves lap against the creek's shore. Tim stood next to her, his fists jammed into his pockets. "How is the counseling?"

"It's good. Good."

"Would you tell me if it wasn't?"

"I would. I'm through keeping secrets. The last one ate a hole the size of a tire in my gut."

A visit to her family doctor had revealed an ulcer. New medications and a bland diet did nothing to improve her mood.

Dr. Kenyon said medical doctors didn't believe stress caused ulcers, but she believed Juliette's stomach pain was a symptom of a spiritual malaise as much as a physical one. Dealing with buried, smoldering anger, fear, and shame would help alleviate her symptoms on both counts.

"I feel helpless. Like I should do something, but I don't know what." Tim scooped up a handful of rocks and began tossing them into the water. With each throw his scowl deepened. "I want to take care of you. Like a friend would."

He tacked on that last piece in a last-ditch effort to keep his distance. Juliette picked up her own rock and skipped it neatly across the water. "Dr. Kenyon thinks it would be good for you to come to counseling in a few weeks."

"I'm willing to do anything that helps you." He stared at the remaining rocks in his hand as if he didn't know how they got there. "But it's really personal. More like couples counseling."

"We are a couple."

"You can't begin to imagine how much I wish that were true. I told you I would never leave you and I won't. I will be your best friend until I die." His voice vibrated with contained emotion. He heaved the rocks far beyond the creek and into the high grass on the other side. "You have no idea—"

"Come to church with me tomorrow?"

"What?"

"Come to my church tomorrow. Pastor David is inviting everyone, including the Amish families, for a joint service of thanksgiving that we're back home and rebuilding."

"And you're going?"

"I met with him yesterday. About joining the church."

Tim's forehead wrinkled. He shook his head as if trying to clear it after a punch to the face.

"Don't think so hard." She patted his chest. "I've been talk-ing to him almost as often as my counselor. She's the one who suggested it. I told Pastor David I'm finished running. God's got me right where He wants me."

"You believe?"

"Deep down, I always did, but I was mad at Him. Furious." She slid her hand into the crook of Tim's arm and leaned her head against his shoulder. "So furious I couldn't see that He was the rock I could cling to when my life imploded. I could rely on Him when no one else came through."

Tim's fingers touched her chin, forcing her to meet his gaze. His blue eyes were filled with emotion. "I'm so happy for you. So relieved."

"That I'm not going to hell?"

He laughed. "That and because I can allow myself to hope."

"What are you hoping for?"

"I think you know, but this isn't about me. As much as I tried to make it about me. Your eternal salvation is way more important than my libido."

"Don't start with the churchy talk again." Juliette poked him with her elbow. "I want to hear more about your libido."

"Let's get you back to church first." His arm came around her shoulders and he moved her into a tight hug. His chin nuzzled the top of her head. "Let Dr. Kenyon know I'll take off work whenever she's ready to see us together. I've waited this long, I can wait as long as necessary."

"Maybe I can't."

"It'll be worth it, I promise you that."

He slid his cowboy hat back. She stretched on tiptoes to meet him. His lips pressed against hers. Her hands slid up his chest. His came around her waist and lifted her up.

Gently, he set her back on solid ground.

"Lord, have mercy." She couldn't help herself. "For a church boy, you do know how to kiss."

"If you hadn't held it against me for barfing all over you, you'd have known that years ago. I'm also a decent dancer." He grinned. "Let's get back to work before I lose any more of my self-control."

"Speaking of work, what do you think about me going back to school?"

His smile faded. "Why would you do that?"

"Mercy has this crazy idea about me teaching."

"That's not crazy at all." His hands caressed her cheeks. "Teachers are always in demand."

"I kind of like the idea too. I—"

His lips covered hers before she could complete the sentence. It could wait. They had the rest of their lives to figure it out. The kiss melted the last remaining vestiges of fear. The wounds would never disappear completely. Scars would remain, but the possibility of healing made joy shimmer on the horizon.

Tim gently disengaged and backed away.

"We have to go back. Now."

Laughing, she tugged on his arm. "One more couldn't hurt."

He stumbled up the incline. Juliette pursued him.

Together they ran toward the Yoders' yard. Laughing and gasping for air.

That life could be good again in the midst of devastation simply provided more proof of God's goodness.

CHAPTER 42

Walking into Kootenai Community Church felt like coming home. Standing in front of a sanctuary packed to the rafters with every family in West Kootenai, Juliette waved at her family and blew Tim a kiss. She did like an audience. A few questions and Pastor David simply said, "Welcome to the fold."

Cheers rang out. Applause resounded. Mom and Dad, neither trying to hide their tears, stood and clapped. Courtney yelled wahoo with her exuberant friends. People Juliette had known since she blew bubbles on the church lawn cheered and clapped. They celebrated with her on the biggest day of her life.

God, it's taken me a while, but I made it. Sorry for being such a big baby about it. Thank You for being patient. Thank You for these people. Thank You for Tim. Thank You.

"I hope you'll stop to congratulate Juliette in the foyer afterward." Pastor David grinned and pumped his fist. "The good Lord caught another one today."

He raised his hands to pronounce the benediction.

"Wait!" Tim left his spot next to Lyle Knowles and made it to the altar in two long strides. "I have something to say."

In his button-down, long-sleeve white shirt, tie, dark-navy slacks, and slick black cowboy boots, he looked almost as good as he did in his uniform. He'd slicked back his hair and shaved. He could say anything he wanted as long as Juliette could stand there and drink him in. She might even listen. He took her hand and mouthed an apology to Pastor David. "Do you mind?"

Pastor David didn't flinch. "Be my guest."

Tim's big hands wrapped around her small fingers. His dark-blue eyes brimmed with unshed tears. Her throat closed. This big, gorgeous teddy bear belonged to her. Only the crowd watching with anticipation kept her from kissing his handsome face right then and there.

He knelt on one knee with startling grace.

"What are you doing?" Sounds died away, leaving a breathless anticipation reverberating in her ears. "Tim?"

His Adam's apple bobbed. His grip tightened. He stared up at her with a face so filled with love, her world shrank until Tim and she were alone. The lights dimmed. Time took a bow. Hurt receded. Hope danced.

"I've loved you since before I barfed all over your lunch in the school cafeteria." A ripple of laughter floated on the air from somewhere far away. "I never thought a guy like me had a chance with a girl so incredibly beautiful and smart and funny. If ever there were a case of beauty and the beast—"

"Tim!"

"Let me finish. Since that day on the highway when I gave you four tickets, I've prayed to God for your salvation and to win your love." He removed one hand and stuck it in his shirt pocket. A second later a sparkling ring appeared. Juliette's body swayed. His grip tightened. "The Shepherd found His lost lamb. We're standing on sacred ground—or kneeling as the case may be. I know we still have a rough road ahead. I know it won't be easy. But I want you to know I'm committed to you and to walking that road with you. I can't think of a more beautiful place to ask this question. Juliette, will you marry me—when you're ready?"

A collective gasp joined with Juliette's.

Everything she'd ever wanted fell into place. She stood with God, her family, her church, and her friends surrounding her and the man she loved on his knees professing his love for her. "I would be honored." The words came easily after all. "I've loved you since you barfed all over my tray. I was just too wrapped up in myself to know it. You are my compass. Without you, I would never have found my way home. Yes, I will marry you."

Wiping at tears that dripped from his chin, Tim stood. He slipped on her finger a silver ring with an arrangement of three tiny diamonds. "This ring has three diamonds—little itty-bitty ones, granted—that represent you and me with God in the middle. The perfect balance." He wrapped his big arms around her and lifted her up for a kiss that brought more applause and shouts of approval.

"There's more where that came from," he whispered in her ear as he set her back on unsteady feet. His breath tickled her cheek and sent goose bumps racing up her arms. "That's a promise."

Juliette leaned against his steadfast body. Together they faced the congregation and the many visitors. Mercy and her family. Christine and Nora and their families. Spencer McDonald and his family all the way from Eureka. Emmett Brody and his brother Paul and their parents from Libby. Many of the volunteer firefighters and Forest Service personnel. This service had been about a new beginning for West Kootenai and all who had lost their homes to the fire.

Now it was her new beginning as well. Today was her birthday. A newborn in Christ, she would spend the rest of her life making up for lost time.

The dark, terrifying, shameful ghosts in her past would always be there, but never again would she face them alone.

Thank You, Jesus.

. . .

The desire to jump up and yell wahoo with the congregation almost overwhelmed Mercy. Only her mother's solid presence on one side and the trio of her own church elders in the seats across the aisle kept her from making a spectacle of herself. She gripped her hands in her lap and tapped her feet. The decision to allow the district's members to attend this joint celebratory service had been a thorny one, not entirely supported by everyone. No sense in making them regret it.

The service had been short and unremarkable. Only an hour at best. Even Juliette's joining of the church had been simple—a few short questions and answers. But Tim's proposal had been more spectacular than a sunrise over the Cabinet Mountains. Joy danced rings around Mercy. Juliette's smile lit up the sanctuary like that same sunrise. For the first time in years, she looked truly happy. The twin sisters of cynicism and sarcasm had disappeared under an avalanche of brilliant expectations honed by painful experiences now overcome.

New beginnings forged in the fire.

Juliette tugged on Pastor David's sleeve. He leaned down

and she whispered into his ear. He nodded and handed her the microphone. She cleared her throat. "I know everyone is itching to get out of here and eat some of my mom's cherry pie, but first I want to say something. Pastor David talked today about everything we have to be thankful for. About the blessing of drawing together as a community to overcome adversity.

"I stand here today so thankful and so blessed." Her voice broke. Tim let go of her hand and put his arm around her shoulder. She smiled up at him and turned back to the congregation. "A few years ago something terrible happened to me. Something I'll never forget. I was so mad and so alone. So ashamed. I didn't tell anyone. I felt betrayed by the church I'd grown up in. I did something stupid. I ran away from God."

Her gaze, unfettered by shame, swept the room. "If there is anyone out there who has experienced something so awful and private you can't put words to it, please, please don't do what I did. I'm here. I've got your back. Come talk to me. Don't let it eat you up from the inside out. If you can't talk to me, talk to someone you trust. I promise you, no one will judge you. Get help. Today.

"It takes time to heal, so the sooner you seek help, the better. I'm only just starting. I've wasted years wandering around in the dark in agony. With the help of a good counselor and my family, I'll get where I need to be, and someday—soon I hope—I'll be Mrs. Tim Trudeau. Together we'll get through this. So will you.

"You're part of a caring community. That's what West Kootenai is. The fire showed us that. This community is part of my DNA. I know everyone who grew up here feels the same. The fire swept through and burned down houses, but it couldn't burn away our fortitude and our connections to each other. We'll continue to rebuild. We'll continue to be a family and a community. There is no place on earth I would rather call home."

More applause erupted. Everyone stood. This time, Mercy clapped so hard her hands hurt. No holding back. Whatever dark shadow haunted Juliette, she was learning to banish it. Not hide it or shove it in a box. It would be destroyed. With it went doubts and fears. If Juliette could embrace a new beginning, why couldn't Mercy?

She stumbled and grabbed the back of a chair. The sun broke through and the shadows parted. She had her faith and her family. She had her scholars. The only piece missing was a man with whom she could share the largesse of a merciful, gracious God who forgave her multitude of sins, beginning with doubting His plan for her.

Mother nudged her. She moved forward.

First things first. She followed her family out the door and into the foyer. Juliette, Tim, and their families made a receiving line. All of Juliette's friends and relatives were hugging and kissing her. "I want to congratulate Juliette. I'll be right back."

Mercy squeezed into the line and waited for her turn. Juliette's face was pink and damp with tears. She wore a corsage of red roses on her white lace dress. "Can you believe it?"

"Yes, I can. I'm so happy for you."

Juliette wrapped Mercy in a rib-breaking hug. "Go get your happiness, you goof," she whispered loudly in Mercy's ear. "You're an idiot if you don't."

Same old Juliette. Mercy broke away. "Thanks for the advice, friend."

"She's good at doling out advice. Not so good at taking it." Tim pumped Mercy's hand so hard the joints in her fingers cracked. "But sometimes she's right."

By the time Mercy had been passed around the entire Knowles family, her own family had disappeared into the reception. Clusters of people stood around talking, but no one she knew well.

Except Caleb. He stood next to the glass doors as if waiting for something. Or someone.

Their gazes collided. He straightened. She started in his direction. Without a word, he opened the door for her and then followed her out. The midday air was fresh and crisp and full of autumn. Neither spoke as they walked toward the buggies that lined the back of the church parking lot.

She climbed into his buggy. He got in and urged Snowy onto the road. Her parents would wonder where she'd gone. It couldn't be helped. Juliette was right. Mercy had let her chance slip away once. Not again.

"I saw you talking to Spencer yesterday."

No small talk then. If Caleb wanted to get straight to the point, she could do the same. "He came to say good-bye. After he finishes with his mom's house, he's going back to Missoula to find the woman he loves."

"He loves a woman in Missoula?"

"Jah."

"I didn't know that."

"Now you do."

"I'm sorry I doubted you."

"I'm sorry I turned down your proposal."

"I understand now why you did."

"Do you?"

"I wasn't all in. I was treading carefully. I reckon a person should never do that with love. You're either all in or a coward."

Caleb was not a coward. Nor was Mercy. "I love you."

He pulled on the reins. The buggy stopped in the middle of the road. "I love you too."

The wind ceased. The dogs no longer barked. The birds stopped chattering. The countryside became so quiet that prayers said in Missoula could surely be heard in the middle of the road in West Kootenai.

Caleb stared at her. His gaze enveloped her. The cool October breeze did nothing to abate sudden heat. She couldn't take her gaze from his face. His insistent eyes and full lips. Nothing stood between them. Not his past. Not her bouts of unbelief.

Certainly not a smoke jumper from Missoula.

Caleb pulled the buggy over to the side of the road and climbed down. He came around to her side and held out his hand. "Come on."

She took his hand. His calloused fingers closed around hers. He led her through weeds that had somehow escaped the billowing flames only a month earlier to a birch tree still standing, still offering shade and the rustling music of leaves. He faced her and took her other hand in his. "I'm standing here in front of you and still I find myself hesitating."

"Because you're not sure." Sudden pain spiraled through her. "Still."

"I've never been surer of anything in my life." He cleared his throat. His grip tightened. "Try to put yourself inside my skin. You turned me down the first time. Women have it easier. They don't have to do the asking."

Mercy grabbed his other hand. Their gazes locked. "We both have our doubts about many things, but not each other.

I needed to know why you couldn't show your affection. Now I know. I know we're meant to be together. Like macaroni and cheese. Like peanut butter and jelly. Like—"

"What are you talking about?" He laughed. His hands let go of hers and grabbed her waist. He whirled her around and swept her up in a hug. "My crazy girl."

"Something Leesa told me when I asked her how she knew Ian was right for her."

"Ah. Well, I know you're right for me."

"Even if I'm not a gut cook and my stitches are a bit crooked."

"Jah, jah, jah. Because you are a gut woman. You're thoughtful and smart and you care about things. About people." Caleb's expression grew pensive. His brown, calloused fingers brushed against hers, then trailed along her arm and up to her cheek. A thrill ran through her. His pale-blue eyes studied her face. "And you are sweet to look at."

She swallowed. "I never thought so."

"Because you can't see what I see." His hands cupped her face. His lips were warm and soft and without hesitation.

She stood transfixed, her body immobilized by feelings that enveloped her from head to toe. Certainty conquered doubt. Light illumined a dark future. No ghosts of old hurts or unrealized dreams came between them. Delicious possibilities banished any fear of loss or failure.

Caleb stepped back, but his hands remained on her shoulders. "Will you marry me?"

Mercy studied every nook and cranny of his tanned face with its high cheekbones and long, noble nose.

The silence stretched.

His eyebrows drew together. His forehead wrinkled. "Mercy?"

"Jah. The answer is jah."

He groaned. "You had me going there for a minute."

"I had to catch my breath." She wrapped her arms around him and kissed him back until her lungs begged for air.

And then she kissed him some more, for good measure.

CHAPTER 43

The phone rang once, twice, three times.

Spencer held his breath.

Pretty Patty's voice, soft, full of sleep, filled the line. "'lo."

"It's me. Spencer."

"I know."

She hadn't dumped his number from her contacts. That was a start. Or maybe an oversight. He sank against the Tundra's leather seat and stared at the vivid stars over Missoula. "I'm ready."

Patty laughed. That same familiar, beautiful, hearty laugh perfect for a full-figured woman like her. "I knew it."

"I don't expect that you waited for me or anything." Big, fat liar. She could be married by now for all he knew. Or at least engaged. Pretty Patty didn't move quickly. She saw joy in the anticipation. "I just wanted you to know."

"I waited."

"How is that possible?"

"When I told you I would wait, I meant it. I prayed for you every night and every day. For you, not for what I wanted, but for what you needed."

"I always knew you were right," Spencer admitted. "Once I

let go of being mad at my mom and God, everything else was easy."

"So you're on speaking terms with Him now?"

"Him and my mom. I just spent almost six weeks at her house."

"You can't imagine how happy this makes me." Patty sounded wide awake now. "I had so many conversations with God about you, and the response was always 'Be patient.' And here you are."

"I'm not perfect."

"Sweetie, no one is. His grace covers every sin you can imagine and even those you can't imagine. We're all works in progress. He never stops working on you or me."

He concentrated on that first word. *Sweetie.* "Does that mean you'll see me?"

"When?"

"I want to ask you to go to a wedding with me."

"Now?"

"It's in the spring. April eighteenth. My mom's getting married."

"Okay. I'll mark my calendar."

"So that means you'll see me?"

"When?"

"Soon. I'm parked in front of your house." He cleared his throat. "Not to be presumptuous or anything."

"Are you coming in or am I coming out?"

"It might be better if you came out." Not that he didn't trust himself. He trusted Patty with everything, including his heart. "We could get something to eat."

"It's midnight. I can make you a turkey sandwich. I have chocolate milk."

"There's an all-night diner on the highway. I'm in the mood for a honking big cheeseburger with those cottage fries you like. I'll buy you a chocolate milk shake. I drove the whole way from Eureka without stopping and I have so much to tell you."

"Give me five minutes."

"I'll be waiting."

Five minutes was nothing.

He'd been waiting his entire life for her.

ACKNOWLEDGMENTS

With every book I write, I learn new things. It's one of the joys of writing. *Mountains of Grace* was no exception. I'd never been to Montana. In anticipation of writing the Amish of Big Sky Country series, my husband and I spent a week driving around northwestern Montana, visiting Amish communities, Glacier National Park, and Kootenai National Forest, attending a powwow in Arlee, and touring the Sky Jumpers' Base and Visitor Center outside Missoula. We're in awe of how gorgeous Montana is and how varied its cultures. I'll never forget this wonderful trip.

I'm so thankful for the people who generously shared their knowledge and expertise with me. My thanks to Lincoln County Sheriff Roby Bowe for taking the time to recollect for me the harrowing days of the Caribou, West Fork, and Gibralter fires of 2017. It helped me to see law enforcement officials involved in the battle against these wildfires as folks with families and the same worries as everyone else. I also gained insight into how well the Amish of this area are respected and liked. While the technical aspects of managing three fires simultaneously were important, the insight into the impact on daily lives was invaluable.

I deeply appreciate the help of Dan Cottrell, operations foreman at the U.S. Forest Service Missoula Smokejumper Base.

Mr. Cottrell's experience includes eighteen years as a smoke jumper after several seasons working as a helicopter rappeller and hand crew member. He kindly answered all my questions with great patience. Learning about the nuts and bolts of smoke jumping was so helpful, but again, even more important was the insight into how smoke jumpers think and why they do this job. My thanks to our tour guide for an information-packed tour of the smoke-jumping school and base.

As always my thanks to the entire team at HarperCollins Christian Publishing, but especially my editor Becky Monds.

I would be totally remiss if I didn't thank my number one supporter and cheerleader—my husband. We put one thousand miles on a rental car in six days and he never complained. He did all the driving and turned a work trip into a couple's retreat filled with good food and lots of laughs—even when my choice of four hotels in seven nights left something to be desired. He was always there to speak up when my introverted nature kept me from starting a conversation. Driving through such gorgeous scenery with someone who appreciated it as much as I did will remain a sterling memory forever. Thank you and love always.

Last but by no means least, thank you to my readers who keep coming back for more. Your kind support is treasured more than you will ever know.

God bless and keep you.

Discussion Questions

1. Several families in West Kootenai lose all their personal belongings. If you have experienced a similar situation with a house fire, how did you overcome the loss? If not, try to put yourself in the shoes of someone like Mercy Yoder. How would you react? What would be hardest for you to accept?

2. Tim Trudeau chooses not to go deeper into his relationship with Juliette because she doesn't profess to be a Christian. Do you think he's right? Have you ever been in a situation where you had a friend who was not a believer and you wanted to help them? What did you do? How do you feel about friend evangelism? Married couples who are "unevenly yoked"?

3. Mercy can't understand why God would allow their home to be destroyed by the fire. She knows she should believe that God has a plan for her and her family but finds it difficult to accept. Have you ever been in a similar situation? How did you resolve your feelings? Why do you think God doesn't stop these painful situations from occurring?

4. Discuss the meaning of Jeremiah 29:11 and how it applies to this situation. "'For I know the plans I have for you,'

declares the LORD, 'plans to prosper you and not to harm you, plans to give you hope and a future.'"

5. Juliette experiences a traumatic assault while on a youth trip to the lake as a high school student. It changes her view of God and her relationship with her church. Why do you think she didn't tell anyone about this event until years later? Why do you think such horrifying events occur in real life and even during church-sponsored trips? Who or what is behind them? Do you think God should stop them? Why or why not?

6. Mercy isn't sure Caleb truly loves her because he hasn't expressed his affection for her in a physical way. He's afraid to stray too far ahead in his feelings for her for fear of rejection. They seem to be at cross-purposes. What would you have done in Mercy's place? What steps could she have taken to let Caleb know how she felt rather than turning down his proposal? Does lack of communication cause problems in your relationships?

7. Spencer has spent years resenting his mother and her alcohol addiction's effect on his childhood. He returns home to find that she has grown and moved on, while he's still stuck in the past. Have you experienced similar situations in your family relationships? How did you deal with them? You know you're called to forgive, but how do you practice forgiveness in "real" life?

8. Tim comes to the realization that he may be selfish in holding on to Juliette, hoping she'll find Jesus so they can be together. He may have to let go. Have you ever experienced a situation where wanting what was best for a loved one

meant letting that person go? How did you react? Were you able to put your loved one's well-being over your own desires? Why or why not?

9. Pastor Matt thought losing his legs was the worst thing that could ever happen to him. Then his girlfriend chose to leave their relationship. The experience brought him closer to God. Do you think that was God's intent? Do you think God uses difficult and traumatic experiences to bring us closer to Him? Do those experiences allow you to help others in similar situations? How does that make you feel?

10. Scripture calls us to forgive. God's Word emphasizes that He will forgive us no matter what we do. Knowing that, how do you feel about Tim's assertion that he and Juliette must not only forgive but love her assailant? Could you do it? Would you try? Why or why not?

ABOUT THE AUTHOR

Kelly Irvin is the bestselling author of the Every Amish Season and Amish of Bee County series. *The Beekeeper's Son* received a starred review from *Publishers Weekly*, who called it a "beautifully woven masterpiece." The two-time Carol Award finalist is a former newspaper reporter and retired public relations professional. Kelly lives in Texas with her husband, photographer Tim Irvin. They have two children, three grandchildren, and two cats. In her spare time, she likes to read books by her favorite authors.

Visit her online at KellyIrvin.com
Instagram: @kelly_irvin
Facebook: @Kelly.Irvin.Author
Twitter: @Kelly_S_Irvin